Love

Feeling h

Praise for three bestselling authors –
Miranda Lee, Cathy Williams and
Anne McAllister

About MARRIAGE IN PERIL:
'Each scene is packed with a lot of sexual
tension and deep, powerful emotions.'
—*Romantic Times*

About CATHY WILLIAMS:
'Cathy Williams pens an emotional tale
with a layered conflict and great
character development.'
—*Romantic Times*

About THE INCONVENIENT BRIDE:
'Anne McAllister's latest must-read,
The Inconvenient Bride, is a larger-than-life
romance with dynamic characters who leap
off the page and witty, fantastic scenes.'
—*Romantic Times*

Love in the City

MARRIAGE IN PERIL
by
Miranda Lee

MERGER BY MATRIMONY
by
Cathy Williams

THE INCONVENIENT BRIDE
by
Anne McAllister

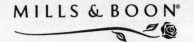

MILLS & BOON®

*MILLS & BOON and MILLS & BOON with the Rose Device
are registered trademarks of the publisher.*
Harlequin Mills & Boon Limited,
Eton House, 18-24 Paradise Road, Richmond, Surrey, TW9 1SR

LOVE IN THE CITY© by Harlequin Enterprises II B.V., 2005

Marriage in Peril, Merger by Matrimony and *The Inconvenient Bride*
were first published in Great Britain by
Harlequin Mills & Boon Limited in separate, single volumes.

Marriage in Peril © Miranda Lee 2000
Merger by Matrimony © Cathy Williams 2001
The Inconvenient Bride © Barbara Schenck 2001

ISBN 0 263 84478 1

05-0805

*Printed and bound in Spain
by Litografía Rosés S.A., Barcelona*

Miranda Lee is Australian, and lives near Sydney.
Born and raised in the bush, she was boarding-school
educated and briefly pursued a career in classical music,
before moving to Sydney and embracing the world of
computers. Happily married, with three daughters, she
began writing when family commitments kept her at
home. She likes to create stories that are believable,
modern, fast-paced and sexy. Her interests include
meaty sagas, doing word puzzles, gambling and going to
the movies.

MARRIAGE IN PERIL
by
Miranda Lee

PROLOGUE

BROOKE steeled herself for her mother's reaction to her news. It wouldn't be good. But there again, she reminded herself ruefully, her mother never approved of any of her decisions.

Not that Brooke was in the habit of being all that assertive. She'd only crossed her mother's will a few times in her twenty-two years, and most of those had been secret transgressions, like reading with a torch under the bedclothes at night. And putting on lipstick the moment she turned the corner on her way to school.

Her only major openly defiant decisions had been taking an apprenticeship in the hospitality industry with a large Sydney hotel rather than doing law at university, followed by her move out of home last year to live by herself in a small bedsit at Bondi.

But neither of those decisions had been as mammoth as planning to marry at a register office ceremony tomorrow morning, *without* breathing a word to her mother about either her husband-to-be or the marriage till this very moment.

Tension built within Brooke while she waited for her mother to say something. But Phyllis Freeman just sat there at the green garden table, smoking. Silent.

The silent treatment was not a tactic her mother adopted very often. She was a highly intelligent and assertive woman, with a sharp mind and an even sharper tongue, who used argument and ruthless logic to get her way. She had definite ideas about everything, but especially the role and rights of the modern woman.

A lawyer who specialised in discrimination cases, Phyllis was an expert in arguing the feminist cause. At forty-two, and with two divorces behind her, she had become a dedicated man-hater, plus the most difficult of mothers.

Brooke had no idea why she loved her. The woman was impossible. She'd driven away two good husbands, and driven Brooke herself to distraction ever since she'd started dating. No boyfriend had ever found favour with Phyllis Freeman. There'd always been something wrong with them.

No wonder when Brooke had met Leo she'd never brought him home to meet her mother. Brooke hadn't wanted to risk spoiling what she knew was the greatest love of her life.

But things had progressed beyond that now—now her mother had to be acquainted with the facts. Her marriage to Leo was about to become a *fait accompli*.

Brook had toyed with the idea of not telling her mother till *after* the event, but had decided that would be too cruel. At the moment, however, she thought it might have been the lesser of two evils.

Brooke's stomach tightened as she watched her mother finally stab out her cigarette in the ceramic ashtray and look up at her with icy blue eyes.

'Was marriage your idea, Brooke?' she asked coldly. 'Or his?'

'His, actually,' Brooke took pleasure in announcing. She'd been over the moon when Leo had proposed straight away on knowing about the baby. Because then she'd known he really loved her, and wasn't just out for a good time.

Her mother had always said actions spoke louder than words. Well, marriage equated with love and commitment in Brooke's mind. It wasn't just her so-called beautiful face and body Leo wanted—something her mother had always gone to great pains to point out about her previous boyfriends.

Brooke wondered if that was what her mother had believed about herself in the past. That the men in her life had been blinded by her looks, that none had ever really loved Phyllis the person. As a young woman Phyllis had been a stunner, with long blonde hair, creamy skin, big blue eyes, full, pouty lips and a body just made for sin. Brooke was often told she was the spitting image of her mother at the same age.

The years, however, had wrought many changes in Phyllis Freeman. Chain-smoking had aged her skin and bitterness had thinned her mouth. Her once lovely long blonde hair was now cut ruthlessly short and going grey at the roots. A dedicated feminist, Brooke's mother never went to the hairdresser's, or wore makeup. She was too thin as well, in Brooke's opinion, living on cigarettes and coffee.

Brooke worried about her mother's health.

'I suppose you refused to consider an abortion,' Phyllis scorned, 'being the hopeless romantic you are.'

Brooke almost hated her at that moment. 'I didn't consider it for a moment,' she said indignantly. 'I love Leo, Mum. With all my heart.'

'I have no doubt you do, darling,' Phyllis returned,

though her eyes remained cynical. 'Why else would an intelligent girl sleep with a man without using protection unless she was in love? But why did he, I wonder?' she mused.

Brooke refused to say a word on *that* subject. No way was she going to admit to being so instantly besotted with Leo that she'd been quite shameless in her swift surrender to his impassioned pursuit of her. Not to mention totally reckless. She'd stupidly deceived him in matters of contraception that first night because she hadn't wanted him to stop, even for a second, and she had genuinely thought it was a safe time. The same thing had applied each night over the following week.

But it hadn't been safe at all. When her period hadn't arrived at the end of that first marvellous week, she hadn't panicked. But when it hadn't made an appearance by the end of another fortnight, and a pregnancy test had confirmed she was going to have a baby, Brooke had been too afraid to confess everything, so she'd pretended that she'd forgotten to take the pill on one of those first tempestuous nights together. At the time she hadn't been trying to trap Leo into marriage. She'd just been unbelievably stupid!

But he'd been so wonderful when she'd confessed her pregnant state. And not at all angry. Comforting and caring when she'd cried. Solid and strong when she'd said she didn't know what to do.

'Don't worry, *mi micetta*,' he'd murmured soothingly as he held her close. He always called her that. It meant little kitten. He said she was like a kitten after they'd made love, practically purring as he stroked her as he liked to do afterwards. 'We'll get married as soon as it can be arranged. But not a big wedding. And no honeymoon, I'm afraid. I do not have time for that right now.'

Only occasionally did she feel a stab of guilt over deceiving Leo, but never when in his arms, never when he called her his *micetta*.

She felt a bit guilty now. Not over Leo. Over her mother. She was probably very hurt by being kept in the dark like this.

But Brooke refused to apologise. Or back down. Once you took a backward step with Phyllis Freeman she went for the jugular.

'So what does your husband-to-be do for a living?' her mother asked abruptly.

'He's a businessman. His family company imports Italian goods into countries all over the world. Leo's in the process of opening an office and warehouse here in Sydney.'

'How enterprising of him,' Phyllis drawled. 'And where did you meet this…Leo? He doesn't sound like your usual style of boyfriend.'

'He's been living in a suite at the Majestic till he can buy a house,' Brooke said, and watched that information sink in.

The Majestic was one of Sydney's most expensive hotels, a lavish, luxurious concern which overlooked the Harbour and the Opera House, and boasted pop stars and presidents amongst its clientele. Brooke had been working on the main desk for just over six months, and it had been there, on a warm summer evening back in February, just over two months ago, that she'd looked up from the computer and straight into Leo's incredibly sexy black eyes.

'So what's his full name?' Phyllis asked sourly. 'This fine, successful businessman called Leo, who's impregnated my daughter but doesn't have the courage to face me himself.'

'He *did* want to face you,' Brooke defended. 'It's me who insisted on coming in alone first.'

'Really?'

'Yes. Really. His full name is Leonardo Giuseppe Parini,' she said proudly, thinking it was a wonderful name, with a wonderful heritage. Leo had told her his family could trace its ancestors back for generations. In the eighteenth century one of his forefathers had been a famous poet.

'He's *Italian*?' Phyllis exclaimed, horrified.

Brooke was taken aback by her mother's reaction. 'Well…yes. He was born in Milan. But he speaks English perfectly,' she hurried on, full of pride and praise for her handsome and clever husband-to-be. 'He travelled a lot with his parents as a child. And he studied business at Harvard. He spent a few years working in New York, then London and Paris. And now he's here in Sydney. He hardly has any accent at all.' Just enough to be very, very sexy.

'His accent isn't the problem, Brooke,' her mother bit out. 'Accent or no accent, he's a born and bred Italian.'

'What's the problem with that?'

'At least I now understand why he's marrying you,' her mother muttered. 'An Australian man would probably have run a mile. Italian men have this *thing* about their offspring, especially sons. I hope you realise, Brooke, how Italians treat their wives once a wedding ring is on their finger and they have them under lock and key at home. Like second-class citizens. Chattels. Italian wives are never partners. Just possessions and producers of children.'

'Leo's not like that!' Brooke defended, her face instantly hot with resentment and fury. Trust her mother to start criticising before she'd even met the man. 'And you're wrong about Italian men. That's an ignorant and very offensive opinion!'

Why, her best friend in high school had been Italian, and her father had been a wonderful man. Brooke had loved going over to Antonia's house. It had been so much warmer than her own. No tension or arguments. Just a whole lot of warmth, and closeness, and love.

'Don't be ridiculous,' Phyllis snapped. 'All men are like that, given the opportunity. But chauvinism is *bred* into Italian men. They think they're gods within their own family circles and demand to be treated as such, no questions asked. Italian women seem to be able to cope. They're brought up with different values and expectations. But you're not Italian, Brooke. You're Australian. You're also *my* daughter. There's more of me in you than you realise, whether you admit it or not. He'll make you miserable. You mark my words.'

'You're wrong!' Brooke lashed back. 'He won't make me miserable because I won't make *him* miserable. And I'm *not* like you. Not in any way. In my eyes, Leo *is* a god. Nothing is too good for him. I'm never going to drive him away like you did Dad, with your constant arguing and criticising. No wonder he

left you. I'm going to give my husband whatever he
wants. I'm going to be there for him whenever he needs
me.'

'Become a doormat, you mean.'

'Not a doormat. A wife!'

'Same thing, in some men's eyes.'

Brooke shook her head in despair and frustration.
'You have no idea how to make a man happy. You
never did.'

'Not if it meant suppressing every thought, wish and
opinion in my head! You're an intelligent girl, Brooke.
And you're quite stubborn and wilful in your own way.
If you think squashing everything *you* are will bring
you lasting happiness, then you're in for a shock one
day.'

Brooke said nothing, gritted her teeth and just
counted to ten. 'Are you going to come to my wedding
or not?'

'Would it make any difference?'

Brooke sighed a weary sigh. 'Of course it would
make a difference. I want you there at my wedding.
You're my mother.'

'Then I'll be there, I suppose. Just like I'll be there
to pick up the pieces when the honeymoon is over. And
it will be over one day, Brooke. I hope you realise
that.'

'Leo and I are *never* getting a divorce, no matter
what!'

'You say that now,' Phyllis said as she lit up another
cigarette. 'I wonder what you might say in five years'
time.'

'The answer will be the same.'

'I truly hope so, darling. Now…' She dragged deeply on the cigarette and let it out slowly. 'Am I going to meet this handsome Italian of yours or not?' The corner of her mouth lifted in a knowing little smirk. 'He *is* handsome, I presume? Never known you to go out with an ugly bloke. Not you, Brooke.'

Brooke's chin lifted. 'He's *very* handsome.'

'Then go get him. I'm beginning to be just a little bit curious about Leonardo Giuseppe Parini.'

Brooke was the one smiling when she led Leo back into her mother's presence, her arms linked tightly around his. For she knew her lover of two months and imminent husband-to-be wasn't just handsome. He was simply magnificent. In every way.

A mature and sophisticated thirty-two, he was tall for an Italian, at six foot two, with an elegant but well-shaped body and a face Valentino would have envied. It combined the best of all things Latin, with slightly hooded and absolutely riveting black eyes, a classic nose and a highly sensual mouth. His hair was even blacker than his eyes, its glossy thickness giving added style and shape to its up-to-date fashion of being cut quite short. Brooke thought him the most handsome man she'd ever seen.

But it was his presentation which really impressed. His utter perfection in matters of dress and grooming. His coolly confident bearing. His grace of movement.

Brooke's smile broadened as she watched her mother's eyes widen and her mouth fall rather inelegantly open.

'This is Leo, Mum,' Brooke said smugly, and ran a possessive hand down his sleekly suited arm.

Phyllis Freeman was rendered totally speechless for the first time in her life.

CHAPTER ONE

Italy…five years later. .

BROOKE stretched out on top of the bed and tried to go to sleep, as everyone else was doing that warm, sultry afternoon. But it was impossible. She'd never been a sleeper during the day. On top of that, she was feeling restless and edgy.

Her gaze drifted agitatedly around the huge and very lavish bedroom, then up at the ornate frescoed ceiling and the elaborate crystal and gold chandelier which hung from its centre.

This was the main guest room, where she and Leo always stayed during their annual visit to the Parini family villa on Lake Como.

'Only the best for my son and his lovely wife,' his mother had said the first time Leo had brought Brooke and their baby son home, just on four years ago.

Brooke sighed at the memory of that first visit, and their subsequent yearly visits. What heaven they always were! With an English-speaking Italian girl to help mind the children, and more time to relax, it was almost like being on a honeymoon each year—the one they'd never had.

Their sex life had always been good—fantastic to start with!—and it was still pretty good. Leo would probably say it was *very* good. But Leo wasn't a stay-at-home mother with two children under five.

Many was the night Brooke just didn't feel like sex.

But she never refused Leo, not unless she was really sick. Of course, that meant faking an orgasm every once in a while. But she did it. For him.

Brooke frowned at the thought she'd been doing that quite a bit lately.

During their Italian stays, however, faking anything was never required. No longer tired from continuous child-minding, Brooke was more easily put in the mood. As for Leo…he would become practically insatiable, wanting her not just at night but during the day as well.

Four years ago, when he'd first suggested they take an afternoon nap at the same time as Alessandro was sleeping—he'd been their only child back then—she'd thought he'd gone crazy. The idea of Leo having an afternoon nap had been just plain ridiculous. The man was a dynamo, needing very little sleep at the best of times.

But he'd insisted, despite her blank look, and she'd finally twigged—courtesy of the knowing gleam in Leo's father's eyes. She'd blushed madly as Leo had practically dragged her up to the bedroom for a couple of hours' torrid lovemaking.

Brooke had been a bit stunned at first. Leo hadn't made love to her like that since before they were married. He'd been gentle and considerate during her whole pregnancy, and hadn't complained at all during the six weeks after Alessandro's birth when the doctor had vetoed any sex. Even when Leo had been given the green light he'd still been tender with her, which she'd appreciated. She'd had stitches and been pretty sore and sorry for herself for a while. He'd also seemed to appreciate the fact she was tired most of the time during Alessandro's first six months. Far too tired for lovemaking marathons.

But that afternoon, although not rough with her, he'd been incredibly demanding. Whilst Brooke had found everything slightly shocking in broad daylight—plus in his parents' house—it *had* been exciting, and she hadn't needed dragging upstairs the next day. Or any day afterwards.

Claudia had been born eight and a half months after their return to Sydney.

But this visit was entirely different in every way. It wasn't their annual holiday which had brought them to Como a little earlier than usual this year, but a funeral. Leo's only sibling, Lorenzo, had been killed in a car accident, losing control of his prized Ferrari on one of the hairpin bends around the lake and crashing to a watery death.

Fortunately, Lorenzo's wife, Francesca, had not been in the car at the time, although maybe she didn't think she was fortunate. The poor woman had been almost comatose with grief at the funeral, unable to function at all. With Francesca's own parents long dead, Leo's mum and dad had brought Lorenzo's widow home to the villa for some tender loving care, and everyone had done their best to offer comfort, despite their own unhappiness.

But it was difficult to know what to say to her. Brooke thought it was a shame the marriage had never produced children. Children would have given Francesca something to live for.

Brooke had tried to talk to her on one occasion, but the woman had just burst into tears and run back to her room, where she'd stayed for the rest of the day. Brooke had felt terrible, and had told Leo's mum about it. Sophia had just patted her hand and smiled a sad smile, telling her not to worry, it wasn't her fault. Francesca was just being Francesca.

Brooke knew exactly what she meant. Francesca was a weak kind of woman, in her opinion. Very beautiful in a dark-eyed, lush-figured way. But she never said much, or exuded much personality.

Not that Brooke had been in their company all that often over their four-year acquaintance. Just the occasional family dinner party, sometimes here at the villa, and sometimes in Lorenzo's plush apartment in Milan.

Francesca would sit silently beside her husband on such occasions, her eyes darting nervously to him all the time, as though waiting to be told what to do, or say. Brooke could never work out if she adored the man or was afraid of him.

Two years older than Leonardo, Lorenzo had been a handsome and charming man on the surface, but Brooke hadn't been able to stand him. He'd given her the creeps. Once, during a party at his place, she'd gone to the powder room. She'd been in there, washing her hands, when he'd come in unexpectedly and made the most disgusting suggestion. She'd been so shocked she hadn't known what to do, except run out of the room and hurry back downstairs.

She hadn't told Leo about the incident. No way.

Brooke wasn't stupid, and she'd sensed there was some angst between the two brothers. They'd been civil on the surface, but nothing more. Brooke had got the impression Leo didn't like his brother's wife much, either, an opinion reinforced by his coldly indifferent stance when Francesca had suddenly upped and gone back to Milan a week ago. To be by herself, she'd said. Everyone had objected, thinking it a potentially dangerous idea; everyone except Leo.

To be honest, Brooke hadn't really been sorry to see Francesca go. Her presence had hung like a pall over the house, bringing tensions she didn't quite understand, not being one of the family.

Leo was actually the lucky one, in her opinion, since he was out of the house most days. He'd been driving back and forth to the Milan office during the working week, going through his brother's desk and sorting out who was going to take charge there now. Brooke had worried his father might ask him to come back and do the job Lorenzo had been doing—Giuseppe had retired with heart problems the previous year—but this hadn't eventuated, thank God.

She was grateful for that, but beginning to resent the amount of time Leo was spending away from her and the children. This past week, the situation had worsened, with her husband getting home later and later each night. After a quick supper and a shower, he would fall into bed, too tired to make love, a most unusual situation for Leo.

If there was one thing Brooke could rely upon with her husband, it was the unfailing regularity of his need for sex. Yet he hadn't laid a hand on her since the funeral, almost three weeks ago.

Brooke was beginning to miss the feelings of love and intimacy Leo's lovemaking always left her with, even when she was faking things. Every woman liked to be wanted that way.

Sighing, Brooke swung her feet over the side of the bed and stood up. Flicking her long fair hair back over her shoulder, she picked up the novel she kept by the bed and padded across the huge Persian rug towards the sliding glass doors which led out onto the balcony. Once outside, in the cooler air, she settled herself in one of the comfy deckchairs and opened her book at the page she'd reached the previous night.

After several minutes scanning the page without a single word sinking in, Brooke closed the book and just sat there, doing her best to relax and enjoy a view coveted the world over.

The first time she'd seen Lake Como she'd been wide-eyed over the scenic beauty of the mountains rising up from the crystalline lake; at the magnificence of the huge villas clinging to the hillsides; at the number of luxury yachts in the water, plus the all-round postcard perfection of the place.

She'd been even more wide-eyed when Leo had pulled up outside his family's summer home.

The Parini villa was not as large as some, but larger than most, showing evidence of the family's long-held wealth. The house had been built in the late eighteenth century, then added to and renovated several times since. Multi-levelled, it had acres of marble flooring, more bedrooms than Brooke could count, huge open-plan living areas, several very formal entertaining rooms, expansive terracotta terraces, a solar-heated swimming pool, and perfectly manicured lawns which sloped down to a private dock where three boats were moored. A speed boat, a cruiser and a racing yacht. Inside, monumental paintings filled the walls, and everywhere there were the most incredible antiques.

Brooke had worried over the years that her boisterous and mischievous son might ruin or break something, but oddly he hadn't, as though he recognised that these treasures were his to inherit one day and had to be preserved.

Although half-Australian, Alessandro was a very Italian child. Openly affectionate, noisy and demanding, he was far too good-looking for his own good, with his father's dark hair and eyes.

Claudia was dark-haired and dark-eyed too, and very pretty, but much quieter and delightfully amenable, content to follow her mother around, or just to play with her dolls. Her brother had to be always on the move, always doing something. Since the age of two, he'd refused to take no for an answer.

Like father like son, Brooke thought ruefully.

Which brought her thoughts back to Leo. Her darling Leo, whom she still adored but who was not the easiest man to live with, she'd found. He really did like his way in everything. Many were the times she'd been tempted to argue with him, to try to get *her* way for once, but she never had.

Except once…when Claudia was born.

Brooke had wanted to call her daughter Chloe. She'd also wanted to call Alessandro Alexander, but had given in when Leo had explained that the heir to the Parini fortune should have an Italian name.

Brooke hadn't really minded, since Alessandro wasn't so different from Alexander. But when she'd had a daughter, she'd expected to be able to choose the name *she* wanted. Not so, she had soon found out. Leo had been adamant about Claudia, then angry when Brooke had argued with him. More angry than she had ever seen him.

'I am the head of this family,' he'd pronounced dogmatically. 'What I say goes!'

For a split second, Brooke had been overwhelmed by a deep, violent anger of her own. *You're just like my mother said,* she'd almost thrown at him.

Thinking of her mother, however, had forced her to get a grip on herself. You don't want to end up like her, do you? Bitter and twisted and lonely. It's only a name, after all. What's in a name? It's not worth getting a divorce over.

So, once again, she'd given in.

But it still hurt a little; his not seeing her point of view on something that was important to her; his not meeting her halfway.

Her mother had warned her she would become a doormat. Well, maybe she had in a way, she conceded. But she was a happy and contented doormat. Most of the time.

A telephone ringing somewhere downstairs had her rising from the depths of the deckchair, only to sink down again when it was swiftly answered.

Determinedly, Brooke picked up her book again, and was doing her best to become absorbed in the story when a voice drifted up from the terrace below. It was Leo's mother. Despite her speaking in Italian, Brooke understood every word.

She'd always been good at languages, and had studied Latin and Japanese at school. After her marriage to Leo, Brooke had made the effort to learn Italian, picking it up quickly from tapes and books, then practising it with Leo in the evenings, plus every time she visited his family. She had no trouble following the conversation below.

'There you are, Giuseppe,' Sophia said. 'I see you couldn't sleep, either. That was Leonardo on the phone.'

Brooke's ears immediately pricked.

'Anything wrong?' came Giuseppe's reply.

'He's going to be late again. Doesn't want us to keep any dinner for him this time.'

Brooke groaned. Just when she'd been wanting him to come home a bit earlier.

'So?' Giuseppe said with a shrug in his voice. 'Why the worried frown?'

'If he has so much work on his plate, Giuseppe, why didn't he ask you to go in with him? It's not as though you couldn't spend a few hours in the office here and there.'

'I offered, woman, but he refused. Told me one death in the family was enough for this year. But you're right. He *did* look tired last night. I'll insist on joining him tomorrow.'

'Tomorrow might be too late, Giuseppe.'

'Too late for what?'

'I don't think he's *in* the office today…' Sophia said in more hushed tones.

Brooke leant forward in her chair.

'…I think he's with Francesca.'

Brooke's heart lurched.

'What?' Giuseppe exploded. 'Don't be ridiculous, woman! Leonardo is not that type of man. He would never be unfaithful to that lovely little wife of his. Never!'

Brooke was glad she was sitting down. If she hadn't been, she might have fallen down.

'Not normally, Giuseppe,' she heard Sophia say. 'But these are not normal circumstances. Leonardo was in love with Francesca long before Brooke came into his life. He never got over Lorenzo stealing Francesca away from him. He might have pretended to, but I know differently. I'm his mother.'

'For pity's sake, that was years ago!'

'Maybe, but Leonardo is not a fickle man. I always knew that when he fell in love it would be for life.'

'Leonardo loves his *wife*!' his father defended, outrage in his voice.

'Has he said as much to you?'

An increasingly stricken Brooke strained forward further, waiting to hear Leo's father say firmly, *Yes, of course. Many times!*

'Men don't talk about things like that, woman. But it's as obvious as the nose on my face.'

Sophia sighed. 'I've no doubt he *does* love Brooke, in a fashion. She's a very beautiful girl. And incredibly sweet. But he was *in love* with Francesca. I will never forget the way he looked at her on the night of their engagement party, with such hunger in his eyes. To find her in bed that same night with his brother must have nearly killed him.'

On the balcony above Brooke was reeling from shock after shock. Leo…*her* Leo, in love with Francesca? Her husband, once *engaged* to his brother's wife? Francesca choosing *Lorenzo* over Leo?

'Unfortunately,' Sophia went on with another sigh, 'Leonardo handled Francesca the wrong way back then, playing the gentleman with her. He thought respecting her virginity was the right thing to do. But he was wrong. Lorenzo, to my eternal dismay, had no respect for anything, or anyone. He simply took what he wanted, and silly, shy, naive Francesca was swept away by his decadent wickedness.'

'You're talking nonsense, woman! Lorenzo was not wicked, just weak in matters of the flesh. If he was truly wicked, he would not have married the girl. Yes, they did wrong, but they couldn't help themselves. They fell madly in love at first sight. Lorenzo told me so himself. He was very sorry he hurt Leonardo, but Francesca obviously didn't really love the boy. Lorenzo said she was only marrying his brother because he was kind, and she was so lonely after her father's recent death. As soon as Leonardo understood that, any feelings he had for the girl died a natural death.'

'If he no longer cared for Francesca,' Sophia scorned, 'then why did he run off to Australia? And why didn't he return for his brother's wedding?'

'He didn't run off to Australia. I *sent* him there! As for not returning for the wedding, give the man some leeway, woman. He has his pride. He did right to stay away.'

'Perhaps so. But I don't think he's staying away now. With Lorenzo dead, Leonardo finally has the opportunity to have what he foolishly denied himself back then. Francesca, in *his* bed.'

'I don't believe a son of mine would dishonour the family name in this way.'

'Why not?' Sophia said, her voice becoming hard. 'Your other son did. Often.'

'Lorenzo may have strayed once or twice. But he was a handsome man, and women threw themselves at him in a shameless fashion. It's unfortunate Francesca never had children. Children keep a man at home, and loyal. But let us talk of Lorenzo no more. The boy is dead. It is not right to speak badly of the dead. And you are wrong about Leonardo. Now, I want to hear no more about this matter.'

'Turning a blind eye will not solve this situation, husband mine,' Sophia said sternly.

'If what you say is true, then turning a blind eye is the *only* answer,' Giuseppe refuted. 'If Leo is fool enough to be having an affair with Francesca, he'll soon get her out of his system and realise there's just as good to be had at home. If I'm any judge, I'd say *better*! Leonardo and his family fly back to Sydney in two more days. Be patient and say nothing. The problem will pass.'

'Maybe you're right. But two days can be a long time…'

CHAPTER TWO

SOMEHOW Brooke made her way back into the bedroom without alerting the couple on the terrace below, there to collapse onto the gold silk quilt. Both her hands lifted to cover her eyes, as though by blocking out the light she could somehow block out the horror of what she'd just heard.

Leo, in love with *Francesca*! Leo, once *engaged* to his brother's widow! Leo, not at the office, but spending time with his lost love...

It seemed unbelievable, and yet it explained so much. The fact Leo had never actually said he loved *her*. Not *ever*! He'd used other endearments, other phrases. Adoration. Desire. Need. But never love.

And then there was his oddly cold behaviour around Francesca. Not dislike or indifference, as she'd imagined. But the other side of love.

Oh, God...

The pain wasn't just emotional. It was brutally physical. A vice clamped around her heart, pressing down till she simply couldn't breathe!

Gasping for air, Brooke struggled off the bed and into the bathroom, where she splashed some cold water over her face, then sucked in great gulps of oxygen before straightening. The distressed face staring back at her in the vanity mirror was hardly recognisable. Chalk-white, with huge, hurt blue eyes and an uncon-

trollably quivering chin. When tears blurred her vision
her eyes dropped and her shoulders sagged. She had to
clutch at the marble vanity-top to stop herself from
sinking to the floor.

Dear Lord, *what* was she going to do?

Suddenly, and perversely, she wanted her mother.

Yet her mother was the last person she could tell any
of this to. She would just say, *I told you so!* in that
scoffing, scornful way of hers.

Brooke could not help thinking that it was almost
five years since her mother had prophesied Leo would
make her miserable. Next week was their fifth wedding
anniversary. And she'd been right!

Or had she?

What if Giuseppe was right and Sophia was wrong?
What if Leo *wasn't* still in love with Francesca, let
alone spending today—or any other day—with her?
What if he didn't give a damn about his brother's wife,
and hadn't since she'd betrayed his love with his
brother?

Brooke's heart clung to this desperate hope.

It was possible, wasn't it? Okay, so Leo *hadn't* proclaimed his undying love for her. But in the five years
she'd known him he'd never given a hint that he was
unhappy, or pining for another woman. He'd always
seemed very happy to come home to *her* every night,
and very satisfied with their life together, especially
their sex life.

Till this last three weeks, that was, she conceded,
with a sickening twist in her stomach. Leo hadn't been
himself in that department since coming home for
Lorenzo's funeral.

She'd thought his unusual lack of desire was due to grief and exhaustion. Now, another more awful reason invaded her mind...

Brooke groaned in despair.

Francesca's abrupt move back to Milan suddenly took on a more sinister meaning, as did Leo's whole-hearted approval of his sister-in-law's decision. He'd wanted the opportunity to be alone with the woman he still loved and wanted, away from the prying eyes of his family, and well away from *her*, his wife.

Francesca's tears that day might not have been grief, but guilt.

She was the type of female to feel guilty, Brooke thought bitterly, but not enough to say no to a determined man. If Leonardo declared his undying love for her, passionately insisting she give him what she'd once withheld, silly, wishy-washy Francesca would probably become as putty in his hands.

Now Brooke's eyes snapped up, and they were no longer quite so haunted-looking. They were angry. No, not just angry. Livid.

Giuseppe might be able to turn a blind eye to his son's adultery, but she could not! She would go and confront the pair of them. Right now! This very moment! Borrow Sophia's car and drive into Milan to Francesca's place.

She knew the way. Leo had often taken her into Milan to shop during previous visits, as well as to his brother's fancy apartment for those dinner parties. She herself had driven home on these occasions, forced to concentrate on the roads involved in a way you didn't when you were a passenger.

Leo liked to have a bottle of wine over dinner, and always gave her the keys at the end of such evenings. It was the only time he allowed her to drive when he was in the car, something which rankled Brooke but which she tolerated. As she'd tolerated Leo's edict shortly after their marriage that he didn't like *her* to drink much. He'd said it made her aggressive.

'Like your mother,' he'd added, when she'd been about to object.

That thought had stopped the automatic protest bubbling up in her throat, after which she'd curtailed her drinking, restricting herself to just one glass or two. Not once during the last five years of their relationship had she ever told Leo it was *his* turn not to drink that evening, that *she* wanted to relax over a bottle of wine for once.

'Silly, weak cow!' she sneered at herself in the bathroom mirror. 'No wonder he thinks he can get away with cheating on you.'

Well, he was in for a shock, wasn't he? In about an hour she would be arriving at Francesca's door, and there would be hell to pay!

If by some remote possibility Giuseppe was right, and Leo *wasn't* with Francesca, if it proved his car was parked safely in the Milan head office car park, and not where she suspected it would be, then she would simply turn round and drive home.

But some inner female instinct told her Leo wasn't going to be at the office, just as his mother knew. Women knew about such things, provided they opened their stupid eyes and saw the signs.

'Well, my eyes are well and truly open now, Leo,' Brooke seethed aloud. 'And God help you!'

With cold fury in her heart, Brooke set about brushing her hair and applying some lipstick before going downstairs in search of Leo's mother.

She found her in one of the large sitting rooms, ostensibly reading a magazine. But her grey head was bowed in a weary fashion, her normally proud shoulders slumped in an attitude of great sadness.

Brooke's heart squeezed tight. She liked her mother-in-law a lot. Sophia was a warm, generous-hearted woman who'd welcomed her into her home and her heart without question. How wretched she must be feeling, with one son dead and the other involved in a potentially disastrous affair.

Protecting Sophia from unnecessary distress became an instant priority with Brooke, her inner fury temporarily pushed to one side. She was still determined to go and find Leo, but whatever happened after that would be between them and them alone. Sophia was not to be told a thing.

Her mind made up, Brooke moved into the room. Sophia's head jerked up at the sound of footsteps on the tiled floor.

'Brooke!' she exclaimed. 'I...I thought you were sleeping.'

Brooke adopted what she hoped was a suitably wan expression. 'I tried. But I have this dreadful headache.'

'Oh, my dear. What a shame. Can I get you something? A tablet? A drink?'

'No. I'm afraid they won't help. It's a PMT thing. My period's due tomorrow.' Which it was, she realised.

Being on the pill, such things were very predictable. 'Happens every month. Sometimes, when I get this back home, I go for a walk or a drive. For some reason that unwinds me and the headache goes away. Would you mind if I borrowed your car, Sophia? I promise to be careful and not to speed.'

'Of course you can, dear. But where will you drive to?'

'Oh…just around.'

'Do you want me to go with you?'

'No, no. I prefer to be by myself. Would you mind the children for me if they wake up before I return?'

'Certainly.'

Five minutes later, Brooke was carefully negotiating the tight corners of the curving road which hugged the lake, only the prospect of leaving her children motherless stopping her from speeding.

She couldn't get to Milan fast enough. She wanted to see the evidence of Leo's betrayal for herself; wanted to see his car outside Francesca's apartment block; wanted to storm inside and find them together.

In her mind's eyes she saw herself tearing strips off Leo, shouting and screaming and doing all those hysterical things she hadn't done during her last five lily-livered years!

The drive took well over an hour, with traffic building the closer she got to Milan. Brooke got a bit lost before finally turning into the wide, tree-lined street which housed Francesca's apartment block.

Brooke had thought she was ready for the sight of Leo's car parked in one of the visitors' bays by the side of the building.

But she'd been wrong.

Her stomach cramped when her eyes landed on its distinctive make and colour, then heaved when the number-plate confirmed there was no mistake. She only just opened her own car door in time for her lunch to land in the gutter and not her lap. As it was, her dress became a little stained.

At last, she sank back against the leather seat, shaken and still shaking. All she could think of was that the man she loved... her husband...her Leo...was inside that building, inside Francesca's apartment, in her bedroom, in her bed.

No use pretending he wasn't. If his presence there was perfectly innocent, why lie about what he was doing today?

He'd probably been lying all week, Brooke accepted, nausea swirling again. He'd probably never been in the office at all. Or only minimally. That was why he'd left his mobile phone number with her, and not the office number.

Perversely, now that she had proof of his lies, her courage failed her. Suddenly she was afraid of what would happen if she did go inside and confront them both.

Because there would be no going back then: no pretending it was just a passing problem—or a passing passion; no turning that blind eye Giuseppe had perhaps wisely said was the only solution.

If she confronted them, her marriage would be over. Even if Leo didn't want that—and Brooke believed that Leo would not want to hurt or lose his children—then pride would come into it.

Her pride.

It was one thing to go on living with a man you knew didn't love you. Quite another to go on living with a man who knew you *knew* he didn't love you. That would be beyond the pale. Totally unendurable.

But she could drive away now, go back to the villa and pretend she knew nothing. Then, if Leo took them back to Australia this Friday—confirming he'd made the decision to give up Francesca for the sake of his family—they might be able to go on as before. Because that would mean he *did* love her, in a way.

Who knew? Maybe his being with Francesca today *was* just a sex thing, a hangover from the past, an old, unrequited passion which he hadn't been able to let go. Maybe he was doing exactly what his father said, getting the woman out of his system.

Much as it killed Brooke to think of Leo in the arms of another woman, it was better he take the creature to bed a few times then ask for a divorce.

The truth was she simply could not bear it if Leo divorced her. Brooke knew she would never love another man as she loved him. On top of that he was the father of her children. They adored him. Heavens, even her *mother* had grown to like him.

Better she swallow her pride and turn that blind eye. Better she ignore the pain, hide the overwhelming feelings of humiliation and pretend nothing had changed.

But oh, dear Lord, it was going to be hard...

Brooke swallowed, reached forward, and turned on the engine. Slowly, wretchedly, she turned the car and made her way back to Lake Como.

'My dear, you look *terrible*!' was Sophia's first remark on her return. 'And what's that on your dress?'

'I...I was sick,' Brooke mumbled, feeling wretched and utterly exhausted. 'Must be a migraine, not PMT.'

'You poor thing. I know how terrible they are. I've suffered from migraines for years. You simply must go back to bed. And draw the curtains. I'll bring you up some very good tablets the doctor prescribed for me. They'll make you sleep, but that's for the best. Now, don't you worry about the children. Giuseppe has taken them out for a boat ride on the lake. Nina's gone with them, so they'll be quite safe.'

Brooke was having a battle not to cry. 'You're very kind,' she choked out.

'Not at all. Leonardo rang again. I didn't tell him you were out driving. I said you had a headache and were having a sleep. I hope I did the right thing.'

Brooke met the woman's worried eyes and wondered why they were both protecting Leo.

For the sake of the children, she supposed.

'Yes, Sophia, you did the right thing,' she said in a flat, dead voice.

'Good. Now, upstairs with you and into a nice refreshing shower. I'll put the tablets by your bed, along with a drink and something light for you to eat. It's not good to take these tablets on an empty stomach. And don't worry about anything. If you're still asleep when Leo comes home, I'll tell him not to disturb you.'

Now the tears came, and Sophia looked alarmed. 'Are you sure it's just a headache, Brooke? There's nothing else wrong, is there?'

Brooke refused to add to the woman's worry. She'd

had enough on her plate lately. This was *her* problem and she would deal with it.

'I think I'm a bit homesick,' she said, not untruthfully.

Sophia nodded. 'It's time Leo took you home.'

Brooke just smiled sadly and turned to go upstairs. Her legs felt like lead, each step a mammoth effort. By the time she came out of the shower, two rather big white pills were sitting on the near bedside table, along with a glass of water. A small and very elegantly set out tray rested on the other table, with two tempting-looking sandwiches and a tall glass of iced milk.

Her mother-in-law's sweet thoughtfulness brought another rush of tears. Brooke knew Sophia would be devastated if she and Leo broke up. So would Giuseppe. Brooke could not do it to them, or to her children, or to herself. She loved Leo. She would always love him, no matter what. Life without him was unimaginable!

Brooke fell asleep with tears still wet on her cheeks. But they had long dried when she woke many hours later to the sounds of someone in the *en suite* bathroom, in the shower.

Her errant husband, it seemed, had finally deigned to come home.

CHAPTER THREE

ODDLY, Brooke's first reaction was fury, not distress.

The room was dark, she noted angrily. Leo must have turned the bedside lamp off when he came in.

She rolled over to check the luminous numbers on the bedside clock and saw it was twenty minutes past eleven. Not *too* late, so a wife wouldn't be suspicious. Certainly not one as stupidly doting and one-eyed as herself!

With a bitter resentment in her heart, she rolled back onto her side, facing the far wall, curling her body up in a foetal position, glad she was wearing one of her more modest nighties.

Leo had a thing for short, slinky black satin nightwear which barely covered her bottom. This particular nightie was much longer, reaching her knees. It was particularly low-cut up top, however, and had only the thinnest shoulder straps keeping it in place. Still, with her back to him, its length was the most important factor.

I'll pretend to be asleep, she vowed savagely as she lay there. That way I won't say anything I might regret in the morning.

Maybe if Leo hadn't stayed in the shower so darned long Brooke might have been able to keep to that vow. But fifteen minutes went by and the water was still running, evoking all sorts of darkly jealous thoughts.

He was trying to wash the smell of her off his body. He probably *reeked* of her, and that heavy, musky perfume she always wore.

By the time the taps were turned off, five minutes later, Brooke had rolled back over and was glaring in the direction of the bathroom, watching and waiting for him to come out.

She was still glowering at the door when it finally opened.

Leo emerged, obviously trying not to make a sound, turning off the bathroom light before carefully closing the door behind him.

But not before Brooke got a good long look at him, framed in the brightly lit doorway.

There was no doubting Leo was an impressive man naked. Brooke had never seen better.

He had it all. Broad shoulders. Deep chest. Flat stomach. Slim hips. Gorgeous olive skin. Not *too* much body hair. Strong arms and lovely muscular thighs...with more than adequate equipment in between.

Brooke had been overawed by him from the first time he'd stripped for her. She was still overawed by him. Even now, when she wanted to hate him.

Her heart began to pound as his darkened silhouette crossed the room, lifted the sheet and slid, still naked, into the bed. Not an unusual occurrence. Leo often slept in the nude.

But the cool, casual arrogance of the man infuriated her. When he rolled over and put his back to her, she wanted to kill him.

Brooke lay there, scowling up at the ceiling, thinking

of the cruellest most uncivilised way of putting him to death for his crimes against her and their marriage. The guillotine was too quick and too kind. The same applied to a firing squad. She wanted him to suffer as she was suffering, to *endure*…in agony.

Hanging, drawing and quartering would do just fine, she decided. Like in past times. But only after a few years' solitary confinement in one of those cold, old prisons, where his only companions would be cockroaches and rats!

Unfortunately, there was no real solace or satisfaction in such thinking, and Brooke's jealous fury was soon sidelined by an equally savage determination to know for sure just how great Leo's crimes against her were: how *far* things had progressed, how many *times* he'd been unfaithful to her that day.

The state of his body, she resolved with a wild recklessness, would be much more telling than the sight of his car in that car park this afternoon.

He flinched when her hand landed on the indent of his waist, then stiffened when it began to slide around further. Abruptly he rolled onto his back, his head twisting on the pillow to face her.

By this time the palm of Brooke's hand was resting provocatively on his stomach, and her heart was racing. With fear of what she'd find, she wondered? Or fear of what he'd do if she dared touch him down there?

'I thought you were asleep,' he said, his voice as cool as his skin.

'I was.' She could just make out his face. The moon was out and the curtains which covered the bedroom windows were light and filmy, letting in enough light to see by once your eyes had adjusted.

Leo was looking at her rather oddly, his eyes narrowed and wary.

'I tried to be quiet,' he said, a measure of defensiveness in his voice.

'Why?'

'Mamma told me you'd had a bad migraine all day. She said she'd given you some pills.'

'Yes. She did. She's very kind, your mum.'

'True.'

There was a moment's awkward silence when Leo said nothing further and Brooke's courage began to fail her. Her hand lay still on his stomach while her heart thudded away.

'You're very late, Leo…'

'Yes. I know. I'm sorry, but Lorenzo's left a damned awful mess behind him. I'm trying to have everything sorted out before we leave on Friday. I haven't finished yet, either. I wasn't as productive today as I would have liked to be. Too many interruptions. So I might have to work late tomorrow night as well.'

'I see,' Brooke said, and another awkward silence fell between them.

'It's not like you to have a migraine, Brooke,' Leo said at last. 'I wonder what brought it on?'

Thinking of you in love with Francesca all these years, she wanted to throw at him. *Thinking of you in bed with her all afternoon and half the night.*

Such thoughts renewed her bitter resolve to see the lie of the land, once and for all.

'I feel much better now,' she murmured, and slid her hand back and forth across his stomach.

He sucked in sharply.

'So I see,' he bit out.

When he made no move to stop her, Brooke's hand changed direction. A little shakily, it began to travel downwards, till it encountered then encircled her intended target.

Shock held her fingers still for a few moments. For never had Leo felt so limp, or less interested in her touch!

As Brooke had already found out this afternoon, it was one thing to *think* something, another to find hard evidence of its truth, even when that evidence wasn't hard, but soft. Crushingly, cruelly soft!

Waves of emotion swept through her. Dismay. Devastation. Despair! How could he betray her this way? Deceive her? *Destroy* her!

And how could Francesca? The bitch! And so soon after her husband's death!

Eventually, surprisingly, the wish to kill them both was sublimated by the mad desire to *make* Leo respond, to show him that she—his wife—knew him better than any other woman, knew what he liked, could give him pleasure unequalled elsewhere. Francesca couldn't possibly do for him what Brooke knew *she* could.

Finally, her frozen fingers began to move once more.

His groan sounded like a protest, but she stubbornly ignored it, using her acquired knowledge of his body to arouse him. After all, hadn't Leo tutored her personally in what he liked during the first few weeks of their relationship, spending long evenings and even longer nights in extending her sexual education, showing her at the same time that her previous lovers had been total ignoramuses?

All they'd wanted were quickies.

But his flesh was depressingly slow to respond, its lack-lustre performance very telling. Her normally responsive and very virile husband must have been making love all day to be like this!

Brooke refused to give up. He *would* respond, she vowed with an icy resolve, her heart hardening against any distracting or distressing emotions.

'This isn't like you, Leo,' she murmured, all the while caressing him intimately.

'I thought you were asleep,' he muttered through obviously gritted teeth. 'I've just had a very long, very cold shower.'

In truth, his skin *was* cold. But she didn't believe his lengthy shower had anything to do with consideration for her.

'Then maybe you need a little extra help,' she said, and, sliding down his body, boldly took the evidence of his recent betrayal between her lips.

This wasn't something Brooke ever did off her own bat. Only at Leo's behest. Even then, it wasn't something he asked for much nowadays. In fact she couldn't remember the last time. Probably last summer, here, in this very room. But in the past it had unfailingly aroused him, no matter how many times he'd already made love to her.

It aroused him now, his flesh swelling quickly. Brooke was merciless, her only aim to make him so excited that he would lose control. She wanted to seduce him so totally that he would forget everything else…and everyone else. Especially Francesca.

At the back of her mind Brooke knew she was acting out of sheer desperation, but she couldn't stop for the life of her. One part of her was almost horrified by what she was doing. Another part remained coldly detached, driving her on to do everything she could think of. And more. Her hands joined her lips in the fray, finding all sorts of erotic areas to torment and tantalise. She was more adventurous than she'd ever been before.

Dimly, she heard him moan, felt his own fingers splay shakily into her hair. When they tightened, she thought for one awful moment he was going to drag her away, make her stop.

But he didn't.

He muttered something in Italian at one stage, his voice low and shaking.

She stopped momentarily to glance up at him. His handsome face was etched clearly in the moonlight, his hooded eyes almost shut, his mouth grimacing.

'Do you want me to stop?' she purred.

When a violent shudder shook his head from side to side, she smiled an amazingly cool smile, dipped her head, and continued.

His breath began coming in raw, panting gasps. He was erect now, all right. More than he'd ever been, his flesh almost cruelly stretched. And straining.

A wave of dark triumph flooded Brooke, bringing its own brand of excitement and satisfaction. For at that moment Leo was hers, totally. He had no will of his own. No ability to think, let alone stop her.

Or so she'd thought.

Brooke was so caught up in her own dizzying sense of power that she didn't notice Leo's hands abandon her hair. When they slid under her arms and pulled her up off him, her cry of shock and frustration was very real.

Ignoring her protest, Leo pushed the satin nightie up to her waist, grasped her buttocks in an iron grip and lifted her till she was kneeling high above him. Before she knew it, his titanic erection was between her thighs and she was being forcibly drawn downwards onto it.

Her lips gasped wide at the swiftness of this turn-around, plus the stunning pleasure as her husband slid, hard and huge, into her. She hadn't realised till that moment how turned on she was.

So much for being removed from the experience!

So much for being the one in control!

Suddenly, all she wanted was to move, to feel him filling and refilling her. But he was holding her too tightly for the riding motion she craved. In desperation, she swayed back and forth, wriggling her hips and squeezing her insides to create some friction, to ease the craven need which was suddenly driving her wild.

'Be *still*!' Leo commanded, his thumbs and finger-tips digging into her flesh.

'But I don't *want* to be still,' she choked out.

'I can see that,' he growled, then smiled the wick-edest smile up at her. 'But I need a little time to compose myself before we continue. Still...maybe I can help *you* out in the meantime.'

His black eyes glittered in the moonlight as he reached up to brush her tangled hair back off her

flushed face, pushing it right back off her shoulders
before slowly sliding the thin straps off her shoulders,
peeling the nightie downwards till her breasts were totally exposed.

Brooke knew, without looking at them, that they
were cruelly swollen, and her nipples as hard as rocks.
She had nice breasts. Big, without being too big.
Breastfeeding had made them drop only a little, and
her nipples were much larger than before.

'I should neglect you in the bedroom more often,'
Leo muttered thickly, 'if this is the result.' Reaching
up, he took both nipples between his thumbs and fore-
fingers, and gave them both a sharp tug.

Shock—and something else—quivered down Brooke's
spine. Leo had never done anything remotely like that to
her nipples before. He was usually so gentle and tender
with her breasts, using his mouth and tongue more than
his hands.

When he did it again, Brooke wasn't sure if the sensation was pleasure, or pain. All she knew was it left
her nipples with the most delicious burning feeling.

She stared downwards and saw they looked longer
and harder than she'd ever seen them, brazenly standing out from her breasts, eager for more of the same.
Leo took possession of them again, none too gently
once more, rolling the still burning flesh between his
fingers in a slow, twisting motion, bringing not a cry,
but a moan. Of the most amazing pleasure.

'Do you want me to stop?' he murmured, echoing
what she'd said to him earlier.

Excitement rendered her speechless. He laughed a

low, sexy laugh and then continued the delicious torment.

In the end she could not bear his eyes upon her, watching her gasp and squirm.

'Leo…please…'

'Please, what?' he drawled, obviously enjoying her breathless arousal. 'Stop? More? Tell me, *mi micetta*. I'll do anything you want. Though you're hardly a kitten tonight. More of a tiger. I think you'd have eaten me alive if I'd let you.'

'Leo, please,' she repeated huskily, her face flaming with both embarrassment and excitement.

'What is it you want me to do? Touch you down here…is that it? Like this?'

She stiffened, then groaned. No, no, not there, she agonised. And not like that.

Leo sometimes made her come first by touching her there. But never before when her body was displayed in such a vulnerable and exposed fashion, never with him watching her responses so blatantly.

Her stomach curled over at the thought.

But he kept touching her in exactly the right spot, and soon she just didn't care.

'Oh God,' she moaned, stiffening and squirming as she tried to hold on, not wanting the magic—or the madness—to end.

'Let yourself go,' Leo urged huskily. 'I want to watch you come. It's the ultimate turn-on for me, don't you know that, seeing you like this?'

Her mind spun at his words.

'Look at me, Brooke,' he commanded forcefully, and she did so, as though pulled by some irresistible magnet. And it was while her eyes were locked to his that her body did exactly what he wanted, splintering apart like fine crystal, her stomach sucking in as her back arched and her lips gasped wide.

Leo made some kind of animal sound, then pulled her down under him, surging into her like a man possessed. His pumping was so deep and wild that he came within seconds, well before her own violently electric spasms had faded away. She called out his name and he scooped her up off the bed, clasping her close, rocking them both to and fro while he shuddered into her. Rapturous tremors ricocheted down Brooke's spine as she clung to him and forgot everything but the moment.

It wasn't till the heat of their animal mating began to cool that sanity slowly returned.

So who seduced who in the end, darling? a coldly cynical voice challenged. Who totally lost control? And what, if anything, did you just prove?

Nothing, Brooke accepted wearily, except that you're still giving Leo the only thing he ever wanted from you besides his children. Your body. Your supposedly beautiful but very weak, traitorous body.

And you'll keep on giving it to him, won't you? You'll keep on humiliating yourself.

Some last pathetic vestige of pride compelled her to struggle against his breast-squashing hold, but she was too exhausted and he was too strong. Defeated, she laid her face back against his chest and began to weep, great racking sobs of despair.

'Hey, hey, what's this?' Leo unwrapped his arms to take her tearstained face in his hands, tipping it upwards.

She couldn't say a word, just looked up into his puzzled gaze with all the love and despair in her heart. *How could you do this to me?* she wanted to wail at him. *I gave you everything!*

I'm still giving you everything.

Her face crumpled anew at the thought.

'There, there,' he crooned, cradling her weeping face back against him and stroking her long hair down her back with tender hands. 'You got too excited, that's all. It happens that way sometimes, if you haven't had sex for a while.'

Gently, he lowered her back to her pillow, and even more gently withdrew.

'Hush now,' he murmured, stroking her hair back from her face. 'Stop crying and try to sleep, or you'll get another headache.' He kept stroking her hair and her head and gradually the tears stopped. Brooke just lay there in his arms, staring blankly up at the ceiling, trying not to feel a thing.

He continued stroking her hair and, speaking softly, gently, said, 'I know I haven't been much of a husband lately, but the past three weeks have been…difficult, to say the least. My brother's death has caused all sorts of problems, problems too complex and numerous to explain. Suffice to say I've sorted them out now.'

Brooke listened to this subtly worded confession without a shred of reassurance or forgiveness. How smooth he was, she realised. How clever. How *patronising*!

She closed her eyes against the temptation to look into his. For she knew she wouldn't see anything re-

vealing there. Leo lied as well as he did everything
else.

'I probably haven't told you this often enough,' he
went on, bending to press his lips into her hair, 'but I
do love you, Brooke…'

Brooke stopped breathing. How could words so
longed for strike like daggers into her heart? And who
exactly was Leo trying to convince with his far-too-
late declaration?

Oh, Leo…Leo…

Brooke's soul wept, but her heart hardened. For she
knew who her husband really loved. His own mother
had said so. Francesca. The woman he'd once planned
to marry.

But it was partly as Giuseppe had said. Leo would
not want to lose his family, even for Francesca. So his
wife was to be kept happy on the home front, keeping
her suspicion-free.

Brooke was prepared to go to great lengths to save
her marriage—hadn't she already shown that?—but she
had to keep *some* self-respect. So she simply refused
to hear the words, or recognise them, pride keeping her
eyes tightly shut as she pretended to be sound asleep.

'Brooke?' Leo prompted softly after a few seconds.

She remained steadfastly silent. Finally he sighed,
then let her convincingly limp body slip out of his
arms.

A bitter resentment burned through Brooke at the
tender way he covered her with a sheet before rolling
away from her onto his side. He really thought it was
that easy, didn't he? Give the missus some great sex
and a few sweet words and she'd be putty in his hands,

never questioning what he did or where he went, leaving him scot-free to have it all. His wife, his children, *and* his mistress.

How he would manage to conduct such an affair from Sydney, Australia, Brooke had no idea. But she was convinced he would. Leo occasionally went overseas on business for a week or two. His father had agreed to his staying and living in Sydney five years ago provided he took on the role of troubleshooter for Parini International. In the early days she'd gone with him, but not now, not with two children in tow.

No doubt there would suddenly be more business trips abroad. Not necessarily to Milan—Leo was no fool!—but to New York, perhaps, or London, or Paris even. Places where the Parini family business had offices and luxury company apartments, places Francesca could fly to at a moment's notice and be bedded without anyone being any the wiser.

It wasn't as if Leo's comings and goings were ever reported in the tabloids or gossip columns. The Parini men had always kept a low profile publicity-wise. No doubt Leo would use the excuse of Lorenzo's death to increase such trips. And no doubt she would never be allowed to accompany him.

'A mother's place is with her children!'

Leo had made that firm statement when she'd brought up the subject of returning to work shortly after Claudia was born. She hadn't meant straight away. She'd meant when both children finally went to school. But Leo had been so adamant—and so shocked she could even *think* of doing such a thing—that she'd never brought the matter up again.

Brooke shook her head in despair over her past weaknesses, as well as her present. Leo would do what he wanted to do. And she wouldn't say a word. That was the truth of it, wasn't it?

But was this bravery or cowardice? There were so many things to be weighed up, so many people's happiness, not just her own. But how did you keep other people happy when you felt so miserable inside? How could you smile when you wanted to cry?

Tears blurred her eyes, but she blinked them away and turned over to face the far wall. She was damned if she was going to cry again. Tears never solved a thing, anyway.

Sleep didn't come for Brooke till just before the dawn, and by the time she woke again Leo had left for Milan, leaving a note on his pillow saying that after last night he would make sure not to be late home tonight.

She groaned at the wave of involuntary excitement which swept through her veins, her self-disgust as sharp as the shards of desire slicing through her. Her nipples went hard with the hot memory of what Leo had done to them last night. And what she'd done to him!

She was clutching the note in her hands, her cheeks burning and her stomach churning, when she remembered her period was due that day.

A sob of sheer relief escaped her lips. She simply couldn't have faced any more self-destructive behaviour.

Or many more days here, for that matter, she thought agitatedly as she swept on her dressing gown and hurried along to the children's rooms. She kept reassuring herself that in just over a day, they would be on their way home.

Once there, maybe she would be able to face Leo making love to her again without feeling so humiliated afterwards. At least Francesca would be thousands of miles away, and, perhaps more to the point, Leo could not have possibly made love to *her* that same day.

Brooke stopped momentarily outside the nursery door to take several deep, steadying breaths. Once composed, she plastered a smile on her face and reached for the doorknob.

Although called the nursery, it was really a large playroom, with wonderfully large windows, a sensibly tiled floor and enough toys to fill a kindergarten. When she went in, Claudia was busily setting up a tea party with three of her dolls. Alessandro was riding a large, life-like rocking horse over in a far corner. Nina, the Italian nanny, was sitting in a window-seat, perhaps admiring the lake.

It really looked very beautiful in the mornings, the water like glass.

Nina's head jerked round at the sound of the door opening. On seeing Brooke, she rose and smiled at her. 'Good morning, *signora*,' she said in English. She liked practising her English, and planned to visit Australia one day. 'You're looking much better today. You have colour in your cheeks.'

Brooke's cheeks coloured a little more at the remark. 'Yes,' she said briskly. 'My headache's gone. Thank you for looking after the children, Nina. I'll take over now.'

'I'll be down in the kitchen if you want me,' she said, still smiling her warm, placid smile. She was twenty, a plump but pretty girl, very sweet, and wonderful with children. Apparently she had several younger brothers and sisters, and helped her mother with them.

'Mummy, you're up very late,' Claudia said, without complaint but with some puzzlement. 'I missed you.'

'I missed you too, darling,' Brooke returned. 'Have you got a hug and a kiss for me?'

Claudia jumped up from the red plastic chair and came running on her solid little legs, hurling herself into Brooke's already outstretched arms.

Claudia was a hugger and a kisser. Alessandro was too, but after Leo's comment one day recently that too much of that would turn him into a Mummy's boy, Brooke had begun holding back a little with her son. Now, she saw Alessandro watching her with his sister, a jealous sulk on his beautiful mouth.

She put Claudia down and walked over towards Alessandro, who promptly jumped off the rocking horse and pretended to polish the saddle, his back to her.

'And do you have a kiss and hug for me too, my darling boy?' she said gently as she squatted down behind him.

He hesitated, then with a sob whirled and threw himself into her arms, his own arms wrapping tightly around her neck. 'What's wrong, Alessandro?' she asked, her heart catching with love and concern.

He pulled back, his big dark eyes glistening. 'I want to go home,' he cried. 'I miss Mister Puss.'

Brooke almost smiled, because she didn't think Mister Puss would be missing *him* too much. A ten-year-old Abyssinian, Mister Puss had been inherited from an elderly neighbour when the woman had had to go into a nursing home and couldn't look after the cat. Alessandro had just begun walking at the time, and had thought the cat was the best toy in the world, a moving, meowing stuffed toy, with a tail to pull, ears to poke and a big, soft furry stomach to sit or lie on.

'He's not a cushion!' Brooke had kept telling her son, but to no avail. Oddly, the cat had taken no steps to avoid his tormentor. He never hissed or scratched, or ran away when sat on, as he so easily could have. It was truly a mystery.

'I miss Mister Puss too,' she said. 'We'll be home soon.'

'Not soon enough!' he grumbled.

Brooke sighed. She couldn't agree more.

CHAPTER FOUR

AT LAST!

Brooke expelled a series of relieved sighs as she carried Claudia swiftly along the passageway towards the jumbo jet which would take them to Sydney. The connecting flight from Milan had been late, and her already strung-out nerves had begun to fray further. But they'd made it just in time.

The last thirty-six hours had been the most difficult of her life. She'd felt as if a bomb was ticking away inside her, about to explode. Outwardly she'd managed to kept her cool, saying all the right things to her in-laws, and acting as normal as possible with Leo.

But it had not been easy. A couple of times he'd given her an oddly puzzled look, as though he knew something was wrong with her but didn't know what.

Thinking of Leo had her glancing over her shoulder at him. He was quite a few paces behind her, walking along as cool and casual as you please, holding his laptop in one hand and Alessandro's hand in the other. The boy was striding out by his side, like the little man he liked to be when he was with his precious father. Nothing sissy for him like being carried.

Leo caught her eye and gave her one of his warm, intimate little smiles, the kind which once upon a time would have made her feel so wonderfully cared for and cared about.

Now, it set her teeth on edge.

She whipped her eyes forward before he could see the instant resentment flash into her eyes, and hurried on.

'Do you want *me* to carry Claudia?' he called after her, something in his voice telling her that he *had* picked up some negative vibe, if not in her eyes then in her manner.

'No, thank you,' she replied crisply without turning round. 'I'm fine.'

As fine as you can be when you're living a lie, she thought bitterly. When the love you once felt for your husband is gradually changing to contempt. When your heart is bleeding to death and your marriage is nothing but a sham!

Unfortunately, Brooke *had* to look back at Leo once she'd stepped on the plane and the flight attendant had put out her hand for her boarding pass. She didn't have it. Leo was carrying all four passes.

'My husband has them,' she tautly informed the very pretty girl, nodding towards Leo as she stepped to one side and turned around.

It was another eye-opening education, watching the flight attendant with Leo. Brooke had always known women found him overwhelmingly attractive. Waitresses rushed to do his bidding without delay. Shop girls simpered all over him. Women on the street would stare openly as he walked by.

This had never bothered her before, because she'd been secure in her marriage and had trusted her husband implicitly. Besides, Leo had never seemed to notice the stares, or the fawning attention. Whenever they were together he'd seemed to have eyes only for her. He'd never done anything to make her jealous, so she'd never *been* jealous.

Not so any more. A black jealousy now festered within her soul, making her fume at the way the flight attendant's face lit up when she saw Leo, the way the woman's green cat-like eyes gleamed in that very female yet predatory way as they raked over him.

Of course Leo was looking superb—and sexy as hell—in a charcoal-grey suit and a black crew-necked top. Any woman would have fancied him.

But did that mean she had to smile at him in that sickening way in front of *her*, his wife? Didn't she have any sense of diplomacy, or decency?

No, Brooke realised ruefully. Where men like Leo were concerned, it was open season these days. Especially if they didn't love their wives...

Brooke suddenly felt sick. Maybe Francesca would prove the least of her problems in the long run. Maybe she was trying to save a marriage and keep a husband who could *not* be kept, no matter what humiliations she endured or how many blind eyes she turned.

'Your seats are on the flight deck, sir,' the attendant purred. 'Up those stairs and to the left. The third row from the front, the two seats on each side of the aisle.'

'Thank you,' Leo returned with his usual polite, pleasant manner. Yet to Brooke his returning smile seemed slightly flirtatious this time, his eyes lingering far too long on the female's moist mouth. Was her imagination playing tricks on her, or was she suddenly seeing the real Leo behind the façade?

When he glanced over at Brooke she hoped she didn't look as despairing as she felt.

A brief frown flittered across his face before he bent down to talk to his son. 'You go up first, Alessandro. And here…you can carry my laptop, if you promise to be very careful with it. Did you hear what the young lady said just now? Our seats are three rows from the front. You can count to three, can't you?'

'I can count to ten!' Alessandro answered, pride in his voice.

'Of course you can. You're a clever boy. In that case, three won't be any problem at all. When you get to three, sit down in one of the window seats and put the laptop on the one next to you. We'll all be with you shortly.'

Alessandro scampered off up the steps to do his daddy's bidding and Leo turned to Brooke. 'Now,' he said firmly, and took his sleepy daughter out of his wife's arms. 'I'll take missie. She's much too big for you to carry up those steps. Especially in that get-up,' he added, with a wry glance down at her outfit.

Brooke gave no reply to this, just whirled round and began mounting the admittedly steep and quite narrow steps.

Immediately she saw what Leo meant. The long, narrow skirt she was wearing restricted movement, despite the split in the back seam, pulling tight around her bottom each time she lifted her foot up to the next step.

'Nice view,' Leo drawled from right behind her.

The sexually charged remark flustered Brooke. For one thing, it wasn't like Leo to make such comments. What flustered her most, however, was her own instant intense awareness of her bottom, and the way it was moving, barely inches from his face.

Brooke wished with all her heart that she was wearing something much less revealing, and much, much looser.

It *had* crossed her mind that morning not to get as dolled up as she usually did when travelling with Leo. But she could hardly stop dressing the way she usually dressed, not if she wanted to pretend nothing was wrong.

Leo always looked a million dollars when in public. Everyone would have thought it very strange if *she'd* shown up today garbed in tracksuit pants and sweatshirt.

So she'd put on the designer suede suit Leo had bought for her the previous year in a boutique in Milan, teamed it with a cream cashmere top and slipped on high heels which matched the colour of the suit—a deep camel shade.

Leaving her hair down would have been impractical, so she'd put it up, made up her face, added gold jewellery, then presented herself downstairs in her usual well-groomed state, if not her usual composed inner self.

She'd imagined—mistakenly—that getting on this plane would solve some of her problems, that she would calm down once Milan—and Francesca—were far behind them. But suddenly Brooke realised that wasn't going to be the case, because she'd brought the problem with her.

Leo was the problem. Leo, who could still make her do things and feel things, almost against her will. Leo, whom she still loved, even while she hated him. Leo, who at that very moment was behind her, coveting her sexually despite being in love with another woman.

What a wicked, ruthless man she was married to!

Face flaming, she reached the top of the stairs, where another attractive female waited in attendance, ready to take jackets whilst pointing out the many added advantages of flying business class on the flight deck. The on-tap galley down at the back. The toilets front and back. The personal televisions attached to each seat.

Brooke handed the woman her jacket, which had been draped over her arm, then proceeded along the aisle to where Alessandro was sitting in his seat, already strapped in. When she went to pick up the laptop and sit next to him, her son gave her a rather disdainful look.

'You can't sit there, Mummy. That's Daddy's seat. Daddy always sits next to me on planes,' he told her.

This was true. Alessandro was not an easy child to contain and control, especially during long flights. He was given to boredom when awake, and became very grizzling and difficult to handle when tired. He didn't drop off to sleep as easily as Claudia, and didn't *need* as much sleep as his younger sister.

They'd found that he was much better behaved if Leo sat next to him.

Leo, unlike some Italian fathers, was not over-indulgent. He gave Alessandro plenty of love and attention, but still expected him to be well behaved when with him, especially in public. He didn't discipline him physically. Just one dark, displeased glare from his father's eyes was enough to curtail the child, and make him think twice about his antics.

Brooke understood just how Alessandro felt when his father scowled at him like that. Leo had a very powerful personality, and a very powerful gaze. When he turned those half-hooded deeply set black eyes on you, he could make you do exactly what he wanted. Either because you wanted to, or because you were afraid *not* to.

When she'd first met Leo, they'd seduced her in seconds, those eyes. She'd been in his bed that very first night.

Brooke suddenly had the ghastly feeling Leo would want to sit next to her on the flight home.

And she simply could not bear the prospect.

Ignoring her son's protest, she swept up Leo's laptop and practically threw it onto the seat opposite. A swift glance down the back of plane showed the flight attendant holding a now wide awake Claudia whilst Leo shrugged smoothly out of his suit jacket. The woman was smiling at him in a similar flirtatious manner to the one downstairs.

Typical! Brooke thought savagely, and plonked herself down next to Alessandro.

'Daddy's sitting next to Claudia this time,' she informed her instantly sulking son. 'And don't you make a fuss,' she warned darkly, 'or you'll be sorry!'

Alessandro stared at this rather frightening new mother with a measure of shock in his big dark eyes.

'What's this?' Leo said when he came alongside, Claudia in his arms. 'Are you sure that's where you want to sit, Brooke?' he asked, and she glared up at him.

'I thought it was time Claudia had a turn sitting next to you,' she said rather sharply.

'Daddy!' Claudia's large velvety eyes lit up in a fashion which Brooke found very irksome. *Your father is just a man, not some god*, she wanted to snap at their daughter.

Leo hesitated, frowning down at Brooke.

She wrenched her eyes away from that penetrating gaze and stared out through the window onto the tarmac below. Not that she could see much except lights winking. It was pitch-black outside.

'Till you go to sleep, perhaps,' Leo conceded. 'Then I think we might change the arrangements. I wish to sit with your mother at some time.'

Brooke's stomach clenched down hard. She knew it. She just *knew* it!

'What about me?' Alessandro wailed.

'A big boy like you doesn't need me to babysit him any longer,' Leo said as he popped the laptop into the overhead luggage rack then bent over to settle Claudia in the window seat. 'Meanwhile, you can look after your mother for me,' he threw over his shoulder at Alessandro. 'She seems a little stressed out today. You know how she hates flying.'

Brooke tried not to stare at the way Leo's trousers pulled tight over his buttocks as he leant over Claudia's seat. But it was a bit hard not to look when she was only a couple of feet away, with her eyes level.

Leo had a great behind. Hell, he had a great everything. That was part of her problem. If only he'd grown flabby and bald and unattractive. If only she didn't still fancy him so darned much!

She was staring at his derrière with ill-concealed lust when Leo's head twisted further around to look right at her. Her eyes jerked up to his, but it was too late, and the hint of a smug little smile began to tug at the corners of his mouth.

Brooke battled to keep from blushing but she failed miserably. Not for the first time during the past couple of days, she was grateful she had her period. For Lord knew what Leo might have persuaded her to do during this flight if she hadn't been indisposed. It seemed finding out that her husband was a liar and an adulterer did not automatically turn her off him in a sexual sense.

Perversely, Brooke was finding she wanted Leo now more than ever before. She wondered if this was Mother Nature's way of making sure the family unit survived. Or was it just life having the last laugh on her for loving a man so blindly, and so obsessively?

'I'll look after Mummy for you, Daddy,' Alessandro said, all puffed up with pride at being asked to do such a grown-up job. 'I can set up her TV for her too. Mummy's not very good at doing things like that. She gets mad with the video at home sometimes, and says naughty words.'

'Really?' Leo said as he sat down, bringing his face almost down to her level. 'I can't imagine that,' he murmured across the aisle, his amused gaze dancing all over her heated face. 'Not *your* mummy. Not your perfect, ladylike mummy.'

'She does too, Daddy,' Alessandro insisted, even

while Brooke's face whipped round to glower at her big-mouthed son.

The sudden movement of the plane backing out of its parking bay, and the captain announcing they would soon be taking off, brought a welcome end to *that* little episode. And none too soon, in Brooke's opinion. She'd been about to combust!

The distraction of take-off and the serving of dinner and drinks soon afterwards was also very welcome. Both parents were fully occupied with their charges, making sure they didn't spill their drinks all over their laps.

After the meal, there were trips to the toilet, shoes to be removed, socks put on, television programmes to be selected, seats to be tipped back. The ever-attentive female flight attendant brought pillows and blankets for the children, fussing over them as if they were *her* children. No doubt she would have liked them to be, Brooke thought sourly as the woman flashed Leo another dazzling smile.

Finally, it was time for the lights to be dimmed in the cabin. Almost immediately Claudia fell fast asleep, and lo and behold so did Alessandro, the little traitor. Brooke could not believe it!

When Leo leant over the aisle towards her, she stiffened in her seat.

'Best we move Claudia over to your seat,' he whispered. 'She won't stir for anything.'

'Why don't we just leave them be, Leo?' she suggested in desperation.

'No,' he said firmly. 'I want to talk to you. And *not* leaning over an aisle all the time.'

Knowing there would be no rest till she agreed, Brooke sighed and stood up, moving out of the way while Leo scooped up an unconscious Claudia and settled her in the seat next to her brother.

Brooke's heart caught as she watched her husband's tenderness with his little daughter. The way he arranged her pillows and tucked her in, the way he kissed her cheek, then Alessandro's.

She knew then that nothing would make Leo ask her for a divorce. He would stay married to her whether he loved her or not.

He straightened and smiled at her. 'Peace at last,' he said with a sigh. 'And privacy. You take the window seat, my sweet. I rather like the thought of having you imprisoned against a wall, with no escape but to climb over my lap.'

Brooke gritted her teeth when he took her by the elbow and ushered her quite forcefully into the window seat.

'Can I help you with that?' he said, leaning over to do up her seat-belt. She sat stiffly in her seat while he did so, trying not to thrill at his nearness, or the brush of his arms across her instantly taut breasts. Afterwards his head lifted, and their mouths were only inches away. She gulped at the look in his eyes, then gasped when he closed the distance between their lips.

It was a long, slow, tongue-in-her-mouth kiss which set her head spinning and her heart racing.

'Leo, stop it,' she protested breathlessly when his mouth lifted momentarily for a breather.

'Stop what?'

'Stop embarrassing me. People might see us.'

'Nearly everyone's asleep,' he murmured as he slid a hand around her neck and stared deep into her eyes. 'Either that or watching television. But I'm not sure I care, anyway. You look so beautiful and sexy today that you've been driving me insane. To be honest, you've been driving me insane since the other night. I can't stop thinking about what you did to me, especially with this lovely mouth of yours…'

His thumb-pad traced over her mouth and her lips fell apart once more, still wet and tingling from his kisses.

'You have such beautiful lips,' he murmured. 'You have no idea how they feel, or how glorious it is to watch your wife do that, to know she *wants* to do it. You've never done that before without my asking you to. God, I can't wait for you to do it again.' He began to insert his thumb into her mouth, and she almost, *almost* sucked it.

'Leo, for pity's sake,' she gasped, slapping his hand away. 'I…I can't. Not here. I *can't*!'

He looked surprised, as though it had never occurred to him that she could, or would. But oh, dear Lord, she might have, if he'd insisted. She was dizzy with the thought of it, drugged by the darkness of her own desires.

Confusion and dismay crashed together to create a very real distress, tears pricking at her eyes. How could she keep wanting him like this when she knew it was only sex with him?

'No, of course you can't,' he murmured, frowning at her distraught face. 'I'm sorry if I've upset you. I didn't mean to. I would never ask you to do anything you didn't want to do. Hell, Brooke, don't *cry*! I misinterpreted the way you were looking at me earlier. I thought... Damn it all, what does it matter what I thought now? Clearly I was wrong.'

He reached out and pulled her into his arms. 'Come here... Hush... Don't cry now... You're tired, that's all... Travelling with the children is always stressful... But we'll be home soon and then we can get back to our normal life. Okay?' He put her away from him and stared searchingly into her tear-washed eyes. 'Forgive me?'

She merely blinked and said nothing.

He sighed. 'You must understand how incredible you were the other night. I wouldn't be a normal man if I didn't want you to do it again. But I honestly didn't mean here. I would never do anything to hurt you or humiliate you. Never!'

At this, Brooke's eyes welled up again, and Leo pulled her back into his arms, apologising profusely.

Brooke *wanted* to forgive and forget—everything! But forgiveness simply would not come. She could feel something else building up inside herself, something cold and alien, something dark and dangerous, something strong and violent.

It was there now, deep inside, muttering away.

You've compromised enough already in this marriage, it growled. Time to make a stand. Time to show this unfaithful lying bastard he can't get away with what he's done. Time to take him on!

Brooke shuddered at where such actions would lead. Straight to the divorce court. Do not pass 'Go'! Do not collect two hundred!

Yet it had its appeal all right, she thought, even as she lay, weeping quietly, in his arms. She would just love to see the look on his face when he found out she knew all about Francesca, then his panic when he realised he might lose custody of his children. Suddenly she understood why people said revenge was sweet.

But it was also self-destructive.

Her emotions were tearing her this way and that. Poor Hamlet really had her sympathy.

To be or not to be, that was the question!

She really needed to talk to someone, someone who would see things more clearly and who wasn't going to have emotion cloud the issues. Someone who might be able to tell her what to do for the best.

Not her mother. Oh, dear heaven, no. She needed someone who wasn't warped and twisted, who would appreciate what she was trying to do: not only save her marriage, but protect her children's happiness.

It would have to be someone else.

But who?

CHAPTER FIVE

LEO had booked a car to be waiting for them at Mascot airport, thank heavens. The last thing she could have coped with at that moment was standing in a taxi queue for ages.

Brooke wondered if she looked as bad as she felt as she traipsed through Customs, a floppy Claudia in her arms. An equally sleepy Alessandro was draped over Leo's shoulder just ahead of them. Their luggage was in a trolley, which Leo was pushing somewhat wearily with his spare hand.

He always said that was the worst thing about living in Australia—the distance they had to travel to see his family, or for him to go overseas on business. But he'd also said he would never want to bring up his children anywhere else. He liked the easy-going lifestyle, the weather, the space, and the relatively low crime rate.

The flight had felt interminable this time to Brooke, despite both children sleeping for most of it. Brooke had slept too, but not for nearly as long as she'd pretended. They'd touched down for a short stop at Bangkok, during which Brooke hadn't even bothered to leave the plane. Leo had, saying he needed to stretch his legs. He'd taken the children with him.

Brooke had been glad to see him go, experiencing an immediate easing of tension the moment he was out of sight.

Was that how it was going to be from now on? she worried as she came through the exit gate. Holding onto herself whenever he was around, then feeling relative relief once he'd gone out through the front door? And all the while having to endure this *thing*, this maelstrom of emotion whirling deep within her, turning tighter and tighter.

Eventually something—or someone—was sure to snap.

The driver from the car company was waiting for them just outside the exit gate, holding a card with their name printed on it. Leo introduced himself and handed the man the trolley with the luggage.

'This way,' the chauffeur said, and set off with the trolley.

'Is the car far away?' Leo asked after they'd followed him some distance through the long arrivals terminal.

'Not too far.' He led them towards a glass-doored exit through which Brooke could see a long, makeshift walkway with high boarded sides.

'I hope not,' Leo returned. 'My family's very tired, poor darlings,' he added, throwing Brooke a soft smile.

Brooke hated herself for deliberately turning her face away from him. But she simply could not stand the loving warmth in his eyes. Was it her imagination again, or was Leo being extra considerate to her? Extra affectionate?

He'd always been a caring husband, when he'd thought to be. But he'd been *so* attentive during the flight it had been almost sickening. Nothing had been too much trouble. If he'd asked her once if she was all right, he'd asked her a thousand times!

Guilt, she decided with a stab of resentment. For what else could it be? Why should he suddenly act differently with her?

'Everything's a bit of a mess here at Mascot at the moment,' the chauffeur explained as they trailed after him through the automatic doors. 'What with all the extensions for the Olympics. Hopefully everything will be back to normal soon. The car's just down here, to the right.'

The air was cool and crisp outside the terminal, with not a cloud in the sky. But the sun was sure to come out later, warming Sydney to a very pleasant autumn temperature.

The car was parked just around the corner, as the driver had said, a white stretch limousine with plush grey upholstery and tinted windows. The luxury of the car surprised Brooke. Leo was certainly pulling out all the stops, she thought sourly.

Brooke climbed into the car first, and deliberately buckled Claudia in on the back seat next to her, leaving Leo to sit next to Alessandro on the seat opposite.

But the ploy backfired when Leo chose the seat facing her, which was more awkward than having him sit next to her. He kept looking straight into her eyes, and frowning his obvious bewilderment at her manner.

Brooke sighed inwardly and turned her face towards the tinted window. It was a relief to be home, she conceded. But being home wasn't going to make everything right overnight.

Claudia stirred beside her.

'Mummy?' she said in slightly worried little-girl voice.

'Yes, sweetie?'

'I want to do a wee-wee.'

'Me too,' Alessandro piped up, before throwing an anxious look up at his father.

Brooke had to smile. At least her children didn't act differently.

'Okay,' Leo said with gritted teeth. 'Everyone out again.'

Whilst waiting for Claudia in the restroom, Brooke tidied her hair and freshened up her face, her reflection in the large mirror showing not a trace of the emotional distress she was still feeling. She didn't even look tired any more.

Brooke was amazed. It just showed the miracles good make-up could perform, though her mother would have said it was her age.

'You can bounce back in your twenties,' she would often moan. 'You can even look good after staying up all night. But wait till you pass forty. You look exactly how you feel in the mornings, or worse. Like you've been dragged through the mill. You mark my words.'

Brooke rarely marked her mother's words. Pity, as it turned out. She'd warned her about Leo but she simply hadn't listened.

Leo and Alessandro were already in the car and buckled up by the time she returned with Claudia.

'You look a hundred per cent better,' her husband said as she climbed in after her daughter. 'I was beginning to get worried about you.'

His comments irked her, as did his ongoing solicitous attitude. Her eyes were cold as they clashed with his. 'We women are easily fixed up,' she bit out before she could stop herself. 'But some repair jobs are only skin-deep, Leo. You'd be wise to remember that.'

Brooke gained no satisfaction from the stunned expression on her husband's face, or his obvious inability to respond to what must seem to him a very strange remark.

Was this the beginning? she thought despairingly. Of the unravelling? Of the end?

Dropping her eyes away from Leo's now frowning face, she attended to Claudia's seat-belt, next to her, then managed to further avoid his penetrating gaze for a while by fiddling with her own seat-belt.

Meanwhile, the car slid away from the kerb, and Alessandro started pestering his father about the cat.

'Can we go past Nanna's place to pick Mister Puss up on the way home, Daddy?'

'Not this morning, Alessandro. Your nanna lives way over town at Turrumurra, nearly an hour's drive from our place. Your mother can take you over there tomorrow to get him while I'm at work.'

Brooke's eyes whipped up to stare at her husband. 'You're going to work tomorrow?' she asked, her suspicions immediately aroused. 'On a *Sunday*?'

Leo *never* worked on a Sunday. A Saturday, maybe, but never Sunday. Sunday was family day. He always spent it with them. Often he took them out somewhere. The beach. The zoo. A picnic. Adventureland. The movies. Why was he rushing to work *this* Sunday? What was so important? Did he need the privacy of his office to telephone his beloved Francesca, to talk sweet nothings in her ear, plan their next romantic rendezvous perhaps?

His expression was weary, she thought. 'Today's Sunday, Brooke. Tomorrow's Monday. We lost a day travelling back.'

'Oh. Oh, yes. I forgot. Stupid me.' Which she was. Stupid, stupid, stupid! Though not as stupid as he thought she was. 'If that's the case,' she said tautly, 'then my mother will be at work tomorrow *too*.'

Leo shrugged. 'Does it matter? You have keys to her place. You can still pick up the cat.'

'Does it occur to you I might like to *see* my mother?' Brooke said waspishly. 'That I might have missed her?'

Leo looked taken aback. 'I think perhaps you *are* still tired. It's not like you to be so snappy. I was just saying it as it is, Brooke. Besides, I wouldn't say you're ever *that* anxious to visit your mother.'

Brooke's chin shot up defiantly. 'My mother and I are a lot closer than you think.' And a lot more *like* each other than you think, buster, came that other dark, hard voice.

It certainly set Brooke thinking. Maybe she'd been wrong to dismiss the idea of confiding in her mother. She was beginning to think her mother's advice might be just what she needed to hear. Because she could not go on like this. Not for long, anyway.

'I'll drive over today,' she said curtly. 'While the children are having their afternoon sleep.'

'But I want to go and visit Nanna too, Mummy,' Alessandro piped up.

'Me too,' Claudia joined in.

'Not today,' Brooke said sharply. 'Today you can

stay at home and your father can mind you. I need to talk to my mother about something. Alone.'

'About what?' Leo asked, his eyes puzzled.

'Mother and daughter things,' Brooke retorted. '*Women* things. I'm sure you wouldn't be interested.'

'Are you referring to that bad headache you had recently? My mother said you told her it might be a PMT problem. I never knew you suffered from PMT, Brooke. You never mentioned it before.'

'What's PMT?' Alessandro asked.

'Poor mothers travelling,' Brooke whipped back as quick as a flash.

Leo laughed and leant forward slightly, bringing his face disturbingly close to hers. 'That was quick,' he murmured, his dark eyes dancing with dry amusement. 'You know, you're much cleverer than you let on sometimes, aren't you?'

Brooke's hands clenched tightly in her lap as she resisted the urge to slap him right across his smugly handsome face.

'You mean considering I'm a dumb blonde?'

He leant back abruptly, his smile fading, his mouth thinning. Leo was an intelligent man, but he was used to his wife not causing any waves in his life.

'You really *are* in a touchy mood. I'll try not to take offence. I'll blame it on the flight and the time of the month. But I sincerely hope you're in a better frame of mind come Wednesday.'

'Wednesday? What's on Wednesday?'

His eyebrows arched. 'It's our anniversary.'

'Oh. Oh, yes. I'd forgotten for a moment.'

His eyebrows arched further.

'What's a nannaversary?' Alessandro asked. 'Is it something to do with Nanna?'

'No, son,' Leo said, his eyes remaining on Brooke. 'It's like a birthday. On Wednesday, it's five years to the day since I married your mother.'

'Are we going to have a big party like when I turned four?'

'No. You don't have a big party till you've been married at least twenty-five years.'

Brooke almost laughed. At the rate they were going, they'd be lucky to make it to six!

'Till then,' Leo continued, 'each year, husbands take their wives out somewhere special for a private party. Just the two of them. This year I have a special treat in mind for your mother. I hope she has something special in mind for me too.'

Brooke stared at him, colour zooming into her cheeks as various images filled her mind.

'Do you get presents?' Claudia asked her father eagerly.

'Of course,' Leo replied, smiling at his daughter.

'Will you get Daddy a present, Mummy?' Claudia asked her mother with bright, excited eyes. Claudia was a born shopper. Present-buying ranked right up there with pretty clothes and dolls.

'We'll see, darling,' she said, glad to have an excuse to look away from Leo's suddenly smouldering gaze.

'Your mother doesn't have to buy me a present this year, Claudia,' Leo said silkily. 'I'll settle for something money can't buy.'

'What's that, Daddy?' Alessandro asked. 'Nonno in Italy says there's nothing money can't buy.'

'Oh, he does, does he? Well, Nonno has been known to be wrong. I'm talking about love, son. You can't buy love.'

No, Brooke thought despairingly. You can't. Otherwise she'd sell or pawn everything she owned to buy her husband's love.

But Leo wasn't talking about love. He was talking about sex. The sort of hot, wild sex she'd given him the other night. Regardless of what he felt for Francesca, he still fancied *her* in bed, maybe now more than ever. She'd shown him a new side to herself the other night, and he was eager to see that side again.

Brooke hadn't really achieved anything by her performance the other night. All she'd done was make Leo think she loved him more than ever.

Perverse as it was, that seemed to be the case. Even worse, she was already looking forward to Wednesday night. How sick could she get?

But it explained why she was being so snakey. Because she despised herself for still loving him.

'That's true, Leo,' she said, a touch bitterly. 'But an actual present might last longer. Ah, here we are. That was a short trip. It's an advantage living so close to the airport, isn't it? Still, there's not much traffic at this time in the morning. Come along, children, undo your seat-belts and let's go see if your rooms are still there.'

Brooke steered her children out onto the pavement and in through the front gate, along the old stone path towards the front steps, doing a quick survey of the front yard as she hurried by. Fortunately, the lawn and garden didn't look too bad for having been neglected for over three weeks. Grass didn't grow much in the autumn, and their garden consisted mostly of flowering shrubs.

She had her house keys ready in her hand by the time she'd mounted the front steps and swiftly inserted the right key in the door, leaving Leo behind to pay the driver and carry in the luggage. As soon as she pushed open the door, the children dashed inside ahead of her and ran up the hallway. Brooke followed more slowly, glancing in the living rooms as she went.

Home at last. *Her* home.

The house wasn't anything flash to look at from the street, just a simple federation-style cottage with a red roof, dark brick and stained glass windows.

Leo had bought the place because it was only a five-minute drive from his warehouse and office complex at Botany, with the added bonus of being close to the airport. He hadn't consulted Brooke in the purchase, and she had the feeling she'd passed some sort of test when she'd loved it on sight, and hadn't complained it wasn't grand enough.

In truth, she thought it was a lovely home, with a warm, cosy feeling to the rooms plus the most beautiful view over Botany Bay from the glassed-in front porch. She would have been happy living in it exactly as it was, but Leo had immediately brought in the renovators.

Initially, there had only been three bedrooms and one bathroom, a largish kitchen, an L-shaped lounge-dining room, a small sunroom, and a separate laundry shed out at the back. All these rooms had been retained in essence, but the back wall had been knocked out and the house extended to include a huge rumpus room, plus a guestroom with a second bathroom attached. The sunroom had become a large internal laundry, and the old laundry a garden shed. The only other change had been to the master bedroom, which was fortunately large enough to have had an elegant *en suite* bathroom included in one corner without sacrificing too much space.

Brooke had had a lot of fun decorating the house from top to toe. Initially, she'd been afraid Leo would insist on filling the house with Italian furniture and artwork, the kind he imported. She'd had visions of the cream-painted rooms filled to overflowing with the sort of dark, heavy, ornate pieces which really needed villa-style rooms in which to look good.

But thankfully Leo hadn't wanted to recreate a smaller version of his family villa out here. He seemed only too happy to have an Australian-style home, and had given Brooke a totally free hand in the decorating, plus a very generous budget. She could have spent a small fortune on furniture and furnishings from the most expensive shops in Sydney, but she had always hated that kind of indulgence, and instead had bought simple but solid pieces from major chainstores. She'd haunted their half-yearly sales and secured some fantastic bargains.

It always gave her pleasure to walk through the house and see what she'd achieved with a relatively small amount of money. Okay, so she didn't have antiques in every corner, or old masters hanging on the walls. But Brooke knew her home was beautiful to look at and comfortable to live in, with a simple style and understated elegance.

As for art… The pictures on the walls had been chosen because they were pleasing to the eye and suited the rooms in question, both in colour and content. Many a time her well-heeled dinner guests had commented on and complimented them, and, whilst the frames were high quality, not one picture was an original.

I would hate to lose my home, Brooke thought as she wandered down the hallway.

And I might, she realised with a sudden pang of dismay, if I don't get a grip on myself. I'm acting like a fool. An irrational, emotional, jealous fool.

But she couldn't seem to get a grip. She was on a roller-coaster ride to hell!

'Mummy, my room's still here,' Claudia trilled, tugging at her skirt. 'And so are all my dollies.'

'Of course your room's still here, silly,' Alessandro said, though he'd just come out of his own room looking as pleased as Punch. 'Mummy was just joking,' he said, and smiled the most incredible smile up at Brooke. So sweet and so open and so innocent.

'Yes, Mummy was just joking, darling,' she said, sweeping her son up into her arms and smothering his dear little face with kisses.

'I can see home's done the trick,' Leo said from the other end of the hallway. He dropped the suitcases he was carrying and walked down towards where the three of them were standing clustered together. 'I hope you've left some of Mummy's kisses for Daddy,' he said to Alessandro.

'No!' Alessandro pouted, and wrapped his arms tightly around Brooke's neck. 'I've taken them all.'

'I have enough kisses for everyone,' Brooke said, thinking of Claudia listening with jealous little ears.

'That's good to hear,' Leo whispered.

Brooke stiffened inside, dark, angry thoughts resurfacing with a vengeance.

So it was back to sex again, was it? Was that all he ever thought about? Or was his revitalised passion for her simply because the woman he *really* wanted was no longer available?

'Could I hope for some decent coffee as well?' he added.

Brooke put Alessandro down before straightening to face her husband. 'You can hope,' she muttered under her breath, 'but you might not get.'

Their eyes clashed. Leo's hardening gaze would have frightened her on any other day. But not *that* day.

'Go wash your face and hands, children,' Brooke instructed them coolly, while Leo glowered at her. 'Then come sit up at the table for some breakfast.'

They raced off to the bathroom, leaving husband and wife momentarily alone.

'What in God's name has got into you?' Leo growled.

'I don't know what you mean,' she said with false sweetness, and swanned off into the kitchen.

Leo was hot on her heels. 'You know *exactly* what I mean,' he muttered from right behind her. 'Don't play dumb with me, Brooke.'

She whirled, her expression scornful. 'Why not? You've always liked it before.'

His face showed true shock.

She smiled. She actually smiled.

She was behaving like a right bitch. But she couldn't seem to help herself.

When she went to walk over to the fridge he grabbed both her arms and spun her round to face him, his fingers digging with bruising strength into her flesh.

She stared down at his hands, then up into his furious eyes, her own like ice. 'Take…your…hands…off…me,' she said, punctuating each word.

He released her immediately, his face anguished as his hands lifted to rake through his hair. Brooke had never seen him look so distressed, and this time she found no satisfaction in it.

'I'm sorry,' he muttered. 'I wasn't trying to hurt you. I just want you to talk to me, tell me what's wrong.'

Brooke genuinely wished that she could, because the thought of his loving Francesca was eating her up alive. She could have borne his having had an affair with her. Like Giuseppe said, that would now have been past history. But to be in love with her. To have been in love with her all these years!

It was inevitable that one day soon she would have to broach the subject of Francesca. But not now. Now was not the right time at all. The children would be back soon, and she had no intention of arguing in front of them.

Thinking of the children brought some sanity back to her troubled soul.

'Leo…please…just leave it for now.'

'No,' he said stubbornly. 'You're angry with me for some reason and I don't know why.'

'I guess that's the problem, Leo,' she said wearily.
'You don't know why…'

'You're talking in riddles, woman!'

It was the wrong thing for him to say.

'Don't you dare call me that,' she snapped once
more. 'My name is Brooke. Brooke! Brooke! Brooke!
I'm not *woman*.'

'Oh, I see,' he sneered back. 'This is some kind of
feminist issue. *That's* why you want to go running to
your darling mother. So what is it, Brooke? You're
dissatisfied with just being a wife and mother now, is
that it? You want more? You want a career, maybe?
Or is it *me* you're dissatisfied with? I haven't been
giving you enough of the sex you suddenly seem to
want? If that's the problem, sweetheart, then believe
me, I'm your man. You don't honestly think I've been
all that thrilled with the way things have been going in
bed this last year, do you? There's just so many faked
orgasms a husband can endure before he starts looking
elsewhere.'

Brooke stared at him, stunned by his attack, *furious*
that he would use such a feeble excuse for his unfaith-
fulness. Okay, so she *had* faked a few orgasms the past
year or two. Wasn't that better than just saying, no, she
didn't feel like it, thank you very much, come back
another night? At least *he'd* been satisfied. He'd certainly rolled over straight away afterwards and gone to
sleep in seconds.

She was opening her mouth to point this out to him
when Claudia ran into the kitchen. 'Mummy, I'm all
clean now,' she said, tugging at her mother's skirt
again. 'I want some Coco Pops and juice.'

Brooke bent down and picked her up, summoning up a smile from wherever mothers summoned up smiles, even when their hearts were breaking. 'Then we'd better get you some Coco Pops and juice *pronto*, hadn't we?' Thank heavens for long-life products, she thought, since they'd hardly had time to do any food shopping since getting off the plane.

'And I suppose we'd better get Daddy his coffee before he has a hernia,' she added ruefully.

'What's a hernia?' Alessandro chirped as he ran into the kitchen.

'What I'm already having,' Leo muttered, his voice clipped and cold. 'You can forget the coffee for now. I'm going down to our bedroom to ring my parents, let them know we've arrived safely.'

'Fine,' Brooke said, infinitely glad to have him out of the room.

By the time he reappeared, some considerable time later, she had herself temporarily under control. Though for how long, she could only guess.

'I won't leave to go to my mother's till the children are asleep,' she told him tautly as she made his coffee. 'They shouldn't be any trouble.'

He stood in the doorway, watching her. 'Brooke, you have to tell me what's bothering you.'

'Yes. Yes, I know,' she admitted. 'Just not now.'

'Why not now? We're alone.'

Which they were. The children had finished breakfast and were at that moment watching some children's programme on television in the rumpus room. Even Alessandro was content to sit quietly this morning, as

he was tired. Brooke could see they wouldn't last too
long before it was nap-time.

'When, then?'

'Tonight. When the children have gone to bed.'

'Tonight, then,' Leo agreed reluctantly, and Brooke
let out a ragged sigh.

CHAPTER SIX

IT WAS a mistake to come here, Brooke thought as she finished pouring out the whole sorry story. The expression on her mother's face said it all. The *I told you so*s were about to start.

'What a bastard!' Phyllis bit out. 'And there I was, utterly convinced Leo was different, that he loved you almost as much as you loved him, that he was a darned good husband and father and nothing like the lying, cheating creeps I had the misfortune to marry. I was almost convinced I'd been wrong about the male species in general. I even started looking favourably at a certain member of the male species I met recently.'

Brooke was speechless. Her mother...looking favourably at a *man*?

'But it turns out darling Leo was just a little cleverer than most men in getting what he wanted,' her mother swept on scornfully, bringing Brooke's mind back from this new mystery man to the man who mattered.

Brooke found herself bristling at her mother's hasty condemnation of Leo. It smacked of a bias and bitterness which was only too ready to jump to the worst conclusions, *never* giving the benefit of the doubt.

'And what, exactly, did Leo want, Mum?' Brooke challenged in brittle tones.

'A beautiful wife who adored him enough to stay home and play full-time housewife and mother, giving him free rein to do exactly what he wanted to do, when he wanted to do it, no questions asked.'

'That's hardly fair. I *chose* to be a full-time house-wife and mother.'

'Did you indeed? I thought you told me once you wanted to go back to work. But I dare say Leo vetoed *that* idea quick-smart. He wouldn't have wanted his beautiful wife out there in the big, bad world. Meanwhile, *he's* out there, having any woman who takes his fancy, including his brother's widow. Oh, yes, don't go doubting him on *that* score. He went to bed with Francesca all right. Men are never to be trusted, Brooke, especially where sex is concerned. Conniving, deceitful, selfish, uncaring bastards, every one of them! I thank you for reminding me.

'Hell, I need a cigarette,' she muttered, and snatched up the unopened packet lying in the centre of the garden table, ripping off the Cellophane and extracting a cigarette with shaking hands. 'Damn, I left my lighter inside. Won't be a moment.'

Brooke just sat there, frowning. How strange, she was thinking. Her mother had only been saying what she herself had been thinking and fearing, but coming from someone else it just didn't sound right. It didn't sound like Leo.

Leo *wasn't* conniving, or deceitful, or uncaring. A little selfish, maybe. But that *was* the nature of the beast. In the main, he was very considerate towards her and the children.

'I've been trying to give up smoking,' her mother snapped on her return.

Brooke blinked her surprise. Her mother had been

smoking sixty cigarettes a day for as long as she could remember. Her even *trying* to give them up was unheard of.

'For this *man*, would you believe? I even went out and had my roots dyed blonde,' she raged on between prolonged puffs.

Brooke's startled eyes jerked up to her mother's hair. Good Lord, she *had*, too.

'Well, it looks good, Mum,' she said truthfully. 'In fact, you're looking darned good all round. Put on a few pounds, haven't you?'

'That's from giving up smoking. I was even going to ask you to help me with my make-up and wardrobe this week. But not now. God, what a fool I've been!' Scowling, she dragged in deeply on the cigarette. 'And what a fool *you've* been,' she directed waspishly at Brooke. 'I warned you Leo would make you miserable. And I was right!'

'You were *wrong*!' Brooke countered. Leaning over, she snatched the cigarette out her mother's startled hand and stabbed it to death in the till then amazingly empty ashtray. 'Leo's made me very happy. He's a wonderful husband and a wonderful father. Please don't use this small personal crisis of mine as an excuse to wallow in old bitternesses, or to start smoking again!'

Phyllis made a scoffing sound. '"Small personal crisis" indeed. Your husband doesn't *love* you, Brooke. He's just *used* you.'

'Don't be such a drama queen, Mum. Leo does love me! He told me so the other night.'

Phyllis shook her head. 'I don't believe I'm hearing this.'

'Well, you are, and you're going to hear more! I've been acting the same way as you, but I can see now how unfair to Leo I've been. I condemned him without a hearing. I was prosecutor, judge and jury. I have no real evidence that he's been unfaithful to me. Or that he's even still in love with Francesca. All I have is gossip and innuendo and suspicion.'

'Are you forgetting the fact he lied to you about where he was that night? And what about the guilty way he crept in? Not to mention the state of his…er…equipment.'

Perversely, the more her mother condemned Leo, the more Brooke felt compelled to defend him. 'Leo explained that. He'd just had a long cold shower.'

Phyllis rolled her eyes. 'For pity's sake, girl, think clearly on this! *Why* didn't Leo tell you he'd once been engaged to Francesca if he no longer loves her?'

'Why should he? That was before he met me. Clearly Leo isn't the type who rakes over the past. If I recall rightly, not once did he ask me about *my* previous boyfriends. And he must have known I'd had at least one! I wasn't a virgin when I met him.'

'Which rather confirms what I said, don't you think?' her mother argued. 'When a man's madly in love with you, he wants to know every single awful detail of every lover you've ever had. I know mine always did. But not Leo, it seems. I wonder why…'

The merciless logic of her mother's argument cut deep. Why *hadn't* Leo asked her about her previous boyfriends?

'I'll tell you why,' Phyllis swept on, before Brooke could think of a single reason. 'Because he didn't care how many men you'd been with. Because he didn't love you. Because he was still in love with Francesca. He only married you because you were pregnant. *And* for the sex.'

Brooke finally saw a chink in her mother's argument and grabbed it. 'I doubt he married me for the sex, Mum. He was *already* getting the sex. And plenty of it. But you're right about one thing. He probably did marry me because I was pregnant. Children *do* seem to mean the world to Italian men. But that doesn't mean Leo didn't love me, or that he was still in love with that stupid Francesca woman. Goodness, she *must* have been stupid to pass up Leo for anyone, especially his brother. Lorenzo was a sleazebag.'

'Sleazebags come in many forms,' Phyllis pointed out. 'Some not so obvious.'

'Leo is no sleazebag. He's a fine man. I'm sorry now that I ever thought he was unfaithful. I should have had more faith in him.'

'Then it would be *blind* faith! So tell me, daughter, what does this Francesca look like? Something tells me she's not ugly.'

Brooke stiffened. 'I won't lie. She's very beautiful.'

'Yet you said Leo hadn't slept with her, despite their engagement. In the past, that is,' came her mother's added tart comment.

'That's right. She was supposed to be a shy virgin back then, and was waiting till their wedding night. Apparently she wasn't so shy once she'd met the sleazebag brother. Leo actually caught them doing it. Did I mention that?'

'No,' Phyllis said, her eyebrows lifting. 'No, you didn't. Which only consolidates what I've been saying. Italian men prize their sexual prowess. Hard for Leo not to take the chance to prove himself the better man once it presented itself...'

Almost despairingly now, Brooke sought reasons not to believe what her mother was saying. 'You're forgetting Francesca in all these suppositions. She does have some say in whom she sleeps with, don't you think? The woman was absolutely besotted by Lorenzo. She was beside herself at his funeral.'

'Maybe. But this Lorenzo's dead, and his widow is undoubtedly very lonely. Do you honestly think she would have been able to resist Leo if he decided to seduce her? Even *I* have to admit that Leo has more sex appeal than any man has a right to.'

'We have no evidence of any such seduction,' Brooke defended staunchly.

'Oh, come now! Leo was *there*, in her apartment! For hours and hours! You told me so!'

Brooke began to get angry, both at her mother, for being so damned smart, and herself, for being so damned stubborn. 'There's loads of reasons why he might have been in Francesca's apartment other than to seduce her. He could have been going through his brother's personal papers.'

'Then why lie about it?'

'I don't know,' she choked out.

'Why, for heaven's sake, don't you just *ask* him?

Why don't you tell him what you overheard as well, and get it all out in the open?'

'Don't you think I've thought of doing just that?' Brooke cried. 'But when did it ever work for you, Mum, confronting your husbands over their sexual behaviour, getting things out in the open? Inevitably it led to bitter arguments, and finally divorce. Once you open that particular Pandora's box, it's impossible to shut it again.'

'You'd really prefer to go on turning a blind eye?' her mother asked, shocked. 'You're happy doing that?'

'I'm not happy at all, Mum. That's why I came over here to talk to you. I had to talk to someone or go stark raving mad. But I have to think of the children's happiness, not just my own silly pride.'

'Yes, of course,' her mother said soberly. 'The children…I'm sorry, Brooke. I'd forgotten about them for a moment. Yes…yes, I see your dilemma.'

'Both Alessandro and Claudia adore Leo. Aside from what might or might not have happened with Francesca, he's a very good father. I don't want a divorce, Mum. I really don't.'

'Then what are you going to do?'

Anguish played across Brooke's face. 'I rather hoped *you* were going to tell me that. I came here desperate for some practical advice, advice that would *save* my marriage, not destroy it.'

'Oh, darling…I'm so sorry…' Phyllis looked both stricken and sympathetic. 'I know how much you love Leo. Too much, I've always thought. But, okay, I'll do my best to help. Just don't jump down my throat if I say things you don't like hearing.'

'I'll try not to.'

'Fair enough. First things first… Let's forget Francesca for a moment, and look at the role *you* chose to play in your marriage. The fact is I never thought you were cut out to be the traditional wife and mother, Brooke, staying at home all the time, bowing to your husband's wishes, stroking *his* ego all the time. Some women can play that part and be perfectly happy with it. But you're much too strong-willed to sustain such an unequal partnership. And much too intelligent.'

Brooke was intrigued by her mother's spot-on observations. But where was she going with this?

'I know you don't see yourself this way, Brooke, but down deep you're a chip off the old block. Your father once told me I was a tiger of a woman, and you're just the same. You *chose* to act like a pussycat in your marriage because you saw what a hopeless mess I made of *my* marriages. But the tiger has escaped now, and I'm afraid you're going to have trouble putting it back into its cage. Now what are you smiling at, daughter? What have I said?'

'That's what Leo called me the other night. A tiger.'

'Mmm. I gather not disparagingly?'

'On, no, he *liked* me being a tiger in bed,' she admitted ruefully.

'Men always like women being tigers in bed. They just don't like it when the tiger doesn't stay there. Look, it probably *would* be better if you could simply ignore what happened in Italy and try to go on as before, but you can't do that now, can you? That's why you're here?'

Brooke nodded.

'I thought as much. I wouldn't be able to, either. So, as a compromise, why don't you start by simply asking Leo about his engagement to Francesca? Say you over-heard someone mention it recently. See what his re-action is.'

Brooke groaned at the thought.

'Don't accuse him of anything further,' her mother went on hastily. 'If you accuse him of adultery and he's guilty he'll just deny it, and your relationship will suffer. If he's innocent he'll be mortally offended, with the same result. It's a no-win situation for a wife.'

Brooke groaned. 'You really think he slept with her, don't you?'

Her mother's eyes carried true sympathy, but her voice was firm. 'There's no use putting your head in the sand, Brooke. You have to admit that, under the circumstances, Leo might have slept with her. But that doesn't mean he loves her. Leo was obviously very happy with *you* when he came home that night. And he said he loved *you*. It's perfectly clear that, whatever happened, he has no intention of leaving you and the children. This Francesca is oceans away. She's hardly an immediate threat to your marriage.'

'You're right,' Brooke said with a burst of well-needed optimism and resolve. 'She's over there and I'm *here*! Frankly, I'd be a fool to even mention her at all. No, I'm going to go home and keep my mouth well and truly shut.' She reached out and took her mother's hand. 'You're a good mum, no matter what you think. And you're not as tough as you make out. Which reminds me... Tell me about this man you've met. He must be something to have you rush off to the hairdresser.'

Brooke could not believe the dreamy look which came into her mother's eyes. 'He's just so gorgeous, Brooke. And only forty-five—two years younger than me. *Very* good-looking. He's a lawyer I met in court. I beat him in a case, actually. Although to be fair his client never stood a chance. I see him quite often around the courts, and he always stops and talks to me. He says I've got a brilliant mind.'

'But it's not your mind you want him to think is brilliant,' Brooke said drily.

Her mother actually blushed. 'I've been so lonely, Brooke. You've no idea.'

'I think I have, Mum. We Freeman women aren't meant for celibacy. We're tigers, both in the bedroom and out. Go get 'im, that's what I say. When do you want to do some clothes-shopping?'

'I'll ring you tomorrow night and we can make a date for later this week. That way I can find out how things are going with Leo.'

'Right.' Brooke jumped to her feet. 'Well, I'd better be going.'

'Aren't you forgetting something, daughter dear?'

Brooke frowned. 'What?'

Phyllis pointed over at the big ginger cat which was at that moment snoozing in the warm autumn sunshine.

Brooke rolled her eyes and slapped her own forehead. 'Lord, I'd forget my head if it wasn't screwed on tight. If I'd gone home without *him*, I'd have been in *real* trouble. Come on, Mister Puss,' Brooke murmured as she scooped him up into her arms, 'time to go home. Time to face the demons.'

CHAPTER SEVEN

IT WAS just after four by the time Brooke turned her navy Falcon into the driveway and eased it into the garage alongside Leo's red Alfa Romeo.

Her mind went to Leo once more on seeing it. Not that it had been far away from her husband during the hour's drive home.

They said you could tell a lot about a man by the kind of car he drove. Leo had chosen the sporty two-seater ostensibly because it was easy to handle in the narrow city streets, and very easy to park. But Brooke knew Leo enjoyed the car's power.

Once, soon after he'd bought it...a few days after they'd met...he'd driven it through the Sydney CBD well over the speed limit, changing lanes like a formula one driver, cornering like a greyhound, racing another car down into the Harbour tunnel and up the other side before spinning round and roaring back into the city across the bridge.

It had been very late on a Monday night—well after midnight—and there'd only been a few other cars on the road, so she supposed it hadn't been as dangerous as it seemed, in retrospect. Still, Brooke had found it a wildly exhilarating and exciting experience, with the top down and her hair streaming out with the wind. When they'd got back to his hotel suite, and Leo had begun undressing her straight away, she'd been as turned on as he was.

She'd chided him breathlessly about his driving while he'd stripped off the last of her underwear, pointing out that if he'd been caught, he would have lost his licence.

'Sometimes,' he'd explained in thickened tones as he'd urged her shockingly naked body across the room and pressed her heated flesh against the large window which overlooked the city streets way below, 'an experience is worth the risk. But don't worry, *mi micetta*,' he'd added, stretching her arms up high above her head and holding her wrists together with a single grasp. 'I'm not a reckless man very often. But why have a fast car without pushing it to the limit at least once?'

His free hand had mercilessly explored her body while he'd watched her breathing become ragged and her lips fall wider and wider apart.

'Much the same could be said for a beautiful woman,' he'd rasped, and had whipped her breathless body round to face the window, releasing her hands to spread them wide and press them, palms down, against the cool glass. She'd dared not move, even when he'd let her hands go, nor protest when he'd eased her legs apart. She had just stood there, quivering with anticipation, while he'd stroked her hair out of the way then kissed her spine from top to bottom, bump by erotic bump.

But he hadn't stopped there; his mouth had moved inexorably downwards…

Brooke's mouth dried at the memory. And at what that night had revealed about Leo.

The truth was her husband could be a reckless man—some might say a *ruthless* man—on occasion. One could conclude that normal moral standards would not stop him seducing a woman if he wanted her badly enough, at least once.

Brooke groaned and buried her face in her hands. During the drive home she'd almost convinced herself that Leo *hadn't* been unfaithful, that he loved *her* and not Francesca. Then she'd seen that car of his and re-membered what he was capable of.

The driver's door being wrenched open sent her head jerking up and to the right. Leo stood there, glaring down at her startled and possibly flushed face.

'What in hell are you doing,' he snarled, 'hiding out here in the car? I've been waiting for you to come inside ever since you drove in. What is it now? Can't you even stand to come inside, in case you're alone with me?'

Brooke had not often seen her husband in such a foul temper. In fact it was a rare occurrence.

But he was in a foul temper now.

In the past she might have quailed, then hastened to smooth down his ruffled feathers. Now, his snarls brought out the worst in her: the tiger.

'*Don't* you raise your voice to me,' she said tersely, pushing him back against the garage wall with the car door as she climbed out. 'And don't go thinking about grabbing me again, either,' she warned when she saw the light of battle flare in his eyes. 'I won't stand for any more bully-boy tactics!' she pronounced, and slammed the car door.

Leo fairly spluttered with outrage.

'And I wasn't *hiding* here in the car,' she informed him curtly. 'I was merely getting my thoughts together before I came inside and told you what was *really* bothering me.'

To hell with common sense, she decided angrily. Or turning a blind eye. Or trying to go on as before. She simply *had* to know what Leo felt for Francesca. Everything hinged on that.

'That's what I was trying to find out this morning,' Leo growled. '*Before* you ran off to your mother's and left me with two of the most tiresome, cantankerous, spoiled little brats I've ever encountered in my life!'

Brooke was taken aback, before realising this was the first time, the very first time, that Leo had been left totally alone with his children for longer than a few minutes. She could well imagine that their over-tiredness from the flight, plus her going off to get Mister Puss without them, might have set another cat among the pigeons, so to speak.

She almost smiled, Francesca momentarily forgotten. 'The children misbehaved?'

'That's putting it mildly,' he grumbled.

'But I put them to bed before I left.'

'Maybe so, but they were *not* asleep, and the moment you drove off all hell broke loose. Claudia started crying for some doll she left in Italy. Then Alessandro started whingeing and whining about Mister Puss.'

Suddenly Leo grimaced, and bent towards the back of the car, straightening with a relieved sigh. 'Thank God you didn't forget the cat! If you had, I would have had to take that infernal child over to Turramurra personally! What is it about that animal he finds so damned indispensable?'

'Mister Puss is like a security blanket and motorised soft toy combined. Your son likes to drag him around by his tail and sit on him while he watches his favourite videos.'

'*Don't* talk to me about videos!' Leo snapped. 'When it became obvious that those two little devils were not going to sleep, I let them get up and put the TV back on, at which point my bossy, demanding son informed me that he wanted to watch *The Wiggles in Concert*. Well! Do you think I could find *The Wiggles in Concert*? Not on your life! And nothing else would do!'

'That's his favourite,' Brooke murmured, trying not to laugh.

'Well, where the hell is it hiding? It's not on the shelves with all the other videos.'

'It's probably in his toy box. He watches that one so much it sometimes ends up in there.'

Leo rolled his eyes. 'I never would have thought to look there.'

'Where are the children now?'

'Oh, they're asleep *now*. I finally got them to sleep around two, after I read them a hundred stories. But they're in *our* bed,' he added wryly. 'It was the only way I could settle them down. They thought it was a wonderful treat, since they're not usually allowed in our bedroom.'

Which they weren't.

'I see,' Brooke murmured.

Leo sighed and gave her a rather exhausted look.

'You know, Brooke, this afternoon has made me realise just how difficult a job you have, minding those two all day every day. And yet you never, ever complain about them. You always look fresh and lovely when I come home, the house is tidy and my dinner's all prepared. I can well understand how tired you must feel sometimes, and why you don't feel like sex. But please, Brooke… I don't want you to pretend with me, either in that area or any other. If you don't want me to make love to you, then just say so. If anything else is bothering you, then, please, tell me that too. I want you to be happy,' he said, reaching out to touch her cheek oh, so gently. 'I can't stand it when you're not.'

This was her chance, yet Brooke hesitated. He was being so nice and understanding. So sweet. How could she bring up a subject like Francesca *now*? It would spoil what they *did* have.

'Aren't you happy being married to me any more, Brooke?' he asked, clearly worried by her silence. 'Don't you love me any more?'

'I could ask the same of you, Leo,' she choked out.

'Of *me*?' He looked stunned.

'Yes. Aren't you happy with me any more? Don't you love me…any more?'

If you ever did…

'Are you mad? I'm very happy being married to you. As for loving you… Why, I love you now more than ever!'

Tears filled her eyes. 'Do you, Leo? Do you really?'

With a groan, he pulled her into his arms. 'Where on earth have you been getting such silly ideas? My God, Brooke, I *adore* you. You're my life, you and the children.' He pulled back abruptly and stared down at her. 'Has anyone said anything to you to make you doubt me?'

Oh, if only he knew…

'The thing is, Leo,' she said carefully, 'you've never actually *said* you loved me before, and I…I did over-hear something while we were in Italy which worried me a little.'

He looked stunned. *Appalled.* 'What?' he demanded to know. 'What did you overhear?'

'That…that you were once engaged to Francesca,' she said in a tiny, scared voice.

His face darkened. 'Who was it who said that?'

'Your mother.'

He swore something in Italian, words she'd never heard before.

'Are you saying it's not true?' she asked fearfully. For if he did she would know he was lying.

'No. No, it's true enough,' he confessed, if reluc-tantly.

Funny. He hadn't lied. But she still didn't feel all that relieved.

'Why didn't you tell me?'

'I didn't want you to know because I thought it might hurt you. That's why I told the family not to ever mention it to you.'

'How could it have hurt me?'

He looked pained. 'Brooke, please…just trust me on this. I love you. I've always loved you.'

'Then why not tell me about Francesca?' she per-sisted. 'Leo, I need a reason for this deception, other-wise I might think really terrible things here.'

He pulled a face. 'Because my engagement to her was so soon before you. I thought you might think... Hell, I didn't want anything to spoil what we had together.'

'How soon was it before me?'

'Must we rake over such ancient history?'

'Yes, Leo, we must.'

He sighed. 'I broke my engagement to Francesca a week before I met you.'

Brooke went white. 'A week. Only a *week*! How could you have been in love with her one week, then me the next?'

'Because I *wasn't* really in love with her. It was nothing more than an infatuation.'

She didn't like that word. Infatuation. It smacked of something uncontrollable. Like an obsession.

Brooke stared at her husband. If he told her the truth about his brother and his fiancée, then maybe she could believe him.

'What led to your engagement breaking up?' she asked, and held her breath.

'My God, what *else* did you overhear?' he exclaimed, his eyes truly troubled. 'Why was my mother gossiping about me and Francesca, anyway, and to whom?'

'She...she was talking to your father. But I moved away and didn't hear any more.' The lie came out swiftly, but was it for her benefit or his? Clearly Leo didn't want to tell her about finding his brother in bed with *his* fiancée. In a way, she could understand that. Leo was a proud man.

'I will speak to Mamma about this,' Leo muttered

angrily. 'I will not have my family making trouble in my marriage where there is none.'

'No, no, Leo, don't say anything. Please, just…just forget about it.'

'But can *you* forget about it? It's clear to me that you've been very troubled by this news. Your tears on the plane. Those strange comments you've been making. Your touchy mood. It's all clear to me now…'

His eyes melted to an expression of incredible sadness and regret. 'How terrible for you to think I married you not loving you, that I might have stood by your side when our son was born not loving you. Let me assure you, Brooke…that's not so. I have *loved* you always, with all my heart. Yes, I'm guilty of not saying so. I have found such words difficult to say in the past. But not any more. I promise. I actually did tell you, you know, after we made love the other night, but you fell asleep and didn't hear me.'

'I…I heard you,' she whispered.

'You—' He broke off, then nodded slowly, sadly. 'You didn't believe me.'

'I didn't know what to think. You hadn't touched me in ages, and when I touched *you* that night, I thought you didn't want me any more.'

'Which was why you pulled out all the stops?'

'Y…yes,' she confessed shakily.

He reached up to run his fingertips over her mouth. 'You're incredible,' he murmured. 'I'll return the favour come Wednesday night, I promise. I presume we *do* have to wait till Wednesday night?' he added ruefully.

She knew what he meant.

'I'm afraid so,' she confirmed, knowing her period would be well finished by then.

'But a kiss or two is not out of the question, is it?'

Brooke gave him her mouth willingly, her heart singing with joy. Leo loved her. He'd always loved her. Francesca was ancient history. It must have been as she'd told her mother. Leo had been going through his brother's papers at his home that day. He just hadn't wanted to say so for fear of starting any gossip. His mother was wrong. Mothers did have a tendency to worry unnecessarily about their children.

Reassured, and full of love for him, Brooke put everything into kissing him back, winding her arms up around his neck and pulling him down hard against her mouth. He responded with a hunger and ardour which literally took her breath away, his tongue thrusting deep into her mouth, echoing what she knew he wanted to do with his body. She could feel his erection against her stomach, his instant arousal bringing Brooke enormous satisfaction.

Whenever his tongue went to withdraw she ensnared the tip between her lips and sucked the whole thing back into her mouth, not wanting him to stop, not wanting the feelings of loving reassurance to end. Only when her own head began spinning did she release him and they both came up for air.

'You're being a wicked little tease, do you know that?' Leo growled, swinging her round and pressing her against the car door.

'You deserve to suffer for making me worry like I did,' she said breathlessly. 'I want you to go on suffering till Wednesday.'

'Is that so?' Casually, he pushed aside her jacket and ran his hands over her soft cashmere top, shaping and kneading her bra-encased breasts till they responded through her clothing, growing full and hard, their nipples aching in their confinement. By the time his hands slid up under the top and took the bra with them Brooke was trembling with desire.

'Leo,' she choked out, half-protest, half-plea.

'Yes, my love?' he drawled, while he did to her nipples what he'd done to them the other night.

'I... I...'

With an abruptness which brought a gasp to her lips, he abandoned her breasts, pulling her bra back to mercilessly enclose and squash their throbbing tips before smoothing down her top and pulling the lapels of her jacket back together.

'And I want *you* to suffer while you wait,' he murmured as he bent to kiss her panting lips. 'I want you so on fire for me come Wednesday night that you won't be capable of faking a single thing. There will be no more secrets between us, my darling wife. And *definitely* no more pretence. From now on when we make love it's going to be real, more real than anything we've ever shared before. *That*, I promise you.'

Suddenly he smiled down at her, his dark eyes dancing with wicked amusement. 'If only I had a camera,' he said. 'I would dearly love to capture that open-mouthed look. Such an incredible mixture of shock and sensuality. It's going to be damned hard to wait. But we will. And the waiting will make it all the better.' He bent to give her one last peck on her stunned lips.

'Now! Let's get this cat out of the car and back into the house before those two little savages wake up.'

Brooke blinked, then dazedly watched her husband coolly set about getting Mister Puss's cage out of the back seat, before making his way from the garage and up the side path towards the front door. She trailed after him, her mouth still open, her nipples still burning.

Leo, however, was striding out confidently, his manner brisk and businesslike. No one would guess that barely a minute before he'd been doing what he'd been doing.

Brooke had always known her husband capable of great self-control when necessary. He prided himself on it. She didn't doubt for a moment it would be *her* who would suffer the most between now and Wednesday. Leo had the distraction of work, for one thing. And he always slept like a log at night, dropping off the moment his head hit the pillow. No tossing and turning for him.

Whereas she…she would think of him all day, every day. Then half the night, every night.

Real, he'd promised. More real than anything they'd shared before…

She wondered what he meant, for surely there was nothing they hadn't shared before. They'd made love in every position *she* knew about.

But then she thought of this new way he'd started playing with her breasts, and she realised there were probably a thousand subtleties and nuances in love-making they'd never tried before. She had to be a babe in the woods in that department compared to Leo.

He'd been thirty-two when she'd met him, a handsome, sophisticated, wealthy man, who'd travelled widely and, yes, been around. Just because he hadn't slept with Francesca it didn't mean he hadn't had hundreds of other very experienced women, whereas she… She had had less than a handful of boyfriends before Leo, all young men with more bravado than technique.

That was why Leo had blown her away in bed. He'd done things to her and made her do things to him which at the time had seemed incredibly exciting. But maybe—on a rating of one to ten—their lovemaking so far had never got above a five. Maybe there was a lot more. Maybe he was going to show her six to ten on Wednesday night.

Brooke choked out a small sound and Leo, who'd been walking on ahead of her, halted and glared over his shoulder at her. 'What *now*?' he said.

Her heart skipped a beat. 'I didn't say a word.'

'I'm sure I heard you say something.'

'It was nothing. Nothing at all!'

His eyes narrowed. 'I thought I said no more secrets.'

'Come Wednesday night,' she reminded him, smiling nervously.

The corner of his absolutely gorgeous mouth curved up slightly. 'All right. You can have a reprieve till then. But come Wednesday night you're going to tell me everything that's been going on in that surprisingly complex mind of yours. You're going to expose your very soul to me, Brooke, before I'm finished.'

Brooke's insides quivered.

She imagined she would.

And quite a bit else too!

CHAPTER EIGHT

COME seven-thirty Wednesday night, Brooke was hopelessly excited, and even more hopelessly nervous.

Leo had rung that morning from work and told her that his plans for their anniversary night had changed and now required her to pack a small overnight bag, since they would not be returning home till the morning.

'Please do not find any objections,' he'd added swiftly. 'I have already made arrangements to have the children minded.'

Brooke had been thrilled, but also slightly worried. The nanny service they used for evenings out *was* very reputable and reliable, but she'd never left the children with anyone overnight before, except her mother.

When she'd mentioned this, Leo had startled her with the added announcement that it was her mother who was going to mind them. He'd just spoken to her by phone and she would be coming straight to their place after she'd finished at the office that day. Brooke was to expect her no later than six, in time to help her get the children bathed, fed and in bed, and for Brooke to then get ready in peace.

Leo had added that he himself would be dressing away from home and would pick her up right on eight. She was to be wearing her red velvet dress, sheer stay-up stockings, strappy gold sandals...

And nothing else.

'*Nothing* else?' she'd repeated, her stomach curling over.

'Make-up and perfume would be acceptable,' he'd drawled.

'But…but…'

'Nothing else, Brooke. Not a damned thing. Not even jewellery.'

She'd quivered all over. 'What about my hair?'

'Put it up, out of the way.'

'Out of the way of what?'

'*Me.*'

She'd begun to go to mush when she'd suddenly pulled herself up. She was doing it again. Losing her will-power. Letting Leo run the show entirely. Letting him run *her*.

'I'll do it, Leo,' she said, managing to find a cool voice from somewhere. Darned difficult when she was in imminent danger of a sexually charged meltdown. 'But only because *I* want to. Only because the thought of being naked under my clothes excites the hell out of me.'

'Mmm. Have I unleashed the tiger again, *mi micetta*?'

'In more ways than you could possibly imagine.'

He laughed. He actually laughed. 'I will look forward to tonight even more than before,' he'd said. 'See you right on eight.' And he'd hung up.

Such false bravado, Brooke thought now, as she glanced down at the meagre amount of clothes laid out on her bedspread. Whatever had possessed her to agree to going out with no panties on? Being braless was bad enough in that particular dress.

It was made in a new kind of stretch velvet which clung like a second skin. Any modesty in its styling— it had a not too deep round neckline, long sleeves and a hemline just a few inches above her knees—would be negated by her lack of underwear. She might as well walk around naked.

At least you won't have to worry about panty lines or straps showing, she told herself drily, trying to re-capture the tiger in her. But it was asleep in its cage at that moment. She was back to being a kitten again, nervy and ready for flight.

Except there was nowhere to run to. Leo would be arriving in less than half an hour. Thank heavens she'd already done her hair and make-up. Still, she would have to get a wriggle on—wriggle being the operative word. You *had* to wriggle to pull that darned dress on. She'd only worn it once, to a dinner party in Milan, *with* underwear. Even so, Lorenzo's lewd eyes had been on her all night.

It hadn't seen the light of day since.

Sitting down on the side of the bed with a sigh, Brooke reached for the stay-up stockings first, the ones she'd had to dash down to the mall this afternoon to buy. It was a struggle pulling them on and getting them high enough. There was a lot of Lycra in them. Finally she snapped the lacy tops into place, just above mid-thigh. Slipping off her robe, she stood up and walked over to the cheval mirror in the corner.

'Oh, dear heaven!' she gasped when she saw herself.

Leo had been right. There was something incredibly

sexy about stocking-encased legs when everything else was nude. It was even turning *her* on. She would look even more wicked with her high heels on, Brooke realised, and let out a long, shuddering breath.

She couldn't take her eyes off her erotic reflection, trying to see it through Leo's eyes. Her hands lifted to travel shakily down over her breasts, her ribs, her stomach. She still had a darned good figure, even if her full breasts had settled a little lower on her chest. Her stomach was flat and her bottom still pert. She'd been so lucky not to get stretch marks during her pregnancies, and naturally—good little wife that she was—she'd done all the exercises she was supposed to do afterwards, all the sit-ups, pelvic floor tightenings and whatnots, so that she'd got her figure back not just outside but inside as well.

'Brooke!' her mother suddenly called through the door. 'It's ten to eight. Are you nearly ready?'

'Won't be long!' she called back, snatching up her robe and holding it nervously in front of her nakedness.

'Shake a leg, then. You don't want to keep Leo waiting, do you?'

Thankfully, her mother didn't come in. Once she'd gone, Brooke threw aside the robe and snatched up the dreaded dress, stepping swiftly into it, then wriggling frantically as she drew it up over her hips. Once there, she slid her arms into the long, tight sleeves before hauling it up onto her shoulders, then, doing contortions as only women can do, she zipped the back up to her neck.

That done, she straightened, smoothed the dress back

down where it had bunched up, and finally dared to glance at herself in the mirror.

Oh, dear God, she thought as she stared at her nipples. They were standing out like nails, open testimony to both her braless and highly aroused state.

As for the rest of her… Okay, so no one would *know* she was naked downstairs, not in this age of G-strings and pantyhose, but she herself was shockingly aware of being naked above and between her stocking-clad thighs. When she walked over to slide her feet into her gold sandals, the silk lining of the dress slid seductively over her nude buttocks. When she sat on the side of the bed to do up the ankle straps on her shoes, it stuck to her like glue.

Leo was a devious and knowing devil, she realised. He knew exactly how dressing like this would affect her.

Once the straps were buckled properly, she stood up and walked gingerly over to the mirror once more, where she stared at the image she presented, at the sexy red dress and the even sexier gold shoes, at the blush in her cheeks and the glittering in her dilated blue eyes. Even her hairstyle was sexy. Though up, it wasn't scraped back tightly, just wound into a loose-ish knot, with bits and pieces left to feather softly around her face.

She looked like a woman just made love to, and expecting to be made love to some more any second. She didn't look like a whore, exactly, but she didn't look like a wife. She looked like some rich man's mistress.

Coward that she was, Brooke left it till the last second before emerging. Thankfully, by this time, the children were safely in bed and sound asleep, and her mother was watching television.

Phyllis glanced up when Brooke walked a little stiffly into the living room, and whistled.

'Mum, *really*,' Brooke said, blushing furiously.

'No, really, darling, you look stunning. And soooo sexy! Remind me to buy something in red when we go shopping together. Remember, you promised to go clothes-shopping with me this week some time?'

'Oh, dear, I *had* forgotten. You should have reminded me when I rang on Monday.'

'Well, we had more interesting things to talk about that day, didn't we? All that good news about Leo and the dreaded Francesca. I was so relieved, I can tell you. I was sick with worry when you left on Sunday. But Leo has restored my faith in men. Which is just as well, because I don't think I could have resisted Matthew much longer. Next time he asks me out, I'm going to say yes. So, could we take the children down to the mall after you get home in the morning and see what we can find? I'm sure to see Matthew again this Friday, and if I can look even a quarter as good as you do tonight, I'll have him lying in the corridor with his tongue hanging out.'

'Shouldn't you wait till you're behind closed doors?' Brooke said with a straight face, though inside she was smiling. She hadn't seen her mother this happy in years.

Both women looked at each other and laughed…till the sound of the doorbell interrupted them.

'That will be Leo,' she said in almost hushed tones, her stomach instantly swirling.

Her mother gave her a stern look. 'None of that doormat nonsense, daughter dear. You're no pussycat any more. Look at yourself. You're a tiger! Let him hear you roar.'

The doorbell rang again, a very lengthy ring.

Now Brooke hurried to the door, because if he kept that up, the children might wake!

Yanking the door open, she was about to chide Leo for being so impatient and thoughtless when the words died in her throat.

Her husband was standing there looking utterly gorgeous. Even more handsome and stylish than usual, if that were possible.

He always looked fantastic, his grooming and fashion sense impeccable. But tonight he'd outdone himself. His sleek black hair lay in perfect symmetry around his well-shaped head and there was not a hint of five-o'clock shadow on his chin. He must have showered and shaved again somewhere, not long ago. Where? she wondered momentarily.

But it was his choice of clothes which drew her eye, all obviously new, since she hadn't seen them before. His suit looked the latest in Italian fashion, coal-black in colour, and not padded in its tailoring, allowing his own marvellous shape to fill out the shoulders of the single-breasted jacket. His shirt was the palest grey and collarless, with small grey pearl buttons done right up to his tanned throat.

When he lifted his hand off the doorbell, his black

onyx and diamond-encrusted dress ring sparkled under the porch light.

'I see the ban on jewellery didn't extend to yourself,' she murmured, smiling. 'And, if I'm not mistaken, they are brand-new clothes you're wearing.'

'I told you I was going to pull out all the stops to-night.' His sexily hooded gaze drank her in for a few smouldering seconds during which Brooke found it difficult to keep standing up straight.

'You look incredible,' he murmured. 'Did you do what I asked?'

She tried to look cool, but it was impossible with him looking at her like that.

He smiled. 'I see by your face that you did.'

'It *feels* wicked,' she whispered, and he laughed softly.

'That's how it's meant to feel. Shall we go, Signora Parini?' he said, picking up the overnight bag she'd placed at the ready by the front door.

Taking a deep breath, she resolved to match his sophistication and insouciance.

'And where are we going to, Signor Parini?'

'Down memory lane. But with a difference.'

'Sounds intriguing. I just have to get my purse,' she told him. 'It's on the hall stand, alongside the beautiful red roses you sent me. I put them there, where I can admire them every time I walk past.'

'And I put your lovely lady on my desk, where I can admire it and think of you every time I look at it.'

First thing this morning Brooke had given him a carving in wood of an elegant lady with long hair. She'd found out from a book that on a five-year anniversary you gave gifts in wood. Leo had given her the longest kiss after opening his present, and told her she would have to wait for her two presents. The first had been the flowers; the second was still to make an appearance.

Obviously he meant to give it to her some time during the evening. Brooke had tried to imagine what it was, but was at a loss. Leo hadn't been all that imaginative a present-giver over the years. He usually resorted to the standbys of perfume and chocolates.

Her mother came out into the hall when they both walked back in.

'My, my,' she said admiringly. 'Don't you two look simply splendid together? Have a wonderful night, darlings. And, Leo…'

'Yes, Phyllis?'

'Don't forget what I told you about the wine.'

'I won't. Don't worry.'

'Mum told *you* something about wine?' Brooke said with surprise in her voice as they walked together out to the red Alfa Romeo waiting at the kerb.

Leo slung Brooke's small bag onto the back seat, a rueful smile on his face.

'She certainly did,' he drawled.

'I can't imagine what. There's nothing you don't know about wine, and Mum is a bit of a Philistine in that department.'

'I doubt that very much. Your mum is a very experienced and intelligent lady. And far more sensible than I ever gave her credit for. Far more sensitive too, I'll warrant. We should visit her more often.'

'Goodness! What brought this on?'

'Let's just say I've realised Phyllis and I have much more in common than I realised.'

'What?' Brooke said laughingly. 'Wine?'

'No, my darling. Our love for you,' he said, and, taking her right hand, he lifted it slowly to his mouth like a Latin lover, narrowed eyes lifted to hers from under his dark brows as his lips made contact with her suddenly trembling fingers.

Brooke had never known what women saw in this type of kissing, or why it should turn their knees to jelly. But as Leo's eyes held hers, and his lips travelled over the back of her hand with a series of feather-like kisses, tingles ran up and down her spine and darts of fire shot between her thighs, reminding her hotly that she was naked there, naked and more than ready for him. Already.

'Is…is this your idea of making me suffer some more?' she choked out.

'Some *more*, my love? Does that mean you've actually *been* suffering?'

'You know I have,' she rasped, and went to pull her hand away. But he held it tight.

'Then that makes two of us, my sweet,' he said. 'But a little erotic torment won't kill us. It will only make everything better in the end. Trust me.'

With that, he helped her down into the low-slung leather seat.

Brooke almost panicked when her tight skirt rode up dangerously high, showing all of her lace-topped stockings and an inch or two of thigh. Brooke glanced up as she wriggled it back down.

Leo smiled a rueful smile, shut the car door and strode round towards the driver's side.

'I have to confess, however,' he drawled as he climbed in behind the wheel, 'that I'm glad I didn't go with my original idea for a chauffeur-driven car and dinner somewhere. The thought of sitting with you as you are at this moment in the back of some roomy limousine while someone else did the driving would have been my undoing. Much better that I have my hands firmly on the wheel and my eyes on the road ahead.' With that, he gunned the Alfa's throaty engine and sped off in the direction of the city.

Brooke decided some distracting conversation would serve them both. She'd never felt this turned on in all her life!

'So, we're heading into the big smoke, are we?' she said brightly.

Leo shrugged. 'I guess there's no point in my keeping it a secret any longer. I'm taking you to the Majestic for the night, to our old suite.'

'Oh, Leo. How romantic!'

He slanted a warm smile her way. 'I hoped you'd think that. Unfortunately it won't look quite the same. They've just refurbished all the rooms. I read about it in the paper over morning coffee and decided on the spot that that was where I wanted to take you. It seemed…appropriate. After all, we did spend our wedding night there.'

'Not to mention just about every night over the previous two months,' Brooke said, smiling at him. Leo could not be taking her anywhere better. She'd been so happy during that time. The place would have wonderful vibes for her. 'But you're not going to drive like you did one night back then, I hope?' she added teasingly.

'Ah. You still remember that night?'

'How could I forget it?'

For some reason he fell broodingly silent after that remark, and she wondered why?

'Did I say something wrong, Leo?' she asked tentatively.

His frown cleared instantly and he threw her a reassuring smile. 'You? You never say anything wrong. I was just off in another world for a moment. Look, I read about something else in the paper this morning too. Something which interested me very much and which I'd like to discuss with you.'

'Oh? What?'

'Firstly, tell me where you think I bought the clothes I'm wearing tonight?'

Brooke blinked her surprise but gave his clothes a second look. 'Well…ummm…they're definitely Italian in design. They have that look about them. And I know you, Leo. Only the best for you when it comes to clothes. But to be honest I can't quite place the style. Not Armani. Or Gucci. Definitely not Brioni. No…I don't know. I give up. You'll have to tell me.'

'It's Orsini.'

'Sorry. I don't know that label. Is it new?'

'Very. But it's about to go out of business.'

'What? But why? Their clothes are wonderful.'

'Lack of money, basically. And the state of the economy. Times are very tough for all the Australian fashion houses at the moment.'

Brooke frowned. 'But I thought we were talking about an Italian fashion house.'

'No. The owner's an Australian/Italian named Vince Orsini. His parents migrated thirty years ago. He's twenty-seven, born and bred in Sydney. He studied design at college here, and with the help of a loan and a small inheritance started up a business in Surry Hills a few years back. But he never had enough for decent advertising and promotion, and now he's going under. There was an article about him in this morning's paper, on the same page as the story about the Majestic's makeover. I was impressed by his obvious passion for fashion, and went to see him.'

'Today!' Brooke was startled.

'Yes, today. I bought this outfit this afternoon for a fraction of what I would have been prepared to pay for it. It made me think that wealthy people all over the world would pay heaps for Vince's clothes too, if only they knew about them, so I offered him a deal. I'd back him financially and we'd go into partnership.'

Brooke was stunned. 'But, Leo…fashion is a long way from furniture and household products.'

He smiled wryly. 'You don't think I can make a success of it?'

'I think you would make a success of anything you did.'

His smile widened. 'I'd hoped you say that. I've worked for my father long enough, Brooke. I have enough money now to strike out on my own. I inherited a substantial sum from my grandmother's estate when I was twenty-five and invested it rather well, even if I say so myself. There's more than enough now to take a chance without bankrupting us, whether the idea succeeds or fails. Parini's won't suffer by my defection. It's a long-established company, with good managers and staff in all its branches. I know exactly the man to put in charge in Sydney. He'll do an excellent job.'

'But what will your father say?'

Leo shrugged. 'I have to be my own man. If he wants me to, I'll keep a personal eye on things for him, play troubleshooter if and when needed. But the rest of the time I want to do something else, something more…challenging.'

'I know what you mean,' she said. 'It's not good to be bored with your job.'

He slid thoughtful eyes her way. 'Which brings me to my next idea…'

'What's that?'

'I want you to help me in this project.'

Brooke could not have been more startled, or more pleased. She'd wanted to go back to work some time. 'In what way?'

'In *every* way. Vince designs women's clothes as well as men's. With your looks and style and intelligence, you'd be perfect to head the PR department in the women's wear section while I do the men's. I've been thinking we could take the collection to Milan each year. I have plenty of business connections over there. You speak Italian like a native, so there's no problem there. And then there's Tokyo.'

'Tokyo!'

'Yes. They're crazy for fashion there, yet they've been neglected by the world at large in that area. I'm sure Orsini's would be a great success in Asia. Of course, I haven't forgotten that you speak Japanese like a native too.'

'I'm pretty rusty on the Japanese, Leo.'

'You'll pick it up again. You're so clever with languages. So what do you think?'

'You've taken my breath away.'

'But you like the idea?'

'I *love* the idea. But…'

'I know exactly what you're going to say. But what about the children. Look, there's no need for you to work full-time to begin with. And a lot can be done from home, you know, with the right electronic equipment. Of course, you *are* going to need extra help in the home, so I rang Italy a little while ago and asked Nina if she'd like to come to Australia and work for us.'

Brooke could not believe Leo had done all this in one day! But it seemed to agree with him. It wasn't just clothes making the man tonight, she realised. It was his energy and his enthusiasm. In a way he reminded her of her mother. He was totally revitalised and absolutely bursting with life.

'So what did Nina say?' she asked. But she could guess. Who could say no to Leo in this mood?

He grinned. 'She can't wait. Said she could be on the next plane.'

'But where will she sleep?'

'I realised that needed addressing. But Rome wasn't built in a day, Brooke, and this project won't get off the ground for a while. Vince has to honour a couple of his present contracts first. So I told Nina she won't be needed for at least three months. Then I contacted our old renovators over lunch and gave them the job of building a small flat over the double garage. They said they could do that for me in *two* months. Easy. Which means it might be done in three.'

'My goodness, Leo, what a busy boy you've been today!'

'You don't know the half of it. Damn, just look at this traffic. It should have cleared by now. I've booked our table in the hotel restaurant for eight-thirty, but at this rate we'll be late.'

'Let's skip the fancy dinner, Leo. If you're really hungry you can order something to be served in the room.'

'You really wouldn't mind?' He flashed her a dazzling smile and she just wanted to kiss him. Right at that moment. When they pulled up at a red light, she leant over and did just that.

'All I have on my menu tonight, Leo,' she murmured against his mouth, 'is you…'

He swore. In Italian. When Leo was really rattled, he dropped into Italian.

'I think you should stop being a tiger and go back to being a kitten,' he grated out. 'At least till we get to the hotel.'

The light turned green just as Brooke laid a provocative hand on Leo's thigh and began to slide it up his trouser leg. When the Alfa Romeo shot abruptly forward she fell back into her seat, laughing.

'I've had about enough of this,' Leo growled, and, whisking the car into another lane with barely inches to spare, he set about making her heart race even faster than it already was.

Brooke was grateful the top wasn't down. Beside being far too cold, her upswept hairdo would not have lasted a minute.

CHAPTER NINE

LEO wasn't as reckless as on that previous occasion over five years ago. Impossible, with the traffic as heavy as it was. Neither did he really speed. But he drove with purpose, using every opportunity to save a few seconds here, a minute there, taking backstreets and shortcuts till they were soon in the inner city and heading for the Majestic.

Brooke could see their destination a few blocks away, rising tall and, yes, majestically above the bulk of the city skyline, although it wasn't quite as tall as the Centrepoint Tower. But the Majestic was almost as high, and circular in shape, a very modern concrete and glass structure, both in architecture and decor.

Brooke could not imagine why the owners of the hotel had felt they needed to refurbish the rooms, but she supposed things did get a little shabby after a while with constant use.

Leo muttered, 'At last,' as he zapped into the Majestic's semi-circular driveway, coming to an impatient halt beside the huge revolving glass doors which steered the hotel's patrons inside its spacious foyer.

Once the engine was cut, Leo swiftly recomposed himself, alighting to hand the valet-parking attendant his keys with his usual smooth panache. Meanwhile the doorman had opened the car door for her, and was about to help her out when Leo intervened.

'I'll do that,' he said, and instructed the doorman to get the overnight bag from behind the seats and send it up to his suite. 'Parini's the name,' he said, before returning his attention to Brooke.

Leo was a stickler for manners of the gallant kind. When she went out with him, Brooke always felt like a queen. Tonight she felt like a sex goddess as well as he drew her out of the car and onto the wide pavement, his darkly smouldering eyes sending prickles of desire rippling down her spine.

'I'm so glad you decided against dinner in public,' he whispered as he guided her into the revolving doors, pressing himself tellingly against her backside. 'The thought of other men enjoying you tonight in any way whatsoever, even vicariously, is simply not on. You are for my eyes only this evening, my love. And for the rest of our lives together.'

Brooke could not help thrilling to his impassioned words, even if he did sound a little over-possessive. But she would forgive him anything tonight.

Tonight was not quite real, she accepted, despite Leo saying the other day it would be. He was bringing a romantic fantasy to life here, recreating the time when they had just met, when Leo had been the dominant erotic master and she his willing love-slave.

But, whilst it had been wonderful at the time, Brooke knew she didn't want that kind of relationship with Leo any more. She wanted a true partnership with him, in the bedroom as well as out of it. Undoubtedly he was beginning to understand that, since he'd already softened his chauvinistic stance with his offer to her of being involved in this fashion project.

But in truth she wanted more from him than just that. She wanted to be Leo's best friend as well as his wife and business partner. She wanted to be his confidante, she wanted *emotional* intimacy, not just of the physical kind.

But these changes could not happen overnight, Brooke realised. And certainly not tonight.

Tonight she would be generous and giving and not make an issue of things. To be honest, it was still very exciting to surrender herself to Leo's will sexually. She just didn't want to have to do it all the time. She wanted the right to say no when she really didn't feel like it, and she wanted the right to take the initiative sometimes.

Brooke hung back a little while Leo collected his key from Reception and ordered some food to be sent up to their room as soon as possible, during which time Brooke tried not to mind the way the attractive redhead behind the desk immediately began making eyes at her husband.

The girl was very lovely, however, and Leo was taking longer than necessary, she thought. Jealousy sent her fingers clutching tighter around her gold evening purse, and she was about to explode when a man in a pinstriped suit materialised by her side and tried the old line of didn't he know her from somewhere?

She dispensed with him with a coldly furious glare just as Leo turned away from the desk. Frowning, he hurried back to take her elbow and usher her towards the bank of lifts.

'I leave you alone for one miserable minute,' he growled, 'and the dogs start sniffing around.'

Brooke bristled at this highly unfair remark.

'Really?' she snapped. 'Well, you'll just have to learn to live with it, Leo, if you want to take me out dressed like this! *I* have to put up with the way women fawn over *you* all the time. The moment you get within three feet of them they begin acting like bitches in heat! If they were on four legs instead of two they'd be wagging their little tushies in your face. As it is, they flutter their eyelashes and smile so much it's a wonder their lips don't set that way, like the Joker in Batman!'

Leo ground to a halt and just stared at her.

Brooke stared right back, angry and unrepentant.

The corner of Leo's mouth eventually lifted into a slow, wry smile. 'Your mother was right,' he said ruefully. 'I have no idea what I've married. But I'm finding out. Come along, tiger woman,' he ground out. 'Sheathe those claws for a while, till we can put them to better use.'

Unfortunately there were other people in the lift riding up, so Brooke could not ask exactly what it was her mother had been saying about her. But she could guess. Her mother must have warned Leo that change was in the air and that he'd better be prepared to go along with things or there'd be trouble in the camp.

And she was darned right!

Brooke smiled as she recalled the exhilaration which had raced through her as she'd let rip just now. Boy, it had felt great letting off steam like that.

'What on earth are you smiling at?' Leo asked as he walked her along to the door of their old suite.

Brooke eyed her wary-sounding husband with renewed confidence. 'Ah…now that's for me to know and you to find out. Later,' she added mischievously, stretching up to give him a provocative lick on his lips.

His eyes gleamed, and he might have grabbed her right then and there if a uniformed waiter hadn't been wheeling a trolley down the corridor towards them.

When he stopped right next to them and said, 'Room service for Mr Parini,' Brooke blinked her surprise.

'Wow,' she muttered under her breath. 'Now *that* was quick!'

'As agreed,' Leo pronounced, and handed the youth a hundred-dollar note. 'Don't worry about setting it up inside,' he said. 'We'll do that.'

The waiter beamed. 'Thank *you*, sir. If there's anything else you require further during the evening, don't hesitate to ring.' He grinned and sauntered off, whistling.

'You gave him a hundred-dollar tip!' Brooke exclaimed, stunned. No one tipped that high in Sydney. It just wasn't expected.

'Amazing what the right financial incentive will do. They told me there would be a half-hour delay in the room service, so I spoke to the kitchen personally and said there would be a hundred dollars for whoever got the food to my room within five minutes. Not that they had to cook anything. I ordered seafood and salad, champagne and strawberries.'

Opening the door, Leo waved her inside while he followed with the trolley.

'So, basically, you subscribe to the same theory as

your father,' Brooke pointed out as she walked in and glanced around the redone rooms with curious eyes.

They'd certainly gone to town on a grand scale, opting for an extremely rich, modern look rather than the cosy country decor of before. The colour scheme was now black and grey and white, instead of blues and greens, with all clean lines and solid colours. Not a hint of floral or stripes anywhere. The carpet was plush grey, the walls white, and the furniture expensive squashy black leather.

'What theory is that?' Leo asked as he wheeled the trolley past the archway which led into the kitchen—a dauntingly modern vision in black marble and stainless steel. He stopped next to the large black sofa which ran along one wall of the sitting area. A long, low glass and black wrought-iron coffee table stood on the black and white rug in front of it, opposite which stood a huge grey-painted entertainment unit, which housed a television, video and hi-fi arrangement, complete with complimentary CDs.

'That money can buy you anything,' Brooke replied, and wandered over to stand at the floor-to-ceiling window where once she'd surrendered to the most erotic experience in her life. It still had the same view, of the Harbour and the Opera House, and whilst the glass was tinted, and too high up for anyone on the city streets below to see anything, she still felt slightly exposed standing next to it.

'Money *can* buy you any *thing*, Brooke. It just can't buy you intangible things, such as love or talent or happiness. It can, however, buy you some damned fine food and the very best French champagne.'

She glanced over her shoulder at him, just as he whisked the covering cloth off the trolley to reveal a mouthwatering array of dishes, plus not one but *two* bottles of champagne, chilling in individual silver ice buckets.

Suddenly the penny dropped with regard to her mother's earlier comment about the wine. She'd told Leo to buy champagne.

Brooke had always been very partial—and susceptible—to champagne, right from her eighteenth birthday, when a friend of the family had bought her a magnum and she'd drunk most of it. She'd had the time of her life. And so had her boyfriend at the time, she'd gathered the next day.

'Are you sure you haven't ordered too much champagne, Leo?' she said cheekily as she sashayed back towards him. 'After all, my limit when I'm with you is two glasses.'

Leo sighed. 'Now, Brooke, about that...'

'Yes, Leo?'

'I'm sorry I took it upon myself to tell you what to drink and how much to drink. It was wrong of me. My only excuse is that I noticed you became somewhat...er...flirtatious when you drank, and I have to confess I was jealous. I promise not to be such a fool in future. And I promise to share the driving when we go out.'

Brooke gaped her astonishment at these unexpected and amazing concessions. 'What in heaven's name did my mother say to you?'

'What should have been said years ago, but what I had already begun to work out for myself. I want you to be happily married to me, Brooke. I don't want to repress you, or control you. I thought I was protecting you, and our marriage, but I went about it the wrong way. Undoubtedly I learned some bad habits from my father, who's a bit old-fashioned in his ideas about marriage. Still, I honestly didn't realise you weren't content till this last week.'

Brooke sighed. 'Now that part's *my* fault, Leo. I should have stood up for myself earlier. I thought I was protecting our marriage too. So I just said yes to whatever you wanted, but sometimes I *wasn't* happy. I just pretended to be.'

'I did notice you pretending in bed, believe me. And I hated it. In future I want you to say no to whatever it is you don't want to do, sex included. Please…don't pretend. Ever.'

When tears suddenly threatened, Brooke steadfastly blinked them away. Tonight was not for tears. 'I…I'll do that in future, Leo. I guess I was afraid that if I was myself I might end up like…like…'

'Like your mother. Yes, I know. She told me all about that today. We had a good long chat, your mum and I. She straightened me out about something else as well.'

For a second Brooke feared her mother had spilled all her concerns about Francesca, about her going to Milan that day and seeing him at Francesca's apartment and jumping to the conclusion he was being unfaithful.

'Like…like what?' she choked out.

'Like the children's names. I rode roughshod over your feelings in that regard, Brooke, and I'm truly sorry. It was incredibly selfish and egotistical of me. But it's too late *now* to change their names, isn't it?'

'Yes, of course it is,' she agreed swiftly, touched by his ongoing concessions but a little agitated over the way this conversation was going. She wished she hadn't thought of Francesca. 'Still, your apology means the world to me, Leo. You've no idea. But let's not get too serious—or sorry—tonight. Tonight is for celebrating only. Why don't you open the first of those lovely bottles of champagne and we'll toast our future happiness?'

He seemed relieved to stop apologising as well.

'You're a wonderful woman, Brooke,' he said as he popped the cork and poured some of the fizzing liquid into the two crystal flutes provided, pressing one into her hand before taking the second for himself. 'To us!' he said, smiling.

'To us,' she echoed. Clinking the glasses, they both drank deeply.

'Another,' he insisted, refilling her glass.

For the next half-hour they devoured the delicious food and drank the truly divine champagne, going through the first bottle in no time and starting on the second. They put on some romantic music and settled themselves comfortably on the deep, squashy sofa with the food at the ready. Between succulent mouthfuls Leo would lean over and kiss her, long, deep, drugging kisses which sent her head spinning. Or was that the champagne already working?

Whatever, Brooke felt more light-hearted—and possibly light-headed—than she had in a long time. And incredibly sexy. She could not wait for Leo to stop eating and start making proper love to her.

They'd disposed of the main course and were down to the last few strawberries when Leo stood up. 'I think now is the perfect time for your present,' he announced.

'Oh, goodness! I'd forgotten all about that.'

'Shame on you,' he mocked. 'Now, you are to go over and stand at that big window right there. Face it and close your eyes.'

Brooke gulped, but she did as she was told.

Tension built in her as she stood there with her eyes tightly shut, trying not to think of the last time she'd stood in that same spot.

She couldn't hear anything except the music. The carpet was very thick and plush and the room was sound-proof. What was Leo doing? What could her present be?

When she suddenly felt his breath on the back of her neck, she stopped breathing; when something cold and metallic slipped round her throat, she gasped.

Her eyes flew open.

'Oh, Leo!' she cried.

The tinted glass in the window provided an excellent reflection and her hands came up to feel what she could already see: a necklace of exquisite delicacy and beauty, the setting like spun gold, into which were set five magnificent ruby-red stones from which fell five more ruby teardrops.

'They're not real, are they?' she said, twisting her head slightly to glance over her shoulder up at him.

His hand cupped her chin and he dropped a tender

kiss on her mouth. 'I told you, Brooke. There's nothing fake about tonight. And that includes this gift. It's as real as my love for you.'

Brooke's head whipped back to stare at it again in the window. 'But, Leo, it must have cost a fortune!'

'It did. Now, don't have a pink fit. I didn't buy it. It's a family treasure. An heirloom. Inherited from my grandmother, as well, to be given to my wife. Frankly, I'd forgotten about its existence till my mother reminded me. I thought it was just the thing to give you this anniversary. I knew it would go wonderfully with that dress, which is why I asked you to wear it.

'And I was right,' he said, curving his hands over her shoulders. 'It looks incredible. *You* look incredible.' His head dropped to her throat, his mouth hungry on her flesh, his voice low and thick. 'God, Brooke… It's been agony keeping my hands off you this long. I keep thinking of what's not under that dress and how much I want to touch you there.'

When his hands slid down her arms and onto her thighs Brooke moaned softly. When they started sliding back upwards, taking her dress with them, she could only stand and stare at the erotic image she made in the window as more and more of her legs were exposed. She could see Leo staring at them as well, his eyelids more hooded than usual. She could hear his heavy breathing in her ear.

Her head began to spin when the dress reached the top of her thighs. He hesitated at that point, then kept going, inch by breathless inch, till she was standing there, naked to the waist.

For several excruciatingly long seconds Leo kept her

that way, whilst he just stared at her. Her heart began hammering against her ribs, a wave of heat flushing the entire surface of her skin.

When his lips moved against her ear, she quivered uncontrollably.

'You look magnificent,' he murmured. 'But I think such a sight requires a lot closer attention…and far less clothing,' he added, smoothing the red velvet back down over her hips once more before lifting his hands to the zipper at the back of her neck.

Brooke gasped as the tightness of the dress abruptly gave way and a rush of cool air invaded her naked back. She watched, her head whirling, as Leo pushed the dress off her shoulders then dragged it downwards, till it peeled off her hands and hips, then dropped, like stone, to the carpet, leaving her standing there, wearing nothing but the ruby necklace, sheer skin-coloured stockings and five-inch gold sandals.

'Incredible,' Leo breathed, his eyes feasting on her image in the window. 'Irresistible.' Abruptly he scooped an arm under her jelly-like knees, lifted her up in his arms and carried her towards the bedroom.

Brooke might not have noticed the room and its contents at all if Leo hadn't stopped to switch on the light. She blinked first at the stark white walls, before dropping her gaze to the plush grey carpet, then finally focusing on the bed.

It was new and huge, with a black wrought-iron bedhead and a shimmering silver spread made of quilted satin.

Leo strode over and spread her heated body across its cool, silky smooth surface, trailing his hands down over her breasts and stomach before stroking her legs apart, then pulling her feet forwards till the heels of her shoes dangled over the edge.

Brooke held her breath the entire time.

'Now, don't move,' he commanded, turning away to walk back and close the door, then switch off the overhead light, plunging the room into darkness.

Immediately Brooke let out a shuddering sigh of relief.

But Leo didn't leave it at that. He drew back the black silk curtains to reveal the lights of the city, then returned to snap on the nearest of the ornate silver-based lamps which graced the glass bedside tables. The black silk shade threw a seductive glow over her entire body, spotlighting it for Leo's gaze, leaving absolutely nothing to the imagination.

Brooke felt both wildly excited and flushingly embarrassed. She wanted to close her legs, yet at the same time ached to open them even wider.

She did neither. She lay motionless, as ordered, watching wide-eyed, heart now thundering, while Leo undressed. He didn't hurry, taking his time to drape his clothes carefully over a chair in the corner. He even set his shoes and socks neatly underneath. But his eyes never strayed far from her body—or for long—yet, oddly, they seemed calm and cool.

At long last he was naked, and Brooke could see he was not nearly as calm—or cool—as he was making out. Far from it. Her own state of arousal was a revelation as well. Already she was on the brink. And he hadn't even touched her. She'd never felt the like in her life. She wanted him. Now! This very second!

Disobediently, her legs dared to part a little further, and she thrilled to the sudden wild flaring in his eyes.

But he made no move to join her, just stood there beside the bed, staring down at her.

'Oh, please, Leo,' she moaned. 'Please...'

'Patience, tiger woman,' he drawled. 'You must learn that the pleasure is more in the chase than the kill.'

She could not believe it when he sat down between her legs, his back to her, and slowly, ever so slowly, removed her shoes and then her stockings. She had never known such an agony of frustration as his fingers feathered over her ankles and toes, her calves, her knees, her thighs. He touched her everywhere but where she wanted him to touch.

She was at screaming point when he finally turned round to face her.

It was then that the real torture began.

'Oh, no, Leo, no,' she choked out when he began touching her where she'd been dying to be touched. Because by then she was wanting something else. She was wanting him, inside her, filling her, loving her.

But he ignored her protest and of course she came almost immediately, one of those electric little climaxes which race through you like lightning but leave you wanting more.

She protested again when he bent to give her more, with his mouth as well as his hands. She thought she could not possibly come again so soon.

But she did.

'Oh, Leo,' she gasped. 'Leo...'

'Yes, my love?' he murmured as he moved over and

into her at last, taking her breath away with the power of his penetration.

But surely it was too late for her to do anything but lie limply in his arms.

Once again, she was wrong.

With each surge of his flesh into hers she stirred a little, till she was clinging to him and moaning with renewed need.

'Yes…*yes*,' she cried out, her nails digging into his back as the exquisite tension built to crisis point in her once more.

'I can't hold on any longer, Brooke,' Leo groaned.

But then they were both there, together, and Brooke was crying out with delight.

Happiness, she decided afterwards, as she drifted slowly down from her rapture, was being made love to by Leo, her darling, wonderful, incredible Leo. The desperation of the previous week was totally forgotten. Her doubts and her fears all gone.

'I love you, Leo,' she whispered, when she could manage to speak.

'And I love you, Signora Parini,' he returned, holding her face while he poured kisses all over it. 'Only you. Only ever you.'

CHAPTER TEN

'THIS is the life,' Brooke murmured as she leant back in the spa bath.

Leo had let her cat-nap while he ran it, kissing her awake before carrying her into the bathroom where the lavish round tub was full to breast height with warm, scented water and the frothiest bubbles she'd ever seen.

Once she was deposited safely in one end, Leo had gone to collect the ice bucket with what was left of the champagne—just enough for one glass each. He'd poured them out, then joined her in the bath, and now they were both lying back, facing each other, enjoying the massaging effect of the water jets on their gentlest setting.

Brooke glanced idly around at the very opulent-looking bathroom as she sipped the last of the lovely bubbly. There hadn't been a spa bath in here five years ago, just the old-fashioned claw-footed variety, in keeping with the then country look. Everything had been cream and green back then, with a large wooden vanity and old-fashioned taps.

Now, all the walls, floors and benches were black marble, the kind which had grey and gilt veins running through it. The bath, basins and toilet were a pearly white, the trim and tap fittings gold, as were the exotic light fittings. The huge mirrored cabinet above the vanity was gilt-edged as well.

141

The effect was very rich and very decadent.

Brooke realised with a measure of surprise that she'd never had a bath with Leo before, not even before they were married. Showers, yes, but not a bath.

It was lovely. Relaxing, yet exciting at the same time. Only their toes were touching at the moment, and they couldn't see too much of each other's bodies. But the knowledge that they were both naked beneath the bubbles added a stimulating edge to the experience.

'I should do this more often,' Leo said.

'Do *what* more often?' she asked, her blue eyes dancing.

'Get the children minded for the night, then take you off somewhere private and romantic where I can make mad, passionate love to you all night.'

'Promises, promises. It's only ten o'clock, and you've only made love to me once so far.'

'Darling wife, I started making love to you the moment I rang this morning and ordered your underwear off. You've been turned on all day, Signora Parini. Why don't you just admit it?'

'What about *you*, Signor Parini?' she countered, refusing to admit a thing. 'Were *you* turned on all day, thinking about tonight?'

'I deliberately distracted myself with one project after another, as you might have noticed. But I still had to have the longest, coldest shower before I came to pick you up. I couldn't afford to disappoint you. Not tonight.'

She smiled softly. 'You never disappoint me, Leo.'

'Really? What about those times you faked things this last year?'

Brooke shrugged. 'I just wasn't in the mood. I don't know why. Tired, I guess. Valentino himself couldn't have aroused me on those nights.'

'I don't think I tried too hard,' Leo muttered. 'And I'm not so sure you were tired as much as discontented. I've been a selfish, self-centred husband, Brooke, and I'm so sorry. But things will be better from now on.'

Brooke was touched by his sincere apology and his promise to do better. If tonight was anything to go by, the future looked very rosy indeed.

'Now!' he said as he lowered his empty glass onto the marble floor then glanced up at her with a wicked gleam in his beautiful black eyes. 'Should I order another bottle of champagne before the next round begins?'

'Mmm. Not unless you're planning on making love to one very sleepy lady.'

'Heaven forbid! In that case, nothing but coffee for you from now on. I have no intention of letting you sleep yet, tiger woman. The night is still young, and you look incredibly desirable sitting there in the water, with your hair slightly tousled, your shoulders bare and that ruby necklace around your deliciously inviting throat.'

'Goodness!' she said, only just remembering it was still there. Hurriedly she put down her near empty glass too, sat up straight and lifted her hands to the clasp at the back of her neck.

'No, don't take it off,' Leo protested. 'It looks gorgeous. Besides, it's made of real gold and real rubies. A bit of soap and water won't ruin it.'

'Really? Are you sure? Oh…all right, then. I suppose you're right.' She touched it reverently with her fingertips. 'I've never owned anything so beautiful before, or so expensive. I just love it, Leo. It was the perfect anniversary present.'

'Yes, I thought so too,' he agreed, his eyes warm and loving. 'Giving it to you tonight worked out very well.'

She was leaning back again when a niggling thought struck. Leo was not the sort of man to forget anything. His memory was second to none. So *why* hadn't he given her the necklace before? Could the delay have something to do with Francesca?

Her stomach curled at this unpleasant idea.

'Leo…' she said, possessed by a sudden determination to find out some more answers about his relationship with Francesca. Such as when *had* he finally got over his infatuation for her? And what did he think of the woman now that Lorenzo was dead? Did he hate her still? Or pity her?

Brooke would also have liked to ask him what, exactly, he had been doing in her apartment that day. But she didn't dare. That would mean admitting she'd been there, which would lead to Leo's asking her why. Then she'd have to explain that his mother had said a good deal more than Brooke had confessed to overhearing.

'Yes, what's the problem?' Leo probed.

Brooke swallowed. 'You…you said there were to be no more secrets between us.'

'Ye…es?' He looked and sounded very wary all of a sudden.

Brooke's courage immediately failed her. Why spoil this wonderful night? she reasoned swiftly, trying to find excuses for her sudden lack of resolve. What more did she want from this man, damn it? He'd said he loved her, only her, always her. What more could he say to reassure her?

'Brooke? What do you want to say?' Leo insisted. 'Come on…you can't hold back now.'

Brooke could, and she would. All she had to do was think of something else to ask instead.

'Why didn't you ever ask me about the boyfriends I had before you?' she blurted out.

His eyebrows arched, then he laughed. 'I opted for blissful ignorance on that score. Besides, I wasn't sure if there was enough time in the world to hear about them *all*.'

'Oh! Oh, you…' She whooshed across to his side of the bath, kneeling on either side of his legs and leaning forward to pummel him playfully on his shoulders and chest. 'You know I didn't have all that many! And you know none of them meant a thing…once I met you.'

'Good,' he growled, grabbing her upper arms and hauling her right up onto him, her soap-slicked nipples grazing over the wet curls which covered his chest. At the same time her stomach rode up over what felt like a very formidable erection indeed.

'Oh, you beast!' she cried out when his grip tightened and he rubbed her up and down against it.

His smile was almost a grimace. 'Lady, you don't know the half of it.'

'Are you telling me that's only *half* of it?' she taunted, doing a little rubbing herself. Heat had instantly licked along her veins at the feel of him, excitement and desire mixing to make her bold.

'Don't tease me, Brooke,' Leo said thickly.

'Who's teasing?' she breathed, and reached down to take him in her hand and insert him deep into her body.

When he groaned, she stretched up to cover his lips with her own, sending her tongue briefly into his startled mouth before retreating and sitting back up straight. He groaned again, and a wave of the most intoxicating triumph washed through her.

She found herself smiling down at him. Who was in control *now*? It was *his* turn to squirm, to be taken to the edge and over, while *she* watched *him*.

'Let's see who can last the longest *this* time,' she challenged, and reached up to take the pins from her hair, shaking her long blonde hair out over her shoulders.

Leo's dark eyes narrowed upon her. Then *he* smiled. 'Loser makes the coffee?' he suggested silkily.

Brooke tried not to look too smug. If Leo thought he had the upper hand this time, then he was in for a surprise. She was on top. *She* would control the action.

Besides, she'd already had three orgasms to his one, Brooke thought with wicked glee. No way would she be coming quickly *this* time!

Slowly, voluptuously, she began to rise and fall upon him, her hard-tipped breasts becoming more and more visible as the soapy bubbles dripped off them. She watched his lips pull back from his teeth as he sucked in sharply; watched his eyes close and his nostrils flare; watched the body language of a man being carried swiftly to the point of no return.

Oh, yes. This time *she* was going to win.

*   *   *

'You look positively wrecked,' were her mother's first words the next day, once Leo had left and the children's maniacal greetings had died down. They had finally been persuaded out into the back yard to play, at which point Brooke sank down on a kitchen stool with a weary sigh.

'Can I get you a cup of coffee?' her mother offered.

Brooke groaned. 'Lord, no. No more coffee. I'm already suffering from caffeine overload.'

'Then how was last night? Or dare I ask? Leo certainly seemed happy enough this morning.'

'That man! Doesn't he ever need sleep? And can't he ever *bear* to lose a bet?'

Phyllis gave her daughter a droll look. 'I take it last night went well, then? For Leo, anyway.'

'For me, too. I won't be a hypocrite and say I didn't enjoy myself. I'm just exhausted.'

'Would that *I* could feel exhausted some morning for the same reason!' Phyllis exclaimed.

Brooke had to laugh. 'Were the children any trouble?'

'Not a bit.'

'You're sure?'

'Positive. As good as gold. Now, are you still up to some shopping this morning? Say so if you're not.'

'Why not? As tired as I am, I haven't a hope of actually sleeping till some of this caffeine wears off. I might get a nap when we get back and the kids go to bed.'

Brooke struggled through the next couple of hours, but it was worth it to see the happiness on her mother's face. She steered her mother into the right kind of dress shop, which had just the thing for the more mature career woman who wanted to look up to date and attractive without crossing the line into mutton dressed up as lamb.

Phyllis splurged out on three three-piece suits which Brooke showed her could carry her through from day to night, depending on what accessories were worn with them. One was red, one black and one cream. Brooke suggested black accessories for all three, conservative pumps and a roomy handbag for daywear, strappy high heels and a clutch purse for after five. She also showed her mother how to mix and match the outfits, and how, by adding a camisole or a scarf, or a little knitted top, or even the right jewellery, she could create an entirely different look.

'You're so knowledgeable about fashion,' her mother complimented her after they'd arrived home and were sitting over a sandwich. 'No wonder Leo wants you to go in with him on this business venture. I think you'll be brilliant! But then I'm biased, I guess. You're my daughter. But I always *did* think you were brilliant. That's why I got mad at your wasting yourself as a glorified clerk.'

'Mum, your intellectual snobbery is showing. Serving the public is a very skilled and demanding job, if you do it properly. Alessandro! For pity's sake, stop teasing poor Mister Puss and go back outside and play. Take Claudia with you.'

'But I don't want to,' he grumbled.

'Do as I say,' she pronounced firmly. 'Or you will go to your room and stay there till your father comes home!'

Her son's eyes widened at this threat of such a long term of punishment. Brooke could see his mind ticking over and wondering if she meant it.

Apparently, he decided, she did.

'Come on, Claudia,' he muttered, taking his sister's hand. 'Mummy's in a bad mood.' He sighed like a little old man and Brooke shook her head.

'Sometimes I think that boy's four going on eighty.'

'He's a darling. But he's going to be a handful when he grows up. You're going to have girls wall-to-wall and running after him.'

'Tell me about it. I have the same problem with his father. You should have seen this redhead behind the desk last night at the hotel, batting her eyelashes at him.'

'Like you once did, you mean?' Phyllis teased.

'Yes…well…that was different.'

'How?'

'He wasn't a married man then. Single girls have no respect for married men these days. Which reminds me, Mum. Your…er…potential boyfriend…'

'Matthew?'

'Yes, Matthew. He's not married, is he?'

'No. Divorced. Like me.'

'How many times?'

'I haven't asked.'

'I think you should.'

'No, Brooke, I'm not going to. I'm going to take him as he is. And hopefully he'll do the same with me.'

'But, Mum, sometimes the past is important.'

'You mean like Leo and Francesca? Goodness, girl, don't tell me you're still worrying about *that*!'

'I…well…yes, I am a little.'

'Then stop it. Right now! Leo loves you. You should have heard him on the phone to me yesterday, wanting to know what else he could do to make you happy. No way would that man look sidewards at another woman.'

Brooke scooped in a deep, gathering breath, then let it out slowly. 'I suppose you're right.'

'I know I am.'

'You've certainly changed your tune.'

'It's a woman's privilege to change her mind, isn't it?'

'Maybe, but when you change yours, you certainly go the whole hog! Next thing you'll be getting married again.'

'Now that's going too far. Some nice companionship and some great sex I could do with. But marriage? No way. Not for me. I'm not that much of a fool.'

'Like me, you mean?'

'Not at all. But I have to be honest, Brooke, men like Leo don't come along every day of the week.'

Brooke wasn't sure if she liked her mother complimenting Leo so much. He wasn't *perfect*. Not by any means. She was almost glad to see him looking the worse for wear by the time he arrived home that night. It was just too irritating for words being married to a superman.

'I take it we shall be having an early night tonight?' she said cheekily over dinner.

His instant alarm amused her. 'No, Leo, that's not

what I meant. I just meant you look as wrecked as my mother said *I* looked all day.'

Leo groaned. 'I don't know how I functioned today. I had to go and see Vince again, like I promised, but I was brain dead as well as body dead. In the end we agreed to meet again this weekend. I invited him over on Saturday. Is that all right with you?'

'Perfectly all right,' she agreed happily. The Leo of last week would not have asked her that. He would have just announced the fact that Vince was coming. Maybe he *was* perfect, after all!

Brooke went to bed that night with good thoughts. Her mother was right. She was silly to keep worrying about Francesca. Leo loved *her*. Francesca was the past, not the present...

CHAPTER ELEVEN

MONDAY was playgroup morning, when Brooke took the children down to a local hall where she mixed with other mothers of pre-school children whilst the children played with each other. Alessandro just loved the company of other boys his age, and expended a lot of energy on these mornings playing chasings, whilst Claudia tended to sit quietly with one or two of the little girls and dress up dollies.

Normally Brooke joined into conversation with the other mothers on these occasions, but on that Monday she found herself often falling silent, her mind going back over the weekend just past.

Vince had come on the Saturday afternoon, arriving around two and not leaving till late that night. Brooke had liked him enormously from the moment he walked in the door. Shortish and quite thin, he was still very good-looking, with spiky blond hair and wicked blue eyes. Obviously gay, he had a charm and a wit which was both engaging and entertaining, and he had made Brooke laugh with his saucy tales of the model and fashion world. He'd been good with the children too, reading them stories while Brooke cooked the dinner.

It hadn't been till the following day that Brooke had realised how much Leo had taken a back seat the day before and let Vince and herself do most of the talking.

152

She'd been touched by his generosity, and had told him so as soon as he woke up on the Sunday morning.

'No need to thank me,' he told her, yawning and stretching. 'I enjoyed watching the interplay between you two. You and Vince are going to make a great team. I can see my investment will be in safe hands. Besides,' he added, smiling, 'with Vince being gay, I have no worries on *that* little score.'

Brooke frowned at that remark. 'Would you ever really worry about me on that score, Leo? What if Vince hadn't been gay?'

'Then I wouldn't have let him within a million miles of you,' he replied in all seriousness.

'But why? Don't you trust me?'

'I trust *you*. I simply don't trust men.'

'But *you're* a man,' she pointed out.

'Exactly.' He grinned and pulled her to him. 'You wouldn't have been safe with me for a minute, even if you'd been married to another man. I had to have you the moment I saw you.'

'Leo, you're not serious!'

'I certainly am. Very serious. Now, do shut up and kiss me. It's Sunday morning and I don't have to go to work.'

'Ah, yes, but *I* do,' she said, and, throwing back the covers, Brooke scuttled out of the bed to see why Claudia was crying.

Now, Brooke kept mulling over Leo's words. Had he meant what he'd said? Would he have seduced her even if she *had* been married? Was he that kind of man? Ruthless? Predatory? *Conscienceless?*

She didn't like that thought, not one little bit.

It plagued her mind from that moment on, so much so that by the time she arrived home, around noon, she was unable to eat, or even open the mail. They were all bills, anyway.

She fed the children and put them to bed for their nap, then sat and idly watched one of the soaps on TV. Not the best thing to watch in her present frame of mind. The characters led such tortured and tangled lives, full of affairs and intrigues, arguments and break-ups. Brooke had always craved a peaceful life, emotionally. She could not bear confrontation or argument.

Eventually she switched off the television, and was about to do some ironing when she heard the phone's soft ring. She always turned the sound down during the children's sleep, and hurried along to the extension in her bedroom to answer it.

'Yes?' She sat down on the edge of the bed.

'Brooke. Leo, here. Look, something awful's happened at home and I have to fly back straight away.'

Brooke immediately thought of Leo's father, with his heart problems. 'Is it your father? Has he had a heart attack?'

'No. Thank God. When I said home, I meant Italy, not Lake Como. It's Francesca. She's tried to kill herself. Took an overdose of sleeping tablets.'

Brooke's head spun. 'But...but *why*?' she blurted out. 'I mean...'

Leo sighed. 'I guess, in the end, she wasn't able to cope. Frankly, I was worried something like this might happen. Would you pack a small case for me, Brooke? Just enough for a couple of days. I've managed to get a seat on the afternoon flight to Rome, then a connecting flight to Milan in the morning.'

Brooke tried to keep calm, but inside all hell was breaking loose. 'But, Leo, why do *you* have to go? What about Francesca's family?'

'She doesn't have any.'

'Then what about your mother and father? Can't they help? They're only an hour away.'

'They can't know anything about this, Brooke. It would probably kill my father.'

'But *why*? I can understand why a grieving widow might attempt suicide, especially when she doesn't have any children. I don't think your parents would be too shocked, Leo.'

'Trust me on this, Brooke. They would be if they knew all the facts. And I can't trust Francesca not to tell them. Unfortunately, I'm the only one who can help Francesca at this point in time. It's a damned nuisance, but that's just the way it is.'

'Tell them what? What are you talking about, Leo?'

'I can't explain everything now, Brooke. There simply isn't time. Pack a bag for me, like a good girl. I'll be by in ten minutes to pick it up.'

He hung up. He actually hung up. Brooke just stared into the dead phone. Her husband was dropping everything and flying off to the other side of the world to be by the side of a woman he supposedly no longer loved!

It was incredible!

Unbelievable!

Unbearable!

Brooke packed the bag in a daze, all the while desperately trying to think of something to say to stop him going.

She was standing at the front gate with the bag at her feet when he drove up and jumped out of his car.

'Sorry about this,' he said, bending to kiss her cheek and pick up the bag at the same time. 'I'll be back by Friday. I've rung everyone I needed to, explaining I've been unexpectedly called away for a few days. If my mother or father ring, make up some excuse for why I'm not there. Tell them I'm talking business with Vince. Tell them anything. They're not to know the truth, Brooke. That's imperative. Promise me.'

'I...I promise.'

'Good girl. Now, don't look so worried. I'll explain everything when I get back. No time right now. I'm only just going to make the plane as it is.'

She followed him over to the car. 'You...you will ring me when you get there, won't you, Leo?'

'What?' he said distractedly as he tossed the bag into the passenger seat and climbed in behind the wheel. 'Oh, yes...yes, of course I will.'

'You can explain everything then,' she pointed out tautly, and he gave her a sharp look.

'You're not still worried about me and Francesca, are you? Yes, I can see you are, but you don't have to be, darling. She'd be the last woman on earth I'd touch. I'm really sorry but I must go or I'll miss the plane. Love you!' He slammed the car door shut and wound down the window. 'I'll ring as soon as I can and tell you the whole long wretched story.'

She watched him roar off, her heart sinking. She wanted to trust him. She really did. He'd sounded so sincere. And he'd said he loved her. He'd been saying that a lot lately.

If only he'd had time to explain *now*.

Regret that she hadn't tackled her husband more forcibly about his relationship with Francesca tormented Brooke all afternoon. She should not have been so weak. She should have asked him for details over their engagement and break-up.

It was well after tea before Brooke finally got round to opening the bills which had arrived that morning. The first was the telephone bill for their home line, and the amount startled Brooke. It was higher than she would have expected, considering they'd spent three weeks away in Italy during the last quarter.

Automatically, she scanned down the list of calls, stopping when she came across two overseas calls on the one day, one far more expensive than the other. The first was to Leo's parents, made on the Sunday they returned. Sixteen minutes.

The second was to a Milan number—one Brooke wasn't familiar with—and it had lasted nearly two hours! The time recorded stated the call had begun at five past two that same Sunday and finished right on four, around the time she'd arrived home from her mother's.

Brooke stared at the number, her heart racing. She knew it wasn't the office in Milan. She knew that number off by heart.

Dread filled her soul as she walked over to the drawer where they kept their telephone and address book. Pulling it out, she flicked open the book to the 'P's, her heart lurching once she saw the number attached to Lorenzo Parini's Milan address. It was one and the same as the number on the bill. Leo had rung Francesca whilst *she'd* been out of the house and talked to the woman for two *hours*!

Brooke burst into tears. How could he? The traitor. The liar. The…the…*bastard*!

Sobbing furiously, she ripped open the second bill, addressed personally to Leo. Again it was a telephone bill, that of his mobile phone, the one he took with him everywhere.

With eyes blurred and shoulders shaking, Brooke searched for the same number amongst the pages. And there it was, not once but three times. Okay, so they weren't long calls, usually only a few minutes, but one really pained her. Because it had taken place on Wednesday night, at eight minutes past seven, the time when Leo would have been getting ready for their anniversary night together.

Yet he'd stopped to ring Francesca. What did that tell her, his wife?

That her husband was a lying, conniving, adulterous bastard, that he'd seduced Francesca at long last—either out of ego or revenge—and was conducting a long-distance affair whilst he soothed his silly wife's suspicion with exactly the same tools he'd probably used with Francesca. Lies and sex.

She didn't believe Francesca had tried to kill herself for a moment. Not seriously. She wasn't dead, *was* she? It was nothing more than a ploy to get Leo to fly back to her and give her some more of what she was now missing. Leo, in her bed. Leo, telling her he *had* to go back to his wife, for his children's sake, but it was *her* he really loved. Her. Always her.

Just as Leo's mother had said.

Brooke went from dismay to distress to despair, then finally to destruction. Not her own. Leo's!

She would not turn a blind eye this time. She would not remain quietly in the background, like a good little girl. She would not roll over and put her legs in the air, like a dead cockroach. Or like the stupid whore she'd been last Wednesday night!

Clenching her teeth hard in her jaw, Brooke looked up their travel agent's number in the book and dialled. She couldn't get a seat on tomorrow's direct flight to Rome, but she could fly with another airline's morning flight to Zurich, followed by a fairly quick connection to Milan. With no unforeseen delays, she would arrive at Francesca's apartment less than a day after Leo.

Provided, of course, she could get her mother to mind the children. It would be a big ask, but this was a real emergency.

'Of course I'll mind the children,' her mother offered as soon as Brooke had poured out the whole story. 'I'll take the rest of the week off. But don't go to the trouble of bringing them over here. I'll come over and stay in your house. Children are best in their own environment if it's going to be for more than a day or two.'

'Oh, Mum, thank you, thank you. I'll never be able to repay you.'

'Nonsense. What are mothers for? Now, don't you worry about a thing at this end, Brooke. Lord knows what's going on between Leo and that woman, but I agree you can't sit back this time and do nothing.

Though I still don't believe Leo's been unfaithful to you. The more I think about it, I think he's being manipulated by a very devious and quite evil woman. She dropped Leo in favour of Lorenzo when it suited her—no doubt because he was the older son and possibly the richer brother—and now that he's dead she's switched her attentions back to Leo.'

Brooke was truly taken aback. She'd never thought of Francesca in that light before. The woman had always seemed such a weak, wishy-washy creature, with no get up and go!

But maybe her mother was right. Maybe, underneath, Francesca played at being fragile to bring out the protective instinct of men, to draw them into her web, so to speak.

Then, once they were there, she kept them captive with the sort of sex men could not resist. Brooke had no doubt Francesca was good in bed. There was an unconscious air of sensuality about the woman which she couldn't hide.

Brooke clutched onto the hope that she'd been directing her anger at the wrong person. Maybe it wasn't Leo she should want to destroy, but Francesca!

But then she remembered the phone calls, and *both* of them lay condemned in her eyes.

'Maybe you're right, Mum,' she said coldly. 'But I wouldn't put my house on it if I were you. Oh, and Mum, when Leo rings tomorrow morning—and he will—don't tell him that I'm on my way there. Tell him I'm sick and that's why you've answered the phone. Tell him I'm in bed asleep and suggest he rings back later in the day. By then I'll be there, and the bastard will wish I wasn't!'

'Oh, Brooke, I hate to hear you sound so hard.'

'There are times in life, Mum, when only hard will do. Now I have to pack and sort out my clothes. See you later.'

CHAPTER TWELVE

BROOKE looked down at her black suit and wondered if, subconsciously, she'd dressed for grieving.

The anger which had carried her onto the plane bound for Zurich had long dissipated by the time she'd arrived, and it had been a very dispirited Brooke who had boarded the connecting flight for Milan. By the time *that* arrived, she'd been close to breaking down, the awful reality of her situation sinking in.

Her husband didn't really love her.

He had deceived her.

Her marriage was probably over.

Once in the taxi on her way to Francesca's apartment, however, Brooke experienced some resurgence of spirit. If she was going to lose her husband to another woman then she would go down fighting. Pride demanded it.

So did the slim hope that her mother *might* be right, and Francesca was the real culprit.

Brooke felt almost flattered when the doorman recognised her and let her into the building without a quibble, and without ringing Francesca's apartment to check if she was expected. Brooke didn't want the illicit lovers to have any time to dress, or arrange the apartment, or even make the bed!

Francesca had never hired live-in servants, despite Lorenzo having been extremely wealthy. She had once confessed to Brooke that she didn't like the feeling of people spying on her, so she hired cleaners and cooks and maids to come in when required. They never slept over.

'My husband is in, is he?' Brooke asked the doorman sweetly in Italian.

She was told that, yes, Signor Parini was definitely in. He hadn't left the apartment since he'd arrived the previous day.

Brooke's stomach churned some more at this news. But she was determined to see things through this time. No more running away.

'Shall I carry your case up for you, Signora Parini?' the doorman offered.

Politely, she declined the offer. She only had a small bag. She wasn't planning on staying long.

Her stomach was in knots by the time she stood outside the solid apartment door on the first floor, her hands on the doorbell. When a perfectly strange woman answered, Brooke was truly startled.

About forty, she was tall and large, with a kind face and an impressive bosom.

Introducing herself in Italian, Brooke quickly found out the woman was a nurse, hired by Leo to help mind Francesca after the 'accident'.

Brooke absorbed this information warily.

So Francesca *had* tried to kill herself. And Leo *had* been of help. That still didn't make either of them innocent.

'Where is my husband now?' Brooke enquired, putting on an innocent expression.

He was upstairs, she was told, sitting with Francesca

in her room. Did the *signora* want her to go up and let Signor Parini know his wife was here?

'No, no,' Brooke said swiftly. 'I'm expected. And I know the way. How *is* Francesca this morning?'

'Much better.'

I'll just bet she is, Brooke thought, all her earlier fury flooding back.

Francesca's apartment was huge, occupying half of two floors. The floors and stairs were all Italian marble, with lots of mirrors and decorative columns everywhere. Brooke had always thought it a showy, gaudy, decadent-looking place, just like Lorenzo.

Francesca's bedroom was to the immediate left of the upstairs landing, and Brooke's heart was squeezing tighter and tighter as she mounted each step. Dread of what she would find behind its door gripped her chest, and her soul.

The door, however, wasn't closed, and from the moment she reached the landing Brooke could see into the room. From where she was standing, all she could see was the foot of the four-poster bed, but if she moved closer and around to the left she might be able to see more. And *hear* more.

A low, muffled voice was drifting through the doorway. A woman's voice. Francesca was talking, saying things that Brooke wanted to hear, *had* to hear.

She tiptoed closer and to the left, into a position where she could see half of Leo. He was sitting in a chair on the other side of the bed, leaning forward, his body language that of an intense and caring listener. She could not see his face, just a side view of the back of his dark head.

Francesca's face was also out of view, but by the position of her feet under the covers she was lying down in the bed, well over to the side Leo was sitting on. Brooke pictured her lying there all pale and wan, a tragic beauty, her wavy shoulder-length black hair spread out on snow-white pillows.

Brooke inched as close as she dared, finding a spot where she could not be seen but from where *she* could see a good deal, plus hear every word.

'You…didn't…*couldn't*…understand,' Francesca was saying in an emotion-charged voice. 'And how could I explain it? But I did love you, Leonardo. You were the only man who'd ever been like that with me. So kind. And caring. So considerate, even when I kept you at arm's length. But I was afraid to sleep with you back then. Afraid you would find out I was not the sweet, innocent virgin you thought me to be. And then Lorenzo turned up, and he…well, you know now what happened with Lorenzo.'

'Yes,' Leo said, sighing. 'I know *now*, Francesca. But I didn't know any of this at the time. How do you think I felt when I came into my brother's bedroom and saw what I saw?'

'Oh, Leonardo,' she cried piteously. 'Don't remind me. It was wicked of us, I know. But then I *am* wicked. I must be, to do the things that I've done. And I'm still doing them. I feel so guilty and so ashamed. Barely two weeks after Lorenzo died and I'm in bed with…' A sob choked off her words.

'Now, now,' Leo soothed. 'Don't upset yourself again. What's done is done. And it was inevitable, Francesca. It wasn't really your fault.'

'You keep saying that, Leonardo, but I can't keep blaming the men in my life. It must be something in *me* which brings out the worst in them. You're the only one who's ever treated me decently. Oh, God...why didn't I marry you when I had the chance?'

Brooke had heard enough. She stepped forward just in time to see Francesca reach out to place a tender hand against Leo's cheek. He was actually covering it with his own and looking sadly down at her when Brooke moved into the doorway and just stood there, watching and waiting for their guilt to manifest itself.

Francesca gasped, and snatched her hand away.

Leo's eyes did snap up and around, but he looked more astounded than guilty. 'Brooke!' he exclaimed, and rose swiftly to his feet. 'What on earth are you doing *here*? Your mother said that...'

'My mother lied to you,' she broke in, in Italian, so Francesca could understand exactly what she was saying. 'I followed you here so that I could catch you and this...*slut*...in the act.'

She actually used the Italian, *puttana*, which encompassed rather more than 'slut'. It was the worst word she could think of.

'I didn't quite manage that,' she went on bitterly, 'but I saw and heard enough just now to know the score.'

'Brooke, you've got it all wrong,' Leo insisted, panic on his handsome face.

'Oh, please...don't take me for a fool any more.' Her voice was hard and cold and scathing in its contempt. But inside her heart was crumbling to nothing. 'To be brutally frank, I already had my suspicions.

Remember the day of my headache? I didn't go to bed that afternoon. I drove in here and sat outside this apartment, being sick in the gutter at what I saw. *Your* car in the car park, Leo. My husband, not working hard at the office, but here, in bed with his sweet sister-in-law.'

Francesca groaned and buried her face in the pillow, while Leo gaped at her. 'What, in God's name, possessed you to even *think* such a thing?'

Brooke's returning look was scornful. He'd stopped denying everything, she noticed.

'Actually, I'd overheard your mother saying a good bit more than I told you, Leo. She expressed concern you were still in love with your old fiancée and that you might not be working late at the office every night. She was afraid you might be here, with Francesca, enjoying what you apparently never enjoyed when you were engaged.'

By this time Leo was ashen, whilst Francesca was shaking her head and sobbing into her hands.

'Lord knows how *that* happened,' Brooke scorned. 'Given you're such a stud and she's the slut of all time. But I could see if that was the case then she would have held some kind of lasting fascination for you. I told myself it was a one-off, that you didn't really love her, it was only an ego or a revenge thing. So, brave little wife and blind, lovesick fool that I was, I determined to get you back, so I…I…'

Brooke's voice broke as emotion threatened to engulf her.

'And *you*,' she threw at Leo as she struggled to fight back tears. 'You let me. You let me humiliate myself in ways which I shudder to think about now. Everyone told me to turn a blind eye, even my own mother. So I did. But I just couldn't do it any longer, not once I found out about the phone calls.'

'The phone calls?' Leo repeated blankly.

'Yes, goddamn it, the phone calls! To this... *creature*! The phone bills came in the day you dropped everything and flew off here. There was one to this number on our account for two bloody hours! So I opened the bill for your mobile and there were more, with one even on the night of our anniversary!'

Leo groaned. 'Brooke, for pity's sake, let me explain!'

'You can't, Leo. It's gone past explaining. I won't believe you, no matter what you say. I want a divorce. And I want the children.'

His chin shot up, determination stamped all over his arrogantly handsome face. 'Well, you can't have them! And you can't have a divorce, either.'

'Can't I just? We'll see about that!' she spat. 'If you recall, my mother is a lawyer, and a damned good one. She'll get my children for me. They won't be allowed anywhere near you and your filthy whore!'

Not once in all the time she'd known Leo had she seen him so shaken. For a split second he just stood there, staring at her.

But then he rallied, his voice strong and reasoned, his eyes intense on hers. 'Brooke, you *have* to listen,' he began. 'For our children's sake, if not for mine. This is not what you think. You've got it all wrong. I love *you*, not Francesca. I've *never* slept with her. All I've been doing is talk to her, try to help her after Lorenzo's death.'

'You expect me to believe that? Then who was it Francesca slept with so soon after her darling husband's death? Who is it who's driven her to *this*!' And she waved a contemptuous hand at the wretched figure weeping in the bed. 'Oh, no, Leo, no...you're quite wrong. I don't *have* to listen to any more lies. I'm out of here. You both make me sick to my stomach.'

She whirled away to leave, but Leo was across the room before she'd taken two strides, grabbing her left arm and whirling her back to face him. Driven to breaking point, Brooke lashed out with her free arm, her hand cracking him across the face with an open palm. He gasped with shock, and so did she, once she saw the ugly red imprint of her blow flare up on his cheek.

'Stop it—stop it!' Francesca screamed as she sat bolt upright in the bed with wild eyes and even wilder hair. 'It wasn't Leonardo I slept with, Brooke. It was a perfect stranger, some man I'd picked up at a bar. I brought him home here and I...I let him do things to me in my husband's bed that nice girls like you don't even *know* about!'

Brooke gaped while Leo groaned. 'Francesca, you don't have to do this. Brooke will understand once I explain everything to her...in *private*.'

'No, no, Leonardo, she has to know it all,' Francesca cried. 'From *me*. And then she'll believe you. I can't bear for you to suffer because of me. Not you. You're the only good man I've ever known.

'But there are bad men out there, Brooke,' she raved

on, madness in her eyes. 'Really bad men. My father was one of them.'

'Your…father?' Brooke echoed.

'Yes. My father. My darling, beloved father whom I adored. When my mother died, I was only twelve. The night she was buried he brought me into his bed to take her place. And the next night. And every night after that.'

Brooke sucked in sharply. She had heard of such things happening, but she'd never actually met some-one it had happened to.

'Can you imagine a father doing that to his daugh-ter?'

An appalled Brooke could only shake her head.

'By the time I was sixteen he had removed me per-manently from school to play wife for him all the time. He was a rich man, you see. He didn't need to go to work if he didn't want to. So we travelled the world together, and he always introduced me as his daughter. But behind closed doors I wasn't his daughter. I was his whore, his very willing little whore.'

Brooke gasped, and Francesca smiled, a chilling lit-tle smile which made Brooke's blood run cold.

'That shocks you, doesn't it? That I would be willing by then. But just think…what else did I know? And we all want to be loved, even if that love is corrupt and evil, like my father's. My mother killed herself, you know, just to get away from him.'

'Francesca, that's enough!' Leo said firmly, but she would not be silenced.

'No, Leonardo! You keep advising me to tell a doc-tor, that talking about it might help. Well, I think telling your wife will help me more. Because she *needs* to know. Because then she'll believe you.'

'Let me at least close the door,' Leo muttered. 'There's no need for anyone else to hear this, surely.'

While he went to do so, a shaky Brooke settled herself on the side of the bed and told Francesca to continue. Leo just shook his head and went over to stare through the bedroom window. Clearly he'd heard the gruesome details before, and didn't want to hear them all again.

Francesca pushed her tousled hair back from her face and propped herself up against some pillows, her expression determined. 'As the years went by, my father's tastes...broadened. He started bringing other men home for me to entertain as well, strangers he picked up in bars, or casinos. One night, when we were staying in Monte Carlo, the man he brought home was Lorenzo.'

Brooke's eyes widened.

Francesca just nodded. 'Yes. Now you're beginning to see. Shortly after this incident my father died suddenly, of a stroke, and I inherited all his money. I stupidly thought I could start all over again, put the past behind me and become a new woman. A *decent* woman. I returned to our family home in Milan and set about trying to be one.

'I met Leonardo quite by accident in the street one day. I'd been clothes-shopping and went sprawling on the pavement with all my bags when I tripped over a small dog. Leonardo helped me up and took me for a cup of coffee. We started dating and I thought he was just wonderful. But every time he kissed me I was afraid; afraid to go further; afraid of what I might do, or reveal about myself. He thought I was shy and innocent, so I let him think it. When he asked me to marry him, I said yes, but resolved to stay out of his bed till after we were safely married. Leonardo was gentleman enough to agree.'

Brooke tried not to think of Leo *so* much in love with Francesca that he'd been prepared to wait till their wedding night. He hadn't been at all that way with her. He hadn't taken no for an answer, right from their first date. She wondered how much that had been to do with genuine passion for her, or fury and frustration at not having pushed the issue with Francesca when he had the chance.

'When Leonardo took me to stay at his family's villa on the weekend of our engagement party,' Francesca went on, 'I could not have foreseen that his brother would be one of the men my father had solicited. On those occasions we never exchanged real names. Unfortunately, Lorenzo recognised me immediately, and didn't waste any time getting me alone. I tried pretending I didn't know what he was talking about, but he wasn't fooled. He blackmailed me into his bed the night of the engagement party, and made sure Leonardo discovered us together. After Leonardo broke our engagement, he forced me to marry *him* instead.'

'But you didn't *have* to marry him,' Brooke said, trying to understand this woman.

Francesca smiled again. This time a sad smile.

'That's the problem. I did. I don't know why. Men like my father and Lorenzo seemed to have this…power…over me. I couldn't say no to them.

Lorenzo used to tell me that the night my father picked him up was the best night of his life, that he'd never forgotten me and couldn't believe it when I turned up at his house as his brother's fiancée. He'd been insane with jealousy till he found out I hadn't done anything with Leonardo. He said he *had* to have me, and he didn't care who got hurt in the bargain. He claimed he loved me, but after our marriage he started bringing home other men, just like my father. He liked watching too…'

Francesca's shoulders sagged, her eyes dropping to the bedclothes. 'I hoped, when he died, I was finally free of all the ugliness. But apparently not. As soon as I was alone I started drinking, then I went out and picked up a creep myself. It seems I've become addicted to that debauched way of life. Maybe I can't live without it. Maybe I need it.'

'That's rubbish!' Brooke said sternly, and Francesca's eyes jerked up. 'You're just mixed up and lonely. A lot of women have one-night stands when they're mixed up and lonely. And you're not *addicted* to that kind of life. You're just conditioned. A good psychiatrist should be able to fix you up. Then, later, a good man. But not *my* good man!' she added firmly.

At this, Leo turned back from the window and their eyes met, his still worried, hers seeing his worry and understanding it. She smiled at him, and slowly he smiled back. A thousand little messages were sent within those smiles. Messages of love and apology, of forgiveness and renewed trust.

Still, Brooke had to admit that Francesca had been dead right. Hearing the truth straight from the horse's mouth, so to speak, had been a lot better than hearing it from Leo.

She would not have believed him so readily. She might have thought he was still lying. But no *woman* would have made up such a horror story, not if she'd set her sights on Leo. For all his worldly experience and sophistication, Leo had a fastidious side to his nature. He hadn't minded Brooke not being a virgin, but that was a long way from a woman having entertained hundreds of men in all sorts of salacious ways.

Privately, Brooke wasn't so sure a psychiatrist *could* solve all Francesca's problems. But it would be a darned good start. Perhaps a *woman* psychiatrist might be a good idea, though. Best not put temptation too close at hand. Francesca was very beautiful, and a man was only a man, after all, even when he was a doctor!

'I think, Francesca,' Brooke continued, 'that what you need is to book into a good clinic with a nice, understanding lady psychiatrist. Leo and I will see to it straight away. Meanwhile, I think you should have a nice, relaxing bath and a change of nightie. I'll send the nurse up to help you, shall I?'

'You're...not angry with Leonardo any more?' Francesca asked warily.

'Not now you've explained everything.'

'He loves *you*,' Francesca choked out. 'Not me. How could he love me after what I did to him? But you...you and the children...they are his life. He told me so, just this morning. He was most unhappy when he called you and your mother said you were sick in bed and couldn't come to the phone. You were worried, weren't you, Leonardo?'

Brooke glanced over at her husband, who nodded. 'Yes, Francesca. Yes, I was very worried.' His gaze met hers and she could see the truth in his eyes.

Brooke felt tears well up at the thought of how close they had come to disaster. But she fought them off. The last thing Francesca needed was for *her* to start crying.

'Well, there's no need for you to worry any more,' Brooke said briskly. 'I'm here, and I believe you. *Both* of you,' she added, swinging a reassuring face back to Francesca. 'Now, Leo and I'll just pop downstairs and send the nurse up...'

'My God, you were impressive up there,' Leo complimented her once the nurse had been despatched upstairs.

They were in the huge main living room, Leo standing at the drinks cabinet, pouring himself a whisky, Brooke sitting on one of the brocade-covered sofas which flanked the marble fireplace. She'd declined a drink, her stomach still churning from all that had happened.

'So sensible,' Leo went on. 'And so strong. I've been having all sorts of trouble trying to get Francesca to see a doctor. And you managed it in five seconds flat. Not just a doctor, either. A clinic, no less! I see now I should have brought you with me in the first place.'

He smiled over at her, and suddenly Brooke's façade of strength crumbled, tears flooding her eyes. She'd forgiven Leo with her head, but her heart was still suffering, her bruised and battered heart.

'Yes, you should have, Leo,' she blurted out. 'You

should have told me everything about Francesca from the word go. And you should have told me you loved me much, much earlier.' With a strangled sob, she buried her face in her hands and wept.

Barely seconds passed before he was sitting beside her and enfolding her shuddering body into his arms, stroking her back and soothing her with softly apologetic words.

'Yes, I *should* have,' he agreed. 'And I'm so sorry I didn't. My only defence is that I'm a man, Brooke. A typically proud, very Italian man. When I arrived in Sydney my ego was still incredibly wounded. I knew nothing of Francesca's or Lorenzo's past history at that time, and I felt betrayed by both of them. It wasn't a feeling I relished, I can tell you. But then suddenly I found myself looking into the most beautiful pair of blue eyes in the world, and they were sparkling at me, sending me the sexiest of messages. So I did what any man would have done in my position.'

'You seduced me,' she sobbed against his chest.

'Ah, Brooke...*now* who's not being strictly honest? I never seduced you. You wanted me as much as I wanted you.'

Brooke thought about that for a few moments, then pulled herself together. By the time she looked up at Leo, a sheepish smile was forming at the corners of her mouth. 'True. I fell in love with you the moment I saw you.'

'And I you, *amore mio*, within the week. No, no, that's no lie,' he insisted, capturing her face between his hands and forcing her to keep looking into his eyes. 'Not in hindsight, anyway. I admit I wasn't capable of recognising my love for you in the beginning. I was still too hurt to appreciate the depth of my feelings. And I was still fancying myself in love with Francesca.'

'Oh…' Her heart and eyes sank, showing how vulnerable she still was to the idea of his having been in love with Francesca whilst he made love to her.

'Hey! I said I *thought* I was still in love with Francesca. The truth was I was *never* in love with her. How could I have been, when I went weeks without making love to her? Do you think I would have been that patient with you, even if you *had* been a virgin? I told you once before I simply *had* to have you. Not because of lust. Because of love!'

Brooke thrilled to the sound of his impassioned words. This was the Leo she'd fallen in love with, her hot-blooded man from Milan with his flashing dark eyes and his all-consuming ardour for her.

'By the time I married you I knew that my so-called love for Francesca had been *nothing* compared to what I felt for you,' he proclaimed passionately. 'When you had Alessandro and I saw you in so much pain I would have offered up my *life*, if it would have lessened your agony. When they put our son in your arms and you smiled down at him, I was so choked up with love for you both I could hardly speak.

'And of course that's been my biggest failing. My inability to say those three little words. I love you. I…love…you,' he repeated, kissing her lips after each word. 'I don't know why I found it so hard. Maybe it's a male thing. We men are strange creatures. But I felt it in my heart, Brooke, and I tried to show you in so many different ways. Remember how after Alessandro was born I couldn't wait to take you home to Lake Como to show you off to my parents? Then, once I got you there, and you were just so warm and wonderful with everyone, I loved you all the more. I couldn't keep my hands off you, remember?'

Brooke's heart contracted. 'Yes…I remember. But to be honest, Leo, after what your mother said I started thinking your extra appetite for sex back then was because you were near Francesca, but couldn't have her. And then this last time, when you stopped making love to me, I thought that was because you *were* having her.'

Leo looked truly aghast, his hands dropping from her face. 'Oh, my God… Oh, Brooke… I promise you that had *nothing* to do with Francesca. I was tired, that's all. Stressed out and worried that Lorenzo's death would change my life. I didn't want my father asking me to go back to Italy. That's why I worked like a dog to make sure I got everything done before we left. The day you saw me here at Francesca's place was the only day I came here. Francesca rang me at the office, crying and saying she was going to tell my parents everything! I had no idea what she was talking about, but she was so hysterical that I went over to her place. It was then she told me the whole sordid story, and I knew that somehow I had to keep it a secret from my parents, especially my father. Lorenzo was the apple of his eye. It would have distressed him greatly to find out his beloved son was so depraved. I didn't tell you because I was ashamed too, ashamed of my brother.

'That's all there was to it, Brooke. I swear to you.

Damn it all, Mamma had no reason to think what she did. I can't understand why she did.'

'Perhaps if you'd told her you no longer loved Francesca at some time it might have been a good idea. Still, in hindsight, perhaps my overhearing that conversation wasn't such a disaster. It made me wake up to myself and stop pretending to be something I wasn't. It made me take stock of our marriage and see things weren't as perfect as I thought they were.'

'*I* thought our marriage was pretty perfect.'

'Did you, Leo? Did you really?'

'In the main. Perhaps not when you pretended in bed.' He smiled a wry smile. 'But things certainly improved in that area once you heard I was a potential adulterer, so maybe I should be grateful to Mamma too. It's ironic, though. I came home that night, after hearing Francesca's horror story, desperate to feel your loving arms around me, only to be told you were sick. Then, when I came into the room and you were lying there, looking so damned beautiful, I had to race into the shower and freeze myself for ages to stop the aching. When I came out and you started touching me, I couldn't believe my good—and bad—luck.'

'I couldn't believe what I felt, either,' she said ruefully.

Leo looked taken aback. 'You mean...you thought...?'

She nodded. 'Uh-huh. I was pretty mad, I can tell you.'

A drily amused light glittered in his dark eyes. 'Try getting mad like that more often.'

'Tell me something, Leo.'

'Anything,' he said sincerely.

'You didn't forget about the ruby necklace, did you?'

Leo sighed. 'No. Not entirely.' He leant forward to scoop up his drink from the coffee table, taking a swig before going on. 'I'd intended to give the necklace to Francesca on our wedding day. When we broke up I couldn't bear to look at it, so I shoved it in the house safe and simply ignored its existence. It was my mother who brought the necklace out on the morning we flew home and told me that it was about time I gave it to you. By then I agreed with her wholeheartedly. In fact, I wished I'd thought of it myself. Remember, I had no idea about what she'd been saying about me and Francesca, or what you'd been thinking. The necklace was just something I could give you to show you my love for you.' His smile was wry. 'We men prefer to *show* our love, rather than speak of it.'

Putting his drink down, he took both her hands in his, rubbing his thumbs softly over her fingers. 'Which is what I've been trying to do lately. *Show* you how much I love you. I am so sorry if you've felt humiliated by anything I suggested, or did. I'll never ask you to do anything like I did the other night ever again. I promise.'

'Oh…' she said, disappointed.

'Unless you want me to, of course,' he added, smiling a wicked smile.

'You're incorrigible.'

'And you're incredibly beautiful.' His hand lifted to stroke her cheek and Brooke's heart turned over.

'Hold me, Leo,' she choked out. 'Just hold me…'

His arms went round her, warm and strong and secure. She laid her head with a sigh against his chest
and listened to his heart beating: beating with love for
her.

A good man, Francesca had called him.

She was right.

He was a good man, her husband. Her Leo.

EPILOGUE

Five years later.

BROOKE peeked around the corner at the top of the hotel's sweeping staircase, smiling her satisfaction at the swiftly gathering crowd below.

'Happy with the turn-out for this year's collection?' Leo said.

'Very. All the main buyers are there, plus the fashion editors from the biggest and best magazines.' Better still, *this* time they'd all paid their own way.

The previous year—Vince's first showing in Milan after three successful years in Sydney and Tokyo—Orsini's had picked up the tab. But it had been worth it to have the *crème de la crème* of the fashion world gather to see what Vince could do. Leo had been right in that regard. You had to invest money to make money. Last year Vince had been declared an up-and-coming new talent. Now, this year, his talent was standing on its own two feet.

'A triumph, then,' Leo pronounced.

'A foregone conclusion, given the quality and class of Vince's clothes.'

'Ah…I do so like a PR lady who has confidence in her product, as well as the producer. Makes me, as the financial backer of Orsini's, a very happy man. Your mother and Matt arrived yet?'

Brooke zeroed in on the spot in the front row reserved for special guests. And there they were, the newly weds, holding hands like teenagers. It had taken both of them quite a while to get over their phobias about marriage. Brooke had taken them to task after they'd been living together for nearly five years and told them that was long enough of a trial, and it was time they went for the *real* thing.

'Yes,' she said happily, on spotting them. 'And they both look a million dollars.'

'Who looks a million dollars?' Vince piped up as he hurried past.

'My mother and Matt,' Brooke called after him.

'Well, naturally,' Vince tossed over his shoulder with a florid wave. 'They're both dressed by Orsini. They're two of my best customers.'

Brooke laughed. 'Vince tells everyone who buys anything in his salons the same thing,' she informed Leo. 'Mum and Matt couldn't *afford* to be his best customers, now that he's Europe's latest most *in* designer. The prices on his designer range are wicked.'

'True. I hear Francesca spends a fortune on them every season.'

'Oh, she does. But then Francesca spends a fortune on everything since she met Carlo.'

'The man's a gigolo, if ever I saw one.'

'He probably is, Leo. But he makes Francesca happy. And he doesn't care about her past.'

'That's because all he cares about is her money!'

'Don't complain. He's a regular on Vince's ten best customers list. Not that *you* should talk, husband mine,' Brooke added, running an admiring eye over her superbly suited husband. 'You've been spending a little in that department.'

'I buy his ready-to-wear. Unlike yourself,' he returned drily. 'If I'm not mistaken that saucy little red silk number you're wearing tonight is an Orsini original.'

'A perk of my job,' she defended haughtily. 'Besides, I wanted to wear my necklace,' she added, touching her most treasured possession and trying not to smile too knowingly.

If only Leo knew…

But she didn't dare tell him. Not yet…

'I commissioned Vince to come up with something especially suited to the occasion,' she said silkily.

'He surpassed himself,' Leo complimented, his gaze drifting down the deep V halter-neckline. 'What a pity we have to go to the after-show party,' he added, his eyes telling her exactly what he was thinking. 'It's going to be almost breakfast by the time we get home to Lake Como.'

'I don't think we need to stay *that* long,' she said. 'But I'm not missing this party for worlds.'

It was just after one-thirty and everything was still in full swing when Brooke tapped Leo on the shoulder. 'The car I ordered is here,' she whispered in his ear.

'Car? What car? I thought it was my turn to drive…'

'Just come along, Leo, and don't argue. Your car will be quite safe in the hotel car park.'

She led a confused Leo from the hotel ballroom and down to where a black stretch limousine with heavily tinted windows waited at the kerb.

'If I'd known there was a hired chariot taking us

back to Lake Como,' he complained, scowling, 'I'd have had a few more drinks.'

'Which is exactly why I didn't tell you,' Brooke said as she steered her disgruntled husband into the plushly upholstered interior. 'I wanted you sober and able.'

He sat, smiling now, in the middle of the long back seat, while she climbed in after him and perched on the equally spacious seat opposite. From there, Brooke leant over and whispered her instructions in Italian to the driver.

Immediately the car moved off, and an opaque screen started sliding up behind her, blocking all view of the driver and the way ahead. Leo's eyebrows arched and he threw his wife an amused look.

'You planned all this?'

'Right down to the dress,' she returned, and pushed a button beside her. A bar slid out, well stocked with chilled champagne and crystal glasses.

'Why don't you pour us both a glass, Leo? It's going to be some time before we reach Lake Como. The driver's taking the long way home.'

A devilish gleam fired his black eyes, but he did as he was told. 'What did you mean by right down to the dress?'

'It's very well lined,' she said coolly, although inside she was far from cool. She'd been thinking about this moment all evening, and the excitement of anticipation was bubbling along her veins with more fizz than the champagne.

'So?'

'So no one could see what was underneath it. Or *not* underneath it, as was the case this time.'

'Happy tenth anniversary, darling,' she said seductively as her hand plucked the soft tie on her right hip undone and the dress fell apart.

'But our anniversary isn't for another three days,' he reminded her.

'Then count this as a dress rehearsal,' she murmured, peeling the dress back off her shoulders and letting it slide to the seat...

Cathy Williams is originally from Trinidad but has lived in England for a number of years. She currently has a house in Warwickshire which she shares with her husband Richard, her three daughters Charlotte, Olivia and Emma and their pet cat, Salem. She adores writing romantic fiction and would love one of her girls to become a writer although at the moment she is happy enough if they do their homework and agree not to bicker with one another.

Look out for Cathy Williams's latest sexy and compelling title:
AT THE ITALIAN'S COMMAND
On sale in November 2005, in
Modern Romance™!

MERGER BY MATRIMONY

by
Cathy Williams

CHAPTER ONE

THE grey-haired man was looking lost and bewildered. From her vantage point in the classroom, and looking over the heads of the fifteen pupils who had shown up for school, Destiny Felt could see him staring around him, then peering at the piece of paper in his hand, as if searching for inspiration which had been lost somewhere along the way. Rivulets of perspiration poured down his face, which was scrunched up in frowning, perplexed concentration, and his shirt bore two spreading damp patches under the arms.

He was ridiculously attired for the belting heat, she thought. Long trousers, a long-sleeved shirt which had been ineffectively rolled to the elbows. The only sensible thing about his clothing was the broad-brimmed hat which produced at least some shade for his face, even though he looked ridiculous in it.

What on earth was he doing in this part of the world? Visitors were virtually non-existent—unless they were photo-happy tourists, which this man didn't appear to be—and as far as she was aware they were not expecting any new medics or teachers to the compound.

She continued viewing his antics for a few minutes longer, watching as he shoved the paper into the briefcase which he'd temporarily stood on the scorching ground at his side before tentatively making his way to the first open door he saw.

Her father would not welcome the intrusion, she thought, continuing to eye the stranger as he knocked hesitantly on the door before pushing through. She fought down the temptation to abandon her class and hotfoot it to her father's research quarters, and instead she reverted her attention to the motley assortment of children.

All would be explained, and sooner rather than later. In a compound comprised of a mere fifteen working adults, nothing was a secret, least of all the appearance of a foreigner obviously on a mission of some sort.

The overhead fan, which appeared to be on the point of total collapse from old age, provided a certain amount of desultory, sulky relief from the heat, but she could still feel the humid air puffing its way through the open windows. No wonder the poor man had looked as though he'd been about to faint from heat exhaustion.

By the time she was ready to dismiss her class, she too was feeling in desperate need of a shower, not to mention a change of clothes.

In fact, she was heading in the direction of her quarters when she heard the clatter of footsteps along the wooden corridor of the school house.

'Destiny!' Her father's voice sounded urgent.

'Just coming!' Damn. She hoped she wasn't about to be palmed off with the hapless man. This was her father's famous ploy. To offload perfect strangers, when they showed up for whatever reason, on her, and whenever she complained about it he would cheerfully brush aside her objections with a casual wave of the hand and a gleeful remark along the lines of how blessed he was to have an obliging daughter such as her.

The three of them very nearly catapulted into one another round the bend in the corridor.

'Destiny...'

She glanced at the man, then turned her full attention

to her father, who favoured her with an anxious smile. 'Just about to go and have a shower, Dad.'

'Someone here to see you.'

Destiny slowly turned to face the man whose hand had shot out towards her. She was at least six inches taller than him. Not an unusual occurrence. She was nearly six feet, and in fact there were only four people on the compound taller than her, including her father, who looked positively towering next to the stranger.

'Derek Wilson. Pleased to meet you.'

'Don't you speak Spanish?' Destiny asked politely, in Spanish.

'Now, don't start that, darling.' Her father remonstrated with her absent-mindedly, and removed his spectacles to give them a quick clean with the corner of his faded, loose shirt.

'Well…people come here expecting us all to speak their tongue…'

'He's from England. Of course he's going to come here speaking English.' There was a lazy, affectionate familiarity to their debate, as though they'd been down this road a thousand times before but were nevertheless more than happy to tread along it once again, through sheer habit if nothing else. 'Apologies for this child of mine,' her father said in impeccable English. 'She can be very well behaved when she puts her mind to it.'

Derek Wilson was staring at her with a mixture of alarm and fascination. It was a reaction to which she'd grown accustomed over time. Nearly every outsider who set foot on the compound regarded her in the same manner, as if, however bowled over they were by her looks, they still suspected that she might target the next blow-dart in their direction.

'What do you want?'

'Social niceties, darling? Remember?'

'It's taken me for ever to track you down.'

The man glanced between the two of them, and her father obligingly capitulated, 'Perhaps we should discuss this somewhere more comfortable. Get some refreshment for you…you must be done in after your trek to get here.'

'That would be super.'

Destiny could feel his eyes on her as the three of them strode through the school house, attracting curious looks from the pupils in disarray as they gathered their scant books and bags together to go home. The noise was a babble of tribal Spanish, a beautiful, musical sound that seemed very appropriate to the beautiful, coffee-complexioned children with their straight black hair and expressive black eyes.

It was why she'd always stood out, of course. Not just her height, but her colouring. Fair-skinned, choppy sun-streaked fair hair, green eyes. And of course, in the depths of Panama, a white face was always a novelty.

'In case you hadn't guessed, this is our local school,' her father was saying, much to her astonishment. Playing the tour guide had never been one of his chosen pastimes. He'd always left that to her mother, whose death five years previously was still enough to make her feel choked up. 'We have a fairly static number of pupils. Of course, as you might expect, some are more reliable than others, and a great deal depends on the weather. You would be surprised how the weather can wreak havoc with day-to-day life over here.'

Derek Wilson's head was swivelling left to right in an attempt to absorb everything around him.

'Just to the right of the school house we have some medical facilities. All very basic, you understand, but we've always lacked the finance to really do what should be done.'

This was her father's pet topic. Money, or rather the lack of it, to fund the medical facilities. He was a researcher and a gifted doctor and had a complete blind eye to anyone who couldn't see that money should be no object when it came to questions of health.

They'd reached the little outer room that served as an office for her father, and he settled the man in a chair then bustled to the stunted and rusting fridge in the corner of the room so that he could extract a jug of juice. A small breeze fluttered through the two large, open windows which were opposite one another so as to maximise air draft, and Derek Wilson attempted to ventilate himself by flapping his shirt at the collar.

Poor man, Destiny thought with a twinge of sympathy. For whatever reason, he'd probably left behind a family in England and all mod cons so that he could tramp halfway across the world to Panama, still a mysterious and unfathomable land virtually behind God's back, and deliver a message to her.

What message?

She felt a little stirring of unease.

Her father handed her a glass of highly sweetened fruit juice, and she attempted to catch his eye for a non-verbal explanation of what was going on, but he was in a strange mood. Nervous, she thought, but trying hard not to show it.

Why?

Another flutter of apprehension trickled along her spine, defying her attempts to laugh it off.

'Well.' Derek cleared his throat and looked in her direction. 'Very nice place you have here…'

'We think so.' She narrowed her eyes on him.

'Brave of you to live here, if you don't mind me saying…'

She shot a look at her father, who was staring abstractedly through the window and providing absolutely no help whatsoever.

'Nothing brave about it, Mr Wilson. Panama is one of the most beautiful countries in the world. Every day there's something new and wonderful to see and the people are very gentle and charming. So you needn't be scared of being captured and tortured or chopped up into little loin steaks and eaten.'

'I never imagined that for a moment…' he protested, and this time when he looked at her his eyes were shrewd and speculative.

'What did you come here for?' she asked bluntly, at which her father tore his attention away from the scenery of grass and dirt and beyond the compound the dense forest that housed the people who seemed as familiar to them as the Westerners who lived and worked alongside them in the compound.

'I've brought something for you.' He rifled through his briefcase and extracted a thick wedge of cream, heavy-duty paper, covered with small type, which he handed to her. 'Have you ever heard of Abraham Felt?'

'Felt…Abraham? Yes, vaguely… Dad…?' she said slowly, scanning the papers without really seeing anything.

'Abraham Felt was my brother, your uncle,' her father interjected tightly. He took a few deep breaths. 'Well, perhaps I'd better let the professional do the explaining.'

'What explaining?'

'Abraham Felt died six months ago. He left a will. You are the main beneficiary.'

'Oh. Is that all? Couldn't you have put it in writing?

Post might take a while to get here, but it arrives eventually.'

'No, Miss Felt, you don't understand.' He gave a small laugh which he extinguished by clearing his throat. 'His estate is worth millions.'

The silence that followed this statement was broken only by the sound of birds and parrots cawing, the muffled voices of people criss-crossing the compound, and the distant rush of the river which provided the only form of transport into the heart of the forest.

'You're joking.' She smiled hesitantly at her father, who returned her smile with off-putting gravity. 'Aren't you?'

'I'm a lawyer, Miss Felt. My line of business doesn't include jokes.'

'But what am I supposed to do with all that money?' Her laugh was a bit on the hysterical side. 'Look around you, Mr Wilson. Do you see anything to spend money on here? We all get a government grant, and some of the locals make things for the tourist trade, but as for spending millions…no shops, no fast cars, no restaurants, no hotels…no need.'

'It's not quite as easy as that.' He rested his elbows on his knees and contemplated her thoughtfully. He'd removed a handkerchief from his pocket and proceeded to give his face a thorough wipe with it. She could see the beginnings of sunburn. In this heat, sunblock was only partially successful. She'd always used it but, even so, at the age of twenty-six, she was as brown as a nut—a smooth, even brown that the average sun-seeker would have killed for.

'Aside from a multitude of small interests, his country estate and a collection of art work, there's his major holding. Felt Pharmaceuticals. It has offshoots in some six

European countries and employs thousands of people. I have the precise figures here if you want. And it's in trouble. Big trouble. Now there's a takeover in the offing, and who's to say how many jobs will be lost globally? As the main beneficiary, nothing can be done without you.'

'I don't know a thing about business,' she said stubbornly, willing her father to chip in with some much needed support.

'Your father says that you were a child prodigy.'

Destiny shifted uncomfortably in her chair and sat on her hands. 'Dad! How could you?'

'You were, my darling, and you know it. Even that boarding school didn't know what to do with you…and perhaps the time has come for you to spread your wings a bit. It's all well and good working out here and…'

'No!'

'Listen to me, Destiny!' Her father's voice cracked like a whip and startled her. She stared at him open-mouthed. 'At least go to England and see what this is all about. You'll have to go there anyway to claim this inheritance…'

'But I don't want any inheritance! I don't want to go *anywhere!*'

The heat in the room began to feel suffocating and she stood up, agitated, lifting her face to the fan so that it whirled her hair back and soothed her hot skin. Her baggy dress seemed to cling to her even though she knew it wasn't. Under it, she could feel perspiration trickle from beneath the heavy folds of her breasts down to the waistband of her sensible cotton underwear.

'If you hate it, you can always come back here,' her father was telling her in a gentler voice, 'but don't turn your back on an experience just because you're afraid.

We've always taught you to see the unknown as a challenge and not as a threat.'

'And besides,' Derek chipped in slyly, 'think of the benefits to your father's research, should you have your hand on the steering wheel of an important pharmaceutical company. Your father has told me that he's working on a cure for certain tropical diseases using special tree saps and plant derivatives. Funding would cease to be a problem. You could help these indigenous tribes far more than you ever could by staying put.' He crossed his legs and began to fan himself with his hat, exposing a balding head that was at odds with his reasonably unlined face. 'Come to England, Miss Felt, for your father if nothing else…'

And that had been the carrot, as the wretched man had known it would be.

Even so, one week later, and sitting bolt upright on an aeroplane which had taken her two days of long-distance hiking to get to, she still couldn't fathom out whether she was doing the right thing or not.

She looked around her furtively and surprised a young tourist staring at her, at which she assumed an expression of worldly-wise disdain.

Ha! If he only knew. She and any form of worldly-wise experience had never so much as rubbed shoulders. Her life had always been a peripatetic journey on the fringes of civilisation, swept along by parents whose concerns had never included the things most normal people took for granted. Occasionally, when one of the members of their team took a trip into Panama City, they would return with a few magazines. She knew about microwave machines and high-tech compact disc players, but only from the glossy pages of the magazines. Firsthand, her experience of twenty-first-century living was lamentably undeveloped.

From Panama City they'd moved gradually onwards and downwards, to more and more remote towns, until they'd finally taken root amidst the wilderness of the Darien forest some eight years previously. In between her education had been erratic and mostly home-grown, aside from one tortuous year at a boarding school in Mexico and then a further three at the Panamanian university, from which she'd emerged, in record time, a qualified doctor and desperate to return to her family and the jungle she had come to love.

She'd hated the veneer of sophistication that seemed an obligatory part of twentieth-century city life. She'd hated the need to wear make-up and dress in a certain way at the risk of being thought freakish. She'd hated the envy she'd encountered from other girls who'd thought her too good-looking and too stand-offish for her own good, and the barely developed young men with their boorish, laddish manners who'd seemed hell-bent on getting her into bed. She'd had no real interest in shopping for clothes whenever she could, and neither school nor university had been able to cope with her prodigious talent at nearly everything she put her hands to.

So what was she going to now?

More of the same, and this time with the horrendous task of walking into a company about which she knew nothing, to attempt to speak to people about whom she knew nothing and all because of an inheritance from an uncle whom she had not known from Adam.

As she stepped off the plane and allowed the unfamiliarity of Heathrow Airport to wash over her like a cold shroud, she felt a wave of terror assault her.

Even her two disreputable cases rolling past on the belt

looked small and scared next to the bigger, brasher items of luggage being snatched up by the horde of weary travellers.

She was to stay at her unknown and now deceased uncle's Knightsbridge house which, Derek Wilson had assured her, was beyond plush.

Right now, all Destiny wanted was to be back home where she belonged.

She had to force her feet forwards, out through the line of watchful uniformed custom officers, past the heaving banks of friends and relatives waiting for their loved ones back from holiday and then, with a surge of gratitude, towards the familiar face of the man who had succeeded in turning her uncomplicated life on its head.

'Got here safe and sound, then,' Derek greeted her, assuming control of the trolley with her bags even though she was more than capable of pushing it herself. 'Did you have a chance to read all the company reports I left with you? Details of your inheritance? My driver's waiting for us outside. You'll probably want to relax after your trip—' he grimaced at the memory of his own '—so I thought I'd drop you straight to your house, let you sort yourself out, have a rest. I've made sure that it's fully stocked with food and you can give me a ring in the morning so that we can start sorting out this business.'

'Where are all these people *going*?' There was barely room to manoeuvre their trolley. In her brightly woven dress, which had been her only item of clothing suitable for long-distance travel, Destiny felt gauche, out of place and utterly lost.

'All over the world.' The man at her side cast a critical look at his companion. 'You'll have to do some shopping, you know. Especially for when you go into the offices…'

'Why? What's wrong with what I've got on?'

'Nothing! It's very charming, I'm sure. Just…not quite suitable…'

'Suitable for what?'

They had now cleared the interminable confines of the airport terminal, but outside things were no less frantic. Destiny felt as though she'd been catapulted onto another planet, where everything operated on the fast-forward button. Black cabs rushed past them; buses were pulling up and pulling away; cars were spilling out their contents of travellers and cases. She allowed herself to be led to a long sleek car quietly purring at the end of the drop-off kerb. It was a far cry from the communal four-wheel-drive Jeep she'd become accustomed to, with its unreliable windows, cracked plastic seats and coughing engine noises.

'Suitable for what?' she resumed, as soon as they were in the back of the car.

Derek coughed apologetically. 'Suitable for the board meeting you'll be attending tomorrow afternoon.'

'Board meeting? *Me? Attending?*' She spoke four languages, had taught any number of subjects over the years, and knew more about medicine and how to deliver it than most doctors, yet the thought of a board meeting was enough to send her into a panic attack. She was only twenty-six! She shouldn't *be* here!

'Well, perhaps *board meeting* is a bit of an overstatement…the directors just want to meet you, actually…'

'Can't *you* go? Or perhaps tell them that I'm ill? Jet lag…?' She could feel her heart lurching about inside her and had to take deep breaths. Inoculation, delivering babies, tending to the ill seemed a faraway excursion to Paradise.

Derek swept past her objections with practised ease. 'Their futures are at stake. Naturally they want to meet the person now in charge of the show…' He cleared his throat and she looked at him, aware that some other piece of not quite so innocuous information was about to come.

'There's also one other person I feel I ought to mention…'

'What other person…?'

'I'm sure you'll be able to handle him…' His voice failed to live up to any corresponding conviction.

'*Handle him?* Is he violent?'

At which Derek allowed himself to chuckle. 'Not violent, my dear girl. Not in the sense you think. His name's Callum Ross…his name crops up in the Company Report I left for you…'

'Sorry, I fell asleep on the plane.'

'He's…how to describe him?…he's a household name over here in the world of high finance and business. Quite a legend, in fact. He's managed to accumulate quite a number of companies in a remarkably short space of time…' He sighed and nervously patted his receding hair. 'The man's quite formidable, Destiny. Some have even described him as ruthless.' His expression conveyed the impression that he included himself in this number. 'When he wants something, he's reputed to go after it, no holds barred.'

'I've met types like that,' Destiny said slowly.

'Have you? Really?'

'Yes. They live in the jungle and they're called cougars. They don't hesitate to go for the kill.'

Derek didn't smile as she might have expected. Instead he nodded and said musingly, 'It's a more fitting description than you might think… At any rate, Callum Ross has wanted your uncle's company for some time now, if gossip in the City is to be believed, and he was very nearly there. Papers had been drawn up, waiting for the signature of your uncle—who had the poor timing to die before he could validate anything. He's engaged to—well…you could say your stepcousin…'

'*I have a cousin?*' She felt a sudden flare of excitement at the thought of that.

'No. Not quite. Your uncle was married four times. Stephanie White was the daughter of his most recent ex-wife by her previous marriage. Stephanie's surname became Felt at the time when her mother married your uncle. At any rate, she has some shares in the company, along with the directors, but the majority of the shares are now under your control. What I'm saying, Destiny, is that Callum Ross badly wants what is essentially *your* company now. He's seen his opportunity slip away from him through a blow of chance and he's going to be a very disappointed man. Disappointed enough to be a thorn in your side.'

'I don't understand *any of this.*' She hadn't been following the progress of the car, but she was now aware that they were pulling up outside a gated crescent. A guard approached them, nodded at something Derek held out for him to see, and the impressive black wrought-iron gates smoothly glided open, like a pair of arms stretching out to reveal a tantalising secret. '*All these people!* I just…'

'Want to go home…?'

She nodded mutely at him, dully taking in what she knew, without really having to be told, was an expensive clutch of houses. They curled in a semi-circular forma-tion around a small, impeccably manicured patch of green. All white, all three storeys tall, all sporting black doors and tidy front gardens sectioned off with more black wrought-iron gates. A few cars were parked here and there and they were all of the same ilk as the one she was currently in. Sleek, long and shiny. She felt a little ill at the sight of all the structured precision.

'You can't. At least not quite yet. Not until the business with the company is sorted out once and for all.'

'Why don't I just sell to this Callum man? Wouldn't that be the easiest thing to do?' She tore her miserable eyes away from her prospective neighbourhood and looked at Derek.

'If you do, there's a good chance he'll split the company up to maximise his profits if he decides to sell. The other thing is this—there's almost no way that he's going to invest in the work your father's doing.'

'But wouldn't *I* be able to fund it all myself? With whatever I make from the company?'

'After all debts have been cleared? Without the back-up of the facilities over here in the Felt labs? Unlikely. Anyway—' he assumed a tone of bonhomie '—enough of all that. You'll be meeting the man himself soon enough. Here's your place! Number twelve. Lucky twelve. In case you haven't noticed, there's no number thirteen. Superstition. Guess there's a lot of that from where you come? Folklore, superstition, etc?' He pushed open his door as soon as the car had stopped, then skipped around to open hers before bounding merrily up three steps to black door number twelve.

'Meeting the man soon enough?' Destiny repeated, as he opened the front door and stepped back to let her pass. 'When?' The driver had followed them with her cases which, on the highly polished black and white flagged

entrance hall, looked even sadder and more forlorn than
they had on the conveyor belt at the airport.

'Shall I do the guided tour?'

'When am I going to be meeting this man, Derek?'

'Ah, yes. Tomorrow, actually.'

'You mean with all the other…directors?'

'Not quite. Tomorrow morning. After you've seen me,
as a matter of fact. Thought it might be best to size up
the enemy, so to speak, before you meet the rest…'

The enemy. The enemy, the enemy, the enemy.

She hoped that Derek Wilson had been exaggerating
when he'd said that, but somehow, she doubted it.
Whoever Callum Ross was, he was obviously good at
instilling fear. It was a talent for which she had no respect. In the compound, she'd become accustomed to
working alongside everyone else to achieve the maxi-
mum. How could they ever hope to help anyone else if
they were too busy playing power games with one another? Only the big cats in the jungle inspired fear, and
that was all part of nature's glorious cycle.

For a man to stride around thinking that he could command other people into obedience was anathema to her.

By the time she'd explored the house, unpacked and
investigated the contents of the superbly stocked fridge
and larder, she had managed to distil some of her apprehension at what lay ahead.

If her father could see her now, she thought, he would
probably faint. Before she left to return to Panama, she
would make sure that he *did* see her. In these grand surroundings. It would give them something to chuckle
about on those sultry, whispering evenings, with the
sounds of wildlife all around.

And if Henri could see her, sitting at the kitchen table,
with a delicate china cup of coffee in front of her—proper

milk! Proper coffee! She smiled. Dear Henri, her soul-mate, just a handful of years older than her, who still flirted with her and jokingly proposed marriage every so often.

Her mind was still sabotaging all her attempts to concentrate on what had to be done before travelling back to Panama, when there was a sharp buzz of the doorbell.

It took a few seconds for her to realise that the buzz corresponded to someone at *her* door, then several seconds more to find herself at the door. Derek, who obviously now saw himself as her surrogate father, had warned her of sharks in the big city which were more lethal than the fishy variety, but she pulled open the door anyway.

It was an impulse which she instantly regretted.

The man standing in front of her, angled in shadows, was taller than she was. Tall and powerful with a sharply contoured, unsmiling face. He was wearing a lightweight suit in a dark colour, appropriate for the mild summer weather, but even his suit did little to conceal the aggressive, muscular lines of his body. She felt her pulses begin to race.

She should have looked through the peephole in the door, a small device pointed out to her through which she could determine whether any unexpected visitors were welcome or not. Despite security, not all visitors were welcome, Derek had told her. Naturally she'd forgotten all about the wretched thing.

'Yes?' She placed her body squarely in the entrance so that the man couldn't brush past her, although, judging from his size, he would have had little difficulty in doing just that if he wanted to.

For a few disconcerting seconds, the man didn't say a word. He just looked at her very thoroughly, lounging indolently against the doorframe, one hand tucked into his trouser pocket.

'Who are you and what do you want?' Destiny said tensely. 'The security guard is within shouting distance so don't even think of getting up to anything.'

'What sort of thing do you imagine I might be getting up to?' he asked coolly. 'A bit of forcible entry, perhaps? Some looting and pillaging?' His voice was deep and smooth.

'Goodbye.' She stepped back and began closing the door to find his hand placed squarely on it. An immovable force.

'Are you Destiny Felt?'

The question froze her, allowing him the opportunity to push the door back and step into the hall, where the overhead light revealed an even more intimidating face than she'd gleaned from the semi-obscure darkness outside. His features were perfectly chiselled and his eyes were a unique shade of blue, midnight-blue. Cold blue eyes fanned by thick black lashes. Lashes that matched the colour of his hair and which, combined with the sensual lines of his mouth, lent him a powerfully masculine attraction. She took a step backwards and glared belligerently at the man standing in front of her.

'What business is it of yours?'

'Destiny Felt, fresh from the Panamanian wilderness? Heir to an unexpected fortune? My, my, my. Lady Luck certainly chose to shine forth on you, didn't she?' He looked around him. 'So this is good old Abe's place. Quite the change for you, wouldn't you say?'

'If you don't tell me who you are, this instant, I'm calling the police.' She folded her arms, unconsciously defensive, and stared at the man. When he returned his wandering gaze to her, it was to inspect her with a thoroughness that bordered on intrusive. It didn't help matters that he was formally dressed while she was in a way too short faded shift, one of the few items of clothing she possessed. Her long legs were too exposed for comfort and, without the reassuring barrier of a bra, her heavy breasts pushed against the dress.

He narrowed his eyes thoughtfully. 'Can't you guess? Surely Wilson must have mentioned my name in passing?'

'You're Callum Ross, aren't you?' she said with dawning comprehension. 'You're Callum Ross, who arrogantly assumes that he can push his way into this house and take control. Am I right?' Her hands shifted from chest to hips and she outstared him with an expression of hostility that matched his own. 'The great and powerful Callum Ross who thinks…what? That he can troop in here uninvited and scare me senseless into doing whatever it is you want? Is that it? Terrify the poor half-witted Destiny Felt because she's all the way from the middle of nowhere and probably doesn't know how to use a knife and fork properly, never mind argue back with the formidable Mr Ross and his reputation for scaring his adversaries senseless?'

'Not quite,' he snarled, but he had flushed darkly in response to her hurled accusations.

'Well, it won't work, Mr Ross. I'm not intimidated by you and I don't intend to be scared into selling you the company if I don't choose to sell. Now, get out of this house before I call someone to throw you out.'

Instead of leaving, though, he moved towards her, and she fought to stand her ground. 'Very fiery,' he murmured, in a change of tone that was much, much more destabilising. He lifted one hand and casually toyed with a few strands of hair, rendering her even more immobile than she had been. 'My mother always told me never to play with fire,' he breathed silkily, 'but I feel on this occasion I might be forced to disregard her advice.' He laughed under his breath. 'Till we meet tomorrow…'

CHAPTER TWO

'Ah, Miss Felt. So we meet again. In the light of day.'

Destiny had spent the previous two and a half hours in Derek Wilson's office, prey to stomach-cramping nerves at the prospect of seeing Callum Ross again, whilst trying to grapple with the complexities of her inheritance. His entrance had been preceded by only the most perfunctory of knocks, and now there he was, looming in the doorway like a dark predator in search of some easy prey. *Her,* in other words.

Derek had half-risen from his seat. 'Mr Ross. Good of you to come.' He looked at both their faces in consternation. 'What do you mean by *we meet again?* Do you two know each other?'

'Mr Ross saw fit to pay me an unexpected visit last night,' Destiny said tightly.

'That, Mr Ross, was quite unorthodox, as you must well know. I have all the relevant papers here and I object to you using intimidation to try and manipulate my client. This matter needs to be discussed in a rational, civilised—'

'Intimidation?' The dark eyebrows rose expressively as he said this and he made his way to the chair next to Destiny, settling into it without bothering to wait for an invitation to take a seat. 'Whatever makes you think that I would resort to intimidation to get what I want, Derek?'

She could feel his presence next to her like a strong, electrical current, hot and lethal, radiating out towards her.

'I didn't *intimidate* you, Miss Felt, did I?'

'Actually, it would take more than you to intimidate me, Mr Ross.' She reluctantly glanced sideways to him and met his eyes with as flat an expression as she could muster.

'Callum. Please. If we're to do business together, we might as well be on a first-name basis. Destiny…' The insolence was there again, softly underlining his slow, velvety pronunciation of her name. She'd dealt with all manner of danger in her life. Real danger. Danger from animals on the many occasions when she'd accompanied her father along the dark river in their *piragua,* to get deep into the heart of the forest to tend to someone. Danger from illnesses with the power to kill. She would not allow him to get under her skin now.

'It has not yet been established that you will be doing business with my client, Mr Ross. Whilst I appreciate that your plans to take over Felt Pharmaceuticals were dashed by Abe's untimely—'

'Perhaps I could have some privacy with…Destiny, Derek?' He tore his eyes away from the tall, striking blonde incongruously dressed in her multicoloured frock—if it could be called a frock—and briefly focused them on the man ineffectively glaring in his direction.

From the minute he'd heard about the existence of a woman who had landed her unexpected prize catch, the catch that he had worked ruthlessly to secure for himself only to see his efforts reduced to rubble, he'd been looking forward to meeting her. Looking forward to a seam-free, ludicrously easy deal. He'd had no doubts that a woman plucked from the wilds of a Panamanian forest would readily agree to the terms and conditions meticulously drawn up for the sale of the company. He had been curious, but not unduly worried by the temporary hitch in his plans.

Having met her the evening before, he was really still not unduly worried, but his curiosity, he'd discovered, now exceeded his original expectations.

Despite his resolve to talk business in as restrained a manner possible, he found that he was itching to be rid of Derek and his patter. Destiny Felt had unexpectedly stirred something inside his jaded soul and he wanted her to himself. Alone.

'I don't think that that's a very good idea, Mr Ross.' Valiant words, Destiny thought, but Derek was looking very twitchy. 'My client needs protecting...'

'Do you need protecting?' Once more the blue eyes enveloped her.

'I think what Derek means is that I've only skimmed the surface of the proposal you had in effect with my uncle. He doesn't want to see me taken advantage of.'

'I should think not!' Derek sounded horrified.

'Oh, nothing could be further from my mind.' His low laugh was not reassuring. In fact, it just upped the tempo of her already skittering pulses. 'So now we all understand each other. I'm not about to take advantage of your client, Derek, so you can leave us alone for a while to discuss matters in privacy.' There was a hard edge to his voice now, although his body was still relaxed and his smile didn't falter.

'It's all right, Derek,' she said, releasing him from his state of nervous tension before he exploded all over his pristine mahogany desk. 'I can take care of myself. If I need you, I can always give you a shout.'

'This is all highly unorthodox,' he faltered, fumbling with his tie and frowning disgruntledly but standing up anyway.

Callum shot him a soothing look from under his dark lashes. At least Destiny, watching him covertly, suspected that it was meant to be soothing. In reality, it just seemed to make Derek even more jittery. Or maybe that was the intention. She'd never had any opportunity to see first-hand how power, real power, worked. She was learning fast.

Her body was rigid with tension as the door closed behind her buffer and Callum slowly positioned his chair so that he was completely facing her now.

She looked at him steadily. For the second time in as few days, she felt utterly disadvantaged in what she was wearing. It had never really occurred to her that the highly coloured clothes she'd brought over with her would make her stand out like a sore thumb in a country where everyone—certainly everyone in the Wilson legal firm—seemed to be attired in shades of black, brown or navy blue. No wonder the man thought that she was a push-over.

'What's Derek told you about me?' he drawled, linking his fingers together on his lap and stretching out his long legs in front of him, so that they were very nearly touching hers, which she had tucked protectively under her chair.

'That you were on the verge of consolidating a bid for my uncle's company. That it all fell apart when he died.'

'That all?' He cocked his head to one side, as though listening for something she couldn't hear.

'What more is there?' she asked politely.

'No character assassination?'

'I'm not in the habit of repeating other people's personal opinions,' she said calmly.

'No, I can understand that. It would be a disaster in a compound of only a handful of people.'

'How do you know…?'

'I made it my business to find out before you came over here. Forearmed is forewarned, as the saying goes.' Actually, he had done nothing of the sort. His mention of a compound had been an inspired guess and he wasn't quite sure what he'd been hoping to achieve with his distortion of the truth. He suspected, darkly, that it was a desire to provoke some sort of reaction from her. He was accustomed to people responding to him, focusing on every word he had to say. He could feel niggling irritation now at his staggering lack of success in that department. She looked back at him with those amazing sea-green, utterly unreadable eyes.

'I hadn't expected you to have such a good grasp of English,' he said bluntly, veering away from the topic, watching as she tucked some hair behind her ears.

Destiny hesitated, uncertain at the abrupt ceasefire. 'My parents certainly always spoke to me in English, wherever we happened to be. They always thought that it was important for me to have a good grasp of my mother tongue. Of course, I speak Spanish fluently as well. And French, although my German's a bit rusty.'

'Isn't that always the case?' he said drily, and she glanced at him, surprised at his sudden injection of humour. With a jolt of discomfort, she realised that, although he had not chosen to display it, there was humour lurking behind the sensual lines of his mouth and she hurriedly averted her eyes.

'There are a number of French workers on the compound, but our German colleagues have been more sporadic so I haven't had the same opportunity to practise what I've learnt.'

'You've studied?'

That brought her back to her senses. Just when an unwelcome nudge of confusion was beginning to slip in. Did the man think that she was thick? Just because her lifestyle had been so extraordinary?

'From the age of two,' she said coolly. 'My parents were obsessive about making sure that my education didn't suffer because of the lifestyle they had chosen. Sorry to disappoint you. Now, getting back to business, I'm not qualified to agree to anything with you. I still have to see the company, meet the directors…'

'Do you know why Felt Pharmaceuticals has been losing money over the past five years?' he cut in, and when she shook her head he carried on, with no attempt to spare her the details. 'Shocking mismanagement. Cavalier and ill-thought-out overinvestment in outside interests with profits that should have been ploughed back into the company, interests that have all taken a beating…'

'How do you know that?'

'I made it my business to know.'

'Just like you made it your business to find out about me before I came over here?'

He didn't like being reminded of that little white lie and he uncomfortably shifted in his chair. 'Unless you've taken a degree course in business management, you might not be aware that taking over a company requires just a touch of inside knowledge on the company you're planning to take over.'

'That's common sense, not business management know-how,' Destiny informed him, riled by the impression she got that he was patronising her.

He swept aside her input. 'For the past five years old Abe, miserable bastard that he was, was bedridden and had more or less been forced to hand over control to his directors—who are good enough men when being told what to do, but on their own wouldn't be able to get hold of a pint of beer in a brewery.'

'What was the matter with him?'

'What was the matter with *whom?*' One minute mouthing off at him with cutting efficiency, the next minute looking like a vulnerable child. What the hell was this woman all about? He had known enough women in his lifetime not to be disconcerted by anything they said, did or thought, for that matter, but Destiny Felt was succeeding in throwing him off balance. How could someone be forthright and secretive at the same time? He nearly grunted in frustration. 'He had a stroke and never really recovered,' Callum said. 'Of course, he remained the figurehead for the company but his finger was no longer on the button, so to speak.'

'At which point you decided to break into the scene, once you'd checked out where the weak spots were,' she filled in, reading the situation with the same logical clarity of thought that she'd inherited from both her parents.

'It's called doing business.'

'Business without a heart.'

'The two, I might as well warn you, in case you're foolhardy enough to stick around, don't go hand in hand.' He hadn't felt so alive in the company of a woman for as long as he could remember. He sincerely hoped that she stuck around, just long enough for him to enjoy the peculiar sparring they were currently establishing that was so invigorating, but not long enough to thwart his plans. His eyes drifted from her face to the swell of her breasts jutting out against the thin dress and he drew his breath in sharply.

Dammit, he was engaged! He shouldn't be looking at another woman's breasts, far less registering their fullness, mentally stripping her of her bra. The thought felt almost like a betrayal and he glared at her with unvoiced accusation that she had somehow managed to lead his mind astray.

'Why did you call him a *miserable bastard?*'

'You won't be able to revive the company, you know,' he said conversationally, standing up and prowling through the office, casually inspecting the array of legal books carefully arranged in shelves along one wall, then moving behind the desk to the picture window and idly gazing through it. 'You haven't the experience or the funds. My offer is wildly generous, as Abe would have been the first to admit.' He turned around to look at her, perching against the window ledge. 'Wait much longer and you'll end up having to sell anyway, for a song, so it's in your interests to give it up sooner rather than later. And then you can get back to your jungle, where you belong. It's a different kind of jungle here. One I don't imagine you'll have a taste for.'

'This is more than just business profit for you, isn't it?' Destiny said slowly. 'You speak as if you hated my uncle. Did you? Why? What was he like?'

'Use your imagination. What sort of man wills his fortune to someone he's never met?'

'I was told that it was because I was his only blood relation. I gather he had no children of his own. He and my father weren't close, but I was his niece.' It had been a straightforward enough explanation from Derek, but Callum's words had given her pause for thought. Abraham Felt, after all, had never met her. He and her father had maintained the most rudimentary of contact over the years. Surely in all that time he should have filled his life with people closer and dearer, to whom his huge legacy would have been more fitting?

'He left it all to you because Abraham Felt was incapable of sustaining friendships.'

'He had hundreds of wives, for goodness's sake!'

'Four, to be exact.'

'Well, four, then. He must have shared *something* with them.'

'Beds and the occasional conversation, I should imagine. Nothing too tricky, though. He was noted for his contempt for the opposite sex.'

'How do you know that? No, don't tell me, you made it your business to find out. I'm surprised you have time to do any work, Mr Ross, since you seem to spend most of it ferreting out information on my uncle and his company.'

For a split second, Callum found himself verbally stumped by her sarcasm. Oh, yes. He had to confess that he was enjoying himself. How on earth the depths of a Panamanian forest had managed to satisfy this woman, he had no idea. She was sharp. He wondered what life on this compound of hers really was like. Having spent his entire life in concrete jungles, he wondered whether a close community in the middle of nowhere might not be a hotbed of conversations stretching into the wee hours of the morning. Not to mention sizzling sex. After all, what else was there to do? For years and years on end? Cut off from civilisation and surrounded by hostile nature?

'Actually, your dear uncle was always very vocal on most things, including his short-lived romances.'

'He left some shares to Stephanie Felt, your fiancée,' Destiny pointed out. 'What about the rest of his stepchildren?'

'There were none.'

She could feel unanswered questions flying around in

her head like a swarm of bees. There was something more personal to his desire to gain control of her company. What? And was her stepcousin all part of his plan? A useful arrangement because she brought shares with her? Not enough to enable him to gain downright control of the company if he married her, but enough to ensure that he remained active in whatever was happening within it. Active and, through Stephanie, with a voice.

Or was her bond to the company simply a coincidence? Was he in love with her?

She realised that intrigue was something she had so rarely encountered it was a job grappling with it all now.

'What is Stephanie like?' she asked guilelessly.

'You'll meet her soon enough. This afternoon, in fact. With the rest of the fools.'

What kind of a non-answer was that? she wondered.

The door was pushed open and Derek's face popped around it. 'Had enough time, Mr Ross?' He didn't wait for an answer. Instead, he walked in and quietly shut the door behind him.

Not nearly enough, Callum felt like saying, but in fact he was already running late. Stephanie would be at the restaurant in under fifteen minutes. He felt an irrational surge of irritation rise to his throat, but he swallowed it and smiled politely at Derek.

'We'll need to continue this conversation after you've met your people,' he addressed Destiny, pushing himself away from the window and almost throwing the little Derek into shadow as he strolled past him towards the door. 'My offer still stands, but, like I said, don't leave it too late or you might find that I'm forced to reduce it.'

At which he saluted them both and left, not bothering to shut the door behind him and affording Destiny the sight of Derek's personal assistant, a woman in her mid-fifties, hurriedly half-rising as Callum swept past her, the expression on her flushed face one of addled confusion.

By the time she arrived at the company, Destiny was feeling addled and confused herself. Over lunch—an intricately arranged fresh tuna salad, the sight of which had nearly made her burst out laughing, so remotely had it resembled anything edible—she had tried to find out a bit more about the much-maligned directors she was to meet. But Derek had not been a source of useful information. His friendship with her uncle stretched back a long way and there was a debt of gratitude to him which ensured his unswerving loyalty. Fighting hard not to be distracted by the comings and goings in the restaurant, she'd discovered that Abraham Felt had helped Derek when he had first struck out, decades previously, on his own. No wonder he was so protective of her and so unofficially antagonistic towards Callum Ross!

Walking into the glass monument to wealth further shredded her nerves.

'You'll get used to it,' Derek murmured staunchly at her side, as they got into the elevator and glided up to the third floor. Destiny doubted it.

'You wouldn't say that if you were in my shoes,' she murmured back, thinking that *in my sandals* would have been a more appropriate description. Three months previously she and her father had made the nine-hour trek to Panama City and had spent two days shopping for essentials, but somehow London was a great deal more daunting than the country she had learnt to love. However, come hell or high water, she would buy some clothes in the morning. Derek had established a bank account for her and she had arrived in England with more money than she had seen in a lifetime at her immediate disposal. Whether she liked it or not, she would have to get rid of her ethnic garb and conform.

'You don't have to say anything if you don't want to,' Derek told her, as the elevator doors slid open. 'Just get a feel for the people, for the company. You already know what the state of their profit and loss column looks like, so to speak, but you can put it all into real perspective once you've met the people in charge.'

Four hours later, Destiny thought that that was easier said than done. All the directors had been there, except the one she was most curious to meet, her stepcousin, and their reactions had run the gamut from suspicion, to relief that she had not summarily announced that she would be selling, to wheedling as they brought out their individual reports and regaled her with why she shouldn't abandon the ship.

They were all men in their late fifties, on the verge of retirement, and she'd inappropriately recalled Callum's scathing description of them as a pack of old fools when Tim Headley had patted her hand and attempted to excuse four years of misguided management under the heading of 'going through a bad patch.'

'I shall go home and read all this,' she had said wearily, as three o'clock had rolled into four, then five, then six. It had been a further hour and a half before she had finally managed to leave and had been told by a beaming Derek that she had *done really well. Buoyed them up. Given them that little injection of hope they needed.*

Her head was throbbing when she at last made it back to her house, for which she felt an inordinate rush of fondness as it contained the two things she wanted most. A well-stocked fridge and a bed.

She'd not managed to attack the first when her telephone rang and she heard a breathless, girlish voice down the end of the line.

'Who *is* this?' she demanded, cradling the telephone between shoulder and head as she fumbled to undo the front fastening buttons of her dress.

'Stephanie. I should have been at the meeting this afternoon, but…somehow my appointments overran…'

Destiny stopped what she was doing and held the telephone properly.

'Anyway, I thought that perhaps we could meet for supper this evening? You could come to my apartment—actually, I only live about ten minutes' drive away from you…?'

'Well…' The thought of slotting in one more piece of the jigsaw puzzle that had become her life was too enticing to resist. 'If you tell me where you are…can I walk to you? No?… How do I get a taxi?… Yes, right… Well, give me about forty-five minutes and I'll be there… Right, yes, that's fine… Yes, I *do* know what Chinese food consists of… Okay, fine, bye.'

As she inspected her wardrobe, selecting the least colourful of her dresses, she wondered what her stepcousin would be like. Her gut feeling warned her that a disaster lay ahead. Callum Ross was made of steel and any fiancée of his would more than likely be made of similar stuff. She was fast developing a healthy streak of cynicism in this bewildering world where scheming seemed to be part of an acceptable game and exploitation was part and parcel of the same game. The healthy streak of cynicism was now telling her that Stephanie Felt had probably been primed by her lover to use every trick in the book to get what she wanted. Her healthy streak of cynicism was going one step further and warning her that the other woman had probably avoided the meeting on purpose, simply so that their first meeting could be on her own territory. Alone. Destiny stared back dejectedly at her reflection in the bathroom mirror and discovered that, despite her lifelong predilection for all things logical and scientific, her imagination was scrabbling frantically now to make up for lost time.

She left the townhouse nervous, but grimly resolved to face down yet one more enemy. The taxi carried her out of Knightsbridge and into the heart of Chelsea, and then stopped in front of a Victorian house, one in a row of many, all of which were as impeccably maintained as the one she had just left.

She sighed involuntarily as she rang the doorbell. Her nervous system couldn't take much more. She longed with a physical ache for the simplicity of her compound, with its heat and wild beauty and unthreatening routines.

From Callum Ross to Stephanie Felt in the space of a few short hours. She wondered what else could hit her. There must be some evil, as yet undisclosed relation somewhere in the background, clutching a potion, a broomstick and a book of spells.

The woman who answered the door almost made her gasp in surprise.

'Hiya.' More of a girl than a woman, just out of her teens from the look of it, with wavy brown hair and huge blue eyes. Even in her heels, she was still small. Small and slender, her heartshaped face smoothly unlined by time.

'Have I come to the right house?' Destiny blustered, trying to peer at the plaque on the door to see whether she had made a mistake with the numbers. 'I'm looking for Stephanie Felt.'

'That's me.' When she smiled, her face dimpled and she stood back to let Destiny walk past. 'I've been dying to meet you, you know. *A stepcousin!* I never even *knew* you existed until Callum told me! Can you believe it? Abraham never mentioned his family, not even to Mum!' Her voice was light and excited as she led the way to the sitting room. 'You'll have to tell me all about where you lived. I've never been to your part of the world—never. Can you believe it? Callum says it's really primitive where you come from. Gosh!' She turned around and looked at Destiny with glowing curiosity and awe. 'This must all seem very strange to you! I love your dress, by the way. Neat. All those swirly colours. Is that what the people over there wear? Is it, like, their native costume, so to speak?'

'No, not really.' Destiny smiled. For the first time since she had set foot on English shores, she felt unthreatened and relaxed. 'Most of the women in the Indian tribes I come into contact with walk around bare-breasted...'

'Which would never do,' came a familiar drawling voice, 'so I should practise that mode of dress only in the privacy of your own house.'

Sure enough, Callum was sprawled in a chair strategically positioned so that Destiny was afforded a full-frontal of the man at leisure. It was the first time she had seen him without the formality of a suit and she was taken aback to realise that he looked younger. Younger yet no less off-putting. His cream trousers made his legs seem longer and the short-sleeved shirt with the top two buttons undone revealed masculine forearms and a sneak preview of dark hair shadowing his chest.

Her mouth felt disconcertingly dry and she almost shrieked her, 'Yes, please!' when Stephanie offered her something to drink. 'Beer, please.'

'Beer?' they both echoed in unison, with varying degrees of surprise on their faces.

'Perhaps not.' She faltered and looked to her stepcousin for support.

'Perhaps some wine?' Stephanie suggested, grinning. 'It's nice and cold.'

'Yes, thank you, that sounds fine.' She breathed a sigh of relief and sat down in the chair facing Callum, more because of its relative proximity than for any other reason, although the badly chosen seating arrangement now guaranteed an uninterrupted vision of him.

'You were talking about your national costume—or, rather, the lack of it,' he said, crossing his extended legs at the ankles and linking his fingers together on his lap.

'What are you doing here?' Destiny surprised herself by asking. This man, like it or not, made her say things and behave in ways that were alien to her. And her skin felt hot and itchy under the intensity of his blue eyes. Was that possible? Could someone make someone else feel hot and itchy just by looking at them? It had certainly never happened to her before.

His eyebrows shot up in exaggerated astonishment at her question. 'Stephanie's my fiancée. Naturally I wanted to be by her side when she met her stepcousin for the first time. She's a very gentle soul.' He lowered his eyes when he said this but there was a tell-tale smile tugging the corners of his mouth. 'I didn't want you to terrify her.'

'*Me? Terrify her?*' Her protesting voice was more of a furious splutter.

'With your aggression.'

'*My aggression?* How can you talk about *my* aggression?'

She reduced the volume of her voice at the sound of approaching footsteps, but the rankled feeling managed to stay with her for the remainder of the evening. Even more infuriating was the fact that her fulminating looks did very little more than provide him with a source of barely contained amusement.

Only Stephanie's cheerful banter, as she dragged out details of Panama from her guest, besieging her with interested questions, squealing with delight when Destiny talked about the children she taught and gasping with little cries of horror at her stories of the jungle and what it contained, saved the evening. Destiny wondered if her stepcousin knew that she would be marrying someone who made the most ferocious jungle animal pale in comparison.

They had spoken not one word of business by the time eleven-thirty rolled around and she stood to leave, feeling woozy from the wine, to which she was in no way accustomed, and exhausted by her jet lag.

'So, what did you make of the buffoons at the company?' Callum asked, standing up as well and shoving his hands into his pockets. 'I suppose they pulled out all the stops? Made you pore over cobwebbed reports of how great and good the firm used to be years ago? Played down what a shambles it's in now?' Despite consuming what had seemed, to Destiny, prodigious amounts of wine during the evening, the man still looked bright-eyed, alert and rearing to attack.

She threw him a wilted looked and stifled a yawn.

'Mmm. *That* interesting, was it?' A wicked glint of humour shone in his eyes.

'I wasn't trying to make a comment on what the meeting was like,' Destiny said with lukewarm protest in her voice. 'I'm tired.'

'Leave her alone, Callum,' Stephanie said sympathetically.

'Business has to be discussed, Steph.'

'Why now? It's so boring.'

'Boring for *you* perhaps, but you want to remember that your finances are tied up with what happens next in this little exciting scenario. I buy the company, play with it a bit until it's running along smoothly, and *your* shares go up. Our Panamanian heiress keeps the company and—'

'Do you mind *not* talking as if I wasn't here?'

'Have you ever been to London before, Destiny?' Stephanie linked her arm through her stepcousin's and ushered her to the front door, pointedly turning her back on her fiancée.

'No. It's all new and—' she glanced over her shoulder and her eyes clashed with Callum's '—a little scary.'

'It would be. You're just so brave to come all this way, on your own. I'd never dream of doing it!'

'No.' Callum's voice behind them was silky. 'It takes a certain type of woman to do that. Some might call it brave, darling; others might just call it—well, let's just say that it's a very *masculine* response.'

At which Stephanie flew around to face him with her hands on her hips and a simmering look in her baby-blue eyes. 'Don't be *horrible!*'

'Me?' He raised both his hands in innocent denial, but the blue eyes that locked with Destiny's were unrepentant. 'Horrible? It was meant to be a *compliment!* A glorious example of how far the women's movement has got!'

'What women's movement?' Destiny asked, her body language echoing Stephanie's. 'I've never been a part of any movement in my life before!'

'No?' He tried to stifle a grin and failed miserably. 'Well, let's just say that feminism has missed out there.'

'Meaning what?'

'Meaning that I'll give you a lift back to your place.' He bent over to give Stephanie a gentlemanly peck on the cheek and a pat on the back. 'That all right with you, darling?'

'Don't badger her, Callum.'

'I wish people wouldn't constantly stereotype me.' He pulled open the front door and gave Destiny an exaggeratedly wide berth to exit ahead of him into a clear night that was considerably more bracing than it had been earlier on in the evening.

'What about tomorrow?' Stephanie asked him, standing in the doorway to see them off, an angelic, diminutive shape that made Destiny feel like an Amazonian hulk in comparison. 'The Holts have invited us to supper. Did you remember? Daisy and Clarence are going to be there as well. Oh, and Rupert.'

Callum paused and frowned, appearing to give the matter weighty thought, then he said with a shrug,

'Meeting. Sorry, darling. You go, though. Don't stay in because of me.'

'You're *always* at meetings,' Stephanie said in a childish, sulky voice. 'He's *always* at meetings,' she addressed Destiny in an appeal to sisterhood, which Destiny took up with sadistic relish.

'If he loved you, he'd cancel, I'm sure.'

'If you loved me, you'd cancel.'

There was a brief silence. 'I'll do my best.' He sighed and Stephanie's face radiated at this unexpected victory.

'Oh, goody!' She blew them both a delighted kiss and shut the front door on them.

CHAPTER THREE

'THANK you. Thank you very much,' he grated sarcastically, as the engine of his powerful car purred into life. He pulled away from the kerb unnecessarily fast and Destiny clutched the car door handle to steady herself.

In the shadows of the car, his averted profile was hard and unsmiling and she had to stifle a desire to burst out laughing. Suddenly, sleep was no longer beckoning at her door. In fact, she felt surprisingly revived, and wondered whether her body might not just have been craving some fresh air.

Not that the London air was particularly fresh. Back in Panama, when she breathed in, she could smell everything. The musky aroma of hot, hard-packed dirt, the rich fullness of the trees and the bushes, the distant freshness of the snake-like river coiling its way lazily into the heart of the jungle. At certain times during the day she could smell the fragrance of food being cooked. Sometimes, when she closed her eyes, she could almost seem to detect the smells of the sky and the clouds and the stillness.

Here, she felt stuffy. Pollution, of course. Not as severe as she had seen in Mexico years ago, where the pollution bordered on contamination, but there nevertheless, unseen but ever-present.

'Thank you for what?' she asked innocently, playing him at his own game, and his mouth turned down darkly at the corners.

'You *know* what for,' he accused, looking away briefly from the empty road to glare at her. 'I'd hoped Stephanie

44

had forgotten all about that damned dinner party. Now I'm going to have to go and spend at least three agonising hours being bored to death by Rupert and his cronies.'

'Oh, dear,' she said unsympathetically, which provoked another blistering look.

'Where,' he asked, 'did you get that?'

'Get what?' Her voice was genuinely surprised.

'Your sarcasm. I always thought that missionaries were supposed to be glucose-sweet.'

Destiny bristled. 'I am *not* a missionary, actually. If you'd done your homework properly, you might have discovered *why* we're on a compound in the heart of Panama, and it has nothing to do with converting anyone to any kind of religion. We're there to help educate people in desperate need of education, and I'm not really talking about reading, writing and arithmetic.'

'What, then?' He could feel himself reluctantly being drawn in, like a fish on the end of a line, curious to find out details of the background that had produced the creature sitting next to him. It felt peculiar to find himself hanging on to a woman's conversation when normally he was the one playing the conversational game, digging into his reserves of wit and charm without even realising it. He wasn't sure whether he liked it or not. He felt himself relax his foot on the accelerator so that the car meandered along.

'We teach them how to use the land they have to maximise their crops—how to be self-sufficient, in other words. We help them with distributing crafts. Some of them make things for the tourist market in the city. And naturally we teach them the usual stuff.'

'*We?*'

'Yes. All of us. We work together. I'm a qualified doctor, but I'm also responsible for the formal classes.

Of course, we have specialists on the compound as well. Not just the children need education; so do the adults. How to use their resources to their best advantage, how to rotate certain crops so that the land is never unused. How to take advantage of the rains when they come. Our agricultural expert is responsible for that side of things, but we all chip in.'

'Like one big happy family.'

Destiny narrowed her eyes on him, but she couldn't read his expression and his voice was mild.

'Something like that.'

'Cosy.'

'Yes, it is. Why are you driving so slowly? I want to get back.'

Callum pressed his foot marginally harder on the accelerator and muttered something inconsequential about speed limits, fines and points on a driving licence.

'What points?'

'Never mind. It doesn't matter.' He felt his jaw begin to ache and realised that he was clenching his teeth. 'So what do you do on those long, balmy evenings, anyway? On your compound?'

'*Long, balmy evenings?* It's not a seaside resort.'

'No, of course not.' Clenching again. He relaxed his jaw muscles and realised, with a twinge of disappointment, that her house was now within view. The guard barely glanced at them. He just waved them through and he pulled up very slowly in front of her house.

'Thank you very much,' Destiny said, fiddling with the seat belt and finally releasing it. 'It was lovely to meet Stephanie. I'm sorry if you think that it's my fault that you're going to have dinner with some boring friends tomorr—'

'Oh, forget it.' He waved aside her apologies irritably

and watched as she walked up to the front door. For a tall girl, she was surprisingly agile, graceful even. She'd never answered his question about what she spent her evenings doing, he realised. He waited, watching as various lights were turned on and switched off, tracing her progress through the house, even though he couldn't see a thing because the curtains were all drawn. When the place was in darkness, he impulsively got out of his car, sprinted up to the front door and insistently buzzed the bell, keeping his finger on the button until he heard the sounds of shuffling behind the door.

This time Destiny looked through the peep hole and reluctantly opened the door. 'What do you want *now?*'

'It's that damned car,' he said, raking his fingers through his hair and casting an accusing look in the direction of the inert lump of silver metal on the road. 'Won't start.'

'What?' She'd pulled on a robe over her long, baggy tee-shirt which served as a nightgown, and now she clutched it tighter around her as she continued to eye him with mounting dismay.

What now? She didn't want him in her house! When he wasn't getting on her nerves he was getting under her skin, and she had enough to cope with without Callum Ross sending her normally well-behaved nervous system into overdrive.

He shook his head and then glanced at her. 'I wouldn't have bothered you… You hadn't got into bed as yet, had you?'

'About to.'

'Well, I wouldn't have troubled you, but it's given up on me and I need to use a phone.'

'A phone? At *this* hour? Who are you going to phone

to fix your car at *this hour?* Do car mechanics work around the clock over here?'

'If I could just come in—it's a bit nippy out here…'

For a few seconds she didn't look as though she was going to budge, but then she reluctantly stepped back and he slipped past her just in case she changed her mind and slammed the door in his face.

'It seemed to be working perfectly fine on the drive over.' Destiny stood where she was and folded her arms.

'Ah, yes. That's the problem, you see. I've been meaning to get it seen to for the past week or so, but I haven't managed to find a spare moment…to book it in to a garage. Didn't you notice that it was going particularly slowly on the way over here?'

Destiny inclined her head to one side and remained silent.

'One minute it's absolutely fine; the next minute it's losing power.' He cleared his throat and attempted to take firm control of the proceedings instead of acting like a schoolboy caught doing something underhand. Smoking behind the bicycle shed.

'The telephone's behind you.'

'Ah, good. Good, good, good.' He lifted the receiver and dialled his driver. He felt a heel, actually, having to rouse the man from a deep sleep, but whoever said that life was fair? 'Bennet's coming over as soon as he gets dressed. Might be half an hour or so.' He wondered whether she'd heard him murmuring indistinctly into the phone that there was no rush, within the hour would be fine. 'Don't let me keep you from bed… You pop along…I'll stay down here. The family silver's safe.'

Destiny clicked her tongue in annoyance and headed towards the kitchen. 'I might as well make you a cup of coffee,' she offered grudgingly.

'Don't put yourself out,' he said, following her and then lounging comfortably on one of the kitchen chairs while she filled the kettle and fetched two mugs down from a cupboard. 'Although,' he said pensively, 'you *do* owe me a favour after your trapping me into tomorrow night's hilarity.'

'I had no idea that seeing your fiancée was a trap.' She pelted a spoonful of instant into each of the mugs, sloshed some boiling water in and topped it off with milk.

'Stephanie isn't the problem.' He hooked out another chair with his foot and proceeded to stretch both legs out in front of him and watch her with his hands behind his head. 'Her friends are the problem. The women titter and giggle and the men talk in booming voices and compare drinking anecdotes.' Despite her attempts to cover herself, her robe slipped open as she handed him his mug of coffee and he was privy to the sight of her long body encased in the least attractive item of clothing he could think of seeing on a woman. A faded and well-worn tee-shirt hanging to her knees with some barely identifiable advertising motif on the front.

She sat down opposite him and blew on the surface of her coffee. 'How long will this car mechanic be?'

'I told him to get here as quickly as possible. Believe me, the last thing I need now is to be sitting here at the ungodly hour of midnight, waiting for someone to come and fix my car. With work tomorrow.' He ferociously gulped a mouthful of coffee. 'And another late night on the horizon.' He looked at her speculatively. 'Why don't you come along?'

'Come along where?' For one bizarre moment she thought he was inviting her to go to work with him.

'Come along to the little dinner party I'm being dragged to? Stephanie would be thrilled and you could meet some people.' He lowered his eyes and sipped some more coffee. 'There'll probably be one or two eligible men there…' He let the offer fall into the silence like a stone dropping into a pond. 'Unless, of course, you're already involved with someone…' He risked a quick look to see how this was registering. 'Someone out there in Panama?'

'That's none of your business.'

'Merely trying to introduce you to a social life.'

'I'm here to sort things out with the company,' Destiny said shortly. 'And then I shall be heading back home. I don't *need* a social life, thank you.'

'Everyone needs a social life. Don't tell me you don't enjoy some kind of social life out there. On that compound of yours.' He tried to imagine it and failed. 'You're a young woman, after all.'

'How long have you and my stepcousin been engaged?'

There was no attempt to disguise the change of topic and Callum cursed under his breath. 'Two years.'

'Two years! And you're not married yet?'

'It's hardly shocking,' he said with a trace of impatience in his voice. He had never considered it a long time. In fact, even now, there were no plans for a wedding on the horizon. Neither he nor Stephanie was particularly adamant on moving the step further. 'Marriage is a serious business. What's the point rushing into it? You know what they say about marrying in haste and repenting at leisure.'

'Yes, but if you're certain about someone, then why hang around?' She rested her elbow on the table and cupped her chin in one hand while the other cradled her mug, idly stroking the ceramic surface as she continued to look at him.

'Two years is hardly *hanging around*.' Silence. 'Is it?' Further silence. 'It's nothing to do with whether you've found the right person or not.' Was it particularly hot in the kitchen? He was perspiring and he ran one finger under the collar of his shirt. 'Marriage is little more than a piece of paper anyway.'

'I thought you said that it was a serious business.'

'This is a ridiculous conversation. I was simply inviting you out to meet a few people and rescue you from the prospect of spending your nights cooped up in this place.' Alarmingly, he could detect pique in his voice. 'Through the goodness of my heart.'

At that, she raised her eyebrows in patent disbelief and he gave her a thunderous look. 'The goodness of your heart? You haven't *got* a heart! You want to buy my company and that's all that interests you! I'm a spoke in your wheel and you would do anything to get rid of it!'

'That's business,' he muttered. 'The fact is, that whether we like it or not, I'm engaged to your stepcousin, so we're going to see one another in the course of things.'

'How can you separate business from pleasure? How can you treat someone one way when you're sitting across a desk from them and then treat them completely differently when you're sitting across a dinner table?'

'Why can't you just accept what's handed to you and not read ulterior motives behind everything?'

'You're the one who showed up at this house unannounced,' she pointed out, 'so that you could try and wheedle me into selling you the company before I'd had time to see the directors or even take advice from Derek.'

'I was not trying to wheedle you into selling anything!' Callum exploded. He stood up and began savagely pacing the kitchen.

'Why don't you just help me get the company into

shape?' she demanded. 'That would be a good solution. And you would still have some shares in it through Stephanie.'

At this, he gave a snort of derisory laughter. 'What, you mean pour some of my own money into your company, money I would never get back? Why the hell would I do that?'

'What would you do with the company if I *did* agree to sell it to you?' She could feel her own thought processes getting agitated and jerky. Her eyes compulsively followed him as he prowled, soaking up his expressive hands, the hard, good-looking face with its sensual, curving mouth.

'Make it a working proposition.'

'Don't you mean chop it up into sections and sell it off individually once it's up and running?'

'Which only shows your ignorance of the facts!' he snapped back at her. 'I intend to incorporate it into my own portfolio.'

'And what about the people who work there?' she demanded.

'Most would stay. Some would be asked to leave.'

'Who? *Who* would you ask to leave?'

'I'm not about to hand over that kind of information to you.'

'Why not?'

'Because we're on opposite sides of the fence!' He realised that he was on the verge of shouting. He was a man who couldn't remember the last time he had raised his voice, because so much more could be achieved with a murmur—yet here he was, practically shouting. He was also breathing hard and fast, as though he had just completed a marathon. 'You,' he grated, approaching her chair, scraping it around so that he was staring down at her, 'are impossible.' He leaned over her, his hands on either side of her chair, caging her in so that she was forced backwards as though the pressure of his personality was a physical force. 'In fact, I would go so far as to say that *you* are the most impossible woman I have *ever* met in my entire life!' His face was inches away from hers and Destiny was suddenly terrified. Not terrified that he might hit her, or even hurl another well-targeted insult at her. She was terrified because something in what he said struck deep into her and caused her pain. The backs of her eyes began to sting and she blinked furiously.

'That's not very kind,' she whispered in a small voice, and then, to her further dismay, a lonesome tear trickled down her cheek. She brushed it aside in a wave of mortification and stared down at her fingers.

'Oh, God. Don't do that. Please don't do that. Here.' He fumbled in his pocket and extracted a handkerchief. 'Take this.'

Destiny blindly grabbed it and wiped her eyes, pressing her fingers into them to staunch any further leakage.

'I'm sorry,' he said roughly. 'I didn't think… Oh, God, say something, would you…? Please?'

She would, she thought, if she could, but she knew better than to rely on her vocal cords right now. Instead, she twisted the handkerchief in her fingers, playing with it for distraction from the appalling situation she was now in.

'I'm sorry, Destiny. I never dreamt…'

'It's all right,' she said on a sigh. 'Would you mind…? I can't breathe with you so close…'

Callum swiftly withdrew, but only to drag a chair in front of hers, which gave her a reprieve of several inches more but not enough.

'Look,' she said in a steadier voice, 'there's no need to apologise. I know I'm not…not what men…' She paused and sucked in her breath, then expelled it a little shakily. 'I realise that I'm not feminine and frilly and the sort of woman that men…I've never known what it was like to date boys and flirt.' A fleeting glance at a face that was far too concerned for her comfort, then some more frantic twisting of the handkerchief. 'I mean, my lifestyle has taught me how to be strong. I've always had to be, you see. Weakness isn't something that goes down too well when you're in the middle of nowhere and someone might be depending on you to administer medicine to them or sew some stitches or draw out toxin from a snake bite.'

He stroked her hair, running his fingers through it in a soothing, rhythmic way.

'You should try looking in the mirror some time,' he murmured.

'Not many of them are long enough to fit all of me in.' She tried an unsuccessful laugh and thought with a certain amount of envy of her stepcousin. *She* was the sort of woman oozing feminine attraction. Soft and small and girlishly sexy. There was nothing feigned about her and nature had kindly lent her a huge helping hand at birth in the form of a tiny, neat body and the kind of face that would always have men running behind her like lap-dogs. Big, strong men like the one in front of her now. She'd read enough articles in magazines about men and their need to act as protector to their women. Not too many about men who liked women who could protect themselves and at a pinch could probably do a passable job at protecting *them* in the bargain.

Perhaps she should just sell the damned company and head back to where she belonged. This big, new world

was too big for her. She felt like the country mouse on
its ruinous trip to visit the town mouse.

The sound of the doorbell clanged into the brief silence
between them and she jumped as though she had been
scalded. He started as well and muttered an oath under
his breath; then he stood up and waited till she had risen
shakily to her feet.

Relief washed over her. She was not one for spouting
forth confidences. When it came to her thoughts and her
feelings, Destiny was adept at keeping her counsel. She
could scarcely believe that Callum Ross had somehow
broken through her reserve and extracted depths of self-
pity which she'd never known even existed.

Now, she just wanted him out. She practically shov-
elled him to the front door.

'Are you sure you won't come with us tomorrow evening?' he asked, taking his time even though he must be
able to sense her urgency to get rid of him.

'Quite sure.'

'When do you expect to come to a decision about the
company?'

Destiny shrugged, back in control of her wayward feelings. 'I'm spending a week there going through things
with the directors and Derek; then I'm going to talk to
the accountant and try and get an honest opinion of
whether the company's salvageable or not.'

'It's not, without a huge injection of capital—which
you haven't got. You don't have to talk to your accountant for that information. You can just talk to me.'

'I hope to have come to some kind of decision once
I've done that,' she carried on, ignoring his interruption.
She reached out to open the front door and he grasped
her wrist. Her eyes, he noticed, were still pink, even
though her voice was steady. She had lost control and he

sensed that she had surprised herself. Surprised herself because she was not a woman who frequently lost control or resorted to any feminine wiles such as the random shedding of tears to stir the heartstrings. For a minute she'd allowed him into her world, and he could taste his own desire to find out more like a drug coursing through his veins.

Her wrist caught between his fingers felt hot and his breathing was sluggish.

'Would you mind letting me go?' Her green eyes were polite and cautious, and for a second he wondered how she would react if he told her that he really *would* mind.

'Why don't we meet over dinner to discuss details of…the company?' he said. He edged towards the door, opened it slightly and nodded to his driver. 'Hate getting you out here at this ungodly hour but it won't do a thing, George. Completely useless piece of machinery. Give it a go, would you?' His hand was still gripping hers.

'There's nothing to discuss until—'

'I want to show you some of the plans I have for the company, should you sell.'

'Could you let me go, please?'

He obediently dropped her hand but remained strategically placed in front of the door, which he had quietly shut back.

'Dinner tomorrow night. I'll pick you up around seven thirty.'

'I have no intent—'

'It's really a good idea to get all your facts in place before you make any kind of decision.'

'Derek—'

'—has no say whatsoever in your decision. He might want to puff himself out and hold your hand but there's no need for you to stroke his ego by going along for the ride…'

'I'm doing no such thing!'

'No? Sure? No girlish, helpless giggles while he pontificates and throws his weight around?'

'I am not a *helpless, giggling girl,*' Destiny informed him hotly.

'Then why are you so afraid of meeting me without him around as a chaperon?'

'I am *not afraid of meeting you,*' she said through gritted teeth.

'Good. Then tomorrow at seven thirty.'

'And what would Stephanie say to that?'

'I'm proposing a meeting to discuss business,' Callum interjected smoothly, gratified to see a tell-tale flush spread across her face. He savoured it for a few seconds, then continued, 'I'm sure she wouldn't have any objections.'

'My wardrobe is a bit scant,' Destiny objected weakly. Had she just been bulldozed into something? It certainly felt like it although, when she recapped their conversation, she couldn't pinpoint *why*.

'You're going shopping tomorrow, though.'

'Oh, so I am. And how do you know that, anyway?'

'You mentioned it to Stephanie over dinner.'

For someone who had not seemed highly riveted at the time, the man had a keen listening ear, she thought.

'You should take her along with you. I know she'd be thrilled. There's very little Steph appreciates more than several hours spent tramping in and out of stores and spending money like water.'

'In which case, I'd better not.' An involuntary smile flitted across her face. 'If there's one thing *I* don't appreciate, it's tramping in and out of stores. I wouldn't know about the *spending money like water,* having never had any, but I suspect I probably wouldn't much like that either.'

There was the sound of the car revving into action, which galvanised Callum into yanking open the door and, before his driver could say a word, she was mystified to see him spoken to in low undertones and then Callum was in the passenger seat and the car was gliding away into the night.

Leaving her, she thought the following morning, facing yet another stressful encounter with a man whose image was proving to have superglue properties when it came to lodging in her head.

Despite that, when, just as she was about to leave the house, her father called, she found herself reluctant to confide anything about Callum. It was the first time she had spoken to him since she'd arrived in England, and he'd had to go to the nearest town for use of a telephone. He told her everything that was happening on the compound, little titbits of gossip that made her smile, passed on a *missing you* message from Henri, and conjured up pictures of heat and jungle that seemed more than a lifetime away. In return, she told him what she had been up to, downplaying her own feelings of inadequacy at being thrown in at the deep end to cope with a situation for which nothing in her life had prepared her. She tried to make London sound exciting, because she knew that her father would worry himself sick if she did otherwise, but really when she thought about London the image became entangled with the image of Callum—whose presence she diluted, for her father's benefit, into *an annoying little man who wants me to sell the company.*

'Don't be bullied into doing anything you don't want to do,' her father said anxiously.

'Oh, I can take care of myself, Dad,' Destiny said. 'I'm not worried at all by Callum Ross.' She conjured up a mental picture of his dark, powerful face, and said with a grin, 'He's really just a silly little chap who thinks he can get his own way.'

'Sounds an unpleasant type, my darling. Why don't you let that Derek man take care of him?'

'Oh, I can handle the man myself,' she said airily.

'Eat him up and spit him out,' her father said with a smile in his voice, which was a compliment, she knew, but managed to reignite those niggling little ideas that had taken root in her mind ever since she had met Callum Ross. Little ideas that being fiercely independent and being able to take care of herself was all very well in the depths of Panama, but somehow out of place in a city where the interaction between the opposite sexes called for an appealing helplessness that she found difficult to muster. In fact, impossible.

She hung up after fifteen minutes, feeling vaguely depressed. She looked in the mirror and saw an ill-dressed, unfeminine, overtall and utterly unsexy woman with hair chopped into no particular cut and a body too well toned by a life that had always involved physical exertion. She had no problem kayaking along treacherous rivers through dense undergrowth, but there were no treacherous rivers in the city of London and that particular talent was useless. She had no use for make-up in the steaming heat, but here her face felt naked. The clothes she had always worn, loose-fitting and functional, were fine on the compound, but she was fast realising that dressing sensibly to cope with heat and mosquitoes was good in the jungle but depressingly laughable in a city. Her hands, strong and hard-working, now seemed like hands a man should have and not a woman.

Had she forgotten somewhere along the way that she *was* a woman? The thought made her even more dejected. She thought of her stepcousin with her beautifully manicured nails painted the pink of candy floss and felt graceless and gauche in comparison.

Henri thinks that I'm attractive, she thought to herself. But did he really? Or did he just think that she was the best of the bunch?

Five hours spent on Oxford Street and the King's Road was no sop to her deflated spirits. She spent a great deal of time wondering which shops were worth visiting and looking around her in a bewildered, confused fashion. Several times she had literally been swept along by the crowds of shoppers like a tadpole caught in a downstream current.

The pace was swift and left no room for uncertain young girls with no particular agenda aside from gathering the skeleton of a wardrobe together.

In the end, she found herself outside Harvey Nichols, took a deep breath and handed herself over to the experience of a shop assistant. She did her best not to convert the vast quantities of money she was spending on clothes into an amount that would have bought a lot more important things in Panama.

She bought two skirts and jackets that would do for when she went into the company to work, jeans and shirts and jumpers for casual wear, and shoes that made her feet feel ten sizes smaller and looked, to her unaccustomed eyes, positively ludicrous. She threw caution to the winds and indulged in lingerie that wasn't sensible. She allowed herself to be persuaded into two dresses which, the shop assistant assured her were perfect, with a firmness that defied contradiction—especially from someone who had no idea what might or might not suit her.

'But they're tight,' Destiny protested weakly, looking at the black dress and the deep green dress with concern. Tight clothes were anathema in blistering heat and she had never possessed anything that clung. Least of all clung to her curves. 'And they're short.'

'They're sexy,' the shop assistant explained, casting a critical eye over her victim and pushing her towards a changing booth.

Destiny emerged feeling like a tree inappropriately clad in a bikini, but when she looked in the mirror she realised with a twinge of pleasure that she was nothing like a tree. Tall, yes, but slim and with curves that had rarely seen the light of day.

Her legs seemed to stretch on and on and on, long and brown and slender, and her breasts, not camouflaged by baggy clothes, jutted out provocatively.

'Of course, you should get your hair cut into something fashionable,' she was told.

It was shoulder-length, and years of DIY home cuts had lent it a rough, uneven edge, all the more apparent because it was so incredibly blonde.

'I like my hair,' Destiny said. 'I'm not going to have it short.' Back in her work gear in Panama, stripped of these wildly glamorous plumes that seemed to turn her into a sexy woman, of sorts, and with a cropped haircut, she really would look like one of the men. No chance. Her mother had always insisted that she have some length to her hair and she wasn't about to abandon that piece of advice now.

But buy the clothes she did. The whole lot. She also bought make-up, which took ages because the choice of colours and shades of everything almost defied belief. At the end of it, the shopping bags seemed as heavy to carry back to the house as a dozen bags of medicine, school-books, containers of plant specimens and the kayak rolled into one.

It was worth it, though.

She knew that when, at seven-thirty, she looked at her reflection and what gazed back at her was a striking woman in a short, tight black dress, wearing smart black, albeit hideously uncomfortable, shoes and a face that was a blend of subtle colours. Blushing Pink on her lips, which made her tan stand out, a hint of Passionate Petal blusher and length enhancing mascara that made her eye-lashes look as though they had taken growth hormones.

She would not give Callum Ross another opportunity to sneer at her for being *impossible*—which really boiled down to *unfeminine*.

She wasn't dressing for him, she insisted to herself, but neither was she going to be treated like someone whose lack of sophistication was an excuse for insults. She had no idea how long she would be in London—two weeks, three, maybe more—and while she was here she would damn well change her colours to match her sur-roundings. Animals did it and so could she.

CHAPTER FOUR

DESTINY felt a surge of disproportionate disappointment when she opened the door to Callum, bursting with smug satisfaction at the figure she presented, and was greeted merely with, 'Oh, good. You're ready. I can't stand waiting around for a woman to get her act together.'

She slammed the door behind her and preceded him to the car. 'Did you bring whatever paperwork you wanted me to have a look at?' One minute he was full of scathing asides on her appearance and inability to cope with life in the fast track, and then, when she *did* make an effort, she noticed petulantly, he didn't even have the good grace to comment on it!

'In the car.' His eyes flicked rapidly over her as she folded herself into the car seat and he added perfunctorily, 'Had a successful day shopping, then, I take it?'

'Very successful, thank you.'

He looked away, turned the key in the ignition and the powerful car roared into life.

'And not too much useless tramping in and out of stores?' he quizzed her with the ghost of a smile on his mouth.

Destiny, pressed against the car door, attempted to compose her features into a mask of unrevealing politeness. If he had the slightest idea how much his opinion meant to her, she had no doubt that he would ruthlessly use the knowledge to get what he wanted.

'Quite a bit of useless tramping in and out of stores, actually.' He was wearing a plain-coloured shirt with some logo almost invisibly embroidered on the front pocket, and dark trousers. She could feel herself going into an undignified trance as she feasted her eyes on him, and with a little twinge of guilt she dragged them away and stared out of the window. She was already beginning to get used to the fact that no part of London was free from crowds. Even at this hour of the evening there seemed to be no let-up from the hordes of people in search of open shops and entertainment. Did no one sleep here? she wondered.

'Mmm. To be expected, considering you don't know where to go. You should have listened to me and gone along with Steph.'

'Does *she* always listen to you?'

'Most people do,' he said comfortably.

'Would that be because you're a bully?'

He frowned at her, and his brief lapse in concentration caused him to brake suddenly behind the black cab in front.

'Could you try not to distract me when I'm driving? London is a bloody obstacle course. The last thing I need is for the two of us to land up in hospital.'

'Which would be *my* fault because I'm trying to make polite conversation?'

'Telling me that I'm a bully is your way of making polite conversation? I don't run around yelling at people and telling them what to do and how to live their lives. I'm very reasonable and usually right.'

'Oh.'

Next to her, Callum simmered silently, barely seeing the crowds overflowing the pavements as they drove through the busy theatre district. He dared not keep his foot on the accelerator and risk another glance at her without opening himself up to a possible crash, but he was itching to. He wasn't idiotic or egotistical enough to imagine that she had put on that sexy little black number for his benefit, but it was having a roller-coaster effect on his senses. Dressed like that, she even *smelt* more womanly. The neckline was scooped and cut low enough to reveal the swelling roundness of her breasts. Not even the thought of Stephanie, with her childishly boyish figure, was enough to put a brake on his wandering imagination. It wasn't disloyalty, he told himself sternly. It was a natural male response to look at a beautiful woman clad in precious little. In fact, he continued his inner dialogue, while his mind carried on its pleasurable games, it would be *unnatural* if the woman sitting next to him didn't evoke a response. He was a red-blooded man of the world merely appreciating what nature had to offer. He was in the middle of reasoning to himself that in fact the desire to feast his eyes on her strikingly tall, voluptuous and entirely womanly body was very similar to a desire to feast his eyes on anything that was aesthetically pleasing, be it a piece of architecture, a stick of furniture or a houseplant in bloom for that matter, when he became aware that she was talking to him.

'What?'

'I asked where we were going to eat.'

'Oh. Just an Italian restaurant I frequent. Five minutes away.' A quick shift of his eyes gathered in brown hands resting languidly on her lap and crossed legs. 'Should make a change from staying in.' He realised when he drew in a shuddering breath that his iron self-control was slipping. 'So tell me about what you do in Panama,' he said, steering the conversation into safe waters that might drown out his wildly soaring thought patterns. 'You never mentioned what you do in the evenings. I don't suppose there's much happening.'

'Depends what you call "not much happening",' Destiny told him. 'If you're asking whether there's much by way of expensive restaurants, clubs and hectic night life, then, no, it's the most boring place on the face of the earth.'

'A simple answer would have been enough.' He pulled sharply into a vacant space that had suddenly become free then turned to face her, one hand lingering on the gear lever between them. 'No need to launch into a biting attack.'

Destiny stared at him for a moment and it occurred to her that she was *never* sarcastic. Now and again, she and Henri would have little ribbing sessions with one another, and they were accustomed to dissecting the magazines that accumulated dust in one of the storage cabins with cutting jokiness, but that was as far as it went. Callum had asked her once before where she had dredged her sarcasm from, but in all truth it was a talent that had only been brought to light with the arrival of the man now sitting next to her, watching her with those cool, disturbing blue eyes.

'I'm sorry,' she apologised.

'Are you?' He didn't give her time to answer, instead twisting round to get out of the car, and she did the same.

'I feel very sorry for whatever man is in your life,' he remarked, holding the door open for her, and she snapped back,

'Funnily enough, I'm only sarcastic when I'm around you.'

'I've had a variety of effects on women in my lifetime,' he murmured into her ear, 'but sarcasm was never one of them.'

Destiny refused to collaborate in his sneering at her expense. Instead, she held her head high and strode ahead of him into the restaurant, for once not feeling overawed by her surroundings.

For starters, she wasn't dressed like someone who had accidentally forgotten the basic rules of fashion.

For another thing, she was so conscious of the man behind her, talking to the head waiter, that she barely noticed her surroundings, never mind how she fitted into them.

She was aware, however, that more than one set of eyes had swivelled in her direction, and she felt a little jolt of pleasure at the minor sensation she had aroused. Even the waiter, as usual a good head shorter than her, was doing his best to hide his interest.

'Your skirt is so damned short—' he leaned across the table as soon as they were seated and looked at her through narrowed eyes '—that even the waiter's staring.'

'It was recommended to me by the sales lady,' Destiny pointed out coolly. '*She* didn't appear to think that it was too short.'

'Well, she should be shot. If you belonged to me, I wouldn't let you leave the house in that get-up.'

He sat back as they were handed two oversized menus, giving her a few seconds for her simmer to reach near boiling point.

'If I *belonged* to you? If I *belonged* to you? People aren't *possessions!*' She stared at him and he gazed back at her, his dark brows meeting in a frown.

'Any woman that was mine would be *my* possession, body and soul.'

'And how would you feel if she felt the same way about you? That she wanted you to dress down because you looked too sexy in what you wear?'

'Are you trying to tell me that you think I'm sexy?'

he asked, turning her well-meaning point on its head and giving her a slow, amused smile.

She muttered something under her breath and resorted to the relative safety of her menu, behind which she could hide. Why ever had she thought that these huge menus were a bit of a joke when in fact they served a very useful purpose as shield from a nerve-jangling dinner companion?

'Well, you still haven't answered my question. Do you?' He pulled down the menu with one finger and peered at her over the top of it, his amused grin much broader now.

'You're an attractive enough man,' she told him—because an outright lie would have probably turned the amused grin into a guffaw of disbelieving laughter. 'If you go for your type of look.'

'*My* type of look?'

He looked neither taken aback nor offended by her postscript. Of course, he *would* she thought irritably. Hadn't she discovered that his ego was roughly the size of Panama? If Stephanie ever sought her advice on the subject, she would tell her in no uncertain terms that scooting around him and never answering back was a sure-fire way to add to the problem.

'I can't read the menu with you dragging it down.'

'Have the fresh fish. It's the best thing on the menu.'

'There you go again,' she reminded him, 'being bossy again,' and blushed when she realised that he had been winding her up.

'So what *is* my type of look?' he persisted, still grinning and still tugging her menu down so that she couldn't conveniently hide behind it.

'Well, if you *must* know, it's that obvious tall, dark-haired, good-looking kind of look.'

'Ah! You mean as opposed to the short, fair-haired, unappealing kind of look...' He released the menu so that her glare of infuriation was lost on the list of starters, and by the time she had decided on what she was going to eat he had his amused gleaming expression safely under wraps.

'I've got all the paperwork here,' he said, whisking a two-inch wad of papers from the briefcase at the side of his chair. He pushed them across to her, then sat back to inspect her at his leisure. 'Naturally you'll need some information on Felt's profit and loss over the past, say, three years. Did you bring it along with you?'

'You know I didn't.' She glanced at the top page and found enough technical terms in the first three sentences to reduce her to bewildered dismay.

'Ah, yes. You were sporting your minimalist look. Not to worry...' He fished into his briefcase again and this time the wad was three inches thick. 'I have everything you need right here.'

'Perhaps you could just sum it all up for me and leave me with this paperwork to read over the next couple of days.'

'You might not understand all the terms and sub-clauses,' he said piously. 'You might find that I have to explain them to you.'

'I'll try my best to get to grips with it.'

'Okay. Just offering my services to speed things up a bit.' He paused just long enough for them to order their meal, his eyes shooting up at her rejection of his fish suggestion, then leaned forward with his elbows resting on the table. 'If you turn to page fifteen, you'll find a listing of all my company's assets.'

Destiny obligingly turned to the required page and was confronted by columns of figures, none of which appeared to have under six noughts in it. His company, or rather his holdings, were hugely profitable. It didn't take a degree in accountancy to see that.

'Now, if you turn to page eighteen of the document underneath, you can have a quick look at how Felt's been performing recently.'

'Get to the point. I *know* they've been struggling over the past few months.'

'Years, actually.'

'Well, years, then.'

'It's going to require a massive injection of cash to come up to scratch. No amount of good intentions and sympathetic man-management is going to haul it out of the red.'

Destiny was busily surveying the papers in front of her, which seemed to have a huge amount of brackets around figures. She sighed and flicked through the rest of the paperwork. Report upon report, all bearing the ominous word *losses*. Without the optimism of the directors, desperate to hang on to their lucrative jobs, the facts staring her in the face were sinister. She looked up to see Callum staring at her and sipping his wine.

'I can see you're beginning to get the picture.'

'Derek seems to think that there's a chance…'

'Derek's a lawyer who doesn't want me to buy the company,' he said bluntly.

'Why? My uncle had agreed to sell…'

'Because he could see sense.'

'Why should Derek care one way or another?'

'Because his links with that miserable uncle of yours stretch back a long way. Felt's started as a family firm and the family firm was good to him. Unfortunately, it's caused him to develop a very unhealthy blind spot when it comes to common sense.'

Destiny shuffled the papers she was holding and shoved them back to him.

'Why are you so keen to buy something that's losing money hand over fist? No one else wants it, apparently, so why do you?'

'Let's just say that I see it as a worthwhile investment.' He drained the contents of his glass in one long gulp, while his eyes flicked over her face. 'You asked me once whether there was anything personal involved and I might just as well tell you the sordid story of your dear, generous uncle.'

'He was never dear to me,' she said swiftly. 'I never knew him.' She too drained her glass of wine, to ease some of the tension building up inside her.

'You should count your blessings.' He scrutinised her face. The green eyes staring steadily back at him were curious but interested. What was it about this woman? She was a good listener, he thought with a jolt of unease. She must be—or why else would he be feeling this irrational urge to start pouring out details of his private life? And she was compassionate. He felt a sudden, weakening spurt of jealousy at all those countless people who commanded her time out there in the wilds of Panama.

'My father and your uncle knew one another. Once. When they were both young men. Felt Pharmaceuticals began its life as a joint venture between two men who'd graduated from the same university. My father was the brains of the partnership but old Abe had the flair.' The interruption of their food arriving was an irritation that suspended his tale for a few seconds but, now that he had begun, he found that he couldn't stop the tide. She dipped into her food, tucking her sun-bleached hair behind her ears as she ate.

'What happened?' she asked, glancing at him, then back to her food.

'Their little venture took off. They both had money and my father invested everything in the scientific side of the company. Everything seemed hunky dory for a while, then something happened. Or at least that's the story my mother told me years afterwards. Your uncle changed. He became greedy. Greedy and bitter.'

'You mean he had a fallout with your father?'

'None that my mother was ever aware of. He just changed. He became bitter with the world and my father was the first to feel it. He had sunk everything he possessed in building the company, only to find that Abe began working against him, pulling the ground from under his feet. In the end, of course, the politics became too much and the company began to run into financial trouble. Three years after it started, it folded. My father was left with debts he could never hope to repay. He discovered later that some creative accounting had gone on. Abe retreated with a huge amount of cash scattered everywhere, cash that couldn't be touched. He drove my father out of the business and then restarted it under his own name and never looked back. My father spent the rest of his days trying to repay debts that should have been shared. He died a broken man and my mother was left having to raise a child in virtual poverty.' He dug into his food and felt all the old resentment weighing him down like an anchor.

'You mean you've spent your life looking forward to the day when you could get your revenge?'

'When I could get back what was rightfully mine.'

'But all of that…was history. How could it motivate you for so long?'

'I saw it as evening the scales of justice.'

'And now I'm the one you want to hurt? Because of my uncle? How could that be right? I haven't done anything.'

'I don't want to hurt you. But I want the company, which is why I'm prepared to pay over the odds for it.'

'And was Stephanie all part of your revenge?' she asked quietly. 'Did you see her as one more step in making my uncle pay his dues?'

'Don't be ridiculous.'

'How did you meet her?' Having done justice to her enormous plate of food, she closed her knife and fork and rested both elbows on the table, on either side of the plate.

Somehow the conversation had run away, and she was fully in control.

'Why don't we stop concentrating on me and start concentrating on *you*,' he said, pushing his plate away and sitting back into his chair with his fingers resting lightly on the table.

'Because my life isn't as interesting as yours.'

'Oh, please!' He shot her a look of reproving disbelief.

'Well, it's not so full of complications and personal sagas.' Which made his life sound, he thought, as if it had been lifted from a tawdry third-rate soap opera.

'Because of course, everyone is brimming over with love and joy where you live.'

'Because most of us don't have the time to get embroiled in each other's lives.'

'Oh, don't give me that.' Now that she had managed to drag his confession out of him, he could feel himself growing resentful and defensive as he tried to claw back some of his self-assurance. What next? he thought. An outburst of weeping? Some ghastly cleansing of the soul? 'You're saying that all of you meander along in a saintlike fashion, smiling and thinking pure thoughts all the time?' He glared savagely at her and she began to laugh. A maddening laugh which she tried to stifle. Tried and failed.

'No, I'm not saying that at all,' she said seriously, although the corners of her mouth were still twitching with repressed amusement. 'We argue and get frustrated just like the next person.'

'And what about the pure thoughts?' he asked slyly. 'Isn't the heat supposed to up the libido?'

'I wouldn't know,' Destiny said primly, flushing. She thought of Henri and wondered whether her libido had ever been active when she had been around him. They knew each other so well. A deep bond of trust and friendship that was half-cultivated by their circumstances. But *desire? Lust?* She had occasionally fancied that she loved him, and had certainly responded to his flirtation, but the temptation to take things one step further had never been there.

She looked surreptitiously at the man sitting opposite her. All dark, dangerous arrogance. Just the sort of man bemoaned by women's magazines. Well, they certainly didn't tell you how much men like that got under your skin and worked away there until just thinking about them was enough to send your pulses into overdrive, did they?

'Oh, surely you must have had a quick kiss and a grope behind the bushes by the river...'

At any other time she would have told him to mind his own business, but the food and the wine had made her mellow. Even the way he was looking at her, with lazy, brooding interest, sent a little dart of excitement shooting around her body. She was beginning to understand any number of the little games that men and women played, games that had no part on their compound.

'Behind the bushes by the river at night is the last place you would want to be, believe me.' She drank some more wine, which was going down more smoothly and more quickly with each mouthful.

'But it would just instil an element of danger, wouldn't it?' He swirled the liquid in his glass round and round and continued to stare at her with languid blue eyes.

'Snakes? Reptiles? Nasty slippery things that wouldn't hesitate to attach themselves to your ankle if you weren't looking out for them? You're telling me that all that adds up to an exciting element of danger?' She made a face and he smiled slowly at her. Conversation with Henri was never like this. He teased her, but his banter was harmless. This didn't feel harmless. In fact, it felt strangely erotic. She blushed with sudden guilty awareness, and reassured herself that it was all in her imagination. Sophisticated men and women, living in big cities, spoke like this to one another, she decided naively.

'Would you care to see the dessert menu?' The waiter was somehow standing by them. She hadn't even seen him approaching.

'Yes, please.'

'You're going to *have dessert?*' He made it sound as though she had committed an unforgivable crime and her outstretched hand paused.

'Shouldn't I?'

'Of course you should. It's just that the women I've dated in the past have avoided dessert like the plague.'

'Why?' She took the menu and looked at it, trying not to salivate at the descriptions of things done with chocolate and fruits and cream.

'Obsession with their figures,' he said drily.

'I have a big frame,' Destiny said defensively. Come to think of it, she *had* noticed the way Stephanie had refrained from piling food onto her plate. Unlike her. Stephanie had taken minuscule amounts, eaten very slowly and declined seconds. Unlike, come to think of it, her. 'And anyway,' she continued, after having ordered tiramisu with lots of cream, 'I don't get to eat food like this. It's a novelty.' Besides, she told herself, eating less wasn't going to reduce her height, was it? It would just turn her into one of those skinny women she saw in the magazines who seemed to have not much of anything.

'So,' she said, when the tiramisu was in front of her, 'I'm not going to feel guilty about this.'

'You shouldn't. It's very refreshing to meet a woman with a hearty appetite.'

'Would you like some?' She held out the spoon, feeling very relaxed and daring, and he leaned forward. At the very moment that his mouth circled the spoon their eyes met, blue tangling with green, and she felt a rush of blood invade her system, burning like a sudden high fever.

'It's very good.' His eyes never left her face, even after he had sat back and was sipping his cup of coffee. He just continued to stare at her over the rim of the cup.

'I have a proposal for you,' he said slowly. He reached forward before she could say anything and his finger brushed the side of her mouth. 'Cream just there,' he said.

'What kind of proposal?' Just where he had touched felt inflamed. What would it be like to have those fingers travel the length and breadth of her body? She felt another hot wave of guilt wash over her. The man was engaged to her stepcousin! He had done nothing inappropriate, so why was her body disobeying her head and behaving as though he had? She pushed the remainder of the dessert away from her and sternly told herself to buckle down and get her act together.

'First of all, tell me why you're so intent on hanging on to the company. I've told you my dark secret, so what's yours?'

'I don't *have* any dark secrets.' She eyed the near completed two bottles of wine and realised that she'd drunk far more than she had imagined. Oh, blessed relief. The wine was the culprit behind her sordid thoughts! 'The truth is that if I hang on to the company, I can help my father with his research. Derek says—'

'Stop referring to Derek as though he's a guru,' Callum inserted irritably.

'Well, my father's working on a cure for certain tropical illnesses using plant products. You'd be surprised how many cures can come from the trees and the leaves of certain plants. We have routine inoculations for the local people against certain diseases, but they still practise an awful lot of home remedies and the majority of them work, if not all. Felt Pharmaceuticals has the technology to help with further research. If I sell the company to you, I won't have access to their specialised equipment, which would be very useful for my father.'

'So we have the insoluble dilemma.' He signalled to the waiter for the bill and settled it with a platinum credit card, barely looking at it in the process. 'Sell to me and lose that possible source of aid or hang on to the company and go down sinking. You've seen the figures. Either way, you're on a loser. But, as I said, I have a proposal…'

'Which is?'

'Has the guru Derek elaborated on everything you've inherited?'

'Well, I have the details in the house somewhere… So

far, I haven't had much of an opportunity to look at them,' she admitted, 'I've been so wrapped up with the company problems.'

'Well, in addition to the house in London, Abe had a country estate. Some of the contents he willed to his various past dependants…'

'How do you know about that?' Destiny interrupted, frowning and recalling some mention of a place in the country.

'Because Stephanie is one of the heirs. The point is this—the actual manor was willed to you, as were the lands.'

'Manor? Lands?'

'Didn't Derek the guru explain *any* of this to you?' Callum asked incredulously.

'Stop calling him "the guru," and yes, he did mention that there was a house somewhere outside London. I didn't pay much attention. I just assumed that it was, you know, a normal little *house*…' Her voice drifted away as his expression changed from incredulity to amusement.

'You mean, something small and detached with a pristine square of grass around it? A hedge or two, perhaps? Maybe a tree?'

'Something like that,' she agreed.

'How right you were when you said you knew nothing of your dear uncle. Abe was always fond of making sure that everyone knew exactly how wealthy he was. He had a mansion in Berkshire, surrounded by twenty acres of land, quite of bit of it cultivated.'

'Oh, right.'

'I gather you're less than impressed.'

'Why would he want two houses?'

'Lots of people in London enjoy having a bolt-hole in the country,' he explained a little too patiently for her liking. 'Abe just liked having a very *large* bolt-hole. Ready to go?' He stood up and she hurriedly scrambled to her feet, tugging down the dress self-consciously while he watched with an inscrutable expression.

'So here's what I propose. In exchange for Abe's country retreat, I'll work with you. I'll plough as much money into the company as I need to so that it's up and running. Of course, I shall have to take a number of your shares from you, but you'll be the head of the company and entitled to your share of whatever profits it makes— which, with the right management, could be considerable. Your father would also have privileged access, naturally, to whatever medical facilities he needs in our own research centres.'

'Would you say that that's a good deal?' she asked dubiously, trying to work out the pros and cons and failing. At the moment, she felt as though trying to do anything logical with her mind was a bit like trying to build a house of cards in a high wind.

'I'd say you should give it very careful thought,' he told her, as they drove slowly back to her house.

'Why would you want a country house?' she asked.

'Why do you ask so many questions?'

'Because it's the way I am. Oh, I think I understand. Is it so that you have somewhere in the country for you and Stephanie, when you begin to have children?' She would have liked children. Of course, she was only young and had all the time in the world, but time had a nasty habit of slipping away when you weren't looking.

'No, that's *not* the reason,' he was saying impatiently. 'Naturally, you'd have to see the house. I wouldn't want you to consider anything until you're in full possession of all the facts.'

'Naturally.' Sooner than expected, the car was pulling

up to the front of her pristine house. Strangely, the place
was beginning to feel a bit like home, even though she
still had an instinctive aversion to the English preoccu-
pation with ordered greenery. She slung open her door
and preceded him to her front door. It was much cooler
now. She unlocked the door, pushed it open and then
turned to face him. His face was all angles and his hair
was raked back so that there was no relief from the chiselled perfection of his features. He was also standing too
close to her. Claustrophobically close.

'Thank you for dinner,' she told him politely, eyes
skirting any possible clash with his by focusing on the
terraced row of houses visible over his right shoulder.
'Do you want me to take the files with me and have a
proper read?'

'So I suggest this weekend. I'll pick you up on
Saturday morning and we can return on Sunday night.
That should give you long enough to have a look around.'

'Pick me up?' she stammered, confused by this alarmingly swift turn of events. Ever since Derek Wilson had
stumbled his way to the compound, her life seemed to
have adopted a galloping speed that was quickly turning
into a sprint.

'You *do* want to see your country place, don't you?
See whether you want my proposal to go ahead?'

'Yes, of course, but…'

'Don't tell me you have plans for the weekend.'

'No, b-but…'

'Then why are you stuttering and acting as though
you've been pushed into a corner?'

'It's all a bit sudden, that's all.'

'I'm a great believer in the saying that there's no time
like the present.'

That, she thought, was glaringly obvious. But a weekend? Alone with him? It wouldn't do. She couldn't face down what the man did to her and she had no intention of being in his company without remission for days on end. She didn't understand what she was feeling, but she knew that it was all wrong. Mild-mannered Henri with his easy ways and his light-hearted flirting was something she could handle. But Callum unleashed different, frightening things in her. A weekend being frightened was not on her agenda.

'I'd like Stephanie to come,' she said bluntly.

'I intended to ask her along,' he lied. 'I'll see you on Saturday. Around nine.' He looked away, showing her his profile. 'We can all get to know one another a little better.'

CHAPTER FIVE

THE following day, Stephanie asked Destiny to lunch. *A gorgeous little wine bar in Chelsea. You'll adore it.*

What was the dress code, she wondered, for gorgeous little wine bars in Chelsea? The flowered dress which she'd bought on her shopping trip made her feel frivolous. It was added to the list of new emotions which she had been accumulating ever since she'd set foot on British soil. Sometimes she felt as though the perfect bliss she had achieved for all those years in Panama had been an illusion. Back there, she'd operated on one level only. She had been calm, useful, productive and down to earth. Devoting her life to other people had left no room for anything else.

Now, it was as if the small world she had busily and happily occupied had grown and swelled into a complex network of different facets. She no longer felt nauseated and overwhelmed by the crowds. She was becoming accustomed to the buildings that rose around her like the tall, lush trees that encroached upon the compound and to the pace of life that left no time to be alone with the privacy of your thoughts for company. She hadn't read a book since she had arrived! In Panama, she had read voraciously every evening, all manner of books, which she stocked up on in quantity whenever a trip to the city was made and, of course, her father's medical journals, which she had started reading for interest from the age of fourteen.

And men had always been her equals. Aside from

Henri, who had worked alongside her for two years and whose gallantry rescued her from total asexuality, she'd had no experience of being aware of them in a sexual manner. She discussed problems with them, joined in their conversations, worked with them—but those peculiar antennae that were so finely tuned to their masculinity had never really got going with her. Callum had been the one to bring that side of her to life. It was a good thing that she was going to see Stephanie. Her stepcousin would put a bit of necessary perspective on what was going on in her head.

Destiny arrived at the wine bar, late but calmly resolved to sort out the problem with Callum and the wayward, puzzling effect he had on her, with the same calm determination that had always seen her through the thousands of minor crises that she had faced in her life. Crises of a more practical nature, but no less surmountable than the problem of Callum Ross. Which, anyway, was an inconvenience but hardly a crisis.

When she cast her mind back to their dinner the night before, she could feel her heart-rate speed up and that would never do.

Stephanie was waiting for her at a corner table of the wine bar. It was obviously a place to go with the fashionable crowd. Rows of men in business suits were lounging by the circular bar, idly drinking but more interested in who was walking through the door. Some of them were with women, who were also smartly dressed in well-tailored suits to match their well-tailored short haircuts. The tables were all occupied, mostly with groups of people talking loudly, gesticulating, and laughing.

The décor was very modern. Pale colours, wooden floor, large abstract paintings on the wall of the kind painted by some of her eight-year-old children on the compound. Just splashes of paint that looked as though some idiot had spilled his palette on a canvas and hadn't been bothered about cleaning it up.

Stephanie stood up and waved and Destiny scurried over to the table and sat down.

'It's very crowded, isn't it?' She leaned forward and glanced around her, smiling.

Her stepcousin grinned. 'I know. It's brilliant, isn't it? Callum hates crowds like this, but I love it. What's the point making an effort getting dressed if no one's going to be around to appreciate it?' She was in a smoky blue fitted dress, very short, and her nails were painted the exact coral shade of her lipstick. This was Callum's fiancée, Destiny reminded herself, and incidentally everything a man like him would want in a woman. Neat, attractive, vivacious, always smiling, always amenable.

'I wouldn't know,' Destiny admitted, breaking off to order some mineral water and a salad, taking the lead from Stephanie and remembering Callum's reaction at her hearty appetite. 'I can't say that dressing up was something that happened much on the compound. No need.' She grinned. 'And no dressing-up clothes either, come to think of it.'

Which revived all the open-mouthed fascination that Stephanie had shown previously. Whenever she leaned forward her wavy brown hair swung over her shoulders, and she would flick it back by running her fingers through it and then tossing her head the way a horse tossed its mane.

She wanted to know everything about Destiny—her life, her education, what it felt like to live so far away from decent shops, what she ate, what she drank, whether she'd ever had malaria, what the people out there looked like, what her father looked like. When the subject came round to Henri, whose name had been mentioned casually, but had been picked up with the perceptiveness of someone well versed in the ways of relationships, Stephanie shot her a coy smile.

'So there *is* more to life there than you let on!' She giggled. 'What does he look like?'

'You've hardly touched your salad,' Destiny said wryly, dodging the questions she could see hovering on the horizon. Stephanie obligingly stuck a couple of lettuce leaves in her mouth and continued to survey her stepcousin with a gleam in her blue eyes.

'Okay. He's about my height, brownish hair, specs, thinnish.'

'Any more *ishes* to add to the description? What about sexyish?'

No, that describes *your* lover, was the thought that flashed through Destiny's head, disappearing before it had time to take root.

'Yes, well…' she said vaguely.

'I can see—' Stephanie sat back and arched her eyebrows meaningfully '—that you're overwhelmed by lust for this man.'

'It's too hot out there to get lusty.'

'Oh, yeah?'

'Too sticky.'

'Right. In that case, I'm surprised anyone has babies.'

'Tell me about Callum,' Destiny said, going red and rapidly changing the subject, which was greeted with another arch of perfectly bowed eyebrows, but Stephanie grinned and relented.

'What about him?'

'You must be very excited at the thought of getting married…' Her salad had already settled in her stomach and steady hunger pangs were beginning to set in. How could anyone exist on a handful of shrubbery with a bit of black pepper on top?

'Well, we're not *getting married*. Least, not yet.' The heart-shaped face suffused with delicate colour.

'Oh.'

'It's just that the time isn't right,' she rushed on, blushing madly. 'You know…'

'Well, not really, but it's none of my business anyway.'

'Yes, it is! I mean, you're the closest thing I have to a relative. At least, a relative of my own age. I have a couple of aunts in Cornwall but they're in their nineties.' She wrinkled her nose, considering the dilemma of her relativeless state, then her face cleared slightly. 'It's just that…you know…Callum and I… Well, he's pretty busy…work and such…'

'Why don't you tell him to make some time for you?'

Stephanie shrugged and chewed her lip. 'It's not as easy as all that.'

Destiny inclined her head to one side and listened. The waiter efficiently cleared their table, routinely asking whether everything was satisfactory, to which she replied, honestly, 'There wasn't enough of it.'

'I shall tell our head chef,' the man said with an expression that told her that he had no intention of doing any such thing.

'I mean,' Stephanie said in a rush, 'Callum's so *overpowering* and he *hates* women who nag. When we first started going out, he used to say that he loathed women who were demanding.'

'So what?' Destiny frowned, trying to work this out in her head. 'If you don't demand certain things, how on earth do you ever get them?'

Another helpless shrug. 'Thing is, we met at a business do that Uncle Abe had hosted before he and Mum divorced, and he sort of swept me off my feet to start with. You wouldn't believe the women who would love to be seen with him…'

'I can't see why if he's that intolerant.' But she could. He drew stares from other people. He was physically commanding. He had the sort of personality that compelled other people's attention.

'Oh, he's so rich and powerful and awe-inspiring.'

'I don't think he's awe-inspiring. Actually, sometimes he irritates the life out of me.'

'But you'd never let him know that, would you?'

'Yes. Why not? He's not going to chop both my arms off if I say what's on my mind.'

Stephanie looked at her as though she had suddenly discovered that she was dealing with a madwoman.

'Anyway,' Destiny said hastily, 'tell me about this wonderful house I shall be going to see on the weekend. Has Callum told you about his offer?' Which he hadn't, unsurprisingly, so she spent a few minutes telling her stepcousin the details.

'So what will you do?' Stephanie asked, while Destiny wondered why her fiancé had chosen to withhold such important news from the woman he loved. 'If he's made such an offer, then you know he'll expect you to accept. He never compromises when it comes to business.' She giggled nervously. 'Or anything else, for that matter.'

'I don't care *what* he expects. I shall have a look around and come to my own conclusions.' Now, from her stepcousin's expression, she was listening to someone from another planet speaking in forked tongue. Destiny gave a little sigh, plunged into an unrevealing conversation about Henri because she knew that it would distract her stepcousin, and left the restaurant half an hour later wondering what exactly was the nature of the relationship between Stephanie and Callum. Was it any wonder that she had no time to read over here? There was far too much drama in her everyday life to leave much room for a bit of mindless escapism.

Whatever the dress code was for a trip to a country house—*her* country house, as Derek had explained in length on the telephone the day before—Destiny didn't care. She packed comfortable clothes. A spare pair of jeans, two tee-shirts, flat walking boots, a pair of wellingtons. She had worked out that she now possessed roughly twice the amount of clothes she had ever had at any one time before. Aside from when she had been boarding in Mexico.

She managed to cram everything she was taking into her rucksack, and Stephanie's first words on seeing her at ten past nine on the Saturday morning were, 'Is that all you're bringing?'

Destiny slung her bag into the back seat and then folded her long body into the car next to it.

'It's only a weekend,' she pointed out. 'Hello, Callum.' She belatedly addressed the back of his dark head. It seemed that meeting Stephanie for lunch had not managed to put some vital perspective on her wayward feelings because, as their eyes met in the rearview mirror, she could feel her skin tingle.

'My make-up takes up nearly as much room as that,' Stephanie was saying cheerfully. 'Doesn't it, Callum?'

'If not more.' He pulled out of the enclosed cul-de-sac, and reached over to hand her an envelope. 'One or two photos of your little house,' he said drily. 'Thought you might be interested.'

The bundle of twenty-odd photos, rescued from

Stephanie's photo album from the times she had gone there years previously, before her mother had joined the line of ex-Felts, showed a sprawling mansion with a series of outbuildings, curling around a swimming pool. From the front seat, Stephanie craned backwards to explain the photos. The outbuildings had apparently been used for stabling horses but were now empty and the swimming pool had been put in at the insistence of her mother, who had seen it as adequate compensation for being deprived of living full-time in the city. The grounds were extensive and included a wood, a stream and orchards of fruit trees.

'Who looks after it now?' Destiny asked, still puzzled by the need her uncle had felt to possess a house of that size in which people could lose each other without a great deal of trouble.

'Derek kept on a skeleton staff,' Callum said from the front. 'He assumed that you'd probably want to sell but, if you didn't, I suppose he thought that you might want the retainers to stay. I have no idea how many people he's kept or what they're doing there for that matter. We haven't been to the place for months. They could have hijacked the silver and cleared off for all I know.'

'I thought you said that the contents were willed to…lots of other people?'

'Certain of the contents, yes. Which would still leave quite a bit *in situ.*'

'So is there anyone there now?' She had visions of arriving at an inhospitable mansion, stone-walled and freezing cold.

'Stephanie got in touch with Harold and his wife to open up and get the place ready. Or, should I say, get a small part of the place ready. A lot of the rooms have never been used.'

'What a waste.'

She noticed that they were now leaving London and was heartened by the sight of greenery. It must be easy to forget the existence of open land when you were constantly surrounded by buildings.

'What would you do with the house if...I decided to go ahead with your proposal?'

'Convert it into something, I expect.'

'Convert it into what?'

'A hotel.'

'You'd convert this beautiful old mansion into a *hotel*?'

'I would convert a beautiful old mansion into a *beautiful old hotel*,' he said, with a trace of impatience in his voice. 'At least it would be used. What difference would it make to you, anyway? Do you intend staying in England?'

'No, of course not.'

'This is all premature speculation anyway. Let's just get to the damned place and see how you feel about it then.' He accelerated as they cleared the outskirts of London and hit the motorway, and Destiny lapsed into silence, watching the scenery flash by. Summer was still holding its own and the blue, cloudless skies made everything seem crisp and fresh.

They were at the village before eleven, and Stephanie, who appeared to have drifted off into a light sleep, was revived at the sight of a few shops and the prospect of getting out of the car and stretching her legs. She launched into an animated conversation about what she'd used to do when she went to stay at the country manor, interrupting herself frequently to remark on the dullness of country life.

'It must be an awful lot more peaceful than living in

London, though,' Destiny pointed out, liking the feeling of space and calm around her. The small village, with its pubs and little stone shops and parish church, had none of the threatening claustrophobia of London. And the air was much fresher. She had rolled down her window, ignoring Callum's comment about the air conditioning in the car, and closed her eyes briefly, enjoying the breeze through the window.

'Stephanie isn't enamoured of peace,' he said drily, speaking about her as though she wasn't sitting next to him—and, in all fairness, Stephanie didn't object.

'And are you?' Destiny asked, looking around her now with interest as the car slowed on the narrow lane and turned left up an avenue lined with trees. Ahead of them, a pair of massive wrought-iron gates were open, and beyond them lay fields and pastures. 'Or do you prefer living in the fast lane, where you can stride around, giving orders to everyone and enjoying having the world bow down to you?'

Stephanie uttered an incoherent squeak of horror and looked around at Destiny, who grinned airily back at her.

'Sorry,' she said politely. 'I shouldn't have said that.'

'Sorry? You? For having said something you shouldn't? Why? Why break habits of a lifetime?' But there was lazy amusement in his voice. 'These are all part of the grounds. The sheep keep the grass down, but there are still six acres of lawned land. Look ahead. You can see the house coming into view.'

She leaned forward and watched as the impressive façade rose up ahead of them, like a matriarch surveying her domain. She had never seen anything quite like it before in her life. The fact that it belonged to her seemed unreal.

'Did you bring a swimsuit?' Stephanie asked suddenly.

'It's hot enough for us to swim and I could do with a tan. I can't bear English weather. All rain and fog and light drizzles.'

'I don't possess a swimsuit,' Destiny told her.

'Not at all?' Her stepcousin sounded horrified.

'No.'

'But how are you going to go into the pool? I'm sure I have a couple here, but you'd never fit into them!'

'I shall have quite enough to do looking around, honestly.' The thought of trying to cram her huge frame into one of her stepcousin's swimsuits wasn't worth thinking about. She looked comical enough next to her as things stood.

In fact, as they all trooped into the overwhelming hall, she wondered whether two days was going to be long enough to see everything. Harold, a wizened middle-aged man with eyes that seemed permanently focused on his feet, welcomed them in and he and Callum conferred in hushed voices for a few minutes, while Destiny continued to stare open-mouthed around her. Stephanie, well accustomed to all the grandeur, stood unimpressed to one side and then, as soon as Harold had disappeared with the cases, announced that she wanted to go for a dip in the pool. *Just in case it decides to rain later. You know what the weather's like over here.*

'Sure you won't come with me and try on one of my swimsuits?' she asked kindly, and Destiny shook her head with a laugh.

'I don't think that would work, do you?' She wanted to tell her stepcousin to run along and have a good time. Even though they were more or less the same age, Destiny felt decades older. There was something very young and childlike about Stephanie, something very much in need of protection. Which brought her round to Callum.

He was standing, watching them with some amusement; and as soon as Stephanie had disappeared up the stairs, lightly running, he turned to her and said in a drawling voice, 'It's hard to believe that you two are roughly the same age. You treat her as though she was your daughter.'

Destiny smiled indulgently. 'Actually, sometimes I feel as though she is. She's so…*young*…in her ways.' She sighed and caught herself. 'Anyway, the house. Should we start now? Looking around? Or do you need time to recover from the car drive? Oh. You may want to go and have a dip in the pool as well,' she added awkwardly. 'I didn't think.'

'No. Playing at being a sun lizard isn't my cup of tea.' He looked at her with a shuttered expression and realised, with a certain amount of confused irritation, that he would have been more than happy to play the sun lizard game if it involved watching her frolic around in a swimming pool with next to nothing on.

He would, he decided, have to speak to Stephanie. Whether he liked it or not, the doubts that had been swelling over the past few months about their relationship were rapidly crystallising into the unpleasantly concrete fact that their relationship was sagging. Sex, which had been satisfactory enough to start with, had been almost nonexistent for months now, and lately had disappeared altogether from the agenda. He could kid himself that his work left him exhausted, but who was he trying to fool? The blunt truth of the matter was that however fond he was of his fiancée, he no longer felt any sexual urges when he was around her.

Why else was he mentally stripping the woman in front

of him now? Wondering what that body of hers would look like uncovered? She was not his type. Too big, too forthright, too damned argumentative and clever. But she was on his mind more than he cared to think. Daydreaming and fantasising about her was obviously a symptom of the malaise in his own personal life.

Realising that he was staring at her, he frowned assertively and said in a clipped voice, 'Right. The house. We'll start with the top and work our way down.'

Destiny vaguely wondered whether two days was going to be enough to complete this daunting task, but she obediently followed him towards the impressive staircase that coiled upwards like a snake. Halfway up, Stephanie came bouncing towards them, towel in hand and a broad smile on her face.

'Off to begin the tour?' she said, pretending to yawn. 'Sitting around the pool would be much more fun,' she said to them.

'Maybe later,' Destiny said, in the sort of placatory voice she used with her children on the compound whenever they asked for something that was patently out of the question. It was the age-old delaying tactic of saying *in a minute,* when a child asked for another glass of juice. And as with a child, it worked, because Stephanie shrugged and grinned and disappeared with a cheerful, *Well, see you both later then* over her shoulder.

What on earth did Callum see in Stephanie? The enigma was enough to bring home to her just how lacking in experience she was. Oh, very experienced when it came to using her brains, and very mature in tackling the day-to-day rigours of living in a jungle, but as green as God's grass when it came to the emotional side of her life.

For goodness's sake, she was still a virgin! She and

Henri had indulged in some light-hearted fondling, but she, for one, had never felt any urge to carry the fondling through to its natural conclusion. Maybe *he* had. Or maybe, she thought, he, like Callum, was really only interested in women who acted like women and not women who were as independent as they were themselves. It was a depressing conclusion. She would never be harbouring these thoughts, she knew, if she hadn't come to this country, and she glared resentfully at the broad, masculine figure ascending the staircase ahead of her because, like it or not, he was the source of her confusion.

Right now, he was giving her a potted history of the house while she continued to scowl safely from behind. Only when they were at the top of the house did she manoeuvre her features into some semblance of politeness, even though she was too aware of him to find the task easy.

'I hope,' he said, turning to her, hands thrust into his pockets, head slightly cocked to one side, 'that I'm not giving you a load of information that you're already aware of.'

'How on earth would I know anything about the history of British architecture?' Destiny snapped edgily.

'You seem to know just about everything else. You speak more languages that any woman I've ever met; you practise medicine; you teach; you single-handedly fight off marauding tigers and crocodiles that have wandered from your river in search of some human dinner.'

'It's not my fault you don't meet the right women,' she retorted sarcastically, instantly regretting her outburst, which wasn't fair because it stemmed from her own sudden lack of self-confidence in her femininity.

'What are you trying to say? That Stephanie is the wrong woman for me?'

'No,' she mumbled, wishing, yet again, that she had controlled her feelings instead of letting him push her into another uncharacteristic response. 'It's very interesting finding out about the house. It's just that knowing about baroque developments in architecture during the Stuart Period isn't exactly handy when you're living in the wilds of Panama. Unless,' she added with a weak stab of humour, 'I intend puzzling those marauding crocodiles into submission.'

He smiled at her, very, very slowly, and she felt as though she had been touched because his smile was so like a physical caress. Her breathing thickened and she looked away quickly. Stephanie was sunbathing downstairs, and wanting to touch this man in front of her was so shocking and so inappropriate that it took her breath away.

For the next couple of hours she meekly followed him from room to room and tried to pretend that he was no more than a tour guide. It helped if she imagined him as a short, fat, bald tour guide.

She didn't glance once at him, which wasn't difficult because there was enough to see in the myriad rooms. From one of them she looked out, and down below she could see the diminutive figure of her stepcousin languidly lying on a poolside deckchair, eyes closed and arms resting over the sides of the chair.

Callum came to stand next to her and immediately the hairs on her arms stood on end.

'What sort of woman do you think would be right for me, then?' he murmured, without looking at her.

During his brisk, factual tour, she had managed to keep everything nicely under control, but now she felt every nerve and pulse in her body stirring and making her feel hot and uncomfortable.

'I think Stephanie's a lovely person.'

'That's not what I asked.'

'You're engaged to my stepcousin. Of course she's the right woman for you.' She didn't dare look at him, but she could feel that he had turned to her and was looking at *her,* and she folded her arms. Her fingernails pressed into her skin.

'You don't believe that. You know you don't.'

'Why are you asking me these questions?' she flung at him, spinning to face him. 'Why does it matter what I think?'

'I'm interested, that's all. I'm not a fool. I've noticed the way you look at us when we're in the same room, seen the expression on your face—as though you're mystified at what I see in her.'

Oh, good Lord. Had she been *that* transparent?

'Maybe you're right,' he said softly, so softly that she wanted to groan. Her body was responding to his nearness, to the low, velvety tone of his voice, to the depths of his eyes resting on her, the way it would have responded if she was standing next to an open fire. An open fire that was slowly but steadily melting her.

The wetness she felt between her legs was such an unknown experience that at first she wasn't even aware of it and, when she was, she was horrified.

This was lust. It bore no resemblance whatsoever to the affection and the tenderness and the light-hearted, detached curiosity she had felt when Henri had occasionally kissed her on the mouth, after a bit of alcohol and under the embrace of a hot starry night. This was like being hit by a sledgehammer.

'Who knows? Do you think I might need a more challenging type of woman?'

'*I* don't know what you need,' she squeaked.

'True. Really, how do any of us know what we need unless we try it out first? Test the water, so to speak?' Then he did something so unexpected and so shocking that for a few seconds her body froze. He touched her. Just with one finger, on her mouth, tracing it, but the touch was so erotic that the ache between her legs shot through the rest of her body like a fast-moving virus. Her breasts actually seemed to hurt and she could feel the pupils in her eyes dilate.

'No!' She pulled back, shaking, and spun round on her heels, staring down at her feet and breathing heavily, while he lounged against the window sill. 'Please,' she whispered, still staring at her feet, 'let's just see the rest of the house. Please.'

Callum didn't answer immediately. He couldn't. He was too busy trying to get his vocal cords into gear. Eventually, more in an attempt to repress the powerful and bloody primal urge he had felt for her than anything else, he said, 'Sure. And if I manage to make it boring enough, who knows? You might just find it useful in boring unwanted animals to death.'

You could never be boring, she wanted to say, but she didn't. He had touched her mouth with his finger and he now felt sorry for her because he must be able to see how inordinately she'd responded. Like the gauche, un-sophisticated primitive that she was. He felt sorry for her and was now trying to put her out of her misery by re-storing some light-hearted humour between them. For that she felt both grateful and mortified at the same time.

But things got easier, and after another hour exploring each room, discussing who'd removed what in accor-dance to the legacy Abe had left, the brief moment of madness, if not forgotten, had been put to sleep. Like a tiger injected with a temporary sedative. She had no doubt that, when she was alone again, the moment would come rushing out at her, like a bat out of hell.

They only managed to cover part of the house, which, if anything, was bigger than it had appeared from the outside, before Callum suggested lunch, and they joined a lazy and slightly browner Stephanie by the pool.

More salad. Destiny looked at her plate, which had been brought out by Deirdre, Harold's other half, with a distinct lack of enthusiasm. At least this time round there was plenty of it, but several helpings went virtually nowhere to filling the gap in her stomach.

'Don't worry,' Callum confided, as they left Stephanie once more by the pool and resumed their tour of the house, 'dinner will be more substantial. It's an old English custom to serve salads on hot summer days.'

'Don't know why,' Destiny said. 'You need a lot of energy in hot weather, especially at lunchtime, and the last thing you get from a bundle of lettuce leaves is an injection of energy.'

An injection of apathy, more like it, she thought when they had finally completed the rounds of the house. In the end they had had to quicken their pace, if the gardens were to be done the following day, but there was lots she wanted to revisit.

At six o'clock, when they found themselves once again at the pool, Stephanie was finally through with her day's exertions.

'You look great,' Destiny said warmly. 'Very brown.'

'Do I?' She contorted her slender body in an attempt to scrutinise as much of it as she could. 'What do you think, Callum?'

'Mmm.' He wasn't looking at her, even though his thoughts were most definitely on her. On her and on the chat they would have to have before the evening was over. He hoped to God that she wouldn't break down on him but, if she did, then whose fault was it? His. His, because he should have ended this relationship a long time ago and not relied on fondness to see them through. He could have kicked himself.

'I think that means *yes,*' Destiny offered lightly.

'And how would you know what I mean?' His voice was cold. They both turned to him with varying expressions of surprise and discomfiture, but it was Stephanie who, amazingly, exploded.

'Why do you have to be so rude? Why can't you just *relax* a little and stop acting as though everyone has to do as you say? You…you…you…' Her brief outburst of valiance tapered off while Destiny groaned inwardly and wondered miserably whether her casual words of advice had been taken to heart. She was now a spectator at a scene in which two opponents faced one another, one with an expression of shock but defiance, the other with grim determination.

'I think, Destiny,' Callum said, looking at his fiancée, 'that it's time you relaxed before dinner. Deirdre is in the kitchen. She'll show you up to your room.'

CHAPTER SIX

WHEN Destiny emerged two hours later, she found Stephanie by herself in the kitchen. The table was set, but for two and Stephanie was busily fussing around the stove with a pair of oven gloves on her hands. She'd pulled her hair back into a high ponytail and was wearing a pair of culottes and a silk blouse.

'Callum's gone,' she said, answering the question that hadn't yet been asked.

'Gone where?'

'Back to London. And I told Harold and Deirdre that there was no need for them to stay and see about dinner for the two of us.'

'So you cooked all of this yourself?' She couldn't help it, but there was incredulity in her voice because the smells emanating from the various dishes were mouthwatering and she had somehow never imagined her stepcousin to be much of a hand when it came to culinary skills.

'Lord, no.' Stephanie looked at her and grinned. 'Are you crazy? Toast and scrambled egg are about the only two things I can manage. No, Deirdre cooked all this up herself and gave me very strict instructions on how long I was supposed to heat everything for. She seemed to think that I would wreck her meal.'

'And you haven't.'

'Well, the soufflé *is* in the bin, actually. Forgot it in the oven, and by the time I remembered it was a sad, deflated black mass.' She brought various dishes to the table, filled their glasses with wine and sat down with a little sigh. 'There's enough food to feed an army here. Hope you're hungry because I've lost my appetite.'

'There was no need for you to rise to my defence back then, Stephanie,' Destiny said awkwardly. 'I'm very sorry if…you know… I mean, I wouldn't like to think that you got yourself into trouble because of me…' She looked at the little figure, ridiculously fragile without her usual make-up and with her hair pulled back, toying with the birdlike proportions of food on her plate.

'Don't be silly. It's not your fault.' Stephanie picked up a few vegetables on her fork and proceeded to survey them without much interest. Then she rested her fork on her plate and gulped back some of her wine instead. 'We really should have called it a day a long time ago, but things have a habit of drifting on. On and on and on. We never really argued, but then we never really *spoke* either. We've just been trundling along for the past few months. No excitement, no magic—just two people who got on reasonably well and saw no reason to have any kind of confrontation.'

Until I came along, was the thought that guiltily occurred to Destiny as she tucked into her food. The spread on the table more than compensated for the lunchtime offering of leaves and cold meats, and it was traditional food. Her meals out thus far, in restaurants, had been small, prettily presented plates of various things drizzled with strange juices and accompanied by delicate titbits of vegetables arranged in appetising but unsatisfactory designs. This was hearty food and manna to a ravenous appetite.

'So it's all over?'

'I gave him back his ring and, to be honest, I was pretty relieved. It was all very civilised, actually. More of a discussion than any kind of argument. Callum hates scenes. You could say that we parted the best of friends.'

'Well, that's something at least.'

'I mean, of course I'll miss him. We kind of got accustomed to one another. But that's not enough, is it? Just liking someone and being *kind of accustomed to them?* What kind of marriage would *that* have been? Without any spark at all?'

'I suppose so.' Destiny thought about Henri—not that marriage had ever been on the agenda, although Henri had jokingly suggested it a couple of times.

'I would have ended up being married to someone who could have been my brother!' Some of the liveliness resurfaced and Stephanie managed to eat a couple of mouthfuls of food before closing her knife and fork. 'I realised that what I wanted was thunder and lightning and fireworks, not just feeling good because I was out with someone most women would give their eye teeth to be seen with. Anyway, I also realised that Callum's always treated me like a child. I think he thought that if he spoke to me in more than two-syllable sentences, I might not understand what he was saying!'

'And did you tell him all of this?'

'What would have been the point? It's not like I felt any urge to fight to hang on. I was relieved that we were going to be parting company. Sad but relieved.' She finished her glass of wine and refilled it. 'So now here I am, back on the market, in search of true love.' She tried to look dramatic and mournful but the effect was ruined by tell tale giggles.

'You'll find a partner in less time than it would take me to kill a snake,' Destiny told her, finally closing her knife and fork with a warm, replete feeling in her stomach. 'Think about me and my problems of finding true love! Out in the middle of nowhere! I shall end up a grey, sad little soul—or should I say big soul?—devoting my life to other people while no one devotes their life to me.'

'You have Henri.'

'You remembered his name?'

'I have a very retentive memory when it comes to certain things.'

'Henri…' Destiny stood up and began clearing the table while Stephanie began washing up. 'Henri is… Well, more of a friend…'

'With or without the spark?'

'We get along so well…'

'You're avoiding the question.'

'He's a lovely person. Kind, thoughtful but not boring or fuddy-duddy.'

'Have you slept with him?'

'Stephanie!' She was frankly shocked by the question. Confidences of that nature belonged to a language she had never spoken.

'Well, have you?' Stephanie persisted.

'I…well… You have to understand…'

'You haven't.'

'Well, no…' Destiny's face was bright red and she made a big production of wiping the kitchen table to try and hid the fact.

'And have you been tempted to?'

'It's awfully difficult on a compound, Steph. It's very comfortable, and we all have our own living quarters, but still…'

'Enough said. I'm beginning to get the message!' And they looked at one another with an instant of perfect comprehension. As if by unspoken but mutual consent, they spent the remainder of the evening chatting about everything under the sun apart from Henri and Callum, and when at ten-thirty Stephanie finally uncurled herself from her chair to head to bed, Destiny thought with a pang that she would miss her stepcousin. Miss the frivolity and gossip and giggling that she never got on the compound. She would miss someone taking an interest in what she wore and how she did her hair and offering advice on colour schemes. She would miss the girlish chat about men and their ways and the cosy, secret bond that seemed to exist between women which was a whole great world away from the one in which she had spent most of her life. For the first time she thought of her compound in Panama with a certain amount of detachment, and realised that she had needs that could never really be fulfilled there.

'I'll stay down here for a while longer,' Destiny said, walking with her stepcousin to the door, and was surprised when she received a hug and a broad smile.

'I'm so glad you're here,' Stephanie said to her. 'You're a darling.'

'Well. Thank you.'

'And don't be late up. A girl needs her beauty sleep.'

Her mother had used to tell her that when she had been alive and the cliché brought tears of nostalgia to her eyes.

Destiny settled into a comfortably maudlin mood, aided and abetted by the glass of port which Stephanie had produced with a flourish and insisted that she drink, and was sitting in the smallest of the sitting rooms when she became aware of the sound of footsteps.

If Stephanie was returning for some more words of comfort, then Destiny had no objection. Comforting people was something she did well. She had enough experience of it, comforting mothers with sick children and the occasional new recruit to the compound pining for what they had left behind.

She looked expectantly at the door and blanched when she saw who her visitor was.

'I thought you'd gone back to London.' She had half stood in shock, but now subsided back into her chair, still cradling her glass of port. The drowsy inertia induced by lots of food and the alcohol disappeared at the speed of light and was replaced by a jumpy edginess that made her breathing jerky and painful and dried out her mouth.

'Forgot something,' he informed her, prowling into the room and circling her chair before sitting down on the sofa and stretching his long legs out in front of him. 'What are you drinking?'

'Port.'

'First wine? Now port? Not getting used to the finer things in life, by any chance, are you?' There was an antagonistic edge to his drawl and it occurred to her that he was looking for a fight. And why not? He had probably got halfway to London, more than enough time to think about what had happened between himself and Stephanie. More than enough time to work out that his fiancée's sudden and uncharacteristic behaviour had only seen the light of day since she, Destiny, had been on the scene. Stephanie might well be relieved that it was all over and, who knew, maybe she had really believed that the feeling had been mutual, but it was evident that Callum was far from a happy man. In fact, he was in a foul mood.

'What did you forget?'

'Oh, I forgot that I was supposed to spend tomorrow showing you around all these extensive acres of land.' He made a sweeping, lazy gesture with his hand while he continued to look at her from under his lashes.

'I think I would have been capable of showing myself around.'

'And leave you with the impression that I'm anything less than the perfect gentleman?' He gave a short, harsh laugh and her jumpy nerves became even more jumpy. 'Now, why don't you go and get me a glass of port? It's been one helluva night, as I'm sure you know.'

'The bottle of port is in the kitchen, and if you want me to feel sorry for you then you're not going the right way about it.'

'Why should you feel sorry for me? No, don't answer that one. Not until,' he said, getting to his feet and heading for the door, 'I have a glass of port in my hand.'

Instead of savouring the few minutes he was gone to try and relax, Destiny found that her nerves were stretched to breaking point by the time he came back with a glass in one hand and the bottle in the other.

'So,' he said, resuming his position of indolence on the chair, 'you were saying…'

'I'm sorry that things didn't work out between you and Stephanie,' she said evenly.

'Are you? Why?'

'It wasn't my fault,' she mumbled defensively, allowing her guilty thoughts to surface.

'I never said that it was.' *But it damn well was,* he thought savagely. She'd moved into his complacent life, which had been running quite smoothly, and blown the whole thing to smithereens. Yes, he'd had misgivings about Stephanie, and, yes, he would have ended the whole thing—which, he'd been relieved to discover, had been met with similar feelings of relief. But he would not now be sitting with a drink in one hand with his well-oiled life in pieces around his ankles.

He'd left the house intent on making it back to

London, but in fact had made it only to the nearest pub, where he had drunk far too much for his own good. It was just as well that the pub in question had only been twenty minutes' drive away and there had been a taxi to get him back to the estate.

It was all right and dandy for her to sit there with those bewitching green eyes and look at him as if he was a madman, but she turned him into one. He'd closed the door on one woman, a long overdue closure, and in the process another door had blown open and he had realised, with the sadistic help of a few glasses of whisky, that what he had considered a harmless enjoyment of this woman's conversation had somehow turned into an addiction. He was falling in love with her, and the mere fact that he'd admitted as much to himself was enough to make him realise that he'd probably gone past the point of no return.

He was not only invigorated by her but she had lodged in his soul and he wanted her out. He wanted his control back. He didn't want to sit at his desk with a stack of files in front of him while his mind played games and sabotaged his every effort to work. To work, to sleep, to think clearly.

The woman who had originally been a temporary thorn in his long-range forecast was now driving him crazy.

'Perhaps you two weren't suited to one another,' she was now saying quietly. 'Perhaps the thunder and lightning and fireworks had gone out of the relationship—and what would have been the point of marriage then?' Anyone would think that she, Destiny Felt, the woman with no emotional past to speak of when it came to the opposite sex, was an expert on the subject.

'And what makes you think that thunder and lightning and fireworks are all that necessary to a good marriage?'

he jeered, calling a halt to the alcohol and resting his glass next to him on the ground. 'In case it's missed you, thunder and lightning and fireworks are all over in the wink of an eye.'

'If you want to try and persuade Stephanie to stay with you, then you're talking to the wrong person,' Destiny said cautiously, and he leaned forward and rested his elbows on his knees.

'You mean you won't go upstairs and try and persuade her that my heart is breaking? That I can't go on?'

Destiny tried to imagine this big, muscular man, made of steel, with a breaking heart, and she realised that it hurt to think that Stephanie might be the one to do that.

'Just as well I don't want you to do any such thing, then, isn't it?' He shot her a ferocious, brooding look. 'Because you're right. Steph and I should have reverted into being just good friends a long time ago.' He got up and began his restless prowling around the room while she watched, mesmerised by the way his body moved. For someone of his size, there was a feline grace about him that she wouldn't have expected.

'Of course,' he said, briefly turning to look at her from across the room, 'it hasn't helped that you've instigated the revolution by telling her that she was a poor, downtrodden female who needed to get in touch with herself and start making a stand for women's rights.'

'I did no such thing!' Destiny protested uncomfortably.

'Well—' he shrugged '—she's been quoting you from dawn till dusk. Oh, *Destiny this,* and *Destiny that* and *Destiny the other.*'

'That's not fair,' Destiny said hesitantly, wondering what exactly these quotes were.

'No, it's not, is it?' he countered, strolling over to where she was sitting and looming over her like an avenging angel. 'Because, stuck out in the middle of no-where, you haven't exactly got the experience to be a guru on all things sexual, have you?'

'I never claimed I was!' Destiny said, rising to the occasion. It took a mammoth effort to stare him down, and in all events she didn't manage it, finally lowering her eyes to his knees, which were altogether less alarming than other, less innocent, parts of him.

'Do you know—' he dropped his voice, which was even more alarming than when it was directed at her with all its implicit menace '—that for someone with little or no experience, you do a pretty damned good job of being a siren?'

'Me? A siren?' She laughed, but what emerged was more along the lines of a hysterical choke. 'You're jok-ing, aren't you? Where do you think I've learnt these amazing skills of being a siren? Do you think I practise daily in front of the howler monkeys in the jungle?' She laughed derisively, thinking of her sheltered, protected background which had left all these loopholes she was now falling headlong into.

'You,' he accused, walking towards her so that she coiled back into the chair. He reached out and dropped his hands to either side. 'So philosophical when it comes to giving advice. I bet you and Steph had a good old heart-to-heart while I wasn't here, while I was in that pub burying myself in a few draughts of whisky, man's most reliable friend...'

'I thought you said you were on your way to London...?'

'I was. But the journey ended prematurely at the vil-lage pub. Funny how these things happen.'

They happen, Destiny thought, because—whether you admit it or not—the break-up was traumatic for you. A man like him would need a submissive woman, a woman who was willing to bend like a sapling to his powerful personality, and the minute that Stephanie began showing signs of rebellion he had reacted with his typical over-whelming intensity. Perhaps the truth of the story was that Stephanie had ended their relationship and pride would not let him try to win her back, so, in her relief, Stephanie had misread his signals for feelings of shared relief that it was over. It all seemed so horrendously con-voluted, but wasn't Destiny fast discovering that nothing here was what it seemed? People dressed, spoke and be-haved in a manner designed to create a certain type of impression, and honesty was something that remained locked away for a rainy day.

'So you've been drinking,' she accused coolly, and he gave a bark of humourless laughter.

'A glass or two of whisky. Is that allowed under the circumstances?'

'You probably need to go to bed,' Destiny said. Her body was beginning to ache from the unnatural angle in which she was sitting, pressed back against the chair in an attempt to ward off the sheer force of his masculinity.

'Is that an offer?'

'No, it's not!' But the suggestion stirred something in her that sent her already accelerated heart into overdrive. Bed? With Callum Ross? Naked bodies coated in per-spiration, writhing in passion on rumpled sheets. The im-age was strong enough to almost make her squeak with terror. 'Look, why don't I make you some coffee?' In other words, Please let me get out of here and away from you so that I can pull myself together.

'You think that's what I need?'

'It might…sober you up…'

'I'm not drunk.'

'No, maybe not, but…'

'Oh, why not?' He pushed himself back and stood up, fists balled in his pockets, watching her.

'Black?'

'Whatever.' He shrugged and she escaped out of the room, and, after a moment of brief orientation in the hall to make sure that she headed in the right direction and didn't amble off to some remote corner of the house by mistake, made for the kitchen.

She didn't hear him enter. In fact, she was only aware of his presence when she turned around with the cup of coffee in her hand to find him standing there behind her. In her shock she took two steps backwards, bumping into the counter, and there was a second's delay between the coffee spilling and the sudden burning pain on her hand, where most of it had gone. This time her yelp had nothing to do with him but with her hand.

She dashed the cup on the counter and half ran to the sink, pushing the plug in and filling it with cold water; then she plunged her hand in, gritting her teeth.

'This is your fault!' she wailed. 'If you hadn't sneaked up on me like that, none of this would have happened.' Through the water she could see the raised red smudge where the coffee had touched. It would come up in a nasty blister and hurt for a bit, but it wasn't serious. When she looked at him, though, his face was deathly pale.

'I'm sorry,' he said roughly. 'Do you need to see a doctor?'

'Don't be ridiculous. It's a burn, not a broken hand.'

'God. Abe must have had some kind of first-aid supplies in this bloody mausoleum.' He began pulling open cupboard doors which were either empty, or else yielded stores of pristine, unused china.

'I'll be fine.'

He swung back to her, raking his hand through his hair. 'There's no need to play the martyr, Destiny.'

'I'm not playing the martyr. Look, why don't you go and sit down? Or make yourself another cup of coffee.'

'You're right. It *was* my fault.' He stood next to her and they both watched her splayed fingers under the water. 'How does it feel now? Is that helping? Should I get a dishcloth and soak it in some water? I've got a first-aid kit in my car. No, forget that, the car's at the pub. We can't even get out of this damned place to get you to a hospital!' he groaned, and Destiny sighed deeply.

'It's a coffee burn, for heaven's sake. Surely you must have dealt with this type of thing before?'

'Not really, no.'

'You've never burnt yourself before?'

'Not that I can remember. My mother always taught me to be careful around hot things.' His anger had dissipated, which was good, she thought, although the humour creeping into his voice was almost as dangerous.

She whipped her hand out of the water and said, in a soothing voice, 'There, it feels much better now.'

'Wait there.' He fetched a dry cloth and gently dabbed the water off, while her heart seemed to do a funny kind of somersault and end up somewhere in her throat. 'You'd better come and sit down.'

'You're overreacting!' Destiny protested fruitlessly, as he led her very slowly back into the sitting room, holding her wrapped hand as though it was made of breakable crystal.

'Now, sit.'

She obediently sat on the sofa and, alarmingly, he sat next to her, so that the sofa depressed under his weight and her body slid an infinitesimal amount closer to his, so that they were lightly touching. He gently rested her hand on his leg and removed the cloth.

'Looks much better,' she said weakly.

'Looks bloody awful.'

'You need to feast your eyes on something truly awful, and you'd agree with me that the hand looks fine.'

'Something…like what?'

'Something…like a human missing a bit because of an overhungry croc? Or something…like a person with a hand infected with snake toxin.'

'I don't know how you do it.' Her hand was still on his leg and she looked at him, her mouth half-open, acutely conscious of the feel of his hard thigh under her fingers, even though he seemed blissfully unaware of it.

'Do what?' she asked, shutting her mouth.

'Live the life that you do.' Their eyes met. To her, they seemed to fuse and she felt a wave of giddiness steal over her.

'You make it sound as though I'm some kind of latter-day heroine,' she said a little breathlessly, 'and I'm not.'

'Do you ever long for escape?'

'Don't we all?' She wished that the lighting wasn't quite so dim, but there was no overhead light. The room was lit by a series of lamps, only two of which were actually turned on.

'How's the hand?'

'Barely feel a thing,' she answered truthfully. She dutifully stared at it, and he lightly traced a pattern along her fingers.

'Will you miss this evil city of ours, then? Or are you itching to get back to your country? God, I make it sound as if you're not English, but of course you are. In fact, you even speak better English than most people over here do.'

She laughed nervously. Her hand had developed a will of its own and was enjoying itself on his thigh. 'That's only because my parents were so adamant about speaking it at home. I never really picked up an accent or slang from anyone else. Can you imagine if you spoke English only to your parents?'

'Oh, I can imagine a lot of things—' he paused '—but not that. You still haven't answered me. *Are* you itching to get back to Panama?'

'Is this your way of asking me whether I've made my mind up about the house as yet?' She withdrew her hand from its compromising position and cradled it on her own lap with her other hand.

'No, it's not!' he shot back at her. 'Damn the house. It's the last thing on my mind at the moment.'

Destiny looked at him warily. 'And what is the *first* thing on your mind?'

For a few seconds he didn't answer. He just looked at her until she could feel every drop of colour leave her face and then rush back in a tidal wave, turning her crimson.

'This is,' he muttered. He put his hand at the back of her neck and pulled her towards him, then his mouth met hers.

Or, rather, his mouth assaulted hers. His lips were hungry and his tongue pushed into the moistness of her mouth. His hand pulled her towards him, fingers buried in her thick hair and, after a split second of confusion, during which she made a feeble attempt to break away, Destiny surrendered to all the powerful, primal feelings suddenly released inside her.

From her near-frozen state of virginal innocence, this awakening was explosive. Had she been conducting her entire life in a state of slumber? she wondered. She coiled

her arms around his neck, moaning in surprise and pleasure when his mouth left hers to trail wetly along the
slim column of her neck.

She knew all about the birds and the bees. Before her
mother had died, she had sat Destiny down and told her.
And, of course, she had studied enough medical journals
to be fully acquainted with the act of mating and repro-
duction. But what she was experiencing now bore no resemblance to all those clinical explanations she had read
about in her youth, and it bore even less resemblance to
what she had felt with Henri, during their occasional am-
ateurish gropings.

A wild animal had taken over her body. She writhed
and groaned and *wanted*. They slipped backwards onto
the huge sofa and she closed her eyes as he pushed up
her baggy shirt, pulling it over her head while she obligingly extended her arms to accommodate him. She had
never been inhibited about her body and the removal of
her shirt felt wonderful, allowed her more movement.

'You're beautiful,' he rasped huskily, and she half-
opened her eyes and smiled.

'Don't talk,' she whispered and those two words sent
a shiver of crazy adrenaline rushing around his body like
a fever. He could feel her breathing heavily beneath him.
Her breathing was an aphrodisiac. In fact, he had never
felt so consumed by lust in his life before. Every experience he'd ever had with any woman now seemed like
minor dress rehearsals for this one big, overwhelming
experience.

Just restraining his urge to rip off the bra that barely
contained her breasts was both painful and wildly intoxicating. He kissed and nibbled the thrusting swell, guid-
ing his tongue into her cleavage and enjoying her abandoned response to his touch.

Love and lust was a heady mixture. He could feel her innocence under his fingers, innocence without the coyness which most women possessed in generous measure. She wanted him and she wasn't hardened enough to try and dissemble. He unclasped the front opening of her bra and moaned in anticipation of the pleasure he would get pulling it aside, freeing those large breasts from their imprisonment. God, he wanted to slow down—but he couldn't. His body wasn't behaving sensibly enough for any such thing.

He was only just beginning to realise how long he had wanted this woman. It felt like for ever.

He slowly pushed aside her bra and his breathing thickened as he feasted his eyes on her breasts. She didn't want talking—oh, no—and nor did he, but if he'd been inclined he could have spent at least an hour expounding on what he was looking at. Firm, big breasts with big, swollen brown nipples, each topped with protruding buds that seemed to be begging for his lips.

This he would not rush, even though his throbbing, stiff manhood, pushing against his zipped trousers, was making its demands very clear.

He bent his head to one breast and flicked his tongue over the protruding bud. This woman's body, like her company, was worth savouring. He wanted to taste every inch of her, and then he wanted to repeat the process all over again.

Her hands moved to his head, urging him to do more than just lick, and he pushed her breasts up with his hands, suckling avidly on the nipples, turned on by the sheen of his saliva on them.

He touched her stomach, placed his hand palm-down on it, and then moved to caress the inside of her thigh.

From the depths of her excitement, Destiny knew

where his hand wanted to be. She wanted it too. Her body was melting, waiting for him. Through her jeans, he began to rub, cupping her while she squirmed against his hand. She felt him undo the button of her trousers, pull down the zipper, and terror made her stiffen.

She had never made love before and this wasn't how she was supposed to lose her virginity. She struggled under him and he looked at her.

'What's the matter?'

'I can't.' They were both still breathing heavily.

'You can't?'

'I'm sorry,' she said helplessly. 'I…I've never…'

'And I'll be gentle, my darling…'

'No. You don't understand.' He had called her *his darling,* but she wasn't, was she? Cold reality gleefully resurfaced. She'd given herself, allowed him to do things, and she'd never stopped to ask herself why. *Why* the sudden physical interest in her? Well, she asked the question now and the answer came immediately. He was a man on the rebound, vulnerable and in need, and she'd been a willing and eager participant in easing his pain after Stephanie.

'What? What don't I understand? I understand what you wanted up to a minute ago…'

'This isn't right.' She wriggled, but he was already drawing back from her, sitting up, watching as she miserably fumbled with her bra, then shoved her shirt back on. Dishevelled, but at least clothed. In a manner of speaking.

'Why not?' Callum demanded. 'We're both adults.'

'I can't just… Look, I'm sorry, but…I'm not a Stephanie substitute…'

'I never accused you of being one!' he exploded; then he drew in a few sharp breaths and eyed her narrowly.

'And I can't... I have to love someone... I'm not the kind of girl who... I realise that there's an awful lot I don't know, and I'm sure if I were a bit more sophisticated...who knows...? But I'm not, and I can't, and I want to go up to my room now. Please.'

'Go ahead,' he said brusquely. 'I'm not about to stop you. But your mother should have warned you about leading men on.'

His words echoed in her head as she finally made it to her bedroom, as did the sensation of his eyes on her back as she had fled in inelegant panic.

Want and lust were all very well, but they weren't enough. She needed stability and security and marriage and babies, and if that was old-fashioned, then it described it down to the last detail.

She lay down on the bed, buried her face in her pillow and knew that she would have to do something about what was happening to her. She could feel herself poised with one foot dangling over the cliff, and she couldn't fall over.

She needed to remind herself of what was real for her and there was only one person who could do that for her.

CHAPTER SEVEN

HENRI arrived in England eight days later.

During the interim, Destiny immersed herself in the company, had daily meetings with various members of the board to discuss flow charts, saw Derek twice, had dinner with Stephanie several times and generally busied herself with anything and everything that could take her mind off Callum.

To a certain degree, it worked.

It was easier not to think of him when she was busy grappling with the complexities of profit and loss accounts and budgets which, even to her unskilled eyes, appeared horrendously optimistic. But the minute her mind wasn't occupied it slipped back to their love-making and, to the even more disastrous Sunday, when they had toured the grounds, keeping a measured distance between them and acting as though nothing had happened. He'd appeared to find that very easy to do. As he'd appeared to be relaxed around Stephanie. In fact, they had seemed more relaxed than when they'd been engaged. Maybe he had been trying to prove a point. The only point he'd ended up proving, through his silence, was that what had happened between them had been a regrettable inconvenience but not much more.

He'd only called her once since then, to find out whether she'd made any decisions about his offer, to which she'd responded with her rehearsed speech about needing a bit more time, needing to consult Derek and informing him that either she or her lawyer would be in touch as soon as possible. It had been a brilliant five-minute exercise in concealment but she'd been shaking after the telephone call.

So, right now, she was banking on Henri to restore her perspective.

When it came to Callum Ross, she seemed to spend half her time banking on someone or something to restore her perspective. She was, she'd thought ruefully, fast becoming a cast member in one of life's soap operas.

Henri emerged into the open walkway along with the rest of the passengers from his flight, trailing his suitcase on a trolley and peering anxiously around to see if he could spot her.

Destiny felt a swell of fondness, waved and gesticulated and, when she had finally made her way over to him, gathered him in a hug.

'You look different, Dessie,' he said, pushing her back to give her the once-over. '*Very smart.* Where's my little girl with the bright clothes and the scrubbed face?' He smiled warmly at her.

'She's temporarily on leave,' Destiny said, speaking in Spanish because she was beginning to feel that her bright, shiny, complicated new life was making her lose touch with the things she had always taken for granted. 'Tell me everything that's been happening on the compound. How's Dad? Has he sorted out his filing system as yet? And how's Martha and John?' She linked her arm fondly through his as they walked to the terminal exit.

She might have changed but dear Henri was still the same. Smaller and thinner than she remembered, but just as appealing, with his small round glasses and his engaging smile.

'I'm really glad you made it over, Henri,' she told him, one hour later when they were standing in the hall of her townhouse. 'Really glad that you decided to use some of your leave here instead of Paris.'

'The temptation to see little Destiny in surroundings other than a jungle was irresistible,' he said, looking around him with interest and then finally turning his attention to her. He was standing less than two feet away from her; their eyes were meeting, but she felt nothing but sisterly affection for the man whose flirting had once aroused the occasional romantic notion in her. It was nothing like what she felt when she was around Callum, the giddiness, the excitement, the feeling of *being alive.*

'And, besides, your father was worried about you,' he confessed.

'Why?' she cried, alarmed. 'Worried for what reason? Everything's going smoothly over here.'

'But you still felt desperate enough to ask me to come over.'

'I wasn't desperate. I wanted to see you. I'm not going to be here for ever and I thought it would be fun for us to see London together. That's all.'

'Sure that's all there is to it?'

'Pretty much,' Destiny mumbled, turning away towards the kitchen while he followed in her wake. 'Do you fancy something to eat? A drink? How was the flight? Are you tired? I can show you up to your bedroom if you like.'

'To answer your questions, no, yes, fine, yes and in a minute.'

But he was still curious about what was really going on with her. He allowed his curiosity to be reined in while they continued to chat about everything under the sun but the expression in his eyes when they rested on her was one of concern.

'I've arranged for you to see the medical facilities of

the company,' she told him, as they headed up to the spare room that would be his. 'I thought you might find it interesting.'

'Not, I gather, that it'll be of much use if you go ahead and sell the company.'

'I might not.' She drew his curtains, flicked her hand over the bedspread and averted her eyes. 'I've had an offer, actually. By the same man who wanted to buy the company. Callum Ross. Have I mentioned him?'

'Not even in passing since I came.'

'No? Well, he's considering helping out financially in exchange for a house in the country I've also been willed.'

'Let me get this right, Dessie… This man, whose name you've studiously avoided mentioning all evening, is proposing to pour millions into a company that's currently losing money in exchange for…a house?'

'It's a big house.'

'Sure it's just the house he wants in exchange?' There was teasing amusement in his voice. 'Sure he doesn't want *you* thrown into the bargain?'

Destiny rounded on him with vigour, hands on hips, thunderous frown on her face. 'No, he most certainly *does not want me thrown into the bargain!* That's an awful thing to say! He's *not my type* and I am very far from being *his!* In fact, the man's arrogant, bossy and pushy!'

Henri held up both his hands in mock surrender but his expression was shrewd. 'Okay! I get the message! Arrogant, bossy and pushy! Just the type of man to get on the nerves of a determined, forceful woman with a mind of her own!'

'Exactly.' She offered him a weak grin. 'Anyway, he's just broken up from my stepcousin—or, should I say, he's just been dumped by her, and not a minute too soon, as far as I'm concerned. Stephanie says it's like a weight being lifted from her shoulders, even though they're still friends.'

'You seem to have become very involved in the lives of the rich and the beautiful, Dessie... Methinks the little chick is maturing...'

'Shut up,' she laughed, 'or I'll hit you over the head with the kettle!'

'I'm cowering!'

'Anyway, you'd better get some sleep now. Tomorrow there's no time for jet lag, not when you've only got ten days over here. I've got an itinerary planned as long as my arm and in the evening we're going to the theatre with my stepcousin. She's dying to meet you.'

'Haven't been telling lies about me again, have you?' he joked. 'Like the time we went to the city and you sent me to collect a shirt you'd bought. Do you remember? Me, standing there, with a flowered blouse in my hand, and you show up and explain to the sales girl that I can't help myself but that there's nothing wrong with men wearing women's clothing if it makes them happy?'

'I was a kid at the time!'

'A kid of nineteen!'

But they ended the evening on a warm note, despite some choppy waters in the middle. Any hint of a relationship with Callum other than a business one would fly back to her father at the speed of light, and then her father *would* be worried. He'd had a long and traditional marriage to his childhood sweetheart and the thought that his daughter might be having any kind of fling with a man he'd never met and whom she barely knew would send him into a frenzy of paternal protectiveness. He'd never said so in so many words, but she knew that Henri was the sort of man her father would approve of for her. The very last would be the likes of Callum Ross.

Not, she thought, guiltily confused, that Callum Ross even entered the equation when it came to her private life. Really.

Of course, *studiously omitting to mention him* would arouse another burst of unhealthy curiosity, so she reluctantly dragged his name up a couple of times during the course of the next day, and was relieved when it was met with a casual air of indifference.

And the evening would be a doddle. They were meeting Stephanie at the theatre at six-thirty, well in time for the start of the play.

When she emerged at five forty-five in her glad rags, she was met with wolf whistles and a one-man round of wild applause.

'Gorgeous, darling, fabulous,' Henri said in an affected voice, approaching her to kiss her hand. 'Where does it all end? Can you tell me? Your father would be very proud!'

'To see me decked out like a clown?' But she laughed at the appreciative gleam in his eyes. She might feel a little clownish, but she knew that she didn't resemble one. Not in the slightest. The wardrobe which she'd initially bought with tentative reluctance, and originally worn with awkward self-consciousness, had now expanded and included a number of dresses of which her first saleswoman would have heartily approved. No more craven concealment of her legs. No more functional, loose garments to cope with stifling heat.

Now, she was wearing a dark green straight dress, caught in at the waist and reaching her mid-calves. The neckline was off the shoulder and scooped low enough to expose the first hint of cleavage. And she was in heels, something she'd never, ever worn in Panama. The heels meant that she was taller than her escort, and she wondered how she'd never noticed Henri's lack of stature before. She could see the top of his head and she had to resist the temptation to give him a quick pat.

They'd booked a taxi to take them to the theatre and they arrived to find no sign of Stephanie. In fact, there was no sign of her at all until they were seated, and then she chose to make her entrance with the panache of someone who thrived on attention. Not that you would ever think it, looking at her, because she approached their row with the vaguely lost and bewildered expression of someone not quite sure of their surroundings.

Destiny grinned wryly and could imagine how many men would be watching the beautiful brunette, wishing that they could leap to her assistance.

She turned to point her out to her companion, only to find him staring at Stephanie with an open-mouthed, befuddled expression. He watched, fascinated, as she made an apologetic fuss of having to make everyone in the row stand to allow her to pass, yet, mysteriously, was not so bothered by the disturbance as to hurry in the slightest.

Unlike Destiny's, Stephanie's dress was brief, and the palest of blue so that every inch of her small, supple body stood out in sharp contrast. The wavy hair had been tamed into perfect sleek straightness and flowed like silk around her face and over her shoulders, halfway down her back.

It was quite an entrance, Destiny thought with amusement, and if it was all part of the partner-searching game, then it was working, because Henri, once the introductions had been made, had been reduced to throat-clearing, speechless wonder.

'Remember the play?' she was forced to whisper halfway through the performance, when she could yet again feel his head staring at the averted profile of the woman sitting to the right of Destiny.

'You should have told me what she looked like,' he said in a responding whisper.

'And you would have prepared yourself by…?'

'Putting on some aftershave.'

'You're wasted as a doctor, Henri. You should be writing sex manuals—especially if your key to mutual attraction can be summed up in one word, *aftershave*.'

'Think of the money I could save all those poor men who spend their time buying flowers and chocolates.'

He fancied Stephanie. Frankly, any passing interest *they* might have had in one another had been, she suspected, the combination of their surroundings and a lack of basic choice when it came to members of the opposite sex. They understood each other and they liked one another, and occasionally that affection had manifested itself in a kiss and a cuddle, but she could see now that there had never been anything beyond that. She could feel him shifting restlessly next to her, responding to the woman on her other side, and there was no jealousy or envy, just amusement.

By the time the interval rolled round, it was a relief to get to the bar. At least there he would be able to talk to Stephanie instead of just breathing heavily and sneaking sidelong glances every three seconds.

But did he talk? Stephanie talked—talked with that animated, endearing eagerness that made her such a warm person. Destiny talked about how wonderful it was to be at the theatre for the first time, about the little plays she'd used to get her children at the school to do, dramatisations of the classics she had read over the years. But Henri could barely manage to piece together three sentences without displaying all the signs of a man bowled over by the sight of a woman.

In the end, it was Stephanie and not Destiny who saved the situation.

'I don't want to intrude on anything you two might have going…' She raised her eyebrows expressively at the both of them, and, while Destiny firmly denied any such thing, Henri stuttered out his version of the same. 'But I'd really like to get to know you, Henri…' She lifted his spectacles gently and smiled at his confusion. 'And this is utterly the wrong place. Too many people, too much going on…'

'We can leave,' he said eagerly. 'Go somewhere for a bite to eat…' In his haste, he slipped partially back into his native French and Stephanie looked delighted.

'We can't leave Destiny here by herself,' Stephanie said quietly, at which point the bell rang and Destiny took matters into her own hands. She had never played match-maker in her life before, but there was a first for everything, and how much could there be in it?

'You two *go*. I'm perfectly capable of enjoying the rest of this performance on my own, and I booked a taxi to collect us after the play. I'll find my way home.'

'Destiny!' Henri looked mildly shocked. 'Taxi? You're—'

'Independent, Henri,' she said, smiling, as the bell rang again and the bar began to clear. 'I was independent in Panama and I'm independent here. You can't keep a capable girl down.'

'But…'

'Come on, Henri.' Stephanie caught him by the tie and tugged him gently, at which he obediently fell into line with her. Only as Destiny was leaving the bar herself did

Stephanie run up breathlessly to say, 'Had to tell you, Dessie. That felt so *good!*'

'What did?'

'Being the one to call the shots!' She dashed back out, pausing to wave at Destiny, and then they disappeared.

The performance had restarted by the time Destiny made her way back to the empty seats, head down in embarrassment at everyone having to shift sideways or lever themselves up to let her through, and it was only when she was sitting that a dark, velvety voice said from one seat along,

'Hope you don't mind if I join you?'

'What are you doing here?'

The question was ignored as Callum shifted one seat along so that he was directly next to her, his elbow resting on the divide between them.

'What are you doing here?' she repeated tensely. The perspective angle hadn't worked at all. In fact, it had monumentally backfired, and she could feel that surge of emotion hit her like a sledgehammer as she glared at his averted profile and breathed in his masculine smell that had nothing to do with aftershave of any description.

'Shh, the play.' He settled back into his seat, while next to him she seethed and tried to figure out how Fate could be malignant enough to throw him into her company at this precise moment in time.

'Aren't you enjoying it?' he murmured in a low voice, 'I can feel you bristling next to me like a steam engine about to explode.'

'I *was* enjoying it.'

'Oh, you mean until I came along.' He didn't appear to be disconcerted by that, and when she opened her mouth again his response was to say, 'Shh!'

So she found herself sitting through the remainder of

the play, which had lost its appeal, while questions piled up in her head. But she restrained herself from saying another word until the performance was ended, the encores had been done and the lights were on. She was barely aware of the crowds of people surging past her towards the exit. Nor was she about to look around to see whether Callum was behind her. In fact, she'd almost convinced herself that he had somehow got lost in the crowd, perhaps even trampled underfoot, when she felt the pressure of his hand on her elbow.

'So where to now?'

'*I've* got a taxi booked...'

'Oh, good. Mind if I grab a lift with you? Taxis can be hell to come by at this hour outside a theatre.' He followed her outside, meekly allowing her to stride towards her taxi, head held high, but once they were inside the car, he turned and said, 'Where were you planning to eat?'

Originally, she wanted to ask, *or now that my escort's vanished?* Then it dawned on her that he was probably aware of exactly why she had been sitting in a row of three on her own. He must have seen her from the start, or else how would he have known where she was sitting? The thought that he'd been watching her made the hairs on the back of her neck tingle. Watching and...laughing?

'Actually, I thought I might just go home and give food a miss,' Destiny said in a stiff, polite voice, head carefully averted.

'*Give food a miss? You?*'

That made her snap round to look at him, although she had a sneaking suspicion that that had been the intention when he had made his gibe.

'I do occasionally skip food,' she told him with glacier-like formality, but the ice in her voice was ambushed by her wide, dilated pupils and for a few heady seconds she was held hostage by his piercing, sexy blue eyes.

It was, he thought, like an attempt to quench a roaring furnace with three drips of water, a token, desperate effort to distance him, and the awareness of that filled him with a crude, primitive sense of triumph. That tentative taste of her one week ago had been like a tantalising aperitif. It had stirred a hunger in him that had been shockingly erotic and one week of absence had done nothing to still it.

Love and animal lust swelled inside him, making his groin ache, and he struggled to let none of it show on his face. The slightest smell of his desire would send her running a mile. In all his life he'd never wanted a woman the way he wanted her, and it was just his luck that she was the one woman whose traditional, principled outlook was like a steel barrier between them.

'Not tonight.' He leaned towards the taxi driver and gave him an address, then he sat back and waited for her inevitable question, which was not long in coming.

'Where are we going?'

'Just a little place I know where we can get something light to eat.'

He sat back against the door and watched her. Watching her gave him a peculiar feeling of pleasure. Watching her, absorbing the expressions that flitted across her face. Even now, as she turned away, hunching her shoulder like someone trying to fend off danger through body language, he still enjoyed the view. Her skin was like satin, smooth and brown, making her hair look even richer and blonder in comparison. He wanted to reach out and gather it up between his fingers, so that he could pull her closer to him. He imagined her weight against him and the bird's-eye view he would have of the enticing swell of her breasts, barely restrained by her low-cut neckline. She had a body that always appeared to be bursting to get out of the clothes she wrapped around it.

That little wimp she had brought with her to the theatre was no match for her. She needed a man, a *real* man. Him, in other words. And she damned well knew it. It was written in every word she didn't say and in every expression she tried so hard to conceal.

Henri. That was his name. Callum had met Stephanie the evening before; their conversation had no longer been strained by the invisible pressure hanging over their heads that they were an engaged couple, and should therefore be frantic to climb into the nearest convenient bed, and he'd managed to pump a fair amount of information out of her.

They would discuss this Henri character just as soon as they had reached their destination. He was pretty good at reading body language, and from what he had glimpsed mutual sexual attraction had not been on the agenda, but still, they had appeared relaxed with one another—and relaxed was always a bad sign.

'Is this a restaurant?' Her voice broke through his reverie and he realised that the taxi had stopped and she was now looking past him to his townhouse.

'In a manner of speaking.' He opened his door, paid the driver, leaving a generous tip and waited impatiently for her to exit the taxi.

'What do you mean, "in a manner of speaking"?'

'I mean there's food inside.' He hustled her along, preparing himself for the inevitable explosion—which occurred just as soon as she was through his front door.

'It's your house, isn't it?' She turned to him, her cheeks flushed with colour.

Instead of answering, he calmly switched on the hall light. 'How do you like it?'

'You brought me to your house! You told me that we were going to a restaurant!'

'I did no such thing,' he demurred. 'I told you that I knew somewhere we could get something light to eat.'

'You lied! I demand to be dropped back to my house! Immediately!'

'Why?'

'Why? *Why?* Because—'

'Promise…no touching…' He held up both hands, palms towards her. 'At least, not unless you want me to…' he added very softly to himself. 'Food and a bit of business. I need to wrap this matter up with the company within the week.'

'You do?' Destiny asked hesitantly. 'Why? You never mentioned a deadline for my decision.'

'Business runs on deadlines,' Callum informed her, improvising as he went along and managing to usher her into the kitchen while she ruminated over what he had said. 'I have my board breathing down my neck, wanting to know whether we'll be acquiring Felt's. My accountants need to know how to distribute the money with year-end coming up.'

'But I can't *give* you an answer,' she said from behind him, while he started extracting pots and pans and cooking ingredients from various cupboards and the fridge.

'Why not? What's the problem? I'm offering to practically bail you out.' Now that he'd managed to get her into the kitchen, it seemed as safe a policy as any not to focus his attention on her. She had forgotten that she'd been brought to his house against her will. No point reminding her of the fact by trying to stare her down.

'Yes, well…' She shuffled over to the kitchen table,

which was constructed of wood and chrome and was very high-tech-looking, and ran her hands over the smooth surface. She sighed and looked at him as he chopped vegetables and expertly tossed things in a frying pan. Whatever he was cooking, there were some very reassuring smells emanating from it.

'Do you need any help?' she asked awkwardly.

'No. Just sit. I'm fully capable of cooking a simple meal for two without help. Don't guarantee how it's going to taste, but it'll be better than nothing.'

'Smells good,' Destiny said politely, raising her voice to compensate for the sound of sizzling, then she lapsed into silence, content to look.

Within ten minutes he began fishing plates out and allowed her to lend a hand by laying the table.

'Now, eat and enjoy,' he commanded when he was finally sitting opposite her with the overhead light dimmed—which he had jokingly told her was a famous ruse of the uncertain chef, who preferred to spare his audience too much clarity when it came to his food.

'It tastes…delicious.' There was a lot of pasta, and he had stir fried vegetables with cream and parmesan cheese which soaked into the noodles like gravy.

'Good. So…I couldn't help noticing at the theatre that you arrived with a man… Looked a nice guy… Who was he? Friend of Steph's?'

'How did you manage to pick us out among all those people?'

'I think everyone in the place noticed Stephanie when she walked in five minutes after everyone was seated. Must have been a bit embarrassing arriving on time with her chap, to find that she hadn't arrived yet…'

'Actually, Henri's staying with me,' Destiny said reluctantly. 'He works with me in Panama and I invited him over for a few days.'

'Oh. *I* get the picture. Bad luck for you. He seemed besotted with my ex—and, of course, he left with her during the interval, didn't he?'

'Were you *spying* on us?' Destiny asked abruptly. 'If you're still that obsessed with Stephanie, then I suggest you tell her—because you might find that someone else is around to pick up the pieces!'

'I wasn't *spying* on you and, believe me, you couldn't be further from the truth as far as my feelings for Stephanie go. I'm more than happy that someone will pick up the pieces—not that there are any pieces to pick up. I'm just sorry that the man in question happens to be *your* man.'

'Henri is not *my* man! He's a friend! Some of us *do* have friends of the opposite sex, in case you hadn't noticed!'

'A very good friend, from the looks of it...'

'So you *were* spying on us!'

'I happened to see you at the start of the play and naturally I found myself glancing over every so often!'

'Who were you there with, anyway?' Destiny asked suspiciously.

'Office people. Finished eating?' He cleared away the table and had to deliver a stern lecture to himself to lighten up. Hadn't she told him what he had already known? That the wimp with the spectacles was nothing more than a friend? Yes. Then why did he still feel jealous? Course, he knew why. He felt jealous because she had admitted that he was a good friend, and now his head was rife with images of them sharing long, intimate conversations, the likes of which she would never share with *him* because she viewed everything he said and did with a liberal pinch of suspicion.

'No dessert,' he said brusquely. 'Sorry.'

'I'll help you wash up.'

'Don't bother.'

'It's no bother.' She came to the kitchen sink and stood next to him, waiting till he filled a bowl with warm, soapy water. His kitchen overlooked a private back garden, now wreathed in darkness. It was far more private than where she was living but, on the other hand, it was also further out of central London, which was much nicer, she thought. Quieter, less frantic. Large French doors led out of the kitchen into the back garden, so that there was an impression of airiness about the room.

'You don't expect me to believe that you and this…man…are…were…*just good friends,* do you? Despite what you say about having friends of the opposite sex, you're a big girl. You must know that such a thing doesn't exist.' Instead of washing, he plunged both his hands into the soapy water and stared at the distorted image they created.

He shouldn't be pursuing this. He knew that she wasn't involved with the man sexually. Dammit, he had eyes in his head and had seen all the signs for himself, but he wanted to hear her say that Henri meant nothing to her. He wanted to be told that he was more interesting, more engaging than his bespectacled and unknowing rival.

Destiny didn't say anything and he turned to look at her, wondering whether she'd even heard what he'd asked. He found her looking right back at him, her green eyes curious and comprehending.

'Are you *jealous* of Henri?' she asked in a faltering voice, at which he forced a bark of laughter out.

'Me? *Jealous?* I've never been jealous of anyone in my entire life and I certainly don't intend to start now!'

The blue eyes that met hers were fiercely proud, but she *knew*. She knew that he had been jealous, even if his jealousy was only based on the sheer egotistical physical grounds of not liking the idea that someone else might have touched her when he was still interested, and the knowledge made her heart flutter wildly inside her.

She wanted to tell him that there was no need, that she'd only ever loved one man and that was him. The admission whipped the breath from her throat and she stared back glassily at him, her lips slightly apart. She turned away, but not before he'd seen that brief flash of hunger that mirrored his own.

'Does it make you feel good?' he taunted softly. 'That a big, strong man like me might be reduced to a pitiful emotion like jealousy?' He lifted one hand out of the water and swung her head to face him. One side of her face was now wet and slippery.

'Yes,' she threw back honestly. 'It makes me feel good.'

Now both hands were out of the water and cupping her face, stroking her cheekbones, and she could feel all her good intentions disintegrating like sand through a strainer. She couldn't fight him any more. What she felt was powerful enough to destroy every item in the feeble armoury she had in reserve. She was sick of looking at him and wanting to touch him and telling herself that she shouldn't, that it was wrong. She was sick of being scared and out of her depth. She loved him and she wanted him and if he was only aware of one of those two things, then that was enough. She would leave England all too soon. Why leave with regrets for things undone?

She ran the tip of her tongue over her lips, aware of the rampantly sexual come-on signal she was giving and, when he bent his head towards hers with a groan, she sighed and offered herself to him with abandonment.

CHAPTER EIGHT

'WHY don't we leave all these dirty dishes and go up-stairs?' he murmured into her ear, and she gave a whim-per in response. She really didn't care where they were, just so long as she could feel his hard body pressed against hers.

They walked up the stairs to his bedroom, with Destiny noticing absolutely nothing on the way. If someone had asked her what the colour of the wallpaper was on the walls, or whether she was walking on carpet, wooden flooring, tiles or red hot coals, for that matter, she would not have been able to give an answer. In fact, she felt as though she were floating, and his fingers laced through hers were like fire against her skin.

By the time they finally made it to his bedroom she knew that she was shaking like a leaf, a combination of excitement and nerves, and she raised her eyes hesitantly to his. At the door, she paused wordlessly.

'I suppose you must be accustomed to this…sort of thing…' Her voice was barely above a whisper and he gazed at her softly.

'I'm not celibate, if that's what you mean. And there's no need to be scared…'

'You don't mind that… I mean, with all your experi-ence… Does it bother you that I'm a…?'

'Virgin?'

Destiny nodded, blushing at the bluntness of the word, now that it was out in the open. Never in a million years would she have imagined that her own lack of experience would have left her feeling so vulnerable. She could stop right now; she knew that. Call a halt and walk right back down those stairs. But she also knew that she wouldn't. This was *right*.

'I have never felt so honoured in my life,' he said huskily, which brought an unsteady smile to her lips. 'Come with me.' He led her into the massive *en suite* bathroom and then sat her down in a wicker chair by the window.

'What are you doing?'

'I'm going to relax you.'

She watched as he began running a bath, testing the temperature every so often with his fingers, adding bubble bath that smelt of cinnamon. The bath was grand enough to suit the dimensions of the bathroom. It was a Victorian masterpiece, with clawed feet. A large, masculine bath that blended well with the forest-green and white tiles surrounding it. She could easily imagine him lying in it, long, indolent, one arm draped lazily over the side, eyes closed. And, of course, naked.

The thought made her pulses begin to race once more.

What, she thought a little hysterically, did one do with a man's naked body? Would he be as big and awesome *down there* as his build suggested? She was so lacking in experience that she doubted she would know what to touch. The idea made her feel faint and she closed her eyes briefly.

'Not dozing off, are you?'

Her eyes flew open to find him standing above her, smiling.

'No,' she squeaked, gripping the arms of the wicker chair.

'Stand up.'

Destiny obeyed. Without saying so, she knew that he

was well aware of the battle raging between her fear at stepping into the unknown and her excitement at the prospect, and he was taking control. She also knew that she could trust him implicitly.

'Now, my darling, just you stand there…' He gently kissed her eyes and stroked her eyebrows with his thumbs.

If only she knew what agony it was, he thought to himself. If only she knew that he was damned nervous himself, though not of the physical act, as she was. Understandably. No, he just wanted to touch her everywhere and in every way that would be right for her, make her the recipient of his glorious passion and feel that body of hers respond to his the way he knew she would. There was something touchingly childlike about this tall woman who could tackle anything life threw at her but this.

He rolled his fingers along her collarbone and very slowly began to undo the long zipper at the back of her dress, feeling her quick, shallow breathing under his hands. It slipped to the ground and pooled around her ankles. God, he was trembling almost as much as she was! He moved to unclasp her bra from the front.

Her breasts spilled out in all their bounty.

He could feel urgency and hunger hit his loins with gut-wrenching force and he forced himself to breathe deeply and evenly. Given his way, he would ravish her right here and now, on the bathroom floor, and, God, he probably wouldn't even have time to strip himself of all his clothes, but she was like a thoroughbred filly that needed to be treated with the utmost care.

The bra was tossed onto the black ash linen basket. Her head was thrown back and her rapid breathing made her chest fall and rise. Her nipples were large and erect, waiting to be touched. And touched they would be, but not yet. He would wait for her to come to him.

The bathroom light was on a dimmer switch, and he had dimmed it so that no harsh light invaded the room. Instead, gentle shadows washed over them with every small movement.

Her body was perfectly toned. Of course, he knew that—had fantasised about it for the nightmarishly long week that had stretched between them since he had last seen her—but, still, seeing her standing in front of him made him feel winded. Naked, with her large breasts resting against her ribcage, the slender waist, beneath which dipped the elastic band of her underwear.

He knelt in front of her and it momentarily flashed through his head that in every respect she had brought him to his knees. Then he curled one finger on either side of her briefs and peeled them down. This time he had to close his eyes and steady himself. Just for a second. Just long enough to get himself and his throbbing body back into some kind of control. He inhaled deeply, breathing in her womanhood, then ran his hands lightly up either side of her thighs, enjoying it as she shuddered beneath him.

'Bath time,' he murmured, standing up.

'Already? Must I?'

'It'll relax you.'

'I feel relaxed already,' Destiny said, tentatively placing her hand on his cheek, then running it up through his dark hair.

'You haven't begun to relax yet,' he promised softly, and she obediently climbed into the water, which was at a perfect temperature. Warm and so full of bubbles that her body was obscured by them.

He slipped round to the back of the bath and for a few

minutes transported her to bliss as he kneaded the muscles at the back of her neck and along her shoulders.

The tips of her hair, hanging in the water, were damp and darker than the halo of blonde he breathed into, kissing the nape of her neck, then he moved and lathered his hands with soap.

This time he didn't have to tell her what to do. She stood up, wet, with an expression of pleasure on her face. When he began sliding his soapy hands along her shoulders and arms, she smiled with the languid contentment of a cat.

The thought of running his hands over her breasts produced such feelings of exquisite anticipation in him that he almost wanted to delay the moment for as long as possible.

But they were waiting for him, like fruit waiting to be savoured, and savour them he did, massaging the soap over them, drawing the pouting nipples to throbbing hardness, while she moaned unsteadily. Then along the flat planes of her stomach, along her thighs and finally, with slow, rhythmic strokes, over the mound of her femininity. He felt it pulsate under the palm of his hand and ran a finger along the crease, finding the nub which he stroked until her moaning became faster and hoarser.

Rinsing off the soap was something she did in record time, and now his hunger was ripening into a steady throb. He dried her and led her into his bedroom and onto the king-sized bed with its tan and terracotta duvet and puffy pillows.

She felt a fleeting sense of wonder at what she was knowingly about to step into. The great big unknown. And then a twinge of alarm that for all her reasoning about enjoying this while it lasted, she was about to jump off a precipice and the fall might prove fatal.

It didn't last long. She lay on the bed, naked and beyond the point of turning back, and watched him greedily as he removed his clothes.

The body she'd imagined was even more impressive than the vague picture she'd conjured up in her newly, irrepressibly fertile head.

Every inch of him was tautly muscled. His limbs were aggressively long and athletic. He watched her watching him and smiled lazily, enjoying her obvious pleasure afforded by the view.

'Let's take our time,' he murmured, when he was lying on his side next to her, their faces almost touching. 'The best things in life need to be savoured for the longest possible time.' He kissed her gently, delicately almost, his tongue licking the contours of her mouth then invading it with supreme thoroughness. Destiny, already on the brink, cradled his head with her hands, then arched back to enjoy the slow path of his mouth as it nibbled and licked her shoulders, finally reaching her aching breasts.

He levered his powerful body over hers, supporting himself with his arms, and devoted all his attention to her full breasts, stroking them with his tongue, sucking the nipples into his mouth, arousing her until she wanted to cry out for satisfaction.

When his head moved inexorably down, so that his exploration of her body could be complete, she thought that she might faint with the intense pleasure of it.

He parted her willing thighs, then after a few teasing nuzzles into the soft down of her hair, he buried his face against her and she gave a little cry of ecstasy as his tongue found its spot and pressed on it in small flicking motions.

Her body seemed to be moving of its own accord. How could she ever have worried that she *wouldn't know what to do?* She raised her hips and curled her fingers into his hair, pushing him down against her, writhing to accommodate his mouth. With wanton lack of inhibition, she rolled the palms of her hands over her nipples, stimulating them, while the lower half of her body continued to do its amazing, erotic dance.

He wasn't about to give her the isolated satisfaction of an orgasm now, though. He could feel mounting need, but before it crested he pulled away, and replaced his mouth with his own fullness, inserting himself gently; after a moment of rigidity, she bucked frantically against him, taking him in and panting as they both came to a shuddering climax.

There was no embarrassment when he eased himself off her and lay next to her, propping himself up on his elbows so that he could inspect her flushed, satisfied face.

Destiny had never felt so free in her life before. Some measure of reason was beginning to set in, but she felt no regrets. Just complete and utter joy that her first act of lovemaking had been with the man she loved. Never mind that he wasn't aware of the fact and never would be. In her own head, and in her heart, she'd not betrayed herself.

'That was…' she said drowsily, searching for just the right word, '…exquisite.'

'Ditto…' He kissed the tip of her nose.

'Don't fib,' she chastised teasingly. 'I didn't *do* any-thing…'

'How can you say that? The proof of what you did was right in front of your eyes! Not to mention in other parts as well…' He gave a slow, sexy chuckle. 'And, in a very short while, there'll be more ample proof of what you do to me clamouring for a bit more of the same…'

'Will there?' Her green eyes widening innocently. 'Or are you just saying that to make me feel good…?'

'Of course, I *do* want you to feel good—' he stroked her legs then dipped his fingers to slide gracefully over her wetness '—and I think I've succeeded…but I think my little beauty needs a rest before…we rediscover each other's bodies…'

'Never mind a rest…I could do with a shower. Would it be all right if I had one?'

'Only if it would be all right if I joined you…'

Later, fresh after a shower which had taken much longer than any of the showers she'd ever had on the compound, due to a mutual lack of conviction that getting out was the object of the exercise, they found themselves back in the kitchen and confronting the forgotten pile of unwashed dishes.

With a bit of imagination, Destiny found that she could create her own little bubble, in which this wonderful domesticity, alongside the man she loved, would be long-lasting. He washed the dishes while she dried them, and their conversation was lazy, relaxed, teasing and utterly unlike what she would have imagined having with this man only weeks previously.

Whoever said that love needed time to flourish? And with all the right environmental conditions? It was more like a weed, capable of sprouting forth in the most hostile of places and, once sprouted, of growing with rapid and tenacious speed.

'I guess I'd better be getting back home,' she said reluctantly, when all the dishes were dried. She neatly placed the cloth over the rail of the Aga and felt him move up behind her until his hands were on her waist and his chin nestled against the crook of her shoulder.

'Why?'

'Why what? Why should I leave?'

'Why *should* you leave?' he murmured provocatively. 'When there's so much left for us to do…? Bit difficult to make love when we're miles apart, isn't it? And I've never been much of a fan of telephone sex… Always seemed like a recipe for frustration to me, although it has to be said that getting dirty down the end of line might have a few attractions…' He slipped his hand underneath the shirt she had borrowed from him and cupped one of her breasts, jiggling it so that it bounced gently against his palm. 'I love your nipples. They're so…' He nibbled her earlobe, sending little shivers of delight racing down her spine, and she leant languorously back against him.

'Big. Everything about me is big,' she said with a little laugh.

'And does that bother you?'

'Not really.' She shrugged and thought about it. 'Sometimes I used to feel a bit awkward at having to talk down to all the other women on the compound, but on the whole it's been to my advantage. If you can call it an advantage to be opted for all the more physical jobs that require a bit of strength.' Now his hands caressed both her breasts, pausing only to rub thumbs over the peaks of her nipples now and again. She felt a familiar stirring down below. The kind of stirring that turned her brain to cotton wool.

'You mean the bespectacled Henri didn't rush to your immediate aid?'

'Doesn't work that way out there, I'm afraid. Women need to be able to do their job usefully and not rely on a man to pull them out of uncomfortable conditions.'

He paused in what he was doing. 'Was your mother as capable as you?'

'If not more.' She sighed. 'My father said that he loved her from the very first moment he set eyes on her.'

'Where did they meet? At a dance? Dinner party?'

'Oh, she was stitching up a young boy whose head had been busted open by a cricket ball.'

'Ah. Unusual circumstances for love at first sight.'

'I guess their eyes met over the needle and nylon.' She giggled.

'So what are you going to do? Stay or stay?'

'Stay?'

'Right choice…'

Was it, though?

She had no idea what time they had finally drifted to sleep. She only knew that she was considerably more experienced in the ways of pleasuring a man than she had been at the start of the evening. And when she wakened several hours later, with needles of light filtering through the curtains, it took her several seconds to remember where she was. Then her eyes flew open to find herself alone on the bed with a mass of crumpled sheets around her.

With the cold light of day came the cold light of reality. Her fragile reasons for sleeping with Callum Ross now seemed ludicrous and naïve. Seductive words and dim lighting, and the overwhelming recognition of her own feelings for him, had worked in devilish ways to banish her reserve, and the prospect of a headlong collision with planet Earth now seemed something that couldn't be reasoned away into non-existence.

What could she have been thinking of?

Had she imagined that she could enjoy the fruition of her love for one night—or maybe one week or even one month, until she left the country—and then take off with her heart and soul intact? What was the remainder of her

life going to be now? Back in Panama, with only her
memories for bitter company?

She groaned silently to herself, wondering if there was
any reasonable chance that she could sneak out of the
house without being caught. Perhaps shinny out of the
window or something.

She tried to picture someone of her stature *shinnying*
and ran up against a mental block. Shinny down and
break her back by crashing thunderously onto the ground
in the process would be more like it.

The thing that really scared her was the suspicion that,
whatever qualms were now dawning on the horizon, she
would still forfeit reason for the pleasure of being with
him, and she knew that the more snatched moments of
happiness she stole now, the greater would be her even-
tual prison sentence.

The thoughts were still churning over in her mind
when the object of them returned to the bedroom, wearing a white bathrobe underneath which was nothing but
his bare body, as she could see every time it swung apart
in rhythm with his tread.

'Breakfast,' he said, raising the tray in both hands
slightly and grinning. 'Full English.' He deposited the
tray on the bed, relieved himself of his bathrobe with an
enviable lack of self-consciousness, then slid next to her.

On the tray was a plate heaped with bacon, sausages,
toast and scrambled egg, two cups of coffee and two
plates with the required cutlery stacked on top of them.

Her onslaught of misgivings evaporated at the sight of
him, as she had known it would.

'Tuck in,' he said, heaping a bit of everything on a
plate and sliding a spare tray from underneath onto
her lap.

'Don't tell me. You're an expert at entertaining women in your bed in the morning.'

'On the contrary. Don't forget, Steph and I were together for two years and I'm a one-woman man.'

'Did you ever love her?' She took a sip of the coffee and waited for his answer.

Love her? Callum almost laughed. Love was anything but the placid affection he had felt for his former fiancée. Love, as he could now testify, was something that took over every pore of your body and left a strong man hesitant and exposed.

'We had fun for a while,' he said slowly, wishing that she was opposite him so that he could read the expression on her face. Her voice implied nothing but a casual interest. 'And I was very fond of her. I still am.'

Just like you're having fun with me for a while? she wanted to ask. Instead, she chickened out of the sickening prospect of putting him in a spot. She wondered whether that would be his future dismissal of her when he was lying on the same bed, bringing breakfast up for another woman.

She ate some of her breakfast in silence, then manoeuvred the tray onto the low oak chest of drawers next to her side of the bed.

'That was good,' she said. 'Thank you very much. The last time I had food delivered to me on a tray in my room was years ago, when I was ill, and my father waited on me hand and foot for a few days. I remember thinking at the time how nice it was not to have to fetch and carry for other people.'

She lay back against the pillow and stared up at the ceiling, feeling the bed shift as he disposed of his own tray then turned on his side to her.

'You're quite something, Destiny Felt, do you know

that?' He pulled the sheet a few inches down so that her breasts were exposed, but he didn't touch her, contenting himself with looking, until his looks were as heady as his touch would have been.

She turned to lie on her side, facing him, half wanting to cover herself, but the desire to do that was a lot less strong than the desire to watch him react to her. She had never known that one man's hunger could be such a powerful aphrodisiac. Eventually, he couldn't resist, and he trailed a finger to circle her nipple, touching it with butterfly lightness, watching as it stiffened and puckered under his finger.

'We need never stop this, you know,' he said gravely, addressing her responding breast, and her breath caught in her throat.

Wasn't this what she had wanted to hear? Some talk of commitment? Of permanence? What else could he mean? They had spent a wonderful night together, and at least as far as she was concerned it was much more than that. Somehow it felt as though their personalities fused. Did he feel it too?

She was no liberated westerner who could gaily conduct an affair as a *fun thing* while it lasted. She was a traditionalist and, although she'd slept with him, she wanted so much more.

She could feel herself holding her breath as she looked at him.

'What, not even to eat or have a bath?' she asked lightly, while her heart pounded like a steam engine inside her. Having Callum at her side, her husband, would raise a few problems—not least those concerning country of residence—but the doubts were soothed as soon as they surfaced. She would be at his side, wherever that might turn out to be.

'I'm being serious.' He lay flat on his back with his hands folded behind his head. He could feel a muscle pulsing gently in his jaw and a light film of perspiration was breaking out over his body. It hadn't been like this with Stephanie, but, then again, he hadn't been toying with his heart then. She'd wanted proof of security and he'd had no trouble agreeing to an engagement because he had felt more real warmth and affection for her than he had ever felt for any of his previous women. Not that talk of marriage had ever cropped up before. It had been something he had purposefully avoided.

But now it was different. He couldn't envisage *not* having this woman by his side for the duration of his life, for better or for worse and all those other vows uttered during a marriage ceremony, vows that he had never given much thought to in the past. And he didn't want an engagement.

But, for all that, the thought of exposing himself and telling her how he felt sent a chill of terror crawling along his veins.

It hadn't escaped him that not once during their love-making had the word *love* been mentioned, not even when she'd been flushed and moaning with pleasure, with every defence down and her head thrown back in abandon. And that in itself said it all. Because, however sharp she was in every conceivable practical area, when it came to emotions she was still finding her way, and there was an openness there that was almost innocent in its demonstrations.

But, God, he still wanted her to be his for ever.

'We could get married,' he said, still staring upwards. 'I mean, it makes sense, don't you think? We're compatible in bed—more than compatible—and it could sort out every niggling area of all this bargaining we've been trying to do over the past few weeks. I can't personally think of a better arrangement than marriage.'

She couldn't fail to see the sense behind his proposal, he thought, and then he would have time on his side. Time to woo her into loving him. He was her first lover and, in a life in which relationships had never made an imprint, she probably wasn't very certain *what* love was. She would only ever have had the example of her parents, and from the sound of it they had been an exceptional couple, both scientists, both fiercely determined to bring their skill and knowledge to a country that needed it. From the start they had been unified in their goals. But with him, well, hadn't it all been a little different?

'Arrangement?' Destiny asked numbly.

'Partnership,' he corrected quickly.

'I'm not sure,' she said, feeling cold all over and very sure indeed. Very sure that the proposition he had put to her had not been the one her romantic, delusional mind had conjured up. Now, it made her feel ill to think that she'd imagined a marriage proposal to have been made with some declaration of love, or at least with some emotion other than the coolly logical one he was displaying now.

She had to get out of here. She couldn't afford to let him start working on her with his arguments of common sense and practicality. He weakened her, and she wouldn't enter into a marriage for all the wrong reasons. That would be a recipe for disaster. Hadn't she made one disastrous error already by sleeping with him and telling herself that it was fine because she loved him? No way would she compound the mistake by adding yet another, and one that she would have a lifetime to regret.

'I need to think it over.'

'What's there to think over?' He rolled to his side and looked at her, his blue eyes urgent and demanding.

She wriggled back a bit. 'I need a few days. Just to get my head around it...to adjust...'

'Adjust to what?'

'We barely know each other!'

'We have been as intimate as two people can be...'

'That's not what I mean.' She edged towards the side of the bed and practically fell off, reaching down for her clothes and sticking on the shirt she had borrowed with her back to him.

'Where are you going?' It was more of a demand than a question. He could feel her ebbing away from him, but the temptation to push harder was something he knew he had to resist. The ebb would turn into outright flight if he did that. She said she needed time, and there was nothing ominous about that. Of course she needed time. Marriage proposals were not things that were sprung on a daily basis. The best thing he could do now would be to curb his savage impatience and let her have the time she needed. With restrictions.

'I need to get back to my place,' she mumbled, not looking at him.

Callum sprang out of bed and pulled a tee-shirt over his powerful torso, followed by boxer shorts.

'You'll need a lift back. I'll drive you.' He kept one eye on her while putting on a pair of trousers, not bothering with a belt so that they hung slightly down his hips. She had sailed into the bathroom, shutting the door, and he waited with increasing frustration for her outside, drumming his fingers on the windowsill.

One desperate part of him was beginning to think that somewhere along the line his impeccably tempting offer, full of the sort of practical advantages that would appeal to someone as clear-headed as she was, was going badly wrong.

And with the desperation, nauseating in itself because it was just so alien to him, came a rush of surly defensiveness. Shouldn't she have jumped to his offer with alacrity? Maybe, he thought, she was disturbed at the thought of cutting ties with the country she'd spent most of her life in. Perhaps she just needed time to sort out the practicalities of the issue.

That line of thought was reassuring, and by the time she emerged from the bathroom, inappropriately clad in her dress, he was prepared to be magnanimous.

'Look,' he said sympathetically, 'I understand that you might be having a few doubts about leaving Panama...' She was virtually scuttling out of the room and down the stairs, running her fingers through her uncombed hair, sticking on her shoes when she got to the front door. 'But you would be able to go over there on holiday whenever you wanted. And of course your father could come and visit whenever he wanted...'

'Oh, yes, right,' she answered in a vaguely surprised voice. She still wasn't looking at him and he positioned himself in front of the door so that she was compelled to look up. 'I hadn't really considered that aspect of it,' she continued, flushing.

'Then *what* aspects are you considering?' he demanded with a trace of aggression in his voice, and she immediately pulled away into herself.

'Please don't push me.'

'I'm not pushing you.'

'You expect me to give you a yes or no answer right this minute...'

'I *told* you I can more than understand that you might need time to think it over,' Callum said repressively.

He steadied himself and stood aside to open the door, following her into the car and starting it with barely contained anger.

'I'm going to be away for the next few days,' he said into the lengthening silence. 'So I won't be around to pester you. Do you think you might have an answer for me by the time I get back?'

'I guess I might,' Destiny told him vaguely.

'You *guess?*'

'All right, then. I will.'

'That's better.'

But when she sneaked a glance at his profile, it was grimly tight. She knew what was niggling him. He'd tossed his proposal to her, expecting her to not be able to resist. A marriage of good sex and good business, without the tricky business of love getting in the way. It made perfect sense, didn't it? And, into the bargain, she would have the pleasure of being wed to the most eligible bachelor in London and all the consequent advantages of limitless money. He must be thinking that the alternative was slinking back to Panama to continue working in a funless vacuum with enough money to fairly do what she wanted, but without the vital medical facilities the company would offer—because she knew that selling the company was virtually a foregone conclusion, despite the fact that so many people would prefer her not to go down that road.

Marriage would be of mutual benefit. He would get the company he had craved, a company that would establish a foothold in the huge, complex world of pharmaceuticals, and she in return would get the benefit of his considerable investments to make it work. Everyone would be happy.

'How long are you planning on being out of the country?' she asked tentatively, and he relaxed fractionally.

'Five days. Maybe a bit longer. Depends on how many problems I have to sort out. Why, will you miss me?'

'Will *you* miss *me?*' She threw the question back at him and felt a treacherous sense of arousal as his mouth curved into a satisfied smile.

'What do you think? Perhaps,' he drawled softly, 'I should find a deserted back road somewhere and stop the car so that I can demonstrate exactly how much I'll be missing you…'

'I don't think so,' Destiny said hurriedly, recognising the familiar road down which all her good intentions tended to go wildly astray.

'No, maybe a little absence is good for the soul.'

A little absence? He was so sure of getting what he wanted, the way he always had, all through his life.

She didn't dare contemplate his shock when he returned from his trip abroad.

'Maybe it is,' she repeated sadly.

CHAPTER NINE

CALLUM stared out of the window of his office which offered an uninspiring view of leaden skies pressing heavily above the grey, claustrophobic confines of the city. He had a meeting in under an hour and he was toying with the notion of delegating it to one of his directors, even though delegation was beginning to become something of a habit—and a habit that was not going unobserved by several of the people who worked for him.

Frankly, he didn't give a damn.

He spun round on his chair and buzzed through to his secretary, telling her to send Peters in his place to the Viceroy meeting at the Savoy.

'But he's already scheduled to see someone,' Rosemary protested uselessly.

'Then he'll just have to cancel, won't he?'

'But…'

'I'm leaving the office. I can't go. That's all there is to it. In case it's missed you, Rosemary, I pay these people to handle important meetings. They'll just have to start earning their keep.'

'Of course, but…' She sighed. 'Are you feeling all right, Mr Ross?'

'Of course *I'm feeling all right*. Is there any reason why I shouldn't be? Do I sound ill to you?'

'Not *ill*, no…' Rosemary's voice trailed significantly down the end of the line and he had to stop himself from clicking his tongue in annoyance. He'd seen enough looks and been privy to sufficient concerned remarks to know what was coming next and he wasn't in the mood for it.

'It's just that you never take time off work, and you have three meetings this afternoon...'

'A simple request, Rosemary, that's all it was. A simple request to cancel my appointments for today so that I can leave the office. I fail to see what the problem is.'

'You haven't been yourself recently, Mr Ross,' Rosemary said in a burst of courage. 'Several of us have been...'

'*Several of you?* I pay you people to work, not to gather into little covens discussing my welfare.'

'How long do you intend to be out of the office, Mr Ross?' she said, returning to her normal brisk voice, and Callum sucked in his breath, realising that an apology was called for but temporarily incapable of dispensing one. Anyone would think that his employees had nothing better to do than shadow his every movement and watch his every expression.

'I have no idea. One day, two days—maybe longer.'

'So what shall I do about...?'

'Rearrange everything in the foreseeable future. When I come back, you can schedule my time.' On which note, he disconnected the internal line and remained sitting for a few minutes longer, staring into space and brooding.

It was becoming an addiction.

Memory lane was now so well trodden that it was beginning to seem more real than what was happening in his life at the moment.

He fished into his trouser pocket, took out his wallet and extracted a crumpled piece of paper from one of the compartments.

It was a fairly pointless procedure, since he knew what was written on the paper by heart, but still he hung on to it, compulsively reading and re-reading the handful of lines that had been waiting for him two months ago on his return from New York.

She had, regrettably, turned down his proposal, she'd written, though she'd appreciated the offer. Under the circumstances, she felt that nothing further would be gained by remaining in England, and was thereby handing over responsibility for the sale of the company to Derek.

He savagely scanned the note, his mouth tightening, as it always did, when he came to the bit about wishing him all the best for the future.

Enraged, as if reading it for the first time, he crumpled the paper, then reluctantly smoothed it out and replaced it in the wallet. Then he strode to the door, flinging on his jacket in the process, and out into the connecting room where Rosemary glanced up from her computer with long-suffering wariness.

'Look,' he said awkwardly, 'I'm sorry if I overreacted just then.'

'That's all right,' Rosemary said quietly.

'I've had a lot on my mind recently…'

'Of course. I understand. Felt Pharmaceuticals has taken a lot of financial resources out of the company profits. Naturally, that would be on your mind…'

'Naturally,' Callum said, going along with that piece of fiction. In truth, the temporary drain on his financial well-being had barely crossed his mind. Within a year things would have evened out, and within a couple of years Felt's would be more than paying for itself. Life would have been a piece of cake if his only worries centred around something as piddling and unimportant as money.

'It would help if you could call me when you're about

to come back,' she said, absently flicking through the diary, which, standing above her, he could see was liberally speckled with entries. Important meetings with important people to discuss important things. Who cared?

'I'll try,' he said slowly. 'But I'm not sure how feasible that will be.' For the first time in a little over two months he managed something resembling a smile, and Rosemary offered a tentative one back in return. 'Where I'm going, the phone lines might be a little bit erratic.' He felt a wild thrill soar through him as his decision was made. No more mindless, brooding introspection, spending every waking moment haunted by images of her while he outwardly attempted to control the reins of his life and convince himself that he was better off without her around. He would go, he would find her and, if nothing else, he would get her to explain how someone could strain in his arms and then hours later bid him farewell via a note and without a backward glance.

She'd gone and he hadn't even told her that he loved her. Pride and fear of being rejected had held him back, and he was willing to shed both even if it meant trekking back to England with nothing but his wounds to nurse in private.

He packed a suitcase like a man demented, remembering her descriptions of the stifling heat and her gentle amusement at Derek's garb when he'd shown up on their compound. He flung in tee-shirts and the only three pairs of shorts he could rustle up, and underwear, and then an assorted selection of other items which he hoped would tide him over.

Then he telephoned the airport and, after an aggressive approach, during which he didn't hesitate to mention every influential name he remotely knew working in the airline industry, managed to secure a seat on the next plane out to Panama the following day.

Destiny eyed her class with a jaundiced and resigned expression. Today, only five children had shown up. The rains had come and the missing faces had caved in at the prospect of a walk in sodden undergrowth in pelting rainfall. Three were ill with the fever, which meant that she would probably have to do the trip with her father later in the evening to make sure that the fever was confinable and not something more rampant and sinister. It was a prospect that made her heart sink.

Ever since returning to Panama she'd found that the simple enthusiasm with which she'd greeted these physical and tiring duties had been difficult to muster. And there was no one in whom she could confide. Henri had taken extended leave and was currently in Paris at his mother's bedside, tending her through the final stages of a cancer about which he'd known nothing until he'd got to England, and to confess to her father that she missed England would break his heart. He needed her and she had to respond to that need, even though her heart was no longer in it. At least, not in the way it used to be. She still efficiently did what she had to do, but in the manner of an automaton, completing functions so that it could then shut down, leaving her private time to think back. Her desperate dash back to Panama, far from assuaging her wounded heart, had been a failure. The torment she'd sought to escape had dogged her right back to the jungle and showed no signs of letting up.

And the weather wasn't helping matters. The rains this time round were considerable, and she felt as though she was literally and figuratively drowning.

'You'd better go home for the day,' she said at a little

after twelve, when the rain was threatening to turn into a storm. She could barely make herself heard above the crashing of the rain against the window panes. 'And, Paolo, make sure that your brothers do some reading.' She managed a weak smile, ushering her little troop to the door and making them don plastic hoods which were fairly useless in a downpour of this nature and anyway would probably be merrily discarded the minute the compound was out of sight.

It was surreal to think that less than three months ago she had been in England, wearing clothes that looked like clothes and shoes that were ornamental rather than useful. She glanced across the open courtyard and through the driving rain saw her father beckoning to her.

'An emergency!' he was yelling, although the noise swept away a good part of what he was saying, and Destiny sighed and nodded, hurrying along the corridors of the wooden building and emerging a few minutes later through the door to her father's office.

'Apologise for disrupting your class, darling.' He ran his fingers through his sparse, greying hair and gave her a worried look. 'I've been radioed from El Real that there's an emergency.'

'What kind of emergency?'

'Lone tourist has bumped into some of our mosquitoes and contracted some kind of parasitic infection. Or, at least, that's what Enrique seems to think, but he's no doctor.'

'What about the medical services there?' Though 'medical services' was something of an overstatement to describe the sole hard-working doctor with whom they had fairly regular communication.

'Pablo's been called away for another emergency a few kilometres away and seems to have become stranded out there by the rains. Dessie, I know you probably don't want to do this, but there's no one else. If Henri had been here I would have asked him, but, really, with me gone I'd need our own qualified doctor here just in case. We've had to deal with two snake bites already in the past couple of days, and Lord knows what's happening towards Cana. I've had reports of fevers.' He looked as weary as she had ever seen him.

'Right. I'll get something packed.' She carried on discussing their method of transport, none too reliable in the current deluge, but she could feel her heart sinking fast. Her father was right. She didn't want to go. There was enough to do here and the trip, which would probably take hours and be a nightmare journey, filled her with sudden dismay.

All she wanted to do was huddle away in her room and let her mind travel back through time.

Within the hour they had told the various other members of the compound what was happening, and were climbing into their four-wheel drive.

The journey would be a combination of road and river and promised to be hellish. Despite the onslaught of rain the atmosphere was stifling and humid, and she knew that, given the muddy nature of the pathways linking all these small towns, they would spend at least a proportion of their time clearing morass from the roads in an attempt to get through. It was always the same during the rainy seasons, and this time it would be a thousand times worse because of the quantity of rainfall.

'It's ridiculous,' Destiny told her father, as they progressed at a snail's pace, with the wipers going at a rate. 'Why do tourists feel that they can travel unaided into this part of the world? What gives them the right to expect help when they get themselves into a muddle?'

'This sounds a little worse than a lost tourist who's got into a muddle,' her father said, craning forward to make sure that he kept to the barely visible marked path.

'We'll get there and he'll have nothing more than a few mosquito bites and a bad cold from getting soaked.'

'Not from what Enrique says.'

'Enrique runs the grocery store and a rooming house!' Destiny grumbled on insistently. 'He's not likely to be much of a gem when it comes to diagnosing illnesses! Did he say what the symptoms were?'

'Raging fever, apparently. The man's hallucinating.'

'I feel like I'm about to hallucinate,' she said, wiping her face with the rag she had brought with her. 'This car is going to self-combust in a minute.' The windows were rolled down, but only very slightly to allow for the rain and the heat inside the car was fierce. Even with the miniature fan affixed to the dashboard she could still feel beads of sweat rolling down her face and making her body feel like oil. She rolled her glass down a few more centimetres and was rewarded with a wash of water across her face. It was better, at any rate, than the humidity.

'I never really asked you this, Destiny, but what exactly happened out there in England?' Her father wasn't looking at her, and she felt a little jolt of shock at his question. He was a reticent man when it came to conversations about feelings and emotions, and for him to encourage one right now showed how much the question had been nagging away at the back of his mind.

'Nothing happened out there.'

'The last time we spoke when you were there, you seemed to have settled in and you were enjoying yourself.'

'I never said that I was *enjoying* myself,' she persisted

stubbornly, staring out of the window as the rain lashed the rainforest around them, making every bending tree and swirling leaf look dangerous. Men thought that they were so big and strong. Well, it only took one show of nature like this to silence them.

'Darling, you don't actually *need* to spell everything out for me. I know I'm an old duffer—'

'Dad! Don't!'

'—but I can occasionally read between the lines, and you were enjoying yourself. Nothing like that time when you were in Mexico and you were so desperate to come back home.'

They both paused as the car was manoeuvred very slowly through a minor flood, densely brown and littered with fallen leaves.

'So why did you suddenly decide to leave?'

'I didn't suddenly decide,' Destiny said awkwardly. 'I just realised that I couldn't accomplish any more over there, so I came back.'

'Henri said something about a man.'

'Henri? What did he say? It's not true!'

'He said something about this Callum character…'

'Henri doesn't know Callum from Adam!' she burst out, cursing her friend for having dumped her in the mire. She hadn't mentioned Callum Ross to her father because there had been no point. It would only have hurt and disappointed him to think that she'd got caught up in a temporary and seedy affair with someone so alien to the sort of man he would have expected for her. Not a doctor, not someone whose life-blood was rooted in environmental issues and helping other people. But a businessman. Someone whose interests were all wrapped up in making money, even when it involved marrying a woman to further his ends.

'What was he like, then?'

'What was who like?'

'You're dodging the question. And you're going into a sulk.'

'Dad, I'm a grown woman. Grown women don't go into sulks. Have you ever known me to go into a sulk?'

'No,' he admitted, but before she could give a triumphant smile, he carried on remorselessly, 'which is why your behaviour has been so odd ever since you returned. You say the right things, and never hesitate to pull your weight, but you've been wrapped up in yourself and I can't help but wonder whether something happened to you over there that you're not telling me about. If I didn't know better, I'd say that you're suffering all the symptoms of love sickness.'

'Oh, Dad, *please.*' Amazing how parents had a knack of making you feel like a child.

'And the only name that's been mentioned in connection with your stay in England, aside from the Wilson man, is this Callum character.'

'Who is just the sort of man I would never fall in love with!' She thought back to that hard, intelligent face, those skilful hands that had explored every inch of her body until she'd thought she would suffocate from desire—and then she thought of his proposal, which had been like a punch in her gut. Cold, logical, without feeling or emotion. Theoretically, the sort of man she really would never fall in love with, which just went to show how huge the gap was between theory and practice.

'Why?' her father was asking in a mildly curious voice. 'Is he cruel? A bore? Stupid?'

'No, none of those things.'

'Ah. I see,' her father murmured.

'He just expects everything to go his way, even when

his plans are…are…' Her cheeks were bright red, and not from the sweltering heat in the car. She stopped abruptly, caught off guard in the middle of her sentence. 'He thinks that because things make some kind of peculiar sense to him everyone will just fall into line and go along with what he has to offer.'

'Are we talking about his purchase of the company? Because, from the sounds of it, it seemed very generous, and it's a great relief to me that you now have more than sufficient funds to retire to England whenever you choose…'

Destiny looked at her father as though he had suddenly taken leave of his senses. What was he talking about? Ever since she had returned to Panama she'd felt as though, subtly but undeniably, things were changing around her. No comfortable Henri, no comfortable routines that she never questioned, and now her father was hinting that she might want to go back to England. Why?

'I don't intend to go back there,' Destiny said quickly. 'Why should I?'

'Why indeed?' her father said, which wasn't much of an answer. 'We should be hitting the station in the next hour or so, if the weather conditions don't get any worse; then we can get a boat to Real. With any luck, the river's going to be all right.'

'If the boatmen haven't all holed up for the rains,' Destiny said gloomily.

By the time they finally made it to the station, the dubious quality of the light was beginning to fade and, as she had feared, they were compelled to spend the night at the ranger station. There was no electricity, and bathing in the creek was out of the question because of the weather, so, after a basic meal, which was brought by them but cooked in good humour by Juan, who refused to see the massive rains as anything other than a minor nuisance, Destiny retired to her cot, sticky, muddy and dishevelled. Her feet felt stiff from the hiking boots she had worn. All around here was fer de lance territory and the thought of a snake bite further complicating things was not even to be contemplated. No one ventured out without the protection of boots. Useful, necessary, but unfortunately very conducive to sweaty feet.

Juan, because he knew them and liked them, had managed to provide two pails of creek water, so at least she found she could go to sleep with clean feet, if very little else.

And the rains, overnight, appeared to have let up a bit. She awakened to more of a persistent drizzle than the torrential, never-ending downpour that had been in evidence over the past few weeks.

'I hope your cousin's going to do the boat trip for us,' Destiny said to Juan once they were outside, 'and he hasn't got himself into one of his alcoholic jags.'

'José's given up the evil drink.' Juan grinned, while Destiny shot him a long, sceptical look. 'No, really!' he said, holding his hands up. 'I think it was after that lecture you gave him.'

'Well, your mother will be pleased.'

'Now all he has to do is find a wife and give her some grandchildren.'

'At seventeen?'

'Never too young to start.' He eyed her cheekily. 'I'd advise you not to leave it too long, old lady.' To which she told him to shut up, but she was in a less oppressed frame of mind by the time they began the second leg of their journey, boxes of provisions and clothes in hand, as well as invaluable medical supplies which were contained in a watertight box and wrapped in several layers of waterproof plastic for good measure.

As soon as they arrived at Enrique's house, her father turned to her and told her to stay put.

'I'll make a diagnosis and then we can discuss what we need to do.'

He vanished inside the room while Destiny remained outside, staring at the fine grey drizzle and trying to come to terms with a life that had been stood on its head and even now was moving at newer and crazier angles with each passing moment. She jumped when her father finally reappeared.

'It's serious, Dessie. Dengue fever. His fever's through the roof and apparently he's been slipping in and out of consciousness. I've washed him a bit, and changed him, but we need to start administering antibiotics in case secondary infections have set in. So…'

She nodded. She knew the routine. She also knew that round-the-clock antibiotics would require them both to take turns at getting up in the early hours of the morning to inject him. Under normal circumstances, and if they'd been in the makeshift hospital area in the compound, they would have had the facilities to give the antibiotics via a drip, but it would be more rudimentary here.

'Will he pull through?' she asked, following her father to the room, and he shrugged and gave a fifty-fifty gesture with his hand.

'Take a look for yourself and then tell me what you think. I haven't seen a case of Dengue this bad for a while…'

Destiny approached the bed, sympathetic to the tourist's plight but exasperated by his foolishness in thinking he could undertake a trek of mammoth proportions in damaging weather.

What she saw made the colour drain away from her face. She felt her breathing thicken. Her father was talking behind her, but his voice was background noise, insignificant next to the roaring in her head.

Callum Ross, ashen and unshaven, lay on the bed. And he was dying. She could almost see the life ebbing away from him as she continued to stare, until the ground began to feel unsteady under her feet and she reached out to support herself on the side of the bed.

'We'll do our best,' her father said quietly, approaching her, 'but it's a bad case.'

'It's Callum Ross,' she whispered, turning stricken eyes to her father. 'The man is Callum Ross.'

'What the…?'

'Please, Dad. Let me give him the antibiotics.' But her hand was shaking so much that she couldn't, and her father swiftly injected him.

She remained with him for the rest of the day, watching the flicker of eyelids over closed eyes, checking him frequently to see whether the tell tale rash that marked the end of the fever was beginning to appear.

'You fool,' she whispered, reaching out to hold his hand. 'What got into your head? Don't die on me, Callum. I'll never forgive you.' One tear spilled down her face and was quickly joined by another. When, later, her father came in to administer the next lot of medicine, she was steady enough to do it herself, and she hustled him out of the door, nodding feverishly when he told her what needed doing.

His body, which had filled every corner of her mind for the past couple of months, seemed vulnerable now that it was under attack. When she washed him, she could see the signs of wasting already beginning to set in. He wouldn't have eaten for days, and the stubble on his face was beginning to resemble the start of a beard.

'I could shave you,' she said, speaking to herself, because thus far she had had no response from him. 'Would you trust me to do that? Why couldn't you have stayed put?' she demanded, swerving away from the subject and glaring at him. 'If you've put yourself in danger because of a couple of questions you wanted to ask about the business, then I'll kill you, Callum Ross. Do you hear me?' No, of course he didn't, but she carried on talking anyway, all through the night, until sleep finally overcame her.

She was awake at the crack of dawn, leaving him alone only long enough to freshen herself and grab something to eat. She was barely aware of her father's battery of questions and offered no explanations.

When she returned to the room, it was to find that Callum at least had changed position on the bed. He was no longer on his back, with his grey face upturned, but on his side, even though his eyes were still closed.

And his breathing seemed easier as well, although she was well aware that that was probably her imagination. It was easy to become accustomed to the varying patterns of an illness until you imagined that they were less severe than they had been at the outset.

She propped him gently up and tried to spoon some liquid food down him.

'Have I told you that you're a fool, Callum Ross?' she said, growing accustomed to the sensation of making conversation into silence to someone who couldn't hear what she was saying. 'Didn't I tell you about the mishaps that happened to tourists who took risks?'

She heard the tremor in her voice. 'Dad's asking a million questions about you and I don't know what to tell him. He wants to know why I'm insisting on doing everything for you when I've explained to him what an arrogant, irritating thorn under the skin you are. He wants to know why I'm running around like a headless chicken and looking like a washed-out rag over someone I told him doesn't matter. He can't understand what you're doing in this part of the world. As usual, I'm in a mess because of you.'

She expertly took his temperature and logged it on the frightening chart that was now clipped to the top of the bed, then she sat back and looked at the man lying on the bed in front of her. 'You risked your life...for what? Some papers I may have forgotten to sign? You stupid man.' Her voice was beginning to sound unnatural again, and she breathed in deeply in an attempt to control it.

She was slowly realising that, even though she'd come back to Panama, even though she'd told herself that Panama was her country and she would remain there for evermore, doing what she'd always done, even if she died a sad, old spinster, a part of her had still believed that one day she would see him again. Because miracles happened. If Callum died now, then there would be no miracles.

Over the next day, she continued with her routine, mopping him, feeding him in a ritual that could take anything up to an hour, watching and waiting and waiting and watching, barely sleeping herself.

All she wanted was one word from him, a signal that he was on the mend.

'He's not going downhill, at any rate,' her father said on the third day, as he stood next to her and performed a number of routine examinations. 'In fact, the fever's beginning to let up a bit.' Instead of leaving the room this time, he walked slowly across to the window and stood there with his back to it.

'And I want some answers from you, young woman.'

'What answers? I can't predict the outcome of this any more than you can, Dad,' Destiny said, deliberately misreading his question, even though she knew that it was no more than a temporary stalling exercise.

'What's the relationship between you and this young man?'

'Relationship? *Relationship?*'

'That's right.' He had an implacable glint in his eye which she met with a mutinous look.

'I'm just looking after him the way I'd look after any idiot who managed to get themselves in this situation because they were too bull-headed to admit that they couldn't cope with the rigours of a journey way beyond their experience.'

Her father didn't say anything. He just continued to look at her patiently, while Callum lay inert on the bed between them.

'Okay!' she half-shouted, glaring at her father and that infernally mild expression of his which had always been more effective when it came to getting what he wanted than any Chinese water torture method. 'So we may have seen one another now and again when I was in England! Is it my fault that the man's pushy?' She folded her arms and watched as her father slowly moved towards the bed so that they were now facing each other with only the width of the bed between them. 'One minute there he was, using every trick in the book to get the company off me, and the next minute…the next minute he's forcing himself on me so that I have no option but to have dinner with him!'

'Ah.'

'Okay! So I may have…may have found him attractive…' She gave her father a weak, apologetic smile. 'Not,' she said, addressing the man on the bed because her situation was all thanks to him, 'that you look very attractive at the moment, Callum Ross! But then whose idiot fault is that?' Panic and worry made her want to strangle him and hold him tightly at the same time.

'So my little girl went to England and grew up,' her father mused slowly to himself.

'If by *growing up,* you call falling in love with the least suitable man on the face of the earth!' She tenderly stroked his forehead.

'I suspected as much.'

'It's not going to come to anything!' Destiny cried. 'He doesn't love me!'

'But you love him.'

'Life's just not fair, is it, Dad? You and Mum just clicked, but me…I had to go halfway across the world and get myself embroiled with a hardheaded businessman who doesn't know the meaning of love.'

'How do you know that?'

She sighed in resignation. 'Because he proposed to me, but *not,*' she carried on quickly, seeing the interruption forming on her father's lips, 'because he loved me. He said that an alliance would make a good business proposition. He wanted my company, we got along, and to him it made sense that we should just tie the two things together and bingo, a marriage made in heaven.' Now she was beginning to feel like a sixteen-year-old child again. Moreover, she didn't want the compassion she could see in her father's eyes. A little bit of shared hostility might have got her going on the right path, but compassion was just going to make her break down.

'So there you go. That's the relationship. I love him,

and now you know I want you to promise not to mention it again.'

They stared at one another, and then, from the bed, Callum said, 'But I was getting really interested in all of this. Please, carry on. Don't mind me.'

CHAPTER TEN

'ARE you sure it's all right for you to be here? Anything could happen.'

'Don't be such a wimp.' Destiny stepped out into the dense, inky blackness and reached out for the hand waiting for her, which slipped around her waist, pulling her against him.

'Wimp? Me? That's not what your father thinks.' Callum buried his face against her hair and reached to cup the side of her head with his hand. 'In fact,' he murmured in a satisfied voice, tickling her ear with his breath, 'if I recall, he told you how lucky you were to meet me.'

'He may have been delusional.' She was grinning as the hot night air wafted aromatically around them. In the compound, everyone was asleep, unlike outside, where the animals of the night had come out to play and could be heard calling from the trees and beyond into the depths of the forest.

They walked slowly and entwined, to one of the three benches which had been recently placed in a circular format under a spreading tree, making it a wonderful place for some of the women to do their craft-making during the day, protected from the full-frontal attack of the sun.

Nine months had changed a lot, not least on the compound, where sensibly-spent money had improved living conditions and amassed more much-needed staff to cope with Henri's departure, her own and, in due course, her father's. He would be working in the medical facilities of the Felt Pharmaceutical subsidiary, which had now only been going for a matter of a few weeks.

Nine months of absolute bliss. It still seemed hard to believe that dreams had come true...

When Callum, supposedly on his death bed and utterly unconscious to anything happening around him, had murmured those words, Destiny had been overcome by the twin emotions of shock and mortification.

They had both stared down at the bed to find Callum looking at them, eyes open and with an expression which, if not perky, had been amused enough to inform her that his brush with death had been successfully outmanoeuvred.

'My boy, you're with us at last.' Her father scurried around, taking all the routine medical checks, making sure that everything was now returning to the land of the living.

All Destiny could think of to say was, 'How long have you been listening to our conversation?'

'Is that any way to greet the man you adore, when he's been on the brink of death?'

Aside from his voice sounding weaker, any near-death experience had certainly left his mind as alert as ever it had been and his sense of humour utterly intact.

'Which,' she hissed, bending down to look at him, at once gutted by such an enormous feeling of relief that he was out of the woods that it was quite possible to allow her embarrassed anger at being eavesdropped to get the better of her, 'he has clearly managed to overcome.' He'd put her through hell, and now here he was, frail, haggard, feeble—yet still capable of rousing within her emotions that left no room for anything else.

What a consummate actor! Lying there on the bed. Had

he heard everything she had told her father? Every word? And had he been aware all along of her presence in the room, hovering over him like a desperate mother hen, not bothering to hide her tears at night because she'd foolishly imagined that he couldn't hear them?

What did it matter, anyway? He had heard enough.

'Don't pester the man, Dessie,' her father ordered, unable to hear their *sotto voce* conversation but more than capable of hearing the tenor of her voice, which contained no hint of any soothing bedside manner.

'Yes, my worshipping nurse, a little sympathy, please.' Callum gave her a weak, pathetic smile, and then added insult to injury by asking her whether she would mind feeding him a little something, because he really was quite hungry now.

'Does he think this is a hotel?' Destiny fulminated to her father, once they were safely out of the choking confines of the room, which seemed to have shrunk to the size of a matchbox the minute Callum opened his eyes. And his mouth, for that matter.

'He may be conscious, but he obviously hasn't had a good look around at his surroundings as yet,' she chuntered on, ignoring her father's lack of input into the conversation. 'He might just have realised that rustling up a few tasty morsels might be a tad more difficult than he thinks!'

'We could see our way to bread and soup, Dessie,' her father reminded her gently. 'There's no need to take it out on the poor man just because he happened to overhear what you were saying to me about—'

'Don't remind me!' Destiny nearly wailed, slopping soup into a bowl, then carefully re-covering it to protect it from the flies.

'He's been through a bad experience. Can you imagine

how hideous this whole thing must have been for him? The man nearly died, for goodness's sake!'

'I'm not saying that I'm not glad he's on the mend. I'm just saying that the two-faced cad had a right to let us know what was going on before I embarked on my soul-wrenching confession. But oh, no! *Typical!*'

She then proceeded to spend the next two days running and fetching for him. In her father's presence he professed to be much weaker than he was, refusing to answer any of her questions with a feeble wave of his hand whilst still being able to insist that she sit with him while he fed himself, taking ages in the process, and that she talk to him because, although he couldn't possibly communicate for any length of time, he still needed to feel the presence of other people around him. By 'other people,' he meant her. And having her around gave him ample opportunity to remind her of the heart-wrenching confession he had wilfully overheard.

He constantly asked her if he really was her beloved darling, and when she refused to answer smiled in an infuriatingly knowing way.

By the end of day two her father assured her that Callum was fit enough to travel back to the compound. The rains had almost completely stopped, he could now walk unaided—even though he still made a great production of it and insisted on clutching her arm whenever she was around—and her father needed to return to his base.

The trip was accomplished in half the time and without the sweltering discomfort of the drive to the outpost, and by the time they arrived back at the compound Destiny was determined to pin him to a wall until he told her why he'd made the trip in the first place.

If he had come for a signature on something, then she

would give it to him and send him on his way, because being so close to him with her feelings so nakedly exposed was tearing her apart. The constant feel of his body against hers as he used her as a propping post sent ragged emotions flying through her, and the whole business was driving her crazy.

She had fled to Panama to escape him, and now found herself in the worst possible spot she could have imagined. He'd discovered how she felt about him and he was determined to wrench every ounce of advantage that he could from the situation.

No opportunity to remind her of her regrettable confession was left unturned. When he wasn't insisting on her personal attention she felt him watching her, but stoically refused to meet his eyes and see the smug knowledge resting there.

If this was his way of getting his own back on her for having run out on him and his cold-hearted marriage proposal, then he had hit jackpot.

As soon as she'd ensconced him in the room he would be having until he was ready to leave, she closed the door behind them and stood there, hands on hips, watching as he indolently took the chair by the window.

'You can stop pretending now,' she informed him without preamble, ignoring the innocently raised eyebrows forming a question. 'And you can stop playing the innocent. You know exactly what I'm talking about.'

'Should you really be taking this tone with someone who's still recovering from a near-death experience?'

'If you don't cut it out, Callum Ross, you'll be facing another near-death experience and it won't be caused by a mosquito! Don't think that I'm too stupid to see through your little games.'

'What little games?' More innocent enquiry in his

voice until she wanted to scream. Instead, she swallowed hard and took a couple of deep, reviving breaths.

'So I ran out on you. Maybe I should have stayed in England and told you to your face that I wasn't about to enter into marriage with someone who saw me as a useful commodity with the added bonus of sex toy until the novelty wore off. I was a coward, but…'

'And now I understand why,' he murmured, in such a soft voice that she had to reluctantly install herself closer to where he was just to hear him properly.

'Yes,' Destiny said bitterly, 'now you know why. And you're basking in the knowledge, aren't you? Your ego must have taken a bashing when you got back from New York to find that I'd disappeared, but you've had your little gloat now. If you came here for me to sign something, then give it to me, let me sign it, and then you can go and leave me alone to get on with my life.' A red mist of self-pity and lurking humiliation formed over her eyes like a cloud.

'And what if I came here to propose to you again?' he asked softly.

'Then you can go back to England and remember what I wrote in that note. The answer is still no.'

'You love me…'

The words were like a dagger jutting into her soft flesh. 'It'll pass,' she told him acidly. 'Like an illness. But there's no way that you'll use what you know to your advantage. Anyway, what would be the point of marrying me now? You got what you wanted all along. I kept the properties and you got the company.'

'Maybe I want the country house as well,' he murmured, looking at her unflinchingly.

'To develop? Something else to add to your portfolio?'

'Maybe I want to live there… It would be a rather

spectacular place for a family…lots of space for lots of kids…'

The words swam seductively around her.

'Then you'd better start looking for a woman you love,' she said in a dull monotone, alarmed by the flight of fancy that had taken her back to the country estate, but this time with this man by her side and children romping around by their feet. A charming little tableau, she thought, were it not for one or two glaring technicalities.

'Why would I do that?' he asked, tilting his head to one side quizzically. 'When I've already found her?'

'Stop it,' she whispered. Tears were gathering in the corners of her eyes and she angrily blinked them away, coincidentally blinking away the vision of him in front of her, looking at her in that way, that way that suggested the impossible, even though she knew that he was still playing games with her.

'No, I won't. I can't,' he said huskily, so that now a desperate kind of hope was beginning to wage war with her grim acceptance. And, like a weed, the hope was sending out shoots everywhere.

'What are you talking about?' Destiny asked in a small, despairing voice.

'I'm talking about you and me and why I trudged halfway across the world to get here. All for you. I don't need your signature on anything aside from on a marriage licence.'

'I told you…'

'You're not listening, my darling.'

It was the tenderness in his voice that did it. She looked at him fully in the face, willing him to say what she wanted to hear but bracing herself in case the words she craved veered off somewhere along the line, just as they had done the last time. She reminded herself viciously that this was but one moment in time, and if it proved a bad moment then it would be washed away eventually and become no more painful than a distant memory. He would go; she would stay; life would carry on the way it always did. Hadn't it been carrying along for the past two months, ever since she had returned from England? She hadn't died from a broken heart, had she?

'I came here to tell you that…' His words dried up and a faint flush began spreading along his neck. 'That…when you ran out on me like that…' He raked long fingers through his hair and told her that he could do with some water, which she refused to get.

'I'm still very weak.'

'Carry on with what you were saying.'

'When you ran out on me like that…' he continued, like a record that had become stuck in a groove.

'Yes?' She had every intention of pushing the needle a bit further.

'I…it was like a punch in the stomach…'

'Oh.'

He tilted her face to his and ran his finger along the side of her cheek. 'No, I'm lying. It was much, much worse than that. It was like watching my life run away down a gutter because…I love you. That's why I came here. To tell you that I love you.'

'To tell me that you love me.' The phrase tasted so delightfully delicious on her lips, did such soaring things to her heart, that she just wanted to repeat it over and over again. She laughed incredulously. 'Because *you* love *me*. Because,' she said, relishing the revelation, 'you love *me.*'

'And because, my darling, I want to marry you. I want to have you by my side and in my bed for the rest of my life. Because I want you to have my babies and be there with them, waiting for me at the end of a long day. To touch, to hold, to caress, to grow old with me, to laugh with me, to do everything under the sun with me.'

'Penny for them.'

The deep voice interrupted her thoughts and she smiled to herself in the dark. 'I was thinking about…everything.' She rested her head against his shoulder. 'About us, the wedding, and now this…'

She patted her stomach and felt a warm glow of contentment.

'We'll have to bring him back here, you know. Or her. To see where I lived for so long. He won't be able to believe it when he's running around the grounds of the house, that his mother ran around different grounds when she was young. And with Dad leaving I feel a little as if part of me is vanishing for ever.'

'It's not vanishing,' Callum said softly. 'It's something that's shaped you and will be with you for ever. It's just given way to something else, a different way of life. And of course we'll be back to Panama often, to see your father when he's here.'

'You mean, your fan?' she teased. Far from disliking Callum, her father had warmed to him instantly, and the pride on his face at their small wedding still had the power to make her feel tearful.

'One of my fans,' he said airily. 'The other one's here next to me and number three will be on the scene in a matter of three months. What more could any man ask for?'

Or woman, for that matter, she thought lazily. Who could ask for any more perfection?

EPILOGUE

'WELL, I think it's time we decided to go for it. There'll be one or two changes to your lifestyle… Could you cope…? Do you even *want* to cope? Am I presuming too much?'

'How can you even think that you're presuming too much? After all the things I've told you, you little fool. I can't imagine any kind of life without you in it…'

'So if I asked you to marry me, your answer would be…?'

'Yes! Yes, a thousand times over! Yes, yes, yes!'

There was much fumbling, then a small box was retrieved from a trouser pocket. The look in her eyes, eyes that could still turn his bones to water, made the unaccustomed and arduous hike through jewellery shops worth every minute of exhaustion.

'My mother is going to be so pleased,' he murmured with blushing pleasure.

'*Only* your mother?'

'Pleased doesn't begin to tell you what I feel now. I'm walking on cloud nine. But…'

'No buts.' She slipped the ring onto her finger and held it up to the light, letting herself be dazzled by the solitaire glow from the diamond.

'Panama is completely different from London,' he said gravely.

'One city is much the same as another when you're with someone you love,' she answered in as grave a voice as his. And she meant every word of it. She closed her eyes and sighed with happiness as he leaned across the small table in the restaurant to place a kiss on her mouth, a kiss that was as tender as it was laden with the heady promise of the life stretching out before them.

Everything was so different and so good. She was even beginning to learn French, to be as bilingual as he was.

'And,' he said, sitting back and leaning with his elbows resting on the table, 'how do you feel about starting a family? I have to admit that when we went to see Destiny and Callum and their baby, I felt a little envious.'

'I know. Little Rosie's perfect, isn't she? Those green, green eyes and black, black hair.' She smiled at the memory of her one-time fiancé and his fierce devotion to the two women in his life. Destiny and baby Rose. He had barely been able to tear his proud eyes away from the two of them.

'Yes, my darling Henri,' Stephanie said dreamily, 'I think starting a family would be a very good idea indeed...'

Award-winning author **Anne McAllister** was once given a blueprint for happiness that included a nice, literate husband, a ramshackle Victorian house, a horde of mischievous children, a bunch of big friendly dogs, and a life spent writing stories about tall dark handsome heroes. "Where do I sign up?" she asked, and promptly did. Lots of years later, she's happy to report, the blueprint was a success. She's always happy to share the latest news with readers at her website: www.annemcallister.com and welcomes their letters there or at PO Box 3904, Bozeman, Montana 59772, USA (SAE appreciated).

Watch out for Anne McAllister's latest emotional and gripping read, on sale next month, in Modern Romance™!

THE INCONVENIENT BRIDE

by

Anne McAllister

Thanks to Jane Dolter and April Collier for helping
Sierra do all that hair!
And for Ann Leslie Tuttle who is everything an editor
should be: helpful, wise, patient and encouraging –
especially when it wasn't even her book!
For Jack and Judy
Happy 30th!

CHAPTER ONE

"YOUR father on line one."

They were the words Dominic Wolfe least wanted to hear.

He sighed and shut his eyes. It had already been a hellish morning.

He liked a brisk walk to his office. The mile trek downtown from his Fifth Avenue apartment was ordinarily exactly what he needed to compose his thoughts, run over his mental list of to-do's and psyche himself up to tackle the day.

Today he'd got drenched halfway there. The "early morning shower" predicted by the weather service had become an eight a.m. cloudburst instead. And by the time Dominic had decided it was more than a sprinkle, taxis had become nonexistent.

He'd arrived, damp and annoyed, to a message that the president of the company with whom he was negotiating a buyout had chosen this moment to rethink his options. While he was trying to sort that out, a supplier in Japan sent a fax saying the shipment would be delayed. His secretary, Shyla, was morning sick, pale and wan and gasping, although trying to mask it with ruthless efficiency.

And Marjorie—the woman he'd been quite sure would never want more from him than his presence in her bed— had just banged the receiver in his ear after delivering an ultimatum: if he wanted to see the inside of her bedroom again, she expected an engagement ring.

And now the old man was on line one?

Dominic did *not* want to talk to the old man.

"Did you hear me, Dominic?" His secretary, Shyla, in-

5

terpreted his silence for distraction, not reluctance. "He said it was urgent."

It was always urgent now that his father was no longer running things.

Douglas Wolfe had far too much time on his hands since he'd retired. He'd gone merrily off to Florida eighteen months ago, telling Dominic he intended to catch up on his reading, fishing and all the other things his years at the top of corporate America had never permitted him to do.

Shuffleboard, Dominic had thought. He'd expected his father to fish and read, to play games and eat Egg McMuffins with his friends.

Instead the old man had spent his every waking moment researching new strategies for the company he was no longer running and attempting to assure its future. That meant he was determined to find the woman who would tempt Dominic to leave bachelorhood behind.

It wasn't going to happen.

Dominic had told him that. They'd been over it a hundred times. More.

Douglas had tried his hand at matchmaking once before. He'd found Dominic a fiancée a dozen years ago. Carin had been absolutely perfect. Young, sweet, gorgeous, and the daughter of one of Wolfe Enterprises' biggest suppliers. Dominic had been young, handsome, ambitious, and naive. He'd thought marriages like that worked out.

He'd never expected Carin to jilt him.

But she had. He'd been left standing at their Bahamas hideaway with a ring, a red face and two hundred intrigued wedding guests, but no bride.

He sure as hell wasn't letting the old man have another shot.

For a dozen years, Douglas had lain low, had let Dominic revel in easy bachelordom. But retirement had apparently pricked his need to meddle again. For the past eighteen months, he'd showed up with a woman every month for Dominic to "look over."

Dominic had assumed it was biological—some sort of urge to become a grandfather that hit men when they turned sixty-five. Thus he'd expected the old man to let up when his youngest brother Rhys had, just this past Christmas, in-advertently provided their father with twins.

But it hadn't mattered. It was May now, and in the past five months Douglas had appeared with one woman after another—each as precise and tailored and businesslike as Dominic himself.

They wouldn't have sex, they'd have mergers, he'd told the old man after the last one. There was no way on earth he would ever consider someone like that!

"Well, what do you want?" Douglas had sputtered.

"To be left alone," Dominic growled and banged down the phone.

He had been for the past three weeks. He'd hoped his father had got the message at last. Now the old man was on line one.

Dominic punched the button and barked into the phone. "What?"

"And a lovely fine morning to you, too," his father's cheerful voice boomed in his ear.

"Not lovely here. It's raining like hell." Dominic scowled out the floor-to-ceiling windows of his office onto the gray damp dismal world beyond.

"I'll tell Evelyn to pack my umbrella and rubber boots."

"Pack—? Why?" Dominic sat up straight, his fingers strangling his Mont Blanc pen.

His earlier vague sense of foreboding was presently slam-ming him right between the eyes. Why should his father's housekeeper be packing Douglas's umbrella and rubber boots, unless—

"I'm having dinner with Tommy Hargrove this evening. Been talking to him about maybe coming on board. So

Viveca and I are catching the noon flight to New York and—''

''Whoa. Stop. Tommy Hargrove is not coming on board.''

If they'd been through this once, they'd been through it a thousand times. Tommy Hargrove's small company might once have been a possible acquisition. It was no longer. ''Wolfe Enterprises isn't in the market for a small outdated communications firm. And who the hell is Viveca?''

''Tommy and I are old friends.'' Douglas ignored the last question, going on smoothly, ''We go back a long way, since before you were in diapers, young man.''

Whenever Dominic became ''young man'' it meant Douglas was meddling again.

''And,'' his father went on, ''it is not a foregone conclusion that Tommy's company isn't just what we need.''

''Yes,'' Dominic said, his voice pure steel. ''It is.''

''We'll see,'' Douglas said enigmatically.

''We won't—''

''It is possible,'' Douglas went on as if Dominic hadn't begun to speak, ''that I could agree with you. If you and Viveca…''

Dominic slammed his pen down on the solid teak desk.

''Haven't I spoken of Viveca?'' Douglas was all mild innocence.

''No,'' Dominic said through his teeth.

''Ah. Well, she's why I called actually,'' Douglas said with determined good cheer. ''Lovely girl. Stunning, really. Pauline Moore's daughter. You remember Pauline. Miss America pageant. Mensa. Phi Beta Kappa. Ran into Pauline and her daughter at the club on Monday. Pauline introduced us. Wondered if I didn't have a son about her age. Of course she meant Rhys. Viveca's much younger than you. Gorgeous girl. Long blond hair. Brilliant. Witty. Charming. Did I tell you she's getting a Ph.D. in art history. She—'' Douglas was gearing up for a long discussion of Viveca Moore's best qualities.

"Cut to the chase," Dominic said wearily.

"Marry her," Douglas said flatly.

"What!"

"You heard me. Get married. To her. You need to get married. To have children. To carry on the line. Marry Viveca," Douglas said, "and I'll tell Tommy we've taken another direction."

"I'll tell Tommy we've taken another direction and I won't have to marry her."

There was a second's silence. "Then I'll tell the board I don't support you."

It was as if all of Manhattan had ground to a halt. For one long moment there wasn't a sound, beyond the pounding of his own blood in Dominic's ears.

And then he said with a calmness he didn't begin to feel, "Is that a threat?"

"Of course it's not a threat," Douglas blustered. "It's a damn promise, boy. You're not getting any younger. You're thirty-six years old! You should have got over that nonsense with Carol—"

"Carin."

"Carol, Carin—whatever her name was—years ago! It's like riding a horse, lad! If you fall off you don't run away and lick your wounds, you damned well get back on again."

"Marry the next woman down the pike, you mean?" Dominic was amazed his voice sounded so mild. He felt like the top of his head was about to come off.

"Of course not. Not just any woman! But there's plenty of damn fine gals around. You've had a dozen years to find one and you haven't done it!"

"Maybe I don't want to."

"Nonsense!" Douglas didn't even consider that. "You need to. For the business if not for yourself. People trust a married man. He seems responsible, reliable. They've given you the benefit of the doubt for years. But you're walking the edge now. Besides," Douglas changed his tack, "you've got the makings of a fine family man. A fine father."

"Like you?" Dominic's voice was scathing, but his father didn't even notice.

"Chip off the old block," Douglas agreed without missing a beat. "That's why I know you'll like Viveca."

"I don't want—"

"You don't know what you want anymore! I bring you a redhead, you want a blonde. I bring you a homemaker, you want a Ph.D. I bring you a—"

"I want you to stop bringing me women!"

"I will."

"When?"

"After tonight. After you meet Viveca. You won't want another woman after Viveca! She's everything you want. A blonde. A homemaker *with* a Ph.D.! And—"

"And if I don't marry her you're going to go to the board with a vote of no confidence," Dominic said through his teeth.

There was a split second's hesitation. Then Douglas said, "You're damn right."

Dominic understood that split second. It was the point-of-no-return. It was the jumping off spot. The last chance to turn back.

Douglas hadn't turned back.

"Viveca and I will be in the city this evening," he said firmly. "Join us—and Tommy—for dinner at Le Sabre's. At eight."

"I've got—"

"At eight, Dominic."

The phone crashed down in his ear.

Dominic stared at it. Then he set it slowly back in its cradle. He tilted back in his chair and shoved it round so that he sat staring at the rain coursing down his window on the world. He drummed his fingers lightly on the arms of his chair and considered his options.

He supposed idly that he should have spiked his father's guns before now. He should have put his foot down years ago, should have said, "Back off," both in terms of the company and in terms of his life.

He hadn't because he'd spent his life admiring his father. He'd admired the old man's determination, his tenacity, his fierce, indomitable will. He'd grown up wanting to be just like him.

He'd dug in and endured the "from the ground up" apprenticeship that his father had deemed necessary for taking over the business. He'd got his hands dirty. He'd worked days and nights, holidays and weekends. He'd done everything that was ever asked of him—and he'd done it well.

A dozen years ago he'd even let the old man pick his bride because he understood why his father wanted ties between his company and Carin's family's. It had been good business sense, and he'd liked Carin—what he knew of her. He'd been sure he would have made a good husband.

It was Carin who had run. Not him.

And when she had, leaving him hurt and humiliated beyond belief, still Dominic had believed in the theory behind his father's actions.

Even now—God help him—he believed Douglas was right. In business married men did seem more trustworthy. More predictable. Less like loners or loose cannons. Some of the CEOs in other corporations he'd done business with recently had implied as much. They'd suggested that he bring his wife to various functions and had lifted a brow just a little when he'd said he didn't have one.

He imagined his father was right, too, that this Viveca, whoever she was, would be the consummate corporate wife. Blonde. Brilliant. Bloodless. Charming. Capable. Clever. The perfect accessory for a CEO to wear on his arm.

Dominic shut his eyes for a minute and saw the future. Saw himself and the bloodless blonde his father had chosen for him.

He opened his eyes and stared out the window at the streaming rain.

It was warm inside, cold out there. The windows were fogging up, reminding him of other foggy windows, of a night out of time—of steam and sex and a woman who wasn't bloodless at all.

And he felt his body harden now at the mere memory of her—and of that night.

For the past three months he'd been doing his damnedest to forget.

He'd been trying since February to pretend it never happened, Then, because he couldn't manage that, he'd tried to convince himself that it would never happen again.

He didn't believe it ever could.

Sex like they'd had that night was a once in a lifetime thing. It had to be. He'd certainly never had it before—or since.

It certainly hadn't happened with Marjorie.

What if—

He tried not to pursue that thought. He couldn't help himself.

What if it hadn't been a fluke? What if they could do it again? And again?

His mouth went dry. His palms got damp. A very unprofessional, unbusinesslike reaction was taking place in his fine worsted charcoal wool trousers. He tugged at his grey-and-burgundy striped tie. It was the same tie…the one she had…

He sucked air.

Then he shoved himself out of his chair, stalked across the room and flung open the door to the outer office.

Shyla held out the phone to him. "Dominic, Mr. Shiguru on line two and Ms. Beecher has been on hold—"

"Not now." He didn't even break stride as he grabbed his raincoat and headed for the door.

"Dominic! Where are you going?"

"To get a wife."

Sierra should have known it was going to be one of those days.

The moment she opened her eyes to see the rain pounding down the tulips in the window box on her fire escape, she should have closed them again and pulled the covers over her head.

Instead she'd pasted on one of her eternal-optimist smiles and told herself how good the rain was for the flowers. She refused to think how bad it was for hair.

Her mistake.

Of course it was bad for hair. It was also bad for tempers and taxis and terminally temperamental clients with the artistic vision of brain-dead walruses, not to mention for photographers whose babies had been teething all night and models with naturally curly locks.

No, it was not a good day.

Sierra did not expect every day to be stress-free. But the bitch-quotient in Finn MacCauley's studio this morning was threatening to blow Manhattan right off the map.

"Hurry up," Finn was saying for the fiftieth time that hour. "Move it! Move it! Move it! Do you know how many damn dresses we've still got left to shoot?"

Sierra didn't know. She didn't care.

The dresses weren't her problem. Her problem was the hair.

Sleek hair. Piled hair. Severe shellacked hair.

"She's frizzing again!" Ballou, the temperamental client pointed at Alison, the goddess from the Bronx. "Look at her!" He grabbed fistfuls of Alison's long wildly curling hair straight out from her head and yelled at Sierra, "She can't frizz! She has to be sleek! Make her sleek!"

It would be easier to make a porcupine bald. Sierra sighed. "Hang on. Let me put on some more gel. Just a little gel."

"Sierra, for Pete's sake!" Finn was tearing his own hair.

"Let's go. Stop messing with her and get the hell out of the way."

"I just need—"

"Sleek," Ballou insisted. "Smooth. Straight as a die." He made up and down knifing motions with his hands.

Then why did you ask for a model with naturally curly hair? Sierra wanted to scream.

"I'm frizzing, too!" Delilah, the other model, complained.

"And not the blue. I don't like her in the blue," Ballou decided, scrutinizing the dress Alison had just put on. "Let's try the yellow."

"I can't wear yellow!" the model objected. "I look dead in yellow."

"You're going to *be* dead in yellow," Finn said, "if you don't shut up. We have thirty of these damn things to get finished and we've only done six! Sierra! Let's go!"

They went. The models stood patiently while Sierra slicked them down again. Ballou fussed and fumed and fretted and changed his mind and Finn griped and growled and cussed and shot.

And all the while Sierra tried to stay up-beat because after all, she told herself, in the greater course of the universe what difference did it make?

It was rain. A yellow dress or a blue one. Curly hair. Frizzy hair. Straight hair. What difference did it make?

It didn't.

Not like Frankie.

That was really what made it a lousy day—thinking about Frankie.

Frankie Bartelli was going to die.

Sierra hated to even think that. Her mind rebelled at the thought. Her emotions rejected it furiously. But for all her rebellion and all her rejection, it was going to happen— unless he got a kidney transplant—and soon.

Sure, some people lived a long time with kidney problems. Some people did just fine on dialysis for years and years.

But they weren't Frankie, who for the last few months had been fading right before Sierra's eyes.

They weren't eight years old, either, with their whole lives ahead of them.

They didn't dream about climbing mountains and going fishing and playing baseball. They didn't draw the niftiest spaceships or the scariest green monsters or detailed plans for the "best tree house in the world."

They didn't love *Star Trek* and root beer floats and double cheese pizza. They didn't have big brown eyes and sooty dark lashes and a cowlick that even Sierra's most determined hair gel couldn't subdue for long. They didn't have the world's croakiest laugh and a grin that melted you where you stood.

Or maybe they did.

Sierra didn't know. She didn't know about anyone—except Frankie.

He and his mother Pam had been Sierra's neighbors since she'd moved into half of the third floor of a four-story walk-up in the Village three years ago.

Frankie had been a lot healthier-looking then. A lot stronger. And Pam hadn't had that hunted, haunted look in her dark brown eyes.

"I don't know what I'm going to do," she'd said, her voice cracking when she'd first told Sierra what the doctors had told her.

To Sierra it was simple. "If he needs a transplant, we'll get him a transplant," she had vowed.

But Pam, desperate but realistic, had shaken her head in despair. "The hospital wants two hundred, fifty thousand dollars up front before they'll even agree to put him on the list."

It seemed like highway robbery to Sierra. Extortion. Every vile thing she could think of. Just because Pam was a self-

employed illustrator whose insurance coverage had managed
to fall through some crack, that was no reason for them to
deny Frankie.

And she said so hotly and furiously more than once.

But they had denied him. Just this morning Pam had repeated it. "They won't even see him unless I come up with
a quarter of a million dollars."

Sierra had almost twenty thousand in savings. Sometimes
it seemed like a lot. But compared to what Frankie needed,
it was a pittance. Even if she begged on the streets she didn't
think she could come up with as much as Pam needed. But
she wasn't ready to admit defeat.

"I'll think of something," she'd vowed and squeezed
Pammie's hands. "Don't worry."

But if she had told Pammie not to, Sierra worried herself.
All morning long, she'd worried. But she hadn't come up
with any ideas at all.

"Okay. Let's go. Long necks, ladies. Lots of chin. Gimme
lots of chin." Finn started moving again, shooting as he did
so. "Don't block each other, for God's sake. Move,
Alison."

Alison moved—right into one of the reflectors. It fell over
with a crash.

Ballou dropped the half dozen dresses in his arms. "Oh,
no! Ohmigod!" He scrabbled for them. "They'll get
creased! Sierra, help!"

"Damn!" Finn's face turned red. "Sierra, get the reflec-
tor."

"I'm frizzing again," Alison wailed. "Sierra! Do something!"

And just when Sierra thought the day couldn't possibly
get any worse, the studio door banged open and in strode
Dominic Wolfe.

Strong, Finn's lady-marine-drill-sergeant office manager
came hurrying, hard on his heels. "Excuse me, sir! *Sir!* You
can't go in there!"

But Strong didn't know Dominic Wolfe.

"The Hotshot With The Cool Head," the *Times* business pages had headlined him just last week in an in-depth profile of the hard-driving, hard-working CEO of Wolfe Enterprises that they'd called "an old-fashioned business with a new-fashioned future."

What they meant was that under his guidance, Wolfe Enterprises, a communications company had moved from radio and television right into the newest electronic and digital media without a glitch.

"Because Dominic Wolfe knows what he wants," the article had said. "And what Dominic wants, Dominic gets."

And that, Sierra could have told them, was the honest-to-God truth.

Strong might have been no more than an angry mosquito as she buzzed after him.

Sierra watched in morbid astonished fascination, aware that her heart was kicking over in her chest. She hadn't seen Dominic Wolfe since her sister Mariah married his brother Rhys three months ago.

She had very carefully *not* seen him since that time—just as he had very carefully *not* seen her.

She had done her damnedest to forget him.

And she'd certainly never expected him to turn up in the middle of Finn MacCauley's studio, heading straight toward her.

But before he reached her, Finn stepped between them. "Wolfe?" He looked perplexed, obviously wondering what his friend Rhys's high-powered CEO brother was doing here.

They all wondered—the annoyed Strong, the slack-jawed Ballou, the starry-eyed models, the makeup artist—and Sierra.

Especially Sierra.

Since he'd pushed his way through the door, he hadn't taken his eyes off her. And whatever amazing electricity had begun sizzling between them the first time they'd met when she'd stormed into his office last summer, demanding the whereabouts of his brother, was still sizzling all these months later—even though they denied it, assuaged it, tried to ignore it.

Now she stepped round Finn and looked up into Dominic's ice-chip eyes. "What do you want?"

"I want you to marry me," Dominic said.

He didn't care that she looked poleaxed or that Finn looked murderous or that everyone else seemed to think he'd just escaped from bedlam.

He repeated the words. "Marry me," in case she wanted to pretend she hadn't heard them.

"Marry...you?"

It was the first time he'd seen Sierra Kelly slack-jawed. But at least she'd finally found her voice. And privately Dominic was satisfied that he'd actually succeeded in shocking her.

"That's what I said." He grinned now, daring her.

And, because she was Sierra, she tipped her sock-it-to-me chin right straight at him and dared him right back. "You'd have to pay me a million bucks!"

"Half a million."

"What!" She went beyond slack-jawed, straight to flabbergasted. "Be serious."

"I am serious." He grabbed her arm and dragged her out into the reception area where half a dozen pairs of prying eyes couldn't oversee and an equal number of ears couldn't overhear. "You want a half a million bucks, fine."

"But—" she started to protest, then looked at him narrowly, suspiciously. "Why?"

"Because."

She laughed. "Because? Oh, there's a reason. This from the man the *Times* calls 'focused, decisive, a man who knows his own mind.'"

Dominic snorted. "One reporter's impression."

"Backed up by pretty solid evidence," Sierra said. "So, I repeat, why do you want to marry me?"

He rubbed a hand over his hair, still damp from the rain and admitted, "I don't."

Sierra's hazel eyes flashed. She folded her arms across her Day-Glo orange rib-topped chest, but not before he'd noted the faintest outline of her nipples. He felt a stirring in his groin.

"Well, then?" Sierra eyed him narrowly. She tapped the toe of her boot.

Dominic gritted his teeth. "I need to get married."

"I thought only women needed to get married."

Damn her smart mouth! He could feel heat climbing up his neck. "It's time I got married. CEOs look more responsible when they're married."

"You're marrying *me* to look responsible?"

"I'm marrying to shut my old man up! I want him to get the hell out of my life! I want *him* to stop trying to find me a wife. I want him to get his claws out of me and out of the company and stay the hell down in Florida playing shuffleboard where he belongs!"

"Like you would be content to play shuffleboard."

Dominic blinked. "What?"

Sierra rolled her eyes. "You wouldn't want to spend your life playing shuffleboard. And you're just like him."

"The hell I—well, so what if I am!" Dominic scowled and kneaded the taut muscles at the back of his neck. Then he found his rationale. "He'd do the same damn thing I'm doing then. He'd do things his own way."

"He'd marry me?" Sierra said skeptically. "He'd marry a woman with magenta hair?"

"It's not magenta," Dominic muttered, giving her tousled locks a quick assessing glance. "It's purple."

Actually it was more of a magenta, now that she mentioned it. A very vivid magenta and not easily ignored, unless you looked the other way, which was what he tried to do. But his eyes kept coming back to it with a certain morbid fascination.

But morbid fascination, to be honest, was a good part of Sierra's appeal. Maybe not the only part, but it would serve the old man right when Dominic introduced Sierra as his wife. He could see what he'd driven his eldest son to!

"Purple, magenta," Sierra brushed his quibble off. She was still looking at him as if he'd lost his mind. "I'm thinking maybe green next week. I did it green for St. Patrick's," she told him with a grin.

She was baiting him and he knew it. "So, what do you say?" he persisted.

"I think you're insane."

"Probably." He waited.

"You're actually serious?"

"I'm serious."

Still she hesitated. She nibbled on her lower lip. Dominic remembered nibbling on that lip. He remembered the taste of her—hadn't been able to forget the taste of her! He smothered a groan.

"Sierra?" he said impatiently.

"Half a million?"

It was the last thing he'd figured she would say. Sierra Kelly—the nearest thing to a free spirit he knew—was not a money-grubber. At least he hadn't imagined that she was. He frowned at her, but she didn't back down. And he had gone too far to back down now himself.

Besides, a half a million to get the old man off his back permanently was a bargain.

He shrugged irritably. "Half a million."

"Now? You'll give it to me now?"

"You want to stop at a bank on the way to the court-house?" He was halfway between sarcasm and disbelief.

But Sierra nodded gravely. "Yes. Please."

He stared at her, wondering what went on inside her magenta-colored head. But he was annoyed enough, and reck-less enough at the moment, not to care. "It's a deal," he said. "For half a million bucks you'll marry me this after-noon."

Sierra only hesitated a second. "Yes."

Any minute now, Sierra figured, she'd wake up.

She'd yawn and stretch and open her eyes to stare at the cracked ceiling above her narrow futon bed. And she would laugh at the craziness of her dreams.

Marry Dominic Wolfe?

Sierra had had some weird dreams in her lifetime, but never one as weird as that. She blinked as she spritzed Alison's hair. She rolled her shoulders and shook her head, trying to wake up. Surely it was time for the alarm to ring!

"What's the matter with you?" Dominic demanded.

The matter was that she was awake.

He lifted his arm and shot back his cuff to glance at his watch. "We need to get moving."

"Can't," Sierra said. "Not yet. I have work to do. A job. A commitment," she explained when she realized that he wouldn't think her job was worth bothering about. He understood commitments at least.

His jaw tightened, and she thought he would object. But finally he nodded. "Then do it. Let's get this show on the road."

And as Sierra stood there, mouth ajar, he pitched in and got things going.

No, that didn't describe it. He didn't pitch in. He com-mandeered. He took one look around and decided what needed to be done.

"You," he said to Alison, "Stop sniveling and get dressed. You, too," he said to Delilah. "And get your fin-gers out of your hair."

To a stupefied Ballou, he said, "Stop standing around like

a moron. Get those dresses out and ready. Shake them out. Have the next one ready as soon as Finn finishes.''

To Finn he said, ''We need to be done by two. And we'll need witnesses. Sierra and I are getting married. Have her—'' he jerked his head toward Strong ''—call Izzy.''

Finn stared, poleaxed, first at Dominic, then at Sierra. ''You're going to marry him?'' He sounded as disbelieving as Sierra felt.

But there were some things Finn didn't know about. Like the chemistry that had been bubbling between her and Dominic for months. Like the night after Mariah and Rhys's wedding. Like the most sizzling sex she'd ever experienced. Like the fact that she hadn't been able to forget the man she'd shared it with even though she knew she should, even though she'd tried. Like Frankie.

Especially Frankie.

''I'm going to marry him, yes.'' She nodded her head.

If Finn considered arguing, a long look into her eyes apparently made him decide not to. ''Right,'' he said. ''Two it is.''

''We can't,'' Ballou protested.

''No way,'' cried the models.

At five of two they were done.

''Let's go.'' Dominic was tapping his foot as she packed up the tackle box in which she carried her gear. Then she grabbed her jacket, stuffed her arms in it, and picked up the tackle box, hugging it against her chest.

''Where are you going with that?'' Dominic demanded.

''It goes where I go,'' Sierra said stubbornly. She looked down at his briefcase. ''Like yours.''

He sighed mightily. ''Fine. Come on.''

''What about a license?'' she asked as he spirited her down the elevator.

''We'll get one.''

''What about a waiting period?'' She was sure there must be one.

"Normally twenty-four hours," Dominic said. "I can get us an exception." He was dragging her out the door, through the rain, and into the hired car waiting at the curb.

"This is insane, you know that, don't you?" she muttered, scrambling in ahead of him. The windows were steamed. She remembered other windows…

"Yes." Dominic climbed in beside her. He was so close she could feel the heat from his body, remembered how very hot that body could be…

"You'll regret it tomorrow," she said with an edge of desperation to her voice.

"Very likely." He banged the door shut behind him.

"*I'll* regret it tomorrow." She clutched the tackle box like it was a life preserver in a storm-swept sea.

"Without a doubt." Then he turned to face her squarely, and she saw a wild, reckless look in Dominic Wolfe's normally cool blue eyes. Hot ice. That was what it made her think of. It was a look Sierra remembered seeing only once before—on the wildest, craziest night of her life.

"So you have to decide—are you in or not?"

For three months she'd tried to forget that night. She hadn't forgotten.

From the glitter in his eyes, she knew Dominic hadn't, either.

Marrying Dominic *was* insane.

She *would* regret it. So would he.

They had nothing but sex between them. Primal attraction. Animal hunger. Lust. A four-letter word that started with L, but hardly the right one on which to base a marriage. But what was the use of being a gambler if you never threw the dice.

They went to the bank.

He got her a check. Made them print it out, spelled out her name. "Sierra Kelly Wolfe," he said, "because you will be when you cash it." And he thrust it into her hand.

He didn't ask what she was going to do with it. He didn't seem to even care. "Satisfied?" he asked as she stared at it, counting the zeroes.

Sierra, trying not to gape, nodded dumbly. "Yes."

"Good." He steered her out of the bank and bundled her back into the car. "City hall," he told the driver.

Sierra hadn't been to city hall since she'd applied for her cosmetology license. She was amazed to find they got their marriage license in the same room. She didn't mention this amazing bit of news to Dominic. He wasn't listening.

He was arranging their wedding.

He gave the clerk information. Then it was her turn. She gave the answers by rote, filled in the forms, signed where she was told. If she'd doubted his ability to arrange an exception to the waiting period, she didn't doubt for long.

He called a friend, who called a friend. In a matter of minutes it was arranged that someone called Judge Willis would perform the ceremony in his chambers.

"Almost there," Dominic said, and taking her arm once more, he hauled her toward the door. "I'll call Finn. Tell him and Izzy where to meet us."

"You don't want to call Rhys?"

Dominic had been best man at Rhys and Mariah's wedding. Sierra had been Mariah's maid of honor.

In the act of opening the door, Dominic stopped and arched a brow. "Do you want to call Mariah?"

Never in a million years! Mariah was sane and sensible. She would throw herself in front of a speeding train before she would let Sierra do something as stupid as marry her brother-in-law on the spur of the moment.

"Didn't think so." Dominic pulled out a cell phone, checked his organizer, and punched in Finn's number. "Finn? All set," he said without preamble. "Meet us in Judge Willis's chambers at five."

He rattled off the directions, then grabbed Sierra's arm again. "It's not in this building. Let's go."

It was two streets over, five flights up, down two long corridors. Dominic's legs were a lot longer than hers, and Sierra was panting by the time they arrived. Finn and Izzy and all four of their kids arrived moments later.

"What the—?" Dominic looked aghast at the sight of nine-year-old twins, Pansy and Tansy, three-year-old Rip and baby Crash. He turned his gaze on Finn's wife, Izzy, his look both accusing and appalled.

Izzy didn't give him a chance to object. She poked her umbrella at him. "You want me to get a baby-sitter, you have to give me more than ten minutes' notice."

Then she turned her eyes toward Sierra. "Are you crazy?" she demanded. To be marrying Dominic, she meant.

It was a question anyone knowing them would ask, and Sierra knew it. She shrugged. "Probably."

It wasn't the answer Izzy was looking for. Scowling, she turned back to Dominic. "Are you coercing her?"

"I am not." His expression went from appalled to offended.

"Then why—"

Finn redirected the umbrella tip away from Dominic's midsection. "I don't think that's our business, Iz," he said to his wife quietly.

"But—"

"You don't have to worry about her," Dominic said firmly. "I'm not going to beat her. I'm not going to mistreat her. I'm not going to tie her up and dye her hair brown. I'm just going to marry her."

Izzy didn't look happy—or convinced.

But before she could argue, the door to the judge's chambers opened just then and a pointy-chinned woman looked down her nose and said, "His Honor will see you now."

Dominic cast one more despairing glance at the assembled group and ushered them all in. He introduced himself, Finn and his wife, then drew Sierra forward.

His Honor took one look at her and his eyes bulged. His

jaw flapped. His gaze went straight to Dominic. "I misunderstood. I thought when Harvey called, he said you wanted to get married..."

"I do."

Sierra felt Dominic's arm come around her as he hauled her close, just in case there was any question in the judge's mind about who the intended bride was.

The judge's eyebrows hiked halfway up his bald head. But at the sight of Dominic's fingers tightening on her shoulder and his steely glare, His Honor nodded his head. "Very well. Come in."

Dominic and Sierra went in. Trailing behind them were a pair of saucer-eyed red-headed twins, then Finn with Rip on his shoulders, and Izzy who carried a wriggling Crash.

The pointy-chinned woman let out an audible sigh, shut the door and left them to it.

The ceremony itself was an anticlimax.

The judge mumbled something about the power vested in him by the State of New York. Then he read lines out of a book.

Dominic repeated them.

Then the judge looked at Sierra and read more lines. She repeated them every time he paused and looked at her.

They were lines she'd heard a hundred times. Richer. Poorer. Sickness. Health. Nothing about obeying, thank God. She didn't think she could ever obey anyone. Not even Dominic.

Especially not Dominic!

She slanted a glance at the man standing so stiffly beside her in his two-thousand-dollar tailored suit and his handmade Italian shoes. She caught just a glimpse of the edge of his subdued gray-and-burgundy striped tie. It was the same tie...

"...till death do you part?"

Sierra jerked her mind away from his tie—the tie that had started it all. She gathered herself together, recollected the solemnity of the occasion and dutifully stared straight ahead. Behind her one of the twins sighed. Rip gave a little hop. Crash gurgled. Finn and Izzy sucked in their breaths.

The judge looked at her over the top of his glasses. She smiled back at him. He cocked his head and looked at her expectantly.

Beside her, Dominic cleared his throat. She glanced over at him. He gave her a speaking look, the sort she was sure he gave underlings right before he put them through the paper shredder.

Sierra gave him one right back.

A muscle in his jaw twitched. His fingers strangled hers. He nudged her clunky boot with his polished black dress shoe. "Well, damn it, do you?" he muttered through his teeth.

Sierra blinked. "Do I what?"

"Take him for your lawful wedded husband, young lady?" the judge said impatiently.

Sierra suddenly realized they'd been waiting for her. "Oh!" she said, then gave them all a blinding smile. "Sure. Why not?"

CHAPTER TWO

SURE. WHY NOT?

As if it were that easy.

It wasn't—as Dominic well knew. He'd tried it once twelve years ago, and had regretted it ever since.

He'd had nightmares for years about that disastrous day— that sunny June morning in the Bahamas when he'd been left at the altar in front of two hundred avidly curious on-lookers.

He knew he could never do it again. Knew he couldn't face a huge production, a mob of people, a bride he had to count on, a wedding he had to wait for.

Well, he hadn't had to wait for this one.

He'd accomplished the whole thing, start to finish, en-gagement to ceremony, in a matter of hours.

And now he was married.

To a purple-haired woman with raccoon eye-shadow eyes.

What had he done?

The words reverberated in his head almost as insistently as Sierra's bright, ''Sure. Why not?'' But he glanced at his watch and knew he didn't really have time to think about it now.

Finn kissed the bride. ''How about we take you out for a champagne toast?''

''Sure,'' Izzy seconded. ''It's the least we can do on such short notice.''

''Great!'' Sierra said brightly.

But Dominic shook his head. ''Thanks, but we can't. An-other time. We've got to meet my father for dinner.''

And with a quick handshake and a few more words of thanks, he spirited Sierra away.

28

''What do you mean, we're meeting your father?'' she protested as he steered her toward the elevator. ''Your father's in town and you didn't even invite him?''

''You think he'd have stood there with his mouth shut, then wished us well?''

Sierra opened her mouth, then shut it again.

Dominic nodded grimly. He'd made his point. She'd met his father when her sister had married his brother. She'd had a glimpse of Douglas then. Not much, but he was fairly sure his trying to commandeer the wedding party and drive them to the reception in his Lincoln Town Car instead of the cars they'd arranged had made an impression.

They rode down in the elevator in silence. Sierra staring at the doors, Dominic at the top of her purple head.

What had he done?

He'd got married, that was all. Exactly what the old man had wanted.

But to Sierra Kelly, of all people!

Sierra Kelly with her purple hair and her Day-Glo spandex, with her clunky boots and ribbed black leggings. Yes, but, as he well knew, that wasn't all she had. She also had mile-long legs and kissable lips and a wicked teasing tongue. She made his blood sizzle and the windows steam.

He'd met a million more suitable women, but he'd never met one who'd set him on fire—except Sierra. He'd never met one he'd wanted to go to bed with more.

Or again.

He could have taken or left any one of the others. But not her.

They'd made wild passionate desperate love one night three months ago. He'd been reliving it every night since.

Half an hour ago he'd married her—to be a sober reliable married man, to put an end to his father's meddling—but mostly so tonight they could set the world on fire again.

But they had to get through dinner with his father first.

He tucked her into the same hired car and got in after her.

Outside, rain slashed against the window. Horns honked as the driver cut into the traffic and began the journey uptown. The faint warmth of the spring afternoon had all but dissipated now. And against the far door Sierra seemed to be shivering inside her denim jacket.

"Are you cold?" Dominic asked.

She shook her head fiercely. "I'm fine." She wrapped her arms around her damned tackle box and sat hugging it like it was some great plastic shield. For an instant she glanced his way long enough to shoot him a quick flippant smile, then stared straight ahead again.

He still thought she looked like she was shaking.

So if she wasn't cold, was she nervous? *Sierra?* Not likely!

He doubted she'd ever been nervous in her life. He studied her out of the corner of his eye—her purple hair, her stubborn chin, her pert nose, her raccoon eyes. He fished in his pocket and thrust a clean handkerchief at her.

"Here. Wipe your face. You've got eye gunk all down your cheeks."

Sierra looked startled. Then, "Thank you so much," she said with false politeness, making him wonder if she'd rather appear in public looking like a raccoon.

But she snatched the handkerchief out of his hand and pressed the button to roll down the window.

"Hey, what are you doing?"

She thrust his handkerchief outside into the rain. "Unless you'd rather I spit in it?"

Dominic flushed. "Of course not."

"I didn't think so." When she decided the handkerchief was sufficiently damp, she put the window back up and scrubbed at her cheeks. It took two more dousings of the handkerchief, followed by so much scrubbing he thought she'd rub the skin off her cheeks.

Finally she quit and turned to look at him. "Satisfied?"

Now she just looked like a prizefighter with two black

eyes. Dominic didn't say so, though. Apparently his silence said it for him.

Sierra shrugged. "Well, let's just hope I get a chance to stop in the ladies' room before your father arrives." She stuffed his handkerchief in the pocket of her jacket, then folded her arms around the tackle box again.

She looked young and innocent—even in her purple-haired insouciance—and he wondered if he ought to coach her so she wouldn't feel out of place.

But, of course, she would *be* out of place—it was part of the reason he'd married her, after all. He felt a twinge of guilt and promptly smothered it.

No one had made her say yes!

Besides, there was no point in telling her how to behave or how to act. If he tried she'd bite his head off, he was sure. And anyway, her very presence, looking as she did, *was* her act.

Still, he couldn't quite leave it there.

"Do you need anything?" he asked her. It seemed like the least he could do. "A briefing?"

She looked at him, incredulous. "To meet your father?"

"Never mind," he said, feeling like a fool. "Well, fine. If there's nothing you need—" he picked up his briefcase, set it on his lap and opened it "—I've got work to do."

She was married.

To Dominic Wolfe.

It would have been funny if it hadn't been so real. If he hadn't been sitting less than a foot away from her in his suit that probably cost more than two months' rent on her apartment. If he hadn't had his nose stuck in papers that Sierra was sure had to do with a merger that would allow him control of more wealth than the average small country.

Had she lost her mind?

Apparently. Never very much given to second guessing

herself, even Sierra couldn't refrain from second guessing this.

What on earth had possessed her? Why had she said yes to Dominic's outlandish proposal?

She knew he didn't love her.

Most of the time he barely acted as if he even liked her! Except in bed.

In bed they were dynamite. In bed things happened that Sierra wouldn't have believed could ever happen—especially between Dominic and herself.

Out of bed, though, she feared they had nothing in common at all.

He was using her against his father. He'd admitted as much.

Well, she was using him to help Frankie, she reminded herself. And she hadn't even admitted that.

Not that he would care. He wouldn't even ask. He'd just cut the check.

Her husband. *Dominic Wolfe!*

"Someday," her mother used to warn her, "you're going to bite off more than you can chew, missy."

"Someday, kiddo," her far more blunt farmer father used to say, "you're going to leap without thinking and land headfirst in the manure pile." Only he hadn't said manure pile. He'd been a little more graphic.

That was about where Sierra felt she'd landed right now.

She shivered inside her jacket and considered opening the door and throwing herself out into traffic. With luck she'd be squashed by a passing taxi.

With *her* luck, she'd be knocked over by a bicycle messenger and Dominic would simply peel her off the pavement, mop her off and trundle her away to meet with his father.

God.

It was as close to a prayer as Sierra had been in a while. She was not big on praying. It wasn't that she didn't believe in God. Or prayer. She did. But for the weak and the down-trodden and the desperate.

Not for herself. And definitely not when it came to asking for things. Asking was for people who couldn't help themselves.

Sierra had always been sure she could.

Until now.

What on earth was she going to do now?

She shot a quick glance at the man sitting next to her. He had his briefcase open on his lap and was running his pen down a column of figures. His *pen* probably cost more than the rent on her apartment!

But it wasn't just about money. It was about style. About values. About their whole very different approaches to life.

Like this restaurant they were heading toward.

She didn't dare hope that Dominic was taking her to an uptown diner or a groovy little club for his little tête-à-tête with daddy.

No, it was bound to be one of those stuffy obnoxious places, all wood-paneling and hunt club prints of dogs with dead birds in their mouths. A muffled elegant place where the maître d' would look down his ski-jump of a nose and seat her behind a potted palm—*if* he even deigned to seat her at all.

What if they didn't even let her in?

A momentary shaft of humiliation and panic stabbed her in the gut before she realized that of course they would let her in.

She was going to be on the arm of Dominic Wolfe. He'd cow them and loom over them and pass them fifty bucks on the side and they might look askance, but they'd let her in.

And then they'd spill soup in her lap.

Or expect that she'd do it herself.

She started to bite her thumbnail, then jammed her hand into the pocket of her jacket. She was *not* going to bite her nails in front of Dominic. It was why she painted them wild and outrageous colors in the first place—so she'd remember not to bite them.

She wasn't going to betray by the slightest flicker that her heart was in her throat and that her stomach was in knots.

No, sir. She wasn't.

She'd learned long ago that fear got you nowhere. Her older sister Mariah had taught her that back when Sierra was only seven years old.

In those days her biggest terror had been water. When she was four, Terry Graff had knocked her into the swimming pool. She'd swallowed half of it before her father had fished her out. For the next three years she hadn't stuck a toe in.

While all the other kids had laughed and splashed and swam and played, she'd stood quaking on the side, watching. Then some of the bigger kids had realized she was afraid—and instead of leaving her alone, they'd dragged her in.

She'd gone kicking and screaming and flailing and floundering. She'd made a complete fool of herself before Mariah had run at them with a stick and scared them off. When she'd dragged Sierra, shaking and crying back out, she'd said the seven most important words anyone had ever told her.

"You can't let them see you're afraid."

Sierra had done her damnedest never to let anyone see her fears ever since.

She'd spent her life making sure she got over them. And, if she had to say so herself, she'd done a bang-up job. She'd outgrown her early panics. She'd discovered the world was a pretty dandy place.

But every once in a while she felt like that little girl on the poolside. But she wasn't going to show it. She was going to march right up to the restaurant and, even if she resembled a Day-Glo raccoon, she was going to look them straight in the eye and never bat a lash.

Dominic might well be sorry he'd asked her to be his bride.

But he'd never feel sorry for her.

She'd see to that!

The maître d' was agog.

His normally impassive features became positively animated at the sight of Dominic and his guest. For a split second his eyes gawped. But then he schooled his features, stiffened his spine and assumed an expression of something that might best be described as "determined indifference."

As well it might be, Dominic thought. If he was willing to pay Le Sabre's exorbitant prices, he ought to able to bring his damn dog to dinner if he so chose!

Gripping Sierra firmly by the arm, he smiled at the maître d'. "Good evening, Flaubert. Has my father arrived?"

Flaubert fixed a thin smile on his face. "He has, Mr. Wolfe. He and the lady and the other gentleman arrived a few moments ago. They've already been seated. I understood you were to be four for dinner?" One brow lifted, but he determinedly did not look at Sierra.

Dominic's back stiffened. "There's been a change in plans."

For a split second the maître d' seemed about to argue. Then his mouth pressed into a tight line and beckoned a waiter. The man scurried to his side. At Flaubert's whispered words, he shot an astonished gaze in their direction, then nodded and hurried toward the dining room.

"It will take just a moment." Flaubert paused. Once more his gaze skated right over Sierra to focus on Dominic. "Would the…young lady…like to…check her coat and er…?" He eyed the tackle box with distaste.

"I'll keep it, thanks," Sierra said before Dominic could open his mouth.

But it was as if she hadn't spoken. Flaubert continued to look at Dominic for an answer.

Dominic's teeth came together and he put an arm around her shoulders. "We will check the box. I think it might get in the way in the dining room, don't you?" He looked to Sierra for a nod which, after a moment's stubbornness, he got. Then he turned back to the maître d'. "My wife will keep her coat, thank you."

Flaubert's jaw sagged as Dominic had been sure it would.

Stepping around him, Dominic handed over the box to the woman behind at the cloak room. Then, pocketing the token she gave him, he steered Sierra into the dining room.

His father, Tommy Hargrove and a sleek blond woman were no longer sitting at the table his father regularly claimed. Instead they were sitting behind a potted palm, looking discomfitted and annoyed as a waiter finished laying an extra place setting and stepped away.

A sound something akin to a smothered snigger emanated from Sierra.

Dominic looked down at her. "Something funny?"

She flashed a grin. "The palm tree. I knew they'd have a palm tree."

And that they'd put you behind it, he finished for her. A corner of his own mouth twisted and his fingers tightened on her arm. "Screw 'em," he muttered and was instantly rewarded when Sierra grinned again.

Just then Douglas spotted them, and Dominic had the pleasure of seeing the old man's jaw rival Flaubert's. Almost instantly, though, it snapped shut again and Douglas took a deep breath as he rose to his feet. His gaze fixed on Dominic and his hard blue eyes glittered. It was belied by his smooth tone.

"How nice that you've brought a guest to join us. I don't believe we've met?" He, at least, was facing Sierra head-on. In fact he stared straight into the magenta and the Day-Glo peeking out from behind the denim and didn't even blink. Dominic was impressed.

"We have, actually," Sierra said cheerfully, offering her

hand. "I'm Sierra Kelly. Mariah's sister. My hair was blonde for the wedding," she added, presumably by way of explaining why he might not have recognized her.

"Oh!" Douglas's relief was palpable as he took her hand and shook it heartily. "Yes! Oh my, yes. Of course. I do recognize you now. The, um, purple threw me for a moment. My son Rhys's wife's little sister!" he explained to Tommy and the blonde who had to be Viveca.

Dominic smiled and corrected this misconception. "Mariah's little sister," he agreed. "And my wife."

He had to give his father credit.

By barely more than a flicker of a muscle in his jaw and a sudden paleness around his mouth, did Douglas betray that Dominic's arrival with a wife in tow was even unexpected, much less a shock.

Instead he kissed Sierra's cheek and introduced them both to Viveca Moore.

She was exactly as his father described her—blonde, brilliant, and sophisticated. The perfect accessory.

A far cry from the woman whom an hour ago he'd made his wife.

Dominic never knew if Viveca had any idea she was supposed to be *his* date this evening. Douglas took hold of her hand and said smoothly that he was sorry they hadn't been able to make the wedding, and then called for a bottle of champagne.

"To toast you both," he said, the glitter in his hard blue eyes the only sign that he was less than pleased.

Champagne, Dominic remembered with a qualm, had been his and Sierra's downfall at Rhys and Mariah's wedding.

It was the champagne that had made them reckless, that had fanned the flames of desire that had been raging between them since the day they'd met. It was the champagne that had made them challenge each other, that had tipped them over the edge and sent them to that hotel room to slake their desperate desire.

"I don't know—" he began.

But Sierra said brightly, "What a lovely idea." Then she explained, "We've been in such a hurry all day, we didn't have time to toast our marriage earlier with our friends." She turned her gaze on Dominic and he saw the challenge in her eyes.

"Then we must do it now," Douglas said firmly. He gave Dominic a hard smile and, when the waiter arrived, poured and passed out glasses of champagne. Then he raised his own, first to Sierra, then to Dominic.

"To my son," he said, "and his new wife. May you share a long, long, long life together."

If he'd said one more "long" Dominic would have throttled him. As it was, he noted there was no wish for happiness. He wondered if Sierra noticed.

Her eyes were laughing as she touched her glass to his. "And a happy one," she said.

Their glasses clinked.

"Hear, hear!" cried Tommy Hargrove.

"We wish you great happiness," Viveca said with etiquette book politeness. "Don't we, Douglas?"

"Yes, of course," Douglas said hastily. "Indeed we do." He poured more champagne, then looked at his son. "Dominic, don't you have a toast for your bride?"

Dominic raised his glass to the challenge, first to his father, then to his wife. "To Sierra," he said gravely, "who has made me the happiest of men."

He meant it as a slap at his father. As a bit of veiled sarcasm. But as he drank, Dominic realized that, in some small way, it was the truth.

For one steamy night three months ago, Sierra had made him happier than he'd ever been in his life.

She'd made him silly and hungry and passionate. She'd made him forget mergers and balance sheets and the rat race he called his life. She'd made him laugh and tease and wrestle and grow sweaty and desperate and, finally, fulfilled.

He hadn't forgotten.

It was, after all, why he'd asked her to marry him. But he wasn't fool enough to expect it to last.

Outside of bed, they had nothing in common. Inside it, for one night at least, they'd had bliss.

"To Sierra," he said firmly. "My wife."

They drank staring into each other's eyes. Hers were no longer laughing, he noticed. They were shiny, as if they held tears. But that was ridiculous. Sierra never cried! She wasn't the type. And she would certainly not get soppy about a marriage like theirs.

"I have a toast," Tommy said suddenly.

Everyone turned to look at the snowy-haired old man as he raised his glass and looked at Dominic over the top of it. "This was a spur of the moment affair, I trust?"

Dominic stiffened, but Sierra laced her fingers through his and nodded. "Yes. Dominic swept me off my feet."

"Ah." Tommy beamed at her.

Douglas fixed Dominic with a glare. But Tommy didn't notice. He was nodding enthusiastically. "Thought so." He raised his glass higher. "Just like Bernice and I. Sometimes," he said with a sweet sad smile, "the best things happen on the spur of the moment. Bernice—God rest her soul—and I knew each other only a week when we eloped." His voice wavered a little and he paused to collect himself. Then, eyes brimming, he murmured, "Fifty-three years. We were married fifty-three years. The best fifty-three years any man could have." His hand shook briefly, but then he drew a breath and it steadied.

Dominic had known Tommy Hargrove his whole life. He'd known Bernice who'd died last year. He supposed he'd never thought about them as young and impetuous. Tommy was a tough-as-nails old man. Bernice had been his dutiful wife—always there with a smile or a gentle laugh. Now

Dominic remembered those smiles, remembered how often they'd been directed at Tommy. He looked at the old man with new and wondering eyes.

"To the surprises in life," Tommy said with a smile. He touched each of their glasses.

"Thank you," Sierra said to him. Then she turned to Dominic and clinked her glass against his. There was a stubborn tilt to her chin and a fierce gleam in those bright blue eyes.

"To us," she said. "And the next fifty-three years."

In high school Sierra had played Alice in *Alice in Wonderland.* She'd fallen down the rabbit hole, chatted with Humpty Dumpty, been spoken down to by a caterpillar, had tea with the Mad Hatter and the March Hare, and had been chased through the forest by a pack of cards while the red queen had screamed, "Off with her head!"

That all seemed downright normal compared to the dinner she'd just survived.

She sank into the back seat of the taxi, clutching her tackle box, and shut her eyes. She was dimly aware that Dominic had climbed in beside her and was speaking to the driver. As the car begin to move, she heard Dominic sigh as he settled back next to her. She kept her eyes shut and waited for him to speak. But he didn't say a word.

Maybe he was as tired as she was.

Acting did that to her. Drained her. Left her limp and exhausted. Playing Alice back in high school had wrung her out.

This had been harder. Lots harder. That she'd rehearsed for. This had been complete improvisation. And while she thought she'd acquitted herself well enough, she was still exhausted. She just wanted to go home and go to bed.

She didn't open her eyes until the taxi stopped.

"We're here," Dominic said.

Sierra hauled herself up and blinked as she looked around.

Then she jerked upright and her eyes went wide. "Where? This isn't my place!"

"Of course not. It's mine.' Dominic was handing the driver some money and opening the door. "Come on."

But Sierra couldn't. She stayed right where she was. "I'm not going to your place!"

Out of the car, he bent down to stare at her. "You're not—*Why not?*" He looked white-faced and furious.

"Because I'm not! I never agreed to—"

"You agreed to marry me. You did marry me." His voice was icy.

"I know, but—"

"Marriage implies cohabitation," he reminded her. He was gritting his teeth.

"Not…not necessarily." It was one thing to have mad passionate sex with Dominic. It was entirely another to get sucked up into his apartment, his world, his life! She folded her arms across her chest. "I'm not getting out," she told the taxi driver. "I need to go downtown."

"The hell you do!" Dominic protested.

But Sierra ignored him and gave the driver her address.

"You can't—!"

The driver flipped on the meter, then glanced at Dominic. "Mister, you gotta shut the door."

"No. I don't. She's not—!"

"Yes, I am. Now. Drive," Sierra commanded the driver. "Go on!"

"No!" Dominic resolutely held the door open, not moving an inch.

The driver looked from one to the other of them, annoyed. "I got a business here."

"So take me—"

"No!"

"D'youse two suppose youse could maybe settle this somewhere else?" the taxi driver said plaintively.

"Yes," Dominic said.

"No," Sierra said.

Their gazes locked. They glared.

"Please!" the taxi driver implored them.

Sierra clutched her box and didn't budge.

Finally Dominic flung himself back into the cab and slammed the door "Fine. Take us to her place." He challenged Sierra to contradict him. "We'll stay there."

"You can't stay here!" Sierra said for the umpteenth time as Dominic followed her up the narrow stairway to her flat.

"You refused to stay at my place," he reminded her. It was getting hard to breathe, and not from the three-floor climb. Rather it was a result of being on eye level with Sierra's curvy bottom the whole way up. Her denim miniskirt barely seemed to cover it. And it didn't matter that the rest of her was discreetly covered in black ribbed leggings, Dominic had a good imagination.

And a good memory.

At last Sierra stopped in front of a tall metal door. She fitted a key into a lock, undid it, moved on to another one, undid that, then unlocked a third, and pushed open the door. "It doesn't mean you had to come here."

"Apparently it does, if I want to spend my wedding night with my bride." He followed on her heels, suspecting that she would shut the door on him if he gave her half a chance.

Apparently the thought had occurred to her, because the color was high in her cheeks and she aimed a disgusted look in his direction when he shut the door himself and leaned against it, arms folded across his chest, smiling at her.

She set down her tackle box and stood glaring at him from the other end of the tiny room. "Well, you can't. Not here. It's not big enough." She waved an arm and practically hit one of the walls. "There's no room."

Dominic shrugged indifferently. "It was your choice."

"It was not my choice! I didn't invite you here."

"But you refused to come home with me," he said reasonably.

"I don't need to come home with you! I went to dinner with you! I shocked your father for you. I stopped Viveca from marrying you. What more do you want?"

"Fifty-three years."

"What!"

Dominic raked a hand through his hair. He shoved away from the wall, wanting to pace, to move, but there was no room. "Nothing!" he muttered. "Never mind. You're the one who said it."

"Tommy's the one who said it."

"And who raised her glass in toast?"

"Would you rather I'd said, 'Oh, how about six months?' Your father would really have taken us seriously then."

"How the hell is he going to take it seriously if you won't come home with me?"

She wrapped her arms across her breasts. "He doesn't have to know that."

"Of course he'll know! He's probably got someone tailing after the cab right now, just watching. I'm surprised he didn't demand to see the license."

Actually Douglas would never do any such thing—not in public anyway. He wouldn't want to admit that Dominic had bested him. "He expects us to be together. I'm staying." He began to loosen his tie.

"Stop that!"

"What?"

"Undressing!"

"You've seen me with my tie undone," Dominic reminded her mockingly as he yanked it off, tossed it on the chair, then undid the top button of his starched white shirt. "You did very creative things with my tie, as I recall." Things that, remembered, could still send shivers straight to his groin.

Sierra turned bright red. "That was then!"

"And now we're married" He arched a brow. "Do you only have sex with single men?"

"I've never had sex with a married one!"

"It's allowed," he told her. "When you're married to him."

He finished unbuttoning his shirt and stripped it off, then tugged his T-shirt over his head. The chill in the room was a shock to his heated flesh. He wanted to go to her and wrap her in his arms.

But all the while she watched him like a fawn caught in headlights. Swell, she was going to turn into Bambi. Sierra, of all people. Who'd have guessed?

Dominic's hand went to his belt. She sucked in a breath. He glared at her, annoyed. "Are you going to pretend this isn't why you said yes?" he asked.

She blinked rapidly, then swallowed, and he thought for a moment she would deny wanting him at all. But finally she gave a jerky nod. "Only partly."

"Right." His jaw tightened. "There was the check, too. The little matter of half a million bucks."

She scowled. "The money had nothing—well, almost nothing—to do with it," she told him defiantly.

He would have liked to ask what the hell she intended to do with half a million dollars, but right now it wasn't important. He didn't care. He wanted another more important answer. "Fine. Then why fight it? It's what we want. What we *both* want. Unless you only believe in one-night stands?"

"Of course not!"

"Then maybe you're a chicken."

Her eyes flashed. "I'm never a chicken!"

"No?" Dominic challenged softly. "Then prove it."

For a long moment she didn't move. Then something changed. A gleam came into her eyes, a gleam he remembered once before. The corners of her mouth turned up in a smile that set his heart to pounding. And quite deliberately

Sierra reached out and snagged his tie from where he'd tossed it on the chair.

She ran it through her fingers as she stepped forward to meet him. And his heart slammed against his chest as she whispered, "How nice of you to remember I had a use for this."

They should have gone to his place.

They wouldn't have to smash together on her hard narrow futon. At Dominic's they could no doubt wallow in sybaritic luxury in Dominic's bed.

But she hadn't been able to do it. Not then.

So she consoled herself that even if they had they wouldn't have noticed.

Once it was clear that neither of them had got the other out of their system during that one night in a Kansas motel— it didn't matter where they were.

The awareness, the attraction, the chemistry—*everything!*—between them simply sizzled!

Something about Dominic brought out parts of Sierra she'd never even guessed were there. Something about his power made her want to challenge him. Something about his starchy conservative demeanor she wanted to muss. And his control—his iron-clad control!—she just couldn't rest until she made it snap.

And she'd made it snap!

She'd moved in on him like a tigress stalking her prey. Circling, smiling, watching him from beneath lowered lids, Sierra had moved closer, turned, stepped and backed him into the futon. Then she'd looped the tie around his nape and slid it back and forth. Silk and skin. Hot damp skin.

She saw him take a quick sharp breath.

She smiled. She gave the tie a tug and drew him toward her, so close she could almost feel his heart pounding against his chest, so close the heat of her breath ruffled the hair that curled there. She touched one flat male nipple with her tongue.

Dominic bit off an exclamation. Then he hauled her hard against him and he was much too close to see.

Her hands pressed against the hot smooth flesh of his back as she lifted her mouth, hungry for his.

Sierra was no stranger to kisses. Since she'd turned thirteen she'd had boyfriends, steadies, casual dates, one after another, men-in-her-life galore. And they'd kissed her—if not one and all, then certainly most.

But she'd never been kissed like this.

There had never been such hunger, such passion, such sheer intensity in any man's mouth on hers. Only Dominic's.

Before that fateful night in Kansas, Sierra had thought that whatever it was that had been sizzling between her and Dominic since they'd met was nothing more than that—an insubstantial, unreal, ephemeral something—like steam.

Just so much hot air.

She'd been wrong. Big time. One kiss and she'd been knocked off her feet—and she'd knocked Dominic off his.

One fierce hungry kiss, almost before they'd got the door closed behind them and had tumbled onto the hard motel bed. They'd practically ripped each other's clothes off in their haste to come together. The kissing, the touching, the stroking, the loving had been hot and fierce.

And their hunger for each other hadn't slacked even after they'd climaxed.

They'd lain in each other's arms, then rolled apart. But within moments they had come together again. They'd touched and taunted, caressed and teased, and kissed and kissed and kissed the whole night long.

In some unspoken agreement, as if they were determined to get enough of each other, to become sated, to be able to happily turn away in the morning and leave each other behind, they had made love again and again.

Once on the plane to New York the next morning, he in

first class and she in economy, they had gone their separate ways, determined to forget.

And they had—but not for long.

Memories of Dominic came back. The desire came back. It slipped into Sierra's mind in the dark of night. It teased her at odd moments in the light of day. When she was cooking spaghetti and getting a face full of steam, she would find herself remembering the heat of Dominic's kiss. When she was combing out someone's hair, she would recall the soft brush of his. When she saw a man in a tux get out of a cab across Broadway, she almost got run over craning her neck to see if it was the man she remembered stripping off his tux and making sweet hot love to her.

She'd dreamed about him.

She'd wanted him again at the same time she'd told herself he couldn't make it happen again. There was no way.

But once more she'd been wrong.

He was making it happen right now!

He turned them around and bore her back onto the futon, his fingers trembling as he fought to unbutton her denim jacket. He muttered when he couldn't manage it easily, and Sierra touched his hands.

"Let me."

He shook his head fiercely. His eyes seemed to glitter and the skin was taut across his cheekbones. "No. I want to."

So she let him.

Though her heart thudded within her chest and she longed to urge him on, she made herself wait, made herself watch, let herself smile at his fervent fumblings, at his mutterings and final sigh of relief when eventually he got the buttons open and peeled the jacket from her shoulders and tossed it aside.

She thought he'd go after her spandex top with equal gusto, but he paused instead and sat back just gazing at her, a rapt hungry look on his face.

"Stop that," she muttered self-consciously and she

tugged at the tie she had still looped against the back of his neck, trying to take back the initiative.

But he just shook his head. Then, with a finger, he traced the line of her top against the swell of her breasts. He bent his head and did it again with the tip of his tongue. It was deliberate, provocative, erotic.

It made her shiver and tug again on his tie. "Wolfe!"

He smiled and slowly peeled her top up, then tugged it over her head and it followed her jacket to the floor. Then with his hands he caressed her breasts. Stroked them. Teased them. Made her wriggle beneath his touch.

"Wolfe!"

"Mmm?" It was somewhere between a growl and a purr and was the sexiest sound she'd ever heard. She remembered it from that night in Kansas when he'd looked down on her, touched her, teased her, eased himself inside her.

She'd lain awake some nights trying to reproduce it. She hadn't come close.

And now Sierra struggled not to clutch at him as he purred again and bent his head to feather kisses across her breasts.

She slid the tie in her fingers and pressed her hands against his shoulders as the kisses moved south.

She felt them lightly on her belly, and at every dip of his head, his soft hair brushed tantalizingly against her sensitive breasts. Her fingers slid up his neck and dug into his hair. It was black as a raven's wing and soft as silk. She lifted her head to touch her nose to it, reveling in the smell of some very costly, subtly masculine shampoo.

There was nothing subtle about the rest of Dominic's masculinity. For all that he had to spend most of his life behind a desk, his body was hard and well-muscled. He made those starched shirts of his look damn good.

But he looked better without a shirt at all.

Without *anything* at all!

Suddenly she was impatient to see the rest of Dominic

again. She had lived on memories for three months. She wanted the real thing.

She eased her fingers out of his hair and began to caress the back of his neck. As he kissed her belly, she rubbed the silk of the tie back and forth against his shoulders.

Then, leaving it there, her hands moved further, sliding down the hot smooth skin of his back until they reached his belt. She traced the line of it around his midsection and felt his muscles tighten. He sucked in his breath at the brush of her fingers against the sensitive skin of his abdomen.

As she eased down his zipper, he tugged off her skirt and cast it aside. Shoes, slacks, socks and leggings followed.

At last they were down to bare essentials. Or nearly bare.

When he peeled off her panties, she didn't demur. When his kisses moved lower, she knotted her fingers and tugged at his hair. The low rumbling purr became more of a growl and he lifted his head to grin at her. "Like that?"

"No," she muttered. "Hate it. What do you think?"

He laughed. It was a smoky laugh, a teasing laugh. And when he bent his head to press the kisses more intimately still, as much as she would have liked to just lie there and savor it, she wasn't giving him that much control.

She plucked the tie up again and slid it down his back. She touched him with it, teased him with it, tantalized him with it. She rubbed it over his body, across his chest, between his legs.

She heard his breath come in a harsh gasp. "Like that?" she purred.

"Tease. Devil. Minx." He was breathing hard, his face was flushed, the skin taut. She could feel the hardness of him, the need. She slid the tie around and over, back and forth.

"Si-errrrrr-a!"

She laughed. It was a throaty laugh, a self-satisfied laugh—and it turned into a gasp, too, when Dominic's mouth caught her unawares.

They twisted, they turned, they tangled and wrestled. Gently but fiercely. Determined to give each other the ultimate pleasure.

And finally, when she thought she could bear it no longer, Dominic parted her legs and slid in.

Sierra welcomed him. Her body stilled, settled, softened.

And Dominic, embraced, shuddered against her, trembling, scrabbling for the last vestiges of control.

And he might have managed to regain it if Sierra hadn't shifted beneath him, hadn't dug her heels against the backs of his thighs, hadn't grinned and said, "What are you waiting for, Wolfe?"

He looked startled. Then he grinned. "Not a damn thing!" He drew back just a little, then thrust deeper.

Sierra met him halfway, her hips rocking, her fingers clenching, her body moving as easily and eagerly as his. He might have lost control, but she wasn't far behind and she knew it.

Two more desperate thrusts and he was over the edge. "I can't—!"

"Shh!" She arched against him, her nails digging into his back as she rode the crest of his climax to an equally shattering one of her own.

It was every bit as incredible as it had been that night in Kansas.

But could you build a marriage on it?

That was what Sierra wanted to know.

CHAPTER THREE

WHEN he awoke there was a woman wrapped around him. Dominic's eyes jerked wide and his whole body went rigid at the shock.

Who? What?

He never slept with the women he had sex with. Never! So how had he—? He eased his head back to peer down at the head resting on his chest.

It was purple.

It all came back like a punch to the gut. His father. Viveca. The ultimatum.

His marriage.

To Sierra.

God.

He was married to Sierra Kelly. He had *slept* with Sierra Kelly! He held himself absolutely still and tried to think. It wasn't easy.

Not with Sierra in his arms.

The sudden tension in his body seemed to disturb her. She sighed and wriggled closer, her fingers curving against his ribs, one of her legs slid over his. Her thigh rubbed against his groin. She tucked her foot between his knees, wiggled it, then slid it down his calf. And up again.

Dominic stopped breathing.

Sierra didn't. She shifted and nuzzled him and he felt her soft breath stirring the hair on his chest. Then her lips brushed one hard nipple.

Dominic sucked air.

He was used to the early morning reactions of his body. He wasn't used to turning into the rock of Gibraltar.

He wanted her now. Again.

Physically. Only physically, he assured himself.

But, ye gods, he sure as heck wanted her physically. What would she think if he woke her and wanted to make love with her again?

He squelched the thought. A glance at the clock on her dresser said it was already ten past seven. He needed to get up and get out now—preferably before she woke.

He didn't know how to deal with morning-after awkwardness. Except for the night in the motel with Sierra, he'd always left before dawn. He didn't know what one did upon waking up with a woman—and he damned sure didn't know how to handle waking up with a wife!

The one thing he did know was that it would be a whole lot easier if he were dressed and not primed to pop at her merest touch.

Carefully, holding his breath, Dominic slid his body out from beneath her. It wasn't easy. Whenever he moved away, she snuggled closer, cuddling in, wrapping her arm around his waist.

Worse, he liked it. He liked the feel of her fingers tucked against his side. He liked the weight of her in his arms. He liked the softness of her skin against the roughness of his own.

He wanted to stay right where he was.

He didn't. One centimeter at a time, he edged his way off the futon, bunching up the comforter and tucking it against Sierra's sleeping form so she wouldn't miss him when he was gone.

His heel touched the floor. He squirmed the last few inches—and came free. Silently he got to his feet—and stood looking down at Sierra.

She looked vulnerable. How odd. With her outrageous hair and wild clothes, not to mention her stubborn chin, smart mouth and flashing eyes, she'd always seemed hard-as-nails and extraordinarily well-defended.

Not now. The purple hair framed a surprisingly innocent-looking face.

Innocent? Sierra?

It didn't seem likely. But she certainly looked it now.

Because, he told himself, at this very moment she wasn't trying to cut him to shreds or shatter every last bit of his control.

She got enormous joy out of doing that. She'd done it again last night.

But he'd done it to her as well, he thought with grim satisfaction. He'd made her crazy—exactly as she'd made him.

The itch to do it again now was almost overpowering.

But he wouldn't.

He was rational this morning. Determined. In control.

He was Dominic Wolfe, after all, and he had more important things to do.

Sierra awoke to see Dominic standing in front of her closet door mirror, knotting his tie at his throat.

"Oh!" she exclaimed, startled because she'd been having luscious, erotic dreams about Dominic Wolfe—dreams in which that tie played a prominent part—and to wake up and realize that those dreams had been based on the night's reality made her cheeks burn.

What was even more shocking was remembering that a few hours before that she'd married him.

At her exclamation he turned, giving his tie one last tug. "Morning," he said briskly. He gave her a quick smile, but didn't look at her.

"Morning," Sierra replied huskily and found herself dragging the sheet more closely around her, though he'd already seen everything there was—and seemed completely uninterested in looking again now.

He was grabbing his suit coat and shoving his arms into the sleeves. "Gotta run," he said. "I'm going to be late."

Sierra scowled at the clock. ''It's just past seven-thirty.''

''Right. But I have to go home first. Change clothes. Shave.'' He rubbed a hand over stubbled cheeks. ''I have a meeting at nine.'' He picked up his briefcase and started for the door. '''Bye.''

''Er…'bye,'' Sierra said. But before he could get away, she hoisted herself to a sitting position, sheet clutched against her breasts. ''Wolfe?''

He glanced back. ''What?'' He was all impatience now, eager to be gone.

As if she'd been nothing more than a good time, not the woman he married! Well, fine. If that's the way he wanted it.

''Nothing,'' she said frostily and gave a toss of her hair. ''Goodbye.''

'''Bye.'' He went out. The door shut. A second later he was back, staring down at her, something hot and hungry in his eyes.

''What?'' she demanded.

''I'll see you tonight,'' he said. ''My place.'' And bang, the door shut after him.

Just like that.

She fumed about it while she showered and dressed. She muttered while she fixed her hair. She supposed she shouldn't have expected anything different from him. It wasn't exactly a love match they had.

She wasn't sure what they did have, besides sex.

She wasn't sure what she wanted—besides sex.

Once upon a time marriage and children were exactly what she wanted. As a teenager she'd had no desperate career plans like her sister, Mariah. She'd never been a whiz kid. No colleges had come banging on her door. And she hadn't gone banging on theirs.

She'd thought that getting married and having babies was a great idea. Only she hadn't really wanted to marry Skip Grimes who was the closest thing she had to a boyfriend at the time. Skip hadn't really wanted to marry her, either, so it never became an issue.

The issue had been what to do after graduation if she wasn't going to go to college. Her aunt Kathy suggested she learn to cut hair.

"You can get a job, make money, get your own place. Move to Kansas City, maybe," her mother's younger sister suggested.

For Sierra, who had never felt she fitted in at home, moving to Kansas City sounded like heaven. Besides, learning to cut hair had to be more interesting—not to mention more useful—than knowing the causes of the First World War. And if she really could earn a living and move to Kansas City, there she might meet the man of her dreams—who would look and act nothing like Skip Grimes.

Everything went exactly the way she'd hoped—except she never met anyone in Kansas City who made Sierra's heart beat faster than Skip Grimes had. So three years later, when Mariah got a job as a staff writer on a New York City based lifestyle magazine, Sierra went with her.

She'd got a job in a trendy salon. They'd shared a tiny fifth floor walk-up in the East Village. They'd been awed by the city—its energy, its bustle, its opportunities—and then they'd plunged in.

The Kelly sisters had thrived in New York. Mariah went from junior staff writer to sought-after freelancer, a well-known writer whose personality pieces and in-depth interviews were snapped up as fast as she could turn them out.

Sierra, too, found a home for her talents.

She was very good at cutting hair. She was very good at styling hair, at studying her clients' bone structure and figuring out how to make them look their best. She wasn't afraid to be daring, to suggest color changes, to be bold. And the results were spectacular.

The salon sent her to Paris to study.

"To take advantage of your talent. So you can learn from the best," her boss told her.

Sierra, never given to study before, had been astonished. And eager. She'd pinched herself all the way to Paris, hardly believing her good luck.

She'd spent a year in Paris, learned everything they could teach her, dated half a dozen charming Frenchmen, but never found one better than Skip.

Still, it was in France that she met Finn MacCauley. He'd been shooting a high fashion layout on the Riviera, and she'd been one of three stylists doing the models' hair. Exacting and demanding and scathing in two languages, Finn routinely reduced stylists to tears.

But not Sierra. She let his tirades blow over her like so much hot air. Then she did what he wanted. They hit it off.

At the end of the week he said, "Let me know when you come back to New York."

When she did, he asked her to work with him. Her reputation grew. Not just for her ability with hair, but for her ability to deal with temperamental photographers, demanding ad agency reps, commercial clients, and the occasional prima donna model.

She was in demand—professionally and personally.

There were always plenty of men wanting to take her out. For years she'd gone—always hoping to find the one man she'd want to be with for the rest of her life.

But she'd never found him. And eventually she'd stopped thinking so much about it. She learned to love what she did, to be content with her life, to savor her friendships, to enjoy the dates she did go out on without looking for happily ever after.

Then along came Dominic.

He did to her heart, to her body, to her mind what legions of Skip Grimes clones had not. Mariah's corporate shark of a brother-in-law was the one man who'd ever made Sierra's heart beat faster, her brain sizzle, and her hormones sing.

What were there, eight million men in New York City? Why him?

She'd tried to resist. She'd steered well clear of Dominic Wolfe after the day she'd bearded him in his office where she'd gone to learn Rhys's whereabouts. And even when she hadn't been able to stay totally away from him, like at Mariah's shower, she'd made it a point not to spare him a glance.

Or she'd tried not to.

It was like trying not to think of giraffes. It was all she'd thought of. Finally, at Mariah's and Rhys's wedding reception, even though she'd done her best to avoid him, the inevitable happened. They had to dance with each other. Rhys's best man, Mariah's maid of honor. And then, of course, they'd drunk champagne.

And danced more. And stared into each other's eyes. And finally had gone to that motel room, determined to get each other out of their systems.

It hadn't worked for Sierra.

Nor for Dominic either, apparently.

So now they were married. For better or worse. For richer, for poorer. In sickness and in health.

"In bed and out of it," Sierra muttered.

In her gut and in her heart she still thought she'd made the right decision.

She just needed to do her darnedest to make sure Dominic thought so, too.

In the meantime, though, she had something to give to Pammie.

Pammie didn't believe it.

Pammie stared at the check Sierra handed her, then she blinked, and stared again. Her jaw sagged and all the color drained from her face. "It's not real," she said. "It can't be real." Her fingers shook. She seemed almost to gasp for air.

"It's real," Sierra assured her. "I was at the bank when

they cut it. It's made out to me, but it's for you—for Frankie—for the transplant.''

"You're not serious," Pam said promptly, then looked at Sierra again and said, jaw sagging, "You *are*." Her breath seemed to almost rattle out of her. "Good lord."

Then as if she just that moment realized they were still standing in the open doorway, she grabbed Sierra and hauled her into her apartment, glancing over her shoulder toward Frankie's bedroom

"How did you—?" She studied the check again. "Who's Dominic Wolfe? And why did he loan you the money?"

"He didn't loan it. He gave it to me."

"*Gave it to you?* Why? In exchange for what?" Pam looked suddenly equal parts nervous and urgent. "What's he going to do to you?"

"Nothing! Nothing I don't want him to do," Sierra qualified. "It's all right. We...we made a deal."

"What deal?"

Sierra shrugged. "I married him."

Pam's mouth opened. And shut. She looked appalled and horrified and then she shook her head fiercely. She thrust the check back at Sierra who put her hands behind her back. "Well, you're not going to do it! Never. You won't. I won't let you! Not even for Frankie. I—"

"Pammie," Sierra said gently, reaching out and folding Pam's fingers over the check. "It's done. I already have."

Her friend's fingers started to tremble, to crumple the check. Her eyes welled. "Oh, Sierra! How could you?"

"How could I not?" Sierra said simply. For Frankie she would have done a lot more terrifying things than marrying Dominic. She was actually feeling pretty good about marrying Dominic. "And stop mashing it! It's real. We'll go cash it at lunch, okay?"

Pam didn't seem to be able to talk. But at least she nodded her head, then swallowed. "You're sure about this?"

"Absolutely."

Tears welled in Pam's eyes. "Oh, my God, you're a life saver!" And she threw her arms around Sierra, and Sierra felt the other woman's body trembling. "I kept telling myself," Pammie babbled, "that if I prayed hard enough, trusted enough, bargained enough… But I didn't expect you to be part of the bargain, Sierra!"

Sierra smiled. "This is my bargain. I wanted to do it."

"Who is he?"

"My brother-in-law's brother."

Pam gaped.

"It's not incest!" Sierra said hotly.

"I know! I'm just…just…surprised. He's not the brother-in-law who's an arrogant jerk, then?" She remembered Sierra muttering more than once about Rhys's bossy know-it-all brother.

"Er, well…he has one or two redeeming qualities," Sierra muttered, cheeks burning.

"He is the jerk!"

"Yes, but he's not *only* a jerk!" Sierra protested. "Besides it was his idea!"

"He just walked up to you yesterday and said, 'Let's get married?'"

"Actually, he did."

Pammie's eyes narrowed. "Why?"

"Because he's madly in love with me?" It was a joke, of course. But Pammie didn't hear that.

She looked vastly relieved. But still she said, "You're sure?"

"Of course I'm sure," Sierra lied briskly. "Now I'm just off to work. But I'll be back this afternoon and we can deposit the check. Is Frankie awake?"

"Yes. Go on in. He'll be really glad to see you. He missed you last night. *Star Trek*," she reminded Sierra.

Sierra banged her palm against her forehead. "I forgot." Two evenings a week Frankie, Pam and Sierra watched old *Star Trek* videos. "We had to go out with his father," she explained. "I'll try not to miss the next one. Put the check away. I'll go say hi to Frankie."

Frankie was eight. When Sierra had moved into the apartment at the other end of the hall he had been a five-year-old bundle of energy—all arms and legs and boundless enthusiasm, his dark hair forever mussed, his blue eyes alight with excitement as every day he stopped by Sierra's flat and told her about his adventures.

In the past year and a half his adventures had become less physical. He'd been home more, in school less. But the adventures he told her had become no less enthralling. He had created his own cast of characters and provided adventures for them. He wrote the stories on the computer, then printed and illustrated them. Frankie had his mother's skill with a pen and pencil.

He was at his desk already, even though it was just past eight. He was still in pajamas, but he was intent on his work, his head bent over his paper.

When he heard her footsteps he turned, and a grin lit his face. "Hey, Sierra. Come see! I'm makin' the most humungous tree house! It's got a sun porch an' a movie theater an' a hangin' staircase." He jabbed the paper in front of him.

Frankie's characters always lived in great places—detailed places that were masterpieces of fantasy and engineering that were actually even more fascinating than the adventures they had.

Sierra crossed the room and bent to study his latest creation. "Wow. I'd like to live in a place like that." She ruffled a hand through his sleep-mussed hair.

"Pretty neat, huh? I'll build you one someday," Frankie promised. "A real one. When I'm an architect."

When he was an architect…

That was his true love. For all that he created fanciful stories, the houses were a bigger passion. Becoming an architect was Frankie's dream. The day she'd first met him, he'd said, "I'm gonna be an architect."

"When I'm an architect…" was almost a daily refrain.

Lately just hearing those words hurt and made Sierra worry that they might not come true. But today they didn't pain her the way they had. Now she could actually smile and tap the end of his nose and say, "A house like that? I'm going to hold you to it, buddy."

Frankie grinned. Then he sobered. "You missed *Star Trek* last night."

"I had to go out."

"Where?"

"To dinner with a…with a friend." She would explain about Dominic later. Now she gave him a tap on the nose. "I'll catch you later, pal. Gotta run. Got to be uptown in— yikes!—twenty minutes."

Pam was waiting in the living room, her cheeks aglow with color for the first time since the doctor had told her Frankie needed a transplant a month ago. Since then she'd been looking like her world was crumbling around her feet. Now she looked nervous, worried, and just the tiniest bit hopeful.

And when Sierra came back into the room, Pammie clutched her hands and started to cry.

"Stop that!" Sierra commanded, horrified. She snatched a tissue from the box on the desk and thrust it at Pammie. "Stop it right now!"

"I can't help it. I know you said he loves you, but do you love him? It's like you're selling your soul and I'm just…just…*letting you!*"

"Of course I love him," Sierra said, and wondered if she was lying or not. "I'm *not* selling my soul! I'm giving Frankie a chance. *Dominic* is giving Frankie a chance."

"And you'll be all right?" Pam was still worried.

"I'll be fine. I'm going to live in a posh apartment and be Mrs. Dominic Got Rocks. How could I not be fine?"

"Money isn't important," Pammie protested, then had the

grace to look abashed because they both knew that in this case—in Frankie's case—it was.

Sierra gave her friend a gentle hug. "I know that. Dominic knows it, too." At least she hoped he did.

Still Pammie shook her head and dabbed at her eyes.

Sierra gave her one last squeeze. "I have to get to work. I'm going to be late. I'll see you later. Call your doctor and tell him it's a go."

"So, did you get a wife?" Shyla grinned as Dominic strode in.

"As a matter of fact, I did." He gave her a blithe smile as he breezed through the reception area, grabbed his mail off her desk and strode into his office. Over his shoulder he saw Shyla staring after him openmouthed.

He shut the door and it banged right open again.

"Who?" Shyla demanded. She'd been his secretary for seven years. She knew him as well as anyone. She didn't stand on ceremony with her boss.

"You don't know her," he said brusquely.

"Not the persistent Marjorie then." Shyla had been deflecting Marjorie for him. Her eyes narrowed. "What did you do, grab the first woman you met?"

"No." He made a pretense of riffling through his mail, hoping if she was ignored, she'd go away.

She didn't budge. "Who?" she asked again.

"Her name's Sierra," he said finally when it was clear she wasn't moving until he answered.

"And who is Sierra? Sounds sort of familiar?" Shyla got a faraway look in her eyes, as if she were mentally going back through all the women in Dominic's address book.

"My sister-in-law's sister," he said grudgingly.

Shyla's eyes went round. "The purple-haired one?" She clapped a hand over her mouth.

Dominic glared. "She's a stylist. It's her image."

Shyla wiped the astonishment off her face. "Of course,"

she said solemnly, but her eyes were twinkling and her lips were twitching.

"You liked her!" Dominic reminded her sharply.

"I said she was the only woman I'd met who could back you down," Shyla agreed, nodding her approval once more.

"Not the only one, obviously," Dominic replied dryly. "There's you."

"Besides me," Shyla said cheerfully. Then she grinned. "You and Sierra. How about that?" She looked positively gleeful. "I'll bet Daddy had a cow."

"Close," Dominic admitted.

Shyla laughed. "I'd like to have seen it. Good for you." Then she sobered. "But surely you didn't marry her just to annoy your father. Did you?" she pressed when he didn't reply at once.

Dominic glowered at her. "Of course not!" There was the sex, too, but he didn't see any reason to be specific.

Shyla looked relieved. She nodded, smiling, and gave him a quick hug. "Then, congratulations. I'm so happy you've fallen in love at last."

In love? Dominic blanched. Not quite! But he didn't think a denial was what Shyla wanted to hear. Edgily Dominic stepped away and pulled out one of the letters from the mail pile. "Get me the file on Harker," he told her. "This is a business. We have work to do."

And God knew he tried, for the entire day, to do it.

He studied the Harker file, twisted his tie around his fingers, and found instead that he wasn't thinking about Harker but about Sierra's activities with his tie the previous night.

He tossed the file aside. Obviously he needed to do something, not just read. So he paced his office, trying to compose a reply, something about the advances of the communications industry, but his mouth went dry as all he seemed to able to think about was the ways Sierra had communicated her desire.

He slammed his fist into his other palm. Then he punched the intercom, and told Shyla to bring the letters she'd finished so he could read and sign them.

He saw—but scarcely read—the words on the page. In his mind he was seeing instead images of Sierra's parted lips, her creamy skin, that tiny dusting of freckles just above her breasts.

"Damn it!" He jumped out of his chair again and stood, hands braced on the desk, head bent, as he took deep lungfuls of air and tried to get her out of his mind.

He couldn't.

But not because he was in love with her, like Shyla thought! Absolutely not. It was just his libido. Hormones. All that testosterone which finally had someplace to go!

He wondered if Sierra was up yet. Maybe he could ring her, get her to meet him at his place for a quickie. God! What was he thinking? He *never* thought things like that!

Well, not never. Today, it seemed, he did.

All the while his assistant Kent Traynor discussed the Harker buyout with him, Dominic's mind wandered. He found himself idly staring at Traynor's solid navy tie and wondering if his wife had ever—

"—don't you think?"

"What?" Dominic jerked back to the moment, aware that he felt oddly flushed and disoriented.

"Think it's a good deal," Traynor was saying. "The Harker buyout," he clarified when Dominic didn't reply at once.

"Oh. Yes, yes. Yes, I do." Which he supposed he did, based on what he'd read in the file yesterday. He sure as hell hadn't been able to focus on it this morning.

"So we should go ahead?" Traynor got to his feet.

"What? Oh, yes, I suppose we should." Dominic checked his watch, still wondering if he would have time for Sierra before a one-thirty meeting.

"I'll get right on it then," Traynor said happily.

"You do that," Dominic said and reached for the phone.

She wasn't home. He supposed she might have gone to his place, but Lupe, his cleaning lady, said there was no one else there. Disgruntled, he called her agent.

"Of course I know where she is," he said. "Right where she's supposed to be. At Gibson Walker's."

"Until when?"

"Until they're finished, of course."

Dominic ground his teeth. "How far ahead is she booked?" Then, hearing the answer, he said, "Unbook her."

"What?"

"She's got other things to do."

"What?"

"She's on her honeymoon," Dominic said and banged down the phone.

He was in Gibson Walker's reception room, when she came out of the studio that evening. Toby Hart, one of the models, had his arm looped over her shoulder and was feeding her one of his ritual lines of bull when she spied Dominic across the room.

He was tapping his foot and glancing at his watch and glaring in annoyance at Edith, Gib's office manager, who stood guarding the inner door with the ferocity of a pit bull.

Sierra smiled. "Hey. Hi!"

"Who's that?" Toby asked.

"My, um, husband?" It wasn't supposed to sound like a question, but somehow it did.

Toby hooted. "A husband? Our Sierra has a husband?" He started to laugh.

Dominic stepped up and with deceptive casualness removed Toby's arm from her shoulders and replaced it with his own. His fingers felt like steel as they curved into her upper arm. "She has a husband," he said with steely smoothness.

Toby grinned, still thinking it was a joke.

Then, "You're late," Dominic growled.

Sierra blinked. "For what?"

"This."

Before she realized what was happening, his lips were on hers. It was a humdinger of a kiss. Fierce, passionate, possessive.

It said, "She's mine," in no uncertain terms. And Sierra, eyes flickering open for an instant, saw that Toby had received the message. As had Edith and Gibson, and Charlee and Cara and Dave, the other models, Sebastian, the ad agency rep, and Lisa, the makeup artist. They stood in a clump in the studio doorway, jaws sagging, as Dominic staked his claim.

Fair enough, Sierra thought. If he could brand her as his, she could do the same to him.

So, shutting her eyes, she returned his kiss with all the fervor, passion and hunger that had been growing inside her all day. She looped her arms around his neck and plastered her body against his—and felt an instant response.

His possessiveness became desire. His passion became hunger. And hers was equal to it. What had started out as a simple branding fire had turned into a full-fledged conflagration. And when they finally pulled apart, it was to stare at each other in wide-eyed astonishment.

"Wow," Toby said, which just about summed it up as far as Sierra was concerned.

Dominic exhaled sharply and grabbed her hand. "We're going home," he said.

CHAPTER FOUR

IF SHE'D had to guess what Dominic's apartment would look like, she'd have imagined acres of polished teak, furniture of chrome and leather and steel, white walls and the perfectly positioned piece of abstract art.

She would have missed by a mile.

His apartment, she knew, was in an elegant pre-war Fifth Avenue building. They were greeted by a doorman who said, "Good evening, Mr. Wolfe," and whose eyes widened only momentarily at his purple-haired companion. They crossed a spacious marble-tiled lobby and walked beneath crystal chandeliers. They rode up five floors in an elevator with exquisite inlaid wood paneling on every wall. They stepped into a graciously appointed vestibule with carpet so thick Sierra felt as if they were standing on a cloud. There were only four doors besides the elevator on the floor. Dominic opened the one facing Fifth and stood back to let her enter first.

Her breath caught in her throat. "You live in a tree house!"

Dominic laughed. "Yeah. More or less." He sounded somewhere between boyish and sheepish and he seemed to be watching her closely.

She couldn't contain her delight at the apartment with its nearly floor-to-ceiling windows that looked right out over the treetops of Central Park. The living room walls weren't white at all, but the soft blue of a spring sky, and the paintings on them were not abstract either. There were several, all almost primitive representational pieces.

The largest was one of a large cottage by a broad sand beach that reminded Sierra of Dominic's house out on Long

Island where she had given Mariah a baby shower. Two more were various aspects of a low-slung peach-colored house with white shuttered French doors. The house was set amongst almost jungly foliage and overlooking a tropical turquoise sea. Two more were beach scenes with children playing in the surf. Sierra didn't know the artist, but she felt an immediate kinship.

"This is your house!" She indicated the painting of the cottage. "How did you get an artist to come and paint your house?"

"My mother painted them all when I was a kid. She wasn't really an artist." There was both pride and defensiveness in his voice.

"She certainly was," Sierra said warmly. "They're all wonderful. I don't know about the others, of course. But she's really captured the spirit of your house."

In fact she could almost feel the love of the Wolfe family home emanating from the painting. It was a feeling she remembered associating with the house the only time she'd visited it. At the time it had seemed odd. Not the sort of feelings she'd ever have expected to get from anything connected to high-powered, hard-edged Dominic Wolfe.

It was, perhaps, one of the things that had made her think there might be more to him than she'd guessed. She remembered she'd come home from the shower even more curious and aware of him than ever.

"Where were the others done?" she asked.

Dominic's expression grew shuttered. "Our family place in the Bahamas."

"It's gorgeous. I love the Bahamas. I've been there on photo shoots. You must go there every chance you get."

"Not anymore." He turned away and she felt as if a wall had crashed down between them.

Too late she remembered Mariah telling her that a long time ago he'd been going to get married in the Bahamas and something had happened. She hadn't been listening then.

She'd been telling herself she didn't want to know anything about Dominic Wolfe. Now she wished she'd paid more attention. Clearly it was still a sore point.

"Well, it's nice to have it because it's your mother's work," she said after a moment. "And you must enjoy remembering that."

He turned back from staring out the window and his smile was only a little strained. "Yeah, I guess."

"So," she said brightly. "Show me the rest."

He showed her a state-of-the-art kitchen, a dining area that was comfortable rather than grand. Then he led her into behind the kitchen to what had once been servants' quarters. One room he had turned into a den with a comfortable sofa, stereo, television and pool table. The other was, he said, "The gear room."

Sports gear, he meant. There was a bin full of soccer balls, footballs, basketballs and baseballs. The walls were lined with racks containing fishing rods, tennis racquets, baseball bats, hockey and lacrosse sticks—all looking well used. There was a serious-looking backpack hanging from a hook on the wall, and beneath it was a row of cleats, skates, both ice and in-line, tennis shoes and hiking boots.

She remembered a profusion of sports gear at the house on Long Island, too, now that she thought about it. But she'd assumed it was left over from childhood or from his brothers, Rhys and Nathan. She'd never imagined Dominic would take time for it.

"You can put your gear in here, too," he said. "Or you can leave it with your stuff upstairs."

"Upstairs?" Sierra echoed as he flipped off the light and led the way back to the living room.

"Mmm. I had it moved." He picked up her tackle box of styling tools and started up the spiral staircase.

It reminded her of Frankie and she knew he would love it. He would love the whole apartment. It looked like it had been designed by a nine-year-old boy. But she barely stopped to think about that now.

She was trying to bend her mind around the "I had it moved" bit.

"I didn't know where you'd want things," Dominic was saying as he led the way up the stairs, "so I just told them for now to put everything in here."

He went into the room directly across from the stairs and flipped another switch. As light spilled into the room, Sierra stopped dead.

It was as if her apartment had been recreated right here. Her futon with its faded striped madras bedspread was against one wall. Against the other was her fish tank, complete with Buster and Gomer.

"Hi, guys," she said in an oddly breathless voice to the imperturbable goldfish swimming around just as if they'd always been here.

Her own bookcase, hand-painted blue, complete with clouds, and filled with her most loved books, was tucked next to the fish tank. She spied her tiny television, her portable stereo. Everything. Even the rather rickety old oak table that she loved—the one that had been in her grandparents' house when she was a child—the one that everyone else she knew was always threatening to throw out.

Dominic hadn't had it thrown out.

He set her tackle box full of makeup gear on it now. "Okay?"

Sierra was still walking around touching it all, wondering at it, awed that, with one wave of Dominic's checkbook her whole life seemed to have moved uptown.

"Did they forget anything?" he asked. "They said they left the stove and refrigerator there, but that your neighbor said they stayed with the apartment."

"They do," Sierra said absently. Then she realized what he'd said. "They asked *Pam*?"

Dominic shrugged. "They asked a neighbor. Someone who came to see what was going on."

"Pam," Sierra said. She'd seen Pam at lunch and her friend hadn't said anything about it. She must have been amazed that Sierra hadn't said anything either. "When did they do all this?"

"This afternoon."

How could they have done it so fast?

As if he'd read her mind, Dominic said, "It didn't take long. There wasn't that much. You can go through it and decide what you want to keep. I told them to bring everything that was yours."

And they'd set it up exactly as it had been in her apartment. Amazing.

Sierra grinned. "So we can come in here anytime and recreate our wedding night?"

He actually blushed, and the heat of the kiss they'd exchanged at Gibson's—which had been burning gently but persistently ever since—flamed suddenly once more to life.

Dominic grabbed her hand and towed her to the door. "Not on your life, sweetheart," he said. "I have a lot bigger bed right this way."

His bedroom was vast. Simple. Almost, but not quite, stark. Unlike the other rooms in his apartment, it had a thick plush carpet on the floor. She could feel her boots sinking into the pile as she stood and stared at the bed.

It was approximately twice the size of her whole apartment. With its hunter-green duvet, it didn't look so much like a bed as a playing field.

And that thought made *her* blush. It sat against the far wall on a raised black lacquer platform. And against the matching black lacquer headboard was a scattering of pillows in toning colors. For an instant Sierra's gaze flickered upward, just to be sure there were no mirrors on the ceiling.

Dominic caught the movement and grinned. "Wishing?"

"No!" She blushed hotly again.

"I always thought it was tacky. But there might be times..." His voice trailed off suggestively, speculatively, and their gazes locked together so fiercely it seemed to Sierra they were almost welded by the heat of the exchange.

After a long moment she cleared her throat. "There might be times," she agreed.

His eyes widened for an instant, and the color in his cheeks deepened. He hesitated just for a second, then he took both her hands in his and drew her close. "I imagine we can manage without."

He knew he shouldn't be so eager.

They hadn't even had dinner yet. And it wasn't like he was going to have to take her home, for God's sake!

She *was* home. In *his* home. Permanently.

But telling himself so made no difference.

He tried to think, to be rational, but he couldn't. It was impossible to think when he had Sierra Kelly—*Wolfe!*—in his bedroom.

There would be plenty of time to be rational—and have dinner—later.

He slid his hands up her arms, then down her back. Then he hooked his fingers under her tube top and peeled it over her head. Her bare breasts brushed against his chest.

He swallowed hard. Then he bent his head and kissed first one and then the other, felt her shiver beneath the cool wet touch of his tongue, and laughed softly.

Her fingers clutched at his hair. "You think you're so hot," she said gruffly, that smoky edge of desire in her voice sending him closer than ever to the edge.

"Mmm," he said and made the sound vibrate against her breast. "Real hot."

Sierra's fingernails dug into his scalp. "Brave man."

He nuzzled her. "You bet." Then he set to work on the leather jeans she was wearing. They were harder to dispose of than her skirts. His fingers felt like thumbs. He fiddled, he wrestled, he groaned.

Sierra grinned. "Thought you might like a bit of challenge."

He steered her back to the bed and toppled her onto it. "I love a challenge." He straddled her and, tongue caught between his teeth, eyes narrowed in concentration, at last he got the button undone and the zip tugged down. Peeling them off was another challenge. They hugged her long legs like a second skin. But finally he smoothed them off and stepped back.

She lay bare before him—but for the merest scrap of lace.

Sierra ran her tongue over her lips and the sight made his hormones jump, made his clothes feel too tight. He tugged at his tie.

"No!" Sierra sat up. "Mine." And she scrambled forward, then knelt on the bed, slid her hands up his shirtfront and unknotted his tie. Then, one by one, she popped open the buttons on his shirt and peeled it slowly away from his chest and down his arms. She was so close that he could feel her breath stirring the hair on his chest. It made him shudder. She smiled and tossed his shirt aside.

"Very nice," she said, her voice a throaty purr. And then her hands were on him again, rubbing up across the crisp hair of his chest, the smooth skin of his shoulders and down his arms. Their fingers locked together, clenched.

And then their lips touched.

That kiss at the studio had been a first course. An appetizer. Heady and passionate, hot and zingy, but insubstantial. This one rocked him back on his heels.

She tasted so good. Ripe and full and warm, as if it wasn't just her mouth kissing him but her whole being, body and soul. She kissed him the way no other woman ever had— as if just doing that was the most important thing in the world, as if she wanted only that—only him.

Her kisses were long and hot, then quick and short. They

were nips and nibbles, tastes and teases. She kissed him on the mouth, on the jaw, on the neck, on the chest. She loosed his hands to knot her fingers in his hair. And he kissed his way down across her chin and her neck. He pressed light kisses once more along the slope of her breasts, then laved her heated skin with his tongue.

"Wolfe!"

"What?"

She wrapped her arms around him and they tumbled together onto the bed. Their bodies tangled, wrestled, squirmed. Her fingers went to his belt and made quick work of it. He let her because he wanted her fingers on him. He yanked off her panties, then held still above her, as she lowered his zipper, knowing she would soon be touching him, flesh to flesh, where he needed her most.

But not yet. Not yet. He took a deep breath and let it out slowly. Slow, he told himself. Go slow.

Then her fingers were at his waist and she hooked her fingers inside his waistband and in one tug, slid both his trousers and his boxers right down to his knees.

"Ah, look what I found," Sierra said softly. Her fingers found him, wrapped him.

He shuddered at her touch. It was exquisite, mind-blowing. He clenched his toes, his fingers, every muscle he owned. He held himself absolutely rigid and prayed to keep his control.

"Si-eeeeerr-ah!" Her name whistled through his gritted teeth.

"Yes, Wolfe?" Her fingers rubbed him lightly.

He swallowed hard. Trembled. Quivered. "Don't. Stop."

His breath came in quick, harsh gasps. And as much as he wanted to go slow, to draw it out, to make her as crazy as she made him, he knew it wasn't going to happen this time.

But he would, he vowed. Later. *Later!*

God!

"Don't?" She smiled against his chest. "Stop? Or, don't stop?"

Her fingers were stroking him, making his body break out in a sweat. Then she followed her fingers with her tongue, licking him, and he was almost gone.

Desperate, he parted her thighs, sought the slick hot center of her, and plunged in, thanking heaven she was as ready as he was.

If she hadn't been, he'd have hurt her or made a fool of himself.

But she was, and she embraced him. "Ah, Wolfe," she whispered, her breath hot against his cheek as she shifted, settling him in.

Dominic's eyes squeezed shut against the overpowering sensation and clung desperately to the last shreds of control. He didn't move. Couldn't. Not yet.

Not if he wanted it to be good for her, too. Not if he wanted to shatter her the way she could so easily shatter him.

He took a careful breath and held it. Held it. Held it.

Sierra went still, too. Silent. Her body wriggled. He bit his lip. Hung on.

A finger touched the small of his back. "Wolfe?"

"What?" He said the word without moving, without breathing.

Muffled laugh. "You are still alive. I thought you were dead!"

"Dead!" He reared up, outraged.

But Sierra held him fast. She wrapped her arms around him, giggling, as she wriggled beneath him, then pressing her heels against the backs of his thighs, urging him closer, seating even him deeper inside her.

And that was all it took.

That small movement. That slight friction—and he was a goner. He surged against her, once, twice—and came with a shuddering, shattering climax that left him weak and wrung out and feeling like a fumbling teenager instead of a thirty-six-year-old man.

"Sorry," he muttered. "Sorry."

He tried to pull away, to come to grips. But Sierra hung on. She kissed his sweat-slick shoulders. She caressed the damp skin of his back. Her fingers kneaded his buttocks. And Dominic felt small shudders course through him at the same time they seemed to ripple through her.

Was she?

Her fingers clenched. Her nails dug into his butt. Her heels pressed hard against the backs of his thighs.

Had she?

Lord, what kind of moron was he that he couldn't tell? Didn't know?

"Ahhhhh," she breathed. "Yessssss." And then she gave a long sigh and her fingers relaxed. She rubbed her foot down his leg, then nuzzled his neck. Her body seemed to settle and soften beneath him. And then he realized that the weight of his body was resting on hers and quickly he rolled away.

This time Sierra let him go. But not far. Just far enough so that she could turn onto her side and snuggle into him. He felt her lips graze one of his nipples and his hand came up involuntarily and stroked her hair.

"Dominic?"

That surprised him as she rarely called him anything but Wolfe. His hand stilled. "What?" he asked warily.

Her eyes were still closed, but he felt her smile against his chest. "That was very nice."

Nice!? As a lover he was "nice"?

Actually he supposed he was lucky she thought that highly of him. He certainly hadn't taken much trouble seeing that her needs were met.

"It will be better," he muttered.

"No." She shook her head slightly. "Couldn't be." She kissed him.

And then she slept.

Dominic didn't sleep.

He lay there and stared at the ceiling, trying to sort things out.

This was the later during which he was supposed to be fixing dinner and going over the papers he needed to look at before morning. But Sierra was asleep in his arms and he didn't want to disturb her.

That was why he didn't move. It had nothing to do with how much he liked just lying there holding her. It had nothing to do with how much he wanted Sierra still.

He didn't like that he wanted Sierra.

Sex was one thing. But just lying here holding her was something else. That felt…committed.

Dominic wasn't about to get committed.

Not in his heart.

He'd be faithful. It was just good sense to be faithful. It was fair. Dominic believed in being fair. He had no intention of looking at any other women. He had no desire at all to sleep around. Even if he should ever feel such a desire he wouldn't do it. Because he'd made a vow.

He believed in vows.

What he didn't believe in was letting anyone into his heart.

He wasn't letting Sierra into his heart.

Even thinking about such a thing annoyed him. He wasn't used to even considering the possibility. He wasn't used to wanting one this much. And he wasn't used to having mixed emotions about it.

He wasn't really used to emotions at all.

After the disaster with Carin, he'd built a good strong wall between himself and the women in his life. He played with them, but he never let them matter. He never fell in love.

And he still hadn't, he assured himself.

Of course he hadn't. Imagine being in love with a purple-haired cosmetologist!

Sierra was his wife, yes. But that was for expediency's sake. He'd wanted to spike his father's guns once and for all, and she had been the perfect woman to do it with.

She was wild, crazy, exactly wrong for him.

And they had great sex.

What could be better?

Outside the sound of sirens headed up Madison Avenue. Sierra snuggled closer and instinctively Dominic's arm tightened around her. Then deliberately, determinedly, he loosened it. She didn't need his protection. Hell, half the time he needed protecting from her!

The sirens receded and, in the silence, he could hear the soft sound of Sierra's breathing. It ruffled the hairs on his chest. Her soft hair brushed his chin and tickled his lips. He held himself still, resisting the impulse to kiss the top of her head.

They were still having great sex, he reminded himself. Tonight they'd had great sex. He wrapped a strand of purple hair around his fingers. It had been fun. Exhilarating. And he didn't even have to grab a taxi and go home afterward.

It was more efficient.

Yes, Dominic decided, pleased with that notion. It was efficient to have married Sierra. Efficient. That's what it was.

Sierra awoke slowly, relishing the end of a lovely dream and snuggling in the soft fine cotton of the sheets. She stretched drowsily, opened her eyes and realized where she was.

Immediately she looked around for Dominic. He wasn't there. She frowned, then glanced toward the bathroom, expecting to see the door closed and hear the shower running. But the door was open and the bathroom was empty. Bright morning sunlight was peeping through the drapes.

Sierra rolled over—and jerked wide awake. It was seven forty-five!

Her alarm clock hadn't gone off!

She scrambled out of bed. Why hadn't he awakened her? Had she forgotten to set her clock? She grabbed it off the table and checked it. Yes, apparently she had. God!

It was what Dominic did to her. He could make her forget her brain if it were trapped inside her head.

She hurried to the bathroom and flicked on the shower. While she waited for the water to warm up, she brushed her teeth. Once she'd done it, she realized that she hadn't needed to wait. In Dominic's apartment, unlike her old one, hot water was plentiful and immediate. She jumped in and just wished she had time to enjoy it.

Sometime she would, she vowed. Maybe tonight. Maybe tonight she would take a long leisurely shower—and not alone. She soaped her body quickly and imagined slicking that wonderful spicy smelling soap over the lean hard planes of Dominic's body. She imagined making him shudder and moan.

Sierra had a good imagination. Way too good. So she flicked the water to cold, yelped and shivered. Then, ardor quenched, she shut it off and jumped out of the shower.

Later, she promised herself. Tonight.

Quickly she toweled her hair dry, wrapped herself in Dominic's plush robe that hung on the door, then went to fix herself some breakfast. Ordinarily, being late, she might have skipped it. But this morning she was ravenous.

They hadn't eaten last night—not food anyway. They'd been far too intent on each other to venture into the kitchen. So now she made oatmeal, fried bacon, and while it was cooking, ate a slice of cantaloupe. There was coffee still hot in the coffeemaker. She blessed Dominic and gulped a cup. Then she poured herself another and carrying it, hurried back upstairs to dress. She had to be at Finn MacCauley's studio a little before nine and now that she was living uptown, she'd have to allow a little more time.

There was no time to do anything clever with her hair, so

she arranged it in a casual tousled style, then went into the bedroom where her things were and opened the closet.

Her clothes weren't there!

None of them. She whipped open the dresser. At least she still had underwear. She grabbed a bra and a pair of panties, then stared once more at the empty closet.

Had Dominic had them throw everything out?

She knew, though he'd never said anything, that he thought some of her clothing was a little over-the-top. But had he married her and then ditched it all?

Incensed, fuming, Sierra stalked back into his bedroom, yanked open the walk-in closet door, ready to do the same to his Brooks Brothers' pinstripes and his long-sleeved dress shirts—and discovered that all her clothes had been hung in there.

Next to a dozen dark conservative suits and jackets and trousers were her denim miniskirts and Day-Glo tube tops. Next to his long-sleeved button-down shirts were her halter tops and camisoles. And there, at the end of a row on the floor, alongside his wing tips and deck shoes were her strapy sandals and clunky boots.

She laughed—and felt oddly, immeasurably lighter.

At least they weren't only sharing sex, they were sharing a closet, too.

She picked out a top, then changed her mind and plucked one of Dominic's shirts off the hanger instead. She slipped it on and flapped the sleeves, then rolled them up to her elbows. It was far too broad in the shoulders and the shirt-tails hit her just inches above her knees. But buttoned, it covered more of her than Sierra normally covered—even if she left the top two buttons open. Besides, wearing it made her feel closer to Dominic. If she rubbed her cheek against the collar she could smell that same clean laundry starch smell she smelled whenever she pressed her face against his chest.

She was going to share his shirt as well. It made her feel good.

She shimmied into a pair of purple leggings, then stuffed her feet into her boots, and cinched her waist with a hot pink belt. Stepping back, she studied her reflection in the full-length mirror on the back of the door.

The new improved Sierra Kelly *Wolfe* stared back at her.

Her lips twitched into a smile, then a full-fledged grin. She felt wonderful. Giving herself a thumbs up and one more saucy grin, Sierra headed off to work.

''What do you mean, you got someone else?'' She stared at Strong, Finn's office manager, her jaw sagging. It was ten minutes to nine. She'd taken the downtown subway and had run the last three blocks. She wasn't late. But Strong had looked astonished to see her and had said Lisa was coming in. ''Why would you get someone else?''

''Because Bruce called and said you were booked out.''

''*What?* Why would he say a thing like that?'' Sierra thumped her tackle box down. ''Give me the phone.''

Furiously she punched in her agent's number. ''Bruce! It's Sierra. What are you doing? Why did you tell Finn I wasn't going to be here?''

''Because you booked out, sweetheart.''

''I did no such thing!''

''Well, not you personally,'' Bruce said. ''But your husband—''

''What? *Dominic* called you?''

''You betcha, sweetheart. Said you were going on your honeymoon.''

Sierra stood speechless. Finally she managed, ''Honeymoon?''

The word stopped her dead. Dominic had called Bruce? Dominic had booked her out? Dominic had said they were going on a honeymoon?

Then why hadn't Dominic told her?

"What *exactly* did my, um, husband say?"

"Just that. He called yesterday morning, looking for you. He seemed to think you had already booked out. But I told him you were working, and he asked how far ahead you were scheduled and then he said to unbook you. You didn't want me to?"

A part of Sierra wanted to tear Bruce's head off. A part of her wanted to tear off Dominic's.

How dare he just call up and cancel her jobs?

But another part of her—the closet romantic part—couldn't quite bring herself to do it. Because he was taking her on a honeymoon.

They would have more than sex and a closet and a shirt shared between them. They would have a real start to their marriage. Time for each other.

For sex, of course.

But for more than that. For getting to know each other. For learning to love each other.

"Oh," she said and sucked in a deep breath, then let it out a little shakily. "No. That's all right. You did…fine. Thanks."

"So you're out, right?" Bruce said, apparently wanting it from the horse's mouth this time.

"I'm out."

"'Till when?"

"I'll let you know," she promised, starting to smile, happiness welling up inside her.

As soon as she'd discussed it with Dominic.

CHAPTER FIVE

SHE went back to the apartment and called Pam. "You and Frankie have to come visit."

"Sierra?" Pam squeaked. "Oh, I'm so glad to hear from you. I was so worried when those movers came. It was so sudden. Of course I should have realized you'd move. I just didn't think—"

"Neither did I," Sierra said cheerfully. "But that's Dominic. He snaps his fingers, the world moves. Or at least I did. You won't believe this place. You've got to see it. Frankie has to see it. Get a cab and come up." She rattled off the address.

"Oh, we can't intrude!" Pammie objected.

"You're not intruding. You're sharing the experience. Besides, you didn't think that moving uptown would get me out of your life, did you? Come on. Grab a taxi and come. I'll pay for it. We'll have a picnic."

"Frankie can't—"

"Inside," Sierra assured her. "Frankie will love it. Trust me."

"But—"

"Pammie," Sierra said sternly. "Don't abandon me." It was underhanded and she knew it, playing on Pam's beholdenness. But it worked.

Pam gave in. "We'll take the bus."

Sierra would have disputed that, but she knew her friend already considered herself beholden for half a million dollars. Pammie would be determined not to add cab fare on top of it.

"I'll see you in an hour," Sierra said.

Dominic's kitchen was as well-stocked as the average restaurant. Sierra had seen that when she was fixing herself breakfast. But she doubted Frankie would care, so she made peanut butter and jelly sandwiches, cut oranges in half, found a bag of "homemade" chocolate-chip cookies in the cupboard, and set everything out on her old madras bedspread in front of the windows in the living room.

"Wow!" Frankie crowed when they arrived. "We are havin' a picnic! See, Mom?" His normally pale cheeks flushed with enthusiasm as he looked around the apartment, then beamed at his mother. His eyes were alight with excitement. "This is great. It's like my tree house," he approved. "Way cool."

"Way cool," Pammie agreed and, looking around, too, actually laughed in delight. "This is amazing."

"Isn't it?" Sierra said. "Come on. Let's eat."

After they finished, she showed them the rest of the apartment. Frankie loved the staircase. He examined it carefully, as if committing it to memory so he could reproduce it on his own designs once he got home. He liked the view and craned his neck to see how far up and down the park he could see. But most of his enthusiasm he saved for "the gear room" and the den next to it. He handled the roller blades and the ice skates and the baseball bats and pounded his fist into Dominic's fielder's glove.

"Next year I'm gonna play baseball," he told his mother and Sierra.

"Yes," Pammie agreed.

"And I'm gonna ice skate this winter."

"Well…"

"I am," Frankie said fervently. "When I get my new kidney. I'm gettin' one," he told Sierra. "My doc said."

"Did he?"

Frankie nodded solemnly. "He said I'll be better'n new then. Didn't he?" He looked to his mother for confirmation.

Pam nodded. "Yes." She smiled at Sierra. "That's what he said."

Sierra wanted to hear more of what the doctor said, but she didn't think Frankie needed to be part of the whole discussion, so she poked through Dominic's collection of videotapes.

"Raiders of the Lost Ark?" She plucked one out, knowing it was one of Frankie's favorites. "Want to watch it on the big screen?" She nodded toward the TV.

Frankie looked at his mother beseechingly. "Can I, Mom?"

"I don't know if we can stay that long," Pam said.

"Let him start," Sierra said. "You can always come back and finish another time."

They left Frankie settled in watching Indiana Jones being chased by headhunters, and she and Pammie went back to the kitchen. Sierra poured them each a cup of tea.

"Tell me what the doctors said?"

"They said he'll be better than new." Pam smiled as she echoed what Frankie had said moments before. "Truly, Sierra. They said if they get a match, he's a great candidate. And because of you, he's on the list. They are going to be doing tissue samples so they will know when a match exists. They're testing me, of course, and my sister. And they'll test Frankie's father if we find him. Not that I think we're likely to. Or," she added grimly, "that Dan would give one up if he knew."

"Of course he would," Sierra said. "Frankie's his son!"

"As if that ever meant a thing to him." Pam gave herself a little shake. "It doesn't matter. What matters is that out there somewhere there's going to be a kidney. I'm sure of it. And Frankie will be well again." She clasped her fingers together and looked heavenward. "Please, God." Then she looked at Sierra, her expression concerned. "Are you really okay here? I mean, it's gorgeous and all that. Almost homey, even. But that's just the trappings. Is he…is he *good* to you? I couldn't stand it if he wasn't good to you."

Sierra took Pam's hands in hers, smiling. "Stop worrying. He's good to me."

"But can you make it work? " Pammie wanted to know. "Really? I know that you probably have—" she blushed "—great sex. But what about…about everything else? Dan and I had great sex," she said grimly.

"No. It's more than that," Sierra assured her. "It started that way," she admitted. "And it's crazy, the two of us are so different. But…we're going on a honeymoon."

Pam's eyes lit up and she squeezed Sierra's hands. "You are?" she said eagerly. "When? Where?"

"I don't know yet. He hasn't said. But…he booked me out. That's why I was off today."

Pam's eyes widened. "He called Bruce and didn't even tell you?"

Sierra shook her head. "It's like him. To do something like that spontaneously. In that way, I guess, we are alike." She grinned. "He'll tell me tonight. He'll have to. Because he didn't tell me this morning and I'm going to have to know. After all I went to work and found out I'd been replaced."

"Whoa! Really?" Pam looked worried.

"Don't," Sierra said, before Pam's natural instinct to think the worst could kick in. "You don't know Wolfe. That's the way he is. Peremptory. Cocky. Determined."

"Nothing like you." Pam·grinned.

Sierra laughed. "It's why we strike sparks off each other, that's for sure. He'll tell me tonight." She hugged her arms across her breasts happily.

And then Pam smiled, too. "I'm glad," she said and gave Sierra a quick hug. "You deserve to be happy, Sierra. Nobody deserves it more."

Dominic had thought yesterday was bad.

Today was a whole lot worse.

Yesterday he hadn't been able to get Sierra out of his

mind, but at least she'd been at work where he knew he couldn't just walk in and grab her and haul her home to bed.

Today he knew she was home.

All day long. Or she would be once she got to Finn's and realized she'd been taken off the books.

He probably should have told her last night, but he hadn't remembered. He'd been much to intent on the Sierra right in front of him to think about tomorrow.

Then this morning, when he'd been tempted to wake her and indulge in making love to her one more time, he hadn't because he knew making love with Sierra would not be quick. Once they got started, they would take their time. They would love each other deeply and intensely and furiously.

And that would be fine for her because she could stay there all day. But he had a meeting about the Harker takeover at eight.

So he'd left her asleep while he'd hauled himself out of bed.

Sierra hadn't stirred. And when he came back after his shower, she'd still been sound asleep. Of course they'd barely slept all night, so she had a right to be tired. And she looked so sweet and peaceful and content that he couldn't bear to wake her up just to tell her she could go back to sleep again.

So he'd reached over and shut off her alarm. There was no sense in her waking up and going in to work when she didn't have to. She would doubtless call Finn's when she woke up, and they could tell her they'd got someone else.

She might be annoyed at finding out that way, but Dominic was confident she'd see the sense in it when he explained.

He shot back his cuff and glanced at his watch. It was now three minutes later than the last time he'd looked at it.

He wanted to go home to Sierra. It was ten minutes after

six. He could certainly leave now. Shyla had left twenty minutes ago. Most everyone else had gone before that.

"You aren't going to keep the bride waiting, are you?" Shyla had said when she'd stuck her head in to say goodnight.

Dominic had looked up from the papers he had spread all over his desk. "Not for long," he'd assured her.

But he would have stayed to work if she hadn't been home waiting. And he wasn't going to disrupt his whole life for her. It would be letting her matter far too much, implying that he cared more than he did.

He had no intention of doing that.

"I'll head home shortly," he said. "There are things that I want to finish up first." He wasn't admitting he'd been aching to leave since lunchtime—or before.

So he made himself focus on the papers on his desk. He read all the specs on the Harker deal, and then he read them over again. He had a fine steel-trap mind and a reputation for attention to meticulous detail. He never went into a business deal unless he understood exactly what he was getting into. He wasn't afraid to take risks, but they were calculated to the nth degree.

Usually such detail consumed him. The more he learned, the more he wanted to learn.

Not tonight.

Tonight his mind kept wandering to Sierra. What had she done all day? Was she eager for him to come home? As eager as he was to be there?

Damn it!

He shoved her out of his head and made himself read the pages aloud. Made himself dwell on every single word. And every few minutes he checked his watch.

Finally at quarter to seven he decided he'd exercised his willpower long enough.

Neatly he put all the papers back into the folder. Then, lining it up with the edge he set it on the corner of his desk.

He checked his e-mail one last time, recorded his thoughts for Kent in case his assistant checked his mail tonight. Then, satisfied that he was once more in control of his life—and his libido—he locked up and made his way home.

She didn't fix peanut butter and jelly for Dominic.

Sierra wasn't a terrific cook, but under the circumstances, she wanted to do her best. So she called her sister Mariah and asked for help.

"What sort of help?" Mariah said warily. Sierra knew her sister loved her dearly, but they were not always on the same wavelength. And considering what she hadn't told Mariah, this was going to be a little tricky.

"I need a recipe or two," she said airily.

"Recipes? What kind? I thought you believed in takeout. Wasn't that your idea of the world's best cookbook? The one filled with phone numbers of take-away joints?"

"Most of the time it is," Sierra admitted. "But I want to do something a little special tonight."

"Who is he?"

Trust Mariah to get right to the point. And trust Mariah not to have heard. How could a woman who made her living interviewing people and doing stunningly perceptive personality pieces miss seeing who made her own sister's heart pound?

Of course that meant that Sierra had camouflaged her feelings incredibly well. She certainly hadn't wanted anyone to know she had a thing for Dominic Wolfe. Unrequited passion wasn't something she had any desire to admit to.

Now she was wishing she'd been a little more transparent.

"It's Dominic," she said.

"Dominic who?" Mariah asked.

Jeez. "Dominic! Your brother-in-law."

"*What!* No! You're joking! Sierra, that's not even funny. You and Dominic? God, Rhys would bust a gut laughing. Who is it really? I mean, I'm glad you've finally found someone who can keep you interested for more than a week and a half. But…'' Her sister's voice trailed off when Sierra didn't say anything.

The silence grew. And grew. And grew.

"You aren't joking." The words fell like stones into still water. Mariah sighed heavily. "Oh, for God's sake, Sierra. He's handsome and clever and smarter than Einstein. But he's made of granite. He's all business—24/7. He probably sleeps in his suit and tie."

"He doesn't."

"He never— What did you say?"

"I said, he doesn't sleep in his suit. The tie is—" Sierra giggled "—optional."

"Oh. My. God." There was a long silence. "Can I just tell you to cut your losses?" Mariah said. "Can I tell you to get out while the getting is good, before you get serious? Because, believe me, sweetie, Dominic is not going to get serious. He's not going to get involved. He's a 100% confirmed bachelor."

"He married me on Tuesday."

She knew she shouldn't just blurt it out like that. She knew she should pussyfoot around, come at it obliquely, maybe try to soften the news a little, prepare her sister. She knew Mariah wasn't keen on surprises.

But it was four o'clock. Dominic would be home in less than two hours. And she wanted to make him dinner—a nice dinner—to celebrate their marriage—and the surprise honeymoon.

She didn't have a lot of time.

"I'm sorry. I must have heard you wrong. I thought you said he *married* you?" Mariah sounded oddly breathless.

"You heard right. We got married. On Tuesday afternoon," Sierra thought that grounding it down to a day might help.

"On Tuesday afternoon. Just like that. *You don't even know each other! You don't even like each other! You threat-*

ened him with his tie when you busted into his…'' Once more Mariah's words died. There was a bit more silence, then a slightly thready, just a little bit hysterical laugh. ''And that's when it began, huh?''

''Not really,'' Sierra said quickly. ''We really stayed well away from each other after that. I mean, he thought I was really going to rip off his family jewels. He wasn't exactly enamored. But he was…''

''Curious?''

''I guess you could say that. And, well, so was I. We ran into each other a few times. At your shower. And then at the hospital after Steve and Lizzie were born. We were just sort of…aware. But nothing happened—until your wedding. We had a little too much champagne at the wedding. And we were on our own after the reception. We had to go back to Kansas City to catch a flight out in the morning and—''

''I get the picture,'' Mariah said. There was a pause. Then she said, ''Why didn't you say anything? If you've been seeing him—''

''I haven't been! It was, like, a one-night-get-it-out-of-our-system event. But it didn't,'' Sierra said. ''I hadn't seen him since.''

''Until Tuesday,'' Mariah said dryly.

''Until Tuesday,'' Sierra agreed. ''And he showed up at Finn's studio and asked me to marry him.''

''Why?'' Then, ''I'm sorry! I'm sorry.'' Mariah backed off at once. ''I didn't mean that. But—wait a minute. Maybe I did. Three months? Sierra, are you—?''

''No! I am damned well not! You're the one who got pregnant, 'Riah,'' Sierra said sharply. ''Not me.''

''Right,'' Mariah said. ''Right.'' This last was a sigh. ''You love him.''

Sierra wet her lips and took a breath. ''Yes.''

Mariah didn't say anything for a moment. She was clearly trying to rethink everything she knew about her conservative, businesslike brother-in-law—*and* her purple-haired impulsive sister.

"Does he love you?" she asked finally, apparently having decided that given everything else she had misjudged, that might be possible, too.

"No," Sierra admitted. "He doesn't. He married me because we're dynamite in bed together. And because—" she sucked in a breath and plunged on, making a full breast of it, "because Douglas kept shoving suitable women down his throat."

"Oh, surely not!" Mariah protested at once.

"He was," Sierra insisted. "Every few weeks he'd have another candidate for Dominic to look over. All marvelous, eminently suitable women. Not like me."

"But that can't be why he married you," Mariah countered. "He couldn't be so dumb."

"Thank you very much!"

"I don't mean that you're unsuitable, but that he wouldn't marry just to spike Douglas's guns!"

"Yes," Sierra said. "He would. He did."

"But—"

"And now we have to make something of it. Something that will work. That will last. I want it to last, 'Riah," Sierra said urgently.

"What does Dominic want?"

"I think he wants it to last, too. He booked me out today. I went to Finn's and I'd been replaced."

"What?" Mariah was somewhere between outrage and astonishment.

"I was furious at first, too," Sierra said, "but then I talked to Bruce. Dominic had called yesterday and booked me out—so we could go on a honeymoon!"

Her sister was silent for a moment. Regrouping. Sorting things out. Thinking. That was Mariah, all over. Steady. Dependable. Insightful.

"So he must want it to work, too," Sierra went on. "Don't you think?"

She didn't realize how badly she wanted Mariah to agree until she asked. It was, she realized, why she'd called her sister in the first place. The recipes had been the excuse, the catalyst that would allow her to tell her sister news she should have told her as soon as it had happened.

But she'd been afraid to then.

She'd been afraid that Mariah would tell her she was an idiot, that there was no way on earth Dominic and she could ever make a successful marriage, that impulsive trips to the city hall, based on no more than lust and a desire to annoy someone else, were destined for divorce court before the month was out.

And she'd had no reason to believe that Mariah would have been wrong.

But now they were going on a honeymoon.

Now it was more than lust and irritation at his father. He was taking time for her. He wanted to be with her, to get to know her. Perhaps to learn to love her.

"Don't you think?" she repeated.

"It's a start," Mariah said. "Yeah, it's a start."

She gave Sierra a couple of good family recipes that she said any idiot could manage. "Do the lasagne," she said. "Rhys loves lasagne. Dominic will, too. Fix a salad. Make garlic bread. Easy. The least of your worries," she said with considerable accuracy. Then she wished Sierra luck.

"Thanks."

"If you need anything—ever—you let me know," Mariah said, her protective big sister determination showing its face. "Rhys will kick his butt for you anytime you want."

Sierra forbore saying that she thought Dominic was a match for his youngest brother.

Even though Rhys was a fireman and worked hard at a physical job much of the time, Sierra had seen enough of

Dominic recently to know he had muscles. Plenty of muscles.

And she didn't think he would suffer much interference in his life.

"We'll be fine," she said. "I hope."

"I hope so, too, kid," Mariah said. "Good luck."

Sierra went shopping for the few things she needed that Dominic didn't have. Then she lugged all the grocery bags home. The doorman had apparently accepted her right to be there for he helped her get them into the elevator.

"You know," he said, "you can have them delivered."

"Really?" It was amazing the things she had no idea about. "Thanks."

She boiled the noodles, browned the meat and grated the cheese. Then she put the lasagne together, made a salad of mixed greens, mushrooms, red onion, black olives and Parmesan-flavored croutons, and made a garlic butter paste for the loaf of fresh bakery French bread she'd bought.

She set the table in the dining el where they could sit and eat, looking out over the park. It was considerably more civilized than the picnic she'd made for Frankie and Pam earlier that day, but it still felt very warm and cozy and tree-house-like. She put wineglasses on the table, dimmed the light slightly, then lit candles instead and shut the light off.

"Yes," she said. It was perfect. Romance in a tree house.

And she would make sure they ate before they adjourned to the bedroom.

Where were they going on their honeymoon? she wondered. Jamaica? Italy? Greece? Cancún?

She had known people who'd gone to all those places. Probably Dominic knew somewhere even better.

She wished he had told her. But then she didn't blame him for keeping it a surprise. The anticipation was lovely.

Even lovelier was the realization that he cared enough to

want a honeymoon with her—that he, too, wanted their marriage to work.

It was six-fifteen. She thought he would be home any minute. She put the lasagne in to bake and opened the wine to let it breathe. She checked his stereo system and discovered that if she put on music in the den, the speakers were rigged so that she could hear it in any room in the house. She put on some soft romantic stuff, hoping that it wasn't music Dominic associated with seducing another woman.

And then she waited for him to walk in the door.

She waited. And waited.

She checked the lasagne. She checked the bread. She fiddled with the salad. She sipped the wine.

Six-thirty became six forty-five. Six forty-five became seven. Then it was seven-fifteen. Finally at almost seven-thirty, the front door opened.

Sierra smoothed damp palms down the sides of Dominic's shirt which she still wore. She'd hadn't felt nervous in years. She'd felt less apprehensive when she'd married him!

But that had just been an impulse.

Now they were getting down to what really mattered.

He wants this to work, too, she reminded herself. Then she drew a deep breath and went to greet her husband.

Something smelled good. Better than good.

Delicious.

As Dominic let himself into the apartment, his stomach growled in anticipation, and his whole being responded with surprise.

He'd assumed Sierra would be there waiting for him. But he'd expected a few threats and not a little annoyance as his reward for having booked her out of work.

In fact, he'd been anticipating the pleasure of charming her out of her irritation. All the way home—all day, for that matter—he'd been looking forward to it. He fully expected to lose his tie and to feel her fingers digging into his ribs.

And he'd imagined catching her hands in his hand holding them over her head while he kissed her senseless. He would be rewarded with a deep flush on her cheeks and a hungry look in her eyes—and all would be forgiven and forgotten as he bore her off to bed.

But if he had to eat a delicious home-cooked meal instead, he supposed philosophically, he could probably manage that. Still, he was a little surprised she wasn't upset.

Maybe she was. He hadn't seen her yet.

"Sier—" Her name dried up on his tongue as she sashayed out of the kitchen.

"Hi!" She gave him a cheery smile and a quick kiss before dancing away toward the dining area.

No complaints? No arguments? No need to charm her into a different mood?

Heck. But then, who cared?

She looked good enough to eat.

She was wearing one of his long-sleeved dress shirts, cinched at the waist with a belt. Dominic had never considered his shirts sexy in the slightest. But he'd never seen one on Sierra before!

Her legs were bare and her knees and several inches of tanned thigh were visible below the tails of his shirt. Even more smooth thigh flashed into view when she turned and he glimpsed the sides where the tails curved upward.

"Hi," he managed. It sounded like a frog's croak.

Enough buttons were undone at the neck and below that she didn't appear to be wearing a bra.

What else wasn't she wearing?

"You didn't tell me you'd called Bruce."

It was what he expected her to say, but her tone wasn't accusing. There seemed to be a soft, wondering, appreciative note in it.

He shrugged. "Well, it's not like I can't afford to support you."

"I know, but I didn't expect it. I'm so glad."

She was? Would wonders never cease? He reached for her, assuring himself that it was okay to do so now. He'd waited all day, after all.

They kissed. It was a long kiss. Eager on both their parts. Deep and hungry. It should have led straight to the bedroom.

But Sierra backed off. "First we eat. Food." She smiled at him. "I got my mother's recipe for lasagne. Mariah gave it to me."

Dominic did his best to tamp down his desire. "Right," he said. "Food."

"I hope you're hungry." She was looking at him hopefully, her expression open and eager.

"Sure," he said. "Even for food."

She laughed as if he'd made a wonderful joke. "Good. Go wash up, then come and sit. It's ready."

He was tempted to suggest they make a quick trip up to the bedroom first. But he didn't. She'd obviously worked hard to make dinner special. The least he could do was enjoy it. Any other time, he was sure he would. It was just that he'd been waiting all day to go to bed with her.

He dried his hands and went back to the dining room. She was serving the meal on his seldom-used dining table in front of the windows overlooking the park. She'd lit candles—tapers on the sideboard and at either side of the table. She'd put their plates directly across from each other. It looked cosy, intimate. A love nest.

Dominic felt edgy, wary, then chided himself. What was he wary of? Being trapped into marriage? Hardly. He was already married to her.

"Sit down," Sierra said. She asked him to pour the wine.

He poured it, then handed her a glass. He was reminded of the last time they'd drunk together—at dinner with his father and Viveca and Tommy Hargrove. He remembered the toasts. Looking at Sierra he thought she did, too. She was looking at him with a bright, eager look in her eyes.

"To you," Dominic said after a moment and touched his glass to hers.

"To us," Sierra replied with a smile. Then she drank.

Dominic drank, too. Then he dug into the lasagne and the salad and the bread. It was excellent. Simple, but delicious. And even though he'd have happily forgone it and headed straight upstairs with her, he ate now with gusto. "Really, really good," he told her, wiping his mouth with his napkin.

She hadn't eaten nearly as much as he had. She seemed to be watching him, waiting. "Good," she said. "I'm glad. I'm not much of a cook. But I'm willing to learn."

"You don't have to cook every night," Dominic said.

"That's a relief. But I intend to do plenty. If it's okay with you. I was wondering what kind of foods you like."

"Most anything. I'm not picky."

"Italian? You like lasagne. Have you been to Italy? I always thought Italy would be a lovely place to go. I never got there, even when I was in France, can you believe it?" She was talking rapidly. Even more rapidly than Sierra usually did.

"You've never been to Italy?"

She shook her head. "There's a lot of places I haven't been. Jamaica. Cancún. Niagara Falls. The Poconos."

Dominic blinked, trying to follow that, wondering what those places had in common. Maybe they were the only places Sierra had never been.

"What about Alaska?" he asked. "Have you been there?"

Her eyes widened. "Alaska? No, never. It sounds…great! Amazing."

"It's beautiful," Dominic agreed. "Rhys and I have gone fishing there several times."

"Oh." She looked a little puzzled, but then she smiled again. "Alaska's great," she said again.

Dominic frowned slightly. Was she angling to go along when he went fishing with Rhys again? He'd never taken a woman along on a fishing trip before. It was a time to be gnarly and grubby and unshaven. But the thought of having Sierra there to share a sleeping bag with made him consider rethinking his decision.

"Maybe we could do that in the summer," he said.

She brightened. "Summer! Oh, yes, that'd be terrific." She plied herself to the lasagne then. When she leaned forward slightly, his shirt gapped at her neck and he could see right down into it. He could watch the shadowed rise and fall of her creamy breasts.

He shifted in his chair, trying to adjust the fit of his slacks. One of his feet connected with Sierra's. Her toes slid up his ankle and rubbed against his shin. She smiled at him over her wineglass.

Dominic raised his and took a hasty gulp of wine, finishing his glass.

Sierra held out the bottle. "More?" Her toes slid slightly higher.

"Not...right now," Dominic said.

"Whenever you want any, then," Sierra said. She wet her lips. "Just help yourself."

"Do you want to finish this meal or not?" Dominic growled.

She giggled. "I'm getting pretty full. I think I might be ready for the next course."

He didn't think she meant food. "About time." His urgency whistled through his teeth. He shoved back his chair and stood.

Sierra stood, too. He saw light and hunger and happiness in her eyes.

"I thought you'd be ticked," he said.

A tiny line appeared between her brows. "Ticked? At what? Why should I be?"

"You shouldn't. But I forgot last night to tell you I'd called your agent and canceled your work."

"Well, I admit it was high-handed of you," Sierra said.

"But under the circumstances, I decided to forgive you."
She came around the table and lifted her arms and looped
them around his neck. She kissed his chin, then his lips.

And he kissed hers, tasting wine and tomato and a hint
of something totally Sierra. It sent his blood pumping
through his veins. "Circumstances?"

"The honeymoon," Sierra said, looking up into his eyes.
"Where are we going? Obviously not Alaska. So where?"

Dominic pulled back and stared at her. "What honeymoon?"

CHAPTER SIX

SIERRA stepped back and stared at him. "What do you mean, what honeymoon? You told Bruce we were going on a honeymoon!"

Dominic looked, for one brief instant, discomfitted. Then resolutely he shook his head. "Perhaps he misunderstood."

"Bruce doesn't misunderstand things like that. He's paid to note details. That's his job. Did you or did you not tell him we were going on a honeymoon?"

"I said *you* were on your honeymoon!" Dominic bit out.

"Just me?" Sierra said after a moment's silent regrouping. "Not *you?*"

"When in the hell would I have time to go on a honeymoon? I've got work to do! Demands. Meetings. Mergers. I have a job!"

"I have a job, too."

"You don't need it now."

"I want it."

He looked surprised. Then he smiled and gave a small laugh. "You want to stand on your feet all day fiddling with peoples' hair? You want to listen to idiots yell at you and tell you what to do and then change their minds five minutes later?"

"Yes," she said fiercely.

He looked incredulous. Then he wiped a hand down his face and stared at her some more. "You're kidding."

She shook her head, wrapping her arms across her chest. "No, I'm not."

"You jumped at the chance to not be there today!"

"Because I thought we were going on a honeymoon!"

He sighed. "You know I can't get away."

"I didn't know that," she said stubbornly.

"Well, I can't."

"You don't want to." That was what it came down to. She was no more than a plaything, a good-time girl. Someone to have fun with in bed, but not to have a relationship with.

He was silent. A muscle ticked in his jaw.

"I notice you're not denying it," she said acidly.

"I'd love to go on a honeymoon with you, Sierra, but—"

"I'd love for you to go to hell all by yourself, Dominic!" And, terrified that she might actually cry, Sierra spun away and snatched up the plates, heading for the kitchen.

Dominic came after her, grabbed them out of her hands, dumped them on the counter, and turned her in his arms. "Don't," he said.

She gaped at him. "*Don't?* Don't get mad? Don't care that you just ripped my work out of my life for no good reason?"

"I was trying to make your life easier. To give you a break. To make you happy."

"Sure you were." She lifted her hands and shoved his off her arms. "You want to make me happy? Let's go somewhere. Let's learn what makes each other tick. Let's find more we have in common than sex."

His jaw grew tight and his expression became shuttered. Watching it happen, Sierra felt as if she were being punched in the gut. There was a physical pain somewhere in her midsection—because she knew he didn't want her.

Not the way she wanted him to want her.

Not all of her.

He only wanted the physical Sierra Kelly—Wolfe, she corrected herself. Damn it to hell!—that made him feel good.

"No? We aren't going to go? Imagine that. Fine. We'll stay here. But I'm going back to work. Tomorrow. And I'm working every damn day I want, and you're not going to stop me."

"Sierra, it's not necessary."

"I'll decide what's necessary!" She grabbed the lasagne pan, slapped some foil on it, then stuck it in the refrigerator. She did the same with the salad, her movements jerky and furious. She banged the dishes into the sink and began to scrub them hard enough to rub the pattern right off.

"I have a dishwasher," Dominic said over the sound of the water.

"And now you have two." Sierra thumped the pasta pot down into the sink and set to work on it, too.

"Sierra." He sounded patient and long-suffering and totally in control.

She wanted to punch him in the nose. Instead she took her rage out on the pot.

"I don't need you to be a dishwasher." He came up behind her and slid his arms around her. She could feel the heat and hardness of his body against her back, and it took all her control not to melt right back against him. Her traitorous body wanted to.

But not her mind. Her mind was furious, and angriest of all was her heart.

"No," she said bitterly, "you just need me in your bed."

"I like you in my bed," he corrected.

"Well, that's just too damn bad, because I'm not going to be there anymore!"

"Oh, for God's sake, Sierra! Stop being melodramatic. You can't tell me you don't like being there, too."

She thumped the pot down and whirled around, shoving him back with wet hands that left an imprint on his suit coat. "Of course I like being there. And once that was dandy. But now we're married. There's more to marriage than that!"

"I can't give more than that."

Once the words were out of his mouth, he looked as if he wanted to call them back. His lips pressed into a tight line and he glared at her. Like it was her fault!

"Why?" She didn't shout the question. She asked it very

calmly, quietly almost. But it didn't mean she didn't want to know.

"I *won't* give more than that," he corrected himself.

"Oh, thank you very much!"

"Christ, Sierra. It's not that I don't like you. I do. It's just…I don't want to get involved!"

She stared at him, openmouthed. "You don't want to get involved? Then why the hell did you marry me?"

He didn't answer.

And that was answer enough.

"For the sex," she said bitterly. She rubbed her palms dry on the sides of his shirt that she wore. It had seemed like such a good idea when she'd put it on. It had made him seem so close—as if they were a part of each other.

And now he was telling her he didn't want that.

He didn't want her.

Except in bed.

She folded her arms beneath her breasts. "I can't do that."

He looked halfway between furious and astonished. "What do you mean you can't do it? We've done it!"

"It isn't enough. Not now. Not anymore."

"So what do you want to do, back out? Run away downtown again? Get a divorce? Give me back my half million?"

Oh, damn.

Because she'd managed to think, *yes, yes,* and *yes* to his first three questions. Her fingernails dug into her arms.

"I can't do that," she muttered.

His eyes widened. "You spent it?"

She stared out the window across the park and saw nothing. "I gave it away."

"What?"

Her gaze snapped back to meet his incredulous one. "I gave it away," she repeated stonily.

"To the homeless? To the starving poor of the Lower East Side?

"To a friend of mine whose son needs a kidney transplant!"

He blinked, then shook his head. "What? What friend? Who?"

"My friend Pammie who lives in my building. Her son Frankie needs one and they fell through the cracks insurance-wise. She needed a quarter of a million to get him on the list. I can give you back half of it now. I'll figure out some way to—"

"The hell you will!" He was shaking his head, pacing the confines of the kitchen like some furious jungle cat, raking his hand through his hair. "Keep the damn money! It's not important!"

"To you—"

"To me!" he shouted, then whirled and glared at her, spitting the words, "Do. You. Want. A. Divorce?"

"Do you?" Sierra asked quietly.

He went stone still. A muscle ticked in his temple and beneath hooded lids his blue eyes were almost midnight. He let out a harsh breath. "I don't know." He slammed a fist into his other palm.

At least, Sierra thought, he was being honest. She supposed she ought to be glad of that. "When you do know," she said politely, "I'd appreciate your telling me."

He snorted. "You'll be the first to know." The words hissed through his teeth.

"Thank you." Her voice sounded frosty, her heart was more so. She felt like ice, brittle and cold, about to crack.

"If you want one…" Dominic began, then stopped.

She shook her head. "I won't be leaving until I can pay my debts."

"I told you—"

"No," she said fiercely. "When I make a deal, Wolfe, I make a deal. I intend to keep it. I married you. For better or worse," she said bitterly.

"But you won't just sleep with me."

They stared at each other, Dominic challenging, Sierra despairing.

"At the present time," she said in a quiet voice that she hoped to God didn't sound as desperate as she felt, "I don't think that would be advisable."

She didn't think it would be "advisable"!

Dominic swore and slammed his fist on the mattress as he stared up at the ceiling above his bed. His very wide, very empty bed.

"Well, you let me know when you think it is," he'd said with his best sarcastic sneer as they'd faced each other in the kitchen hours before. And then he'd stalked out. He'd grabbed his briefcase and holed up in his study, trying to do the work he'd brought home so he wouldn't obsess over Sierra every minute he was with her.

Yeah, sure.

He hadn't got a damn thing done. He'd spent the rest of the evening staring at meaningless drivel on paper while his mind played and replayed everything that had happened that evening over again.

And while he played it over he heard her crashing dishes and pots and pans around in his kitchen. Slamming cupboards. Banging drawers.

Like she had a right to be angry because he didn't want to go on a honeymoon. Because he didn't want them to spend every minute in each other's pocket. Because he didn't want what she wanted in this marriage!

If she'd wanted that sort of marriage, damn it all, she shouldn't have married him!

Why would she do anything so stupid as say yes to a man she'd only spent one glorious night with—if she wanted a traditional marriage?

It didn't make a bloody bit of sense.

Nor did it make sense that she was sleeping down the hall and he was here alone in his bed!

But that's where she was. She'd come upstairs while he was working in the bedroom he used as a study, and when he went past the room where he'd had the movers put her stuff, the door was closed and locked.

He knew it was locked because he'd tried the handle. Lightly. Carefully. So she wouldn't even notice. It hadn't moved.

He'd debated just walking on by and ignoring it, but finally, annoyed, he'd said loudly, "You're being juvenile, Sierra."

She didn't reply.

He rattled the door handle.

No response.

"Childish," he said loudly.

Still nothing.

Damn her! How could she do this? He'd waited all day for her!

Well, fine, if that was the way she was going to be, she could just lie in there by herself all night. He didn't need her.

He didn't need anyone!

Five hours later he was still telling himself the same thing.

And pretty well convinced that Sierra was stubborn enough not to think going to bed with him was going to be "advisable" tonight.

He rolled over onto his side, pounded the pillow and thumped his head down onto it. Then he stared across the expanse of bed that, last night, he had shared with Sierra. One night and she had infiltrated his bedroom as if she'd been there forever.

He rolled over again, turning his back on the side where she'd slept—and remembered how she'd snuggled up behind him and slid her arms around him, how her hand had—

Cripes! He had to stop this!

His body remembered even better than his mind. And certain parts of his body were not happy at all.

And lying there thinking about what he wasn't getting wasn't making them any happier. He threw off the covers, threw a T-shirt on over his boxers, and went out into the hall. Not a sound emanated from behind Sierra's locked door.

He wondered if she was asleep.

He hoped she wasn't.

He wanted her suffering as much as he was. That would show her how ''advisable'' sleeping alone was!

''Well, that was the shortest honeymoon on record,'' Bruce said when she called him about working the next morning.

''We decided it would be better to wait,'' Sierra said, which was about the kindest thing you could say about what had happened between her and Dominic the night before.

Bruce grunted. ''I'll let Finn and Gib know you're working again. I'm sure Finn will want you tomorrow. He was grumbling last night when I told him you were going to be gone. So count on him. I'll be in touch, and I'll put you back on the books for everyone else.''

Which left her today to get through. Yesterday had been easy. She'd been dancing on air yesterday, delighted with life and with the prospect of her marriage.

Today it was harder to be sanguine. Today it was damned difficult even to muster a Sierra Kelly trademark smile.

Of course she wasn't Sierra Kelly anymore. Technically.

But in every other way, apparently, she was. Dominic certainly didn't want to make a real marriage out of what they had. He only wanted a live-in bed partner.

The very thought made Sierra want to spit.

Well, really, she chided herself. What did she expect?

Love.

It was as stupid and simple as that.

She was such a foolish optimist, such a ridiculous Pollyanna, that she'd expected he'd fall in love with her the way she was falling in love with him.

At the very least, she expected he would try.

Sierra gave points for trying.

Dominic wasn't getting any points at all. In fact he was so far in the hole that she thought he would probably never reach zero again if it took him the rest of his life.

Not that he was trying.

He'd stalked off to his study after their little blowup—and he'd still been there when she'd gone up to her room. He'd stayed there a good long time, too, immersed in his files and his mergers and his papers.

It was well past midnight when she heard his footsteps outside her door.

She'd heard him stop, then try the handle.

As if!

Like she would have left the lock undone so he could just come in and grab a quickie before he barricaded himself in his own little business world once more!

And then he'd had the audacity to tell her she was being childish. She was tempted to throw a pot at the door. If he wanted to see childish, she would be only too happy to show him!

But she hadn't. She'd glared in stony silence at the locked door, and finally he'd gone away.

She'd heard him banging around in his room, making plenty of noise, letting her know how displeased he was.

Well, he could take his displeasure and shove it, Sierra thought. She'd be glad to help!

Finally the noise had abated. The room had quieted. And Dominic, no doubt, had gone right to sleep.

Sierra had spent the rest of the night fuming. If she slept at all, it was close to dawn and she only dozed fitfully, dreaming alternately about making love with him and throttling him. The latter dreams gave her far more satisfaction. And then, close to five-thirty, she heard the shower go on in his bathroom.

"Getting an early start?" she muttered sourly.

Undoubtedly. He wouldn't want to let more than a couple of hours go by when he wasn't totally consumed with his work. Still furious, she rolled over, pulled the pillow and the blanket over her head and shut out the sound of Dominic.

Not until she was sure he was gone to work did she get up and unlock the door.

Then she took a leisurely shower, dressed in her own clothes this time. There was nothing romantic or sexy or remotely enticing about wearing one of Dominic's shirts. In fact she was tempted to burn the one she had worn. Fortunately she had just enough maturity not to do anything quite that stupid.

Pity she had been stupid enough to marry the man.

Pity she'd been stupid enough to bare her heart to Mariah, too. Now her sister would be worrying and, worse, very likely meddling.

Sierra decided she would have to put a stop to that before Mariah even got started. So she took a bus to the West Side and, fetching Reuben sandwiches from Mariah's favorite deli, she turned up on her sister's doorstep for lunch.

"You're not going to be morning sick, are you?" she asked when her sister opened the door. Last year Mariah had opened the door, taken one whiff of the corned beef and sauerkraut sandwiches and dashed for the bathroom.

"Blessedly no," Mariah said. "Not yet. Good grief. Stephen and Lizzie aren't even six months old. Come on in. How did dinner go?"

"That's what I want to talk to you about." Sierra came in and shut the door.

Of course Mariah was furious. "That jerk!" she exclaimed when Sierra gave her a brief and reasonably objective rundown of last evening's encounter. "He actually *said* he doesn't want to get involved?" She paced around the living room of the brownstone apartment she and Rhys shared, Stephen bouncing on her hip.

"That's what he said." Sierra was spreading out the lunch so they could picnic on the coffee table.

"Humph." Mariah lifted her small son up and looked squarely into his eyes. "Your uncle's an idiot," she told him. "You will *not* grow up to be like him!"

"Of course he won't," Sierra said firmly. "He'll be just like Rhys."

"Oh, there's good news," Mariah said dryly. "Rhys is so enlightened."

"He's come around," Sierra reminded her. Rhys hadn't wanted to be involved either. He'd literally run the other way when he'd discovered Mariah was expecting the twins. Now, though, you couldn't ask for a more doting husband and father.

"So there is hope, then." Mariah sat cross-legged on the floor and set Stephen down beside her. "Let's eat quick," she said. "Before Lizzie wakes up." She took a bite out of her sandwich.

Sierra sat down opposite her sister and unwrapped her own. Maybe there was hope, but she wasn't going to kid herself anymore. She was done being Pollyanna where her relationship with Dominic was concerned.

"He'll come around," Mariah promised, "just like Rhys did."

"You say that now." Sierra poked glumly at a piece of sauerkraut sticking out of her sandwich. "You didn't sound so confident six months ago."

"Well, I wasn't," Mariah admitted. "But Rhys had reasons not to want to get involved."

"Presumably Dominic does, too."

"His wife didn't die," Mariah said. "He didn't lose an unborn child."

Which Rhys had, Sierra knew.

"He got dumped at the altar though. That must have hurt."

Silently, simultaneously, they both considered the awfulness of that. Sierra couldn't imagine a man as proud as Dominic suffering it easily. And she could see very clearly why he wouldn't want to get involved again.

It wasn't a comforting realization.

Stephen waved his arms and rocked back and forth, trying to reach his mother's sandwich until finally he toppled over and started to cry. Mariah scooped him up and hugged him, then, when he'd stopped fussing, she set him back on the floor.

"You've got to do that with Dominic."

Sierra blinked. "What? Pick him up, brush him off and assure him he's going to be fine? I don't think so."

"You have to be there for him," Mariah insisted. She coaxed a smile out of Stephen. He gurgled and batted at her.

He had his father's and his uncle's blue eyes and Sierra wondered what it would be like to share a child with Dominic. The thought actually hurt. But it made her say, "Like you were there for Rhys, you mean."

"Yes."

"And you think Dominic, like Rhys, will see the light?"

"Yes," Mariah said more slowly.

"I can just hear all the confidence in your voice," Sierra said dryly.

"Well, he and Rhys are different. He's a little harder. More businesslike. But I can't believe he'd feel worse about being jilted than Rhys did about Sarah dying, for goodness' sake!"

"Maybe not. But that doesn't mean he's going to fall in love with me. Rhys was your friend at least...first."

"You have to start somewhere."

"Well, Dominic and I started in bed—and I don't think the success rate is as high as if you're friends."

"But not nonexistent, surely. Where's your innate optimism? Where's your supreme self-confidence?"

"I think they died last night."

"Don't let them," Mariah said urgently. "You can't."

"Yesterday you were telling me he was a lost cause."

"He's not."

"How do you know?"

"Because he married you. He wouldn't have married you if he hadn't felt something."

"He might have married me because he felt nothing and preferred it that way!"

"Do you really think so?"

And Sierra, confronted with the blunt question, hesitated a long moment, then shook her head slowly. "No. But—"

"So bear with him. Give him a chance."

"Pick him up and dust him off?"

"Just be there. Propinquity."

"I don't know those big words."

"The nearness of you," Mariah translated.

Sierra wanted to believe in it. She wanted to hope. But she was afraid. "What if…what if it doesn't work?" Her throat seemed to close on the words.

"What have you lost by trying?" Mariah asked gently.

When you put it like that…

"You're right," Sierra said.

Something smelled delicious when he opened the door that evening.

Just like last night.

God, he didn't want a rerun of last night.

Not that he was likely to get one. He figured she had probably cooked for herself and he was smelling what she'd already eaten an hour or two before.

It was after eight when he got there. He'd had a meeting with Kent and a couple of the men in his office that lasted until six-thirty. Then he'd taken his time going over what they'd discussed, making notes, leaving a recording for Shyla to type up tomorrow morning. He'd done it with the thorough deliberation with which he had always worked in his pre-Sierra days—those days when his mind had been blessedly unfogged by lust and desire and a woman with purple hair.

He tried telling himself that it had been unfogged tonight. But that wasn't true. He still thought about her every minute or two. He just resisted the thoughts now. He refused to allow himself to dwell on what they'd do when he got home tonight.

He knew what they'd be doing. He'd be in the study working and she'd be in her room. *If* she even stayed home.

It was wondering if she'd be there that finally got him out of the office and hurrying on his way home. Not that he'd go looking for her if she wasn't!

But he couldn't deny he'd wanted to know.

And he couldn't deny the shaft of pure relief he felt when he turned the key in the lock and pushed open the door to be greeted by mouth-watering smells emanating from the kitchen, and the soft Caribbean sounds of Jimmy Buffett on the stereo.

He set down his briefcase, then picked it up again, intending to take it to the study straight away. But before he could move, Sierra came out of the kitchen.

She wasn't wearing his shirt.

No surprise there, of course. But he felt oddly bereft to see she was wearing a pair of faded denim jeans and a scoop-necked, long-sleeved pale pink T-shirt. She looked…normal. Except, of course, for the hair.

"I fixed some beef bourguignonne this afternoon," she said casually. "Would you like some?"

What was he going to say? No?

"That'd be…good." He hoped he didn't sound as awkward as he felt. "I'll just put my briefcase away."

"Sure. We're eating in the kitchen." She disappeared again, leaving him to stare after her for a long minute before he gave himself a shake and carried his briefcase to his study and left it there. He washed up, then went back to the kitchen where Sierra had served the meal. She was already sitting on one side of the small table.

She looked up fleetingly when he came in and gave him a vague smile, then focused on her plate again.

Dominic sat down opposite her. "Looks good." His voice sounded too loud for the small room. "Is this another of your mother's recipes?"

He usually had no trouble at all making small talk. He'd been raised to make social conversation by both his parents. He could do it in his sleep. He couldn't seem to do it with Sierra without feeling like a fool.

But she nodded gravely. "Mariah gave it to me. I was never interested enough in cooking before."

Dominic wanted to ask, *before what?* but he didn't dare. He took a bite of the meat dish and savored it. "Tastes even better than it looks."

This time he got more of a real smile from her.

"There's plenty," she said, then sighed. "It makes enough to feed the French Foreign Legion. We'll probably be eating it for a week."

He took heart from that. She'd said *we,* and she'd said *week.* That didn't sound like she was planning to leave him. The meal tasted even better after that.

He ate two big helpings and, she was right, there was still a lot left. Besides that, there was salad and some leftover garlic bread from last night, too. Also the rest of the bottle of the wine they'd drunk.

Neither of them mentioned last night.

Sierra, in fact, didn't talk at all, which meant that things were definitely not normal. Still, he was glad she wasn't holed up in her room, shutting him out, which is what he'd expected.

He studied her silently over his wineglass. Most of the time when he watched Sierra, it was with an eye to what was going to happen next—or more bluntly, he was busy gauging when he was going to get her into bed and what was going to happen when he got her there.

They were thoughts worthy of consideration, to be sure. But Dominic was smart enough to know he wasn't going to get her in bed tonight.

Still he couldn't stop looking at her. His gaze seemed drawn to the soft curve of her cheek, the creamy length of her neck, the pulse beating at the base of her throat. Her gaze was hooded. She gave the meal her full attention and didn't pay any attention to him at all.

He started to talk, to tell her about something that had happened in the office, then didn't. She wouldn't care. And he didn't really want to tell her. He'd just be making conversation. He, too, focused on the meal.

When they were finished eating, Sierra stood up at once. "I'll clear up," she said briskly. "I'm sure you have work to do."

You're dismissed. She couldn't have said it more clearly without using the words.

And it was true, he did have work to do, but something stopped him. "I'll help you with the dishes."

His willingness surprised her no more than it did him. What was he, a glutton for punishment? He wasn't getting anything out of her tonight—and he had a briefcase full of papers he needed to go over.

Still, he didn't like being superfluous. Didn't like being dismissed. He helped clear the table, and when she scraped the dishes, he loaded the dishwasher.

As they were finishing, and he put the last pan in, she wiped her hands on a towel. "I'm going back to work tomorrow. At Finn's."

There was a note of determination in her voice, followed by a moment's pause, as if she was waiting for him to object and for the battle to begin to rage again. Dominic inclined his head to show he'd heard.

When he didn't immediately reply, she added stiffly, "I

just thought I should tell you ahead of time.'' There was just enough hesitancy in her voice to make him wonder if her words were a slap at his way of having handled things or an attempt at being conciliatory.

''Suit yourself,'' he said, and tried for the same neutral expression that she'd used.

''I intend to,'' she said quietly. For just an instant their gazes met. Instantly both of them looked away.

''Good night, then,'' Sierra said. She turned and headed for the stairs.

Dominic stared after her, watching the gentle sway of her hips in those skintight jeans, and felt an ache he knew all too well.

''Sierra?'' Her name was out of his mouth before he realized it.

She stopped, one hand on the banister, looked back at him. ''Yes?''

A moment of silence washed over them both. He shook his head. ''Nothing. Good night.''

CHAPTER SEVEN

"SHORT honeymoon," Finn said when Sierra walked into work the next morning. "Everything okay?"

Sierra smiled her best sunny smile. "Of course. Dominic just had something come up. You know how these corporate hotshots are. We decided to postpone."

"Well, go somewhere," Finn advised. "Izzy and I and the girls went to Bora Bora."

"Bora Bora? I didn't know that! Whyever did you—"

"Started out as a joke." Finn grinned. "Remember when my sister dumped Tansy and Pansy on me? It was so she could take off to Bora Bora with a guy. Izzy and I were stuck with the kids while she went out to have a good time. We had a pretty good time ourselves, eventually," he recalled with a smile. "After Izzy and I finally decided to tie the knot, I said we'd go to Bora Bora on our honeymoon and take the girls."

He shrugged. "She held me to it."

Izzy would, Sierra thought. Izzy was a force.

"Nothing like a little sea and sand and sun to get a marriage off on the right foot," Finn went on, a faraway look of longing in his eyes.

It sounded heavenly to Sierra, too. "That's an idea," she said. She didn't tell him that Dominic had no intention of getting their marriage off on any foot at all.

She got home late that evening because the ad agency rep kept changing his mind. It was nearly seven when she arrived.

Dominic was standing in the doorway to the kitchen when she pushed open the door. His normally neat hair was ruffled, as if he'd been running his fingers through it. His tie was jerked loose, and one shirt button was undone at his neck.

"Where were—" he exhaled sharply, words coming to a complete stop as she set her tackle box on the floor. He took another breath, then said, "Worked late?" in an almost casual tone.

Almost, Sierra thought. Not quite. Had he been worried? Had he thought she'd left? He couldn't have. All her things were still upstairs.

But why else would he be looking so frantic?

She nodded. "Yes. It was Ballou again. Never make one decision when five will do."

Dominic grinned faintly. "I've had managers like that. Briefly."

"Well, I wish he worked for you. You could fire him." She flexed her shoulders wearily. It had been that sort of day.

"I picked up Chinese," Dominic said. "I figured it was my turn in the kitchen, and I got home too late to want to bother figuring out what to cook."

Sierra had trouble keeping her jaw from dragging on her toes. They were going to be taking turns cooking?

Dominic had stopped and got dinner?

"I hope you like Mongolian beef and cashew chicken," he said. "I got some spring rolls and some wontons and some bird's nest soup, too." He looked like he wasn't just making conversation but was waiting for a reply.

So Sierra nodded. "Sounds…fantastic. I'll wash up."

The table was a sea of small white cardboard boxes when she entered the kitchen a few moments later. Dominic gestured for her to sit, then sat down opposite her.

Sierra hadn't eaten all day and she was as hungry as she was exhausted. The first bite was ambrosial and she whimpered.

"What's wrong?"

She shook her head. "N-nothing. I…it's so good. Thank you." She smiled at him.

Dominic smiled back. And for a few seconds Sierra felt an even deeper connection than she had all those times that their hormones had been in sync. Then Dominic bent his head over his bowl and began to eat.

Once her initial hunger was sated, she started to talk. For one night, perhaps, she could keep silent. But it wasn't her way not to talk during meals. She told him about Ballou. She could write a book of hair-pulling stories about Ballou. And telling them, she made Dominic smile, and then she made him laugh.

And when they'd finished, she said, "I'd like a cup of coffee. Would you?"

He hesitated, then nodded. "All right."

They cleaned up the kitchen together while the coffee was brewing. Sierra took hers out to stand and look over the park bathed now in late evening shadows. Across the way she could catch just a glimpse of the tiny white lights that marked the Tavern on the Green. They looked magical. Like fairy lights. Or stars.

When she'd been a child she'd lain out on the grass in their front yard in Kansas and stared up at night into a sky awash with stars. She'd never been sure which was the first one—the wishing star—so she'd always wished on all of them.

Most nights she couldn't see stars here in New York City. There were too many other lights.

But it didn't stop her wishing.

She clutched her coffee cup, held it against her mouth and let the steam rise, blurring her eyes. And she pretended the lights across the park were wishing stars.

And she said inside her heart, *I wish it would work.*

She felt more than heard Dominic come to stand beside her. He didn't stand close. There had to be a foot separating them in physical space. She didn't even want to think how much emotional space there was.

Before their blowup he would have taken the coffee cup out of her hands and turned her in his arms and kissed her. He would have run his hands up under her shirt and rubbed his fingers over her sensitive nipples. And she would have responded in kind.

She would have made quick work of those buttons and that half-mast tie. She might have teased him with it. She surely would have pleased him with it.

She stood absolutely still. She even stopped breathing, praying that he wouldn't try, that he wouldn't touch. She wanted him as much as she ever had.

But she wanted more of him than he was ready to give. So she would have to pull back. Say no.

He shifted his weight from one foot to the other and sipped from his mug. ''Good coffee. Thanks.''

''Thank you...for dinner.''

They stood still and silent in the darkened room, side by side, not looking at each other.

Then Dominic said, ''Gotta get to work.''

And Sierra said, ''Of course.''

Lying alone in bed that night, she tried to think positive thoughts.

He tried not to think about her.

It didn't work.

He tried to tell himself that it didn't matter whether she was in his bed or not, marrying her had accomplished what he'd wanted it to—his father had gone back to Florida and there were no more phone calls about women Dominic ought to consider making his wife.

Because he had a wife.

Living down the hall from him.

It set his teeth on edge. It made him clench his fists and

want to pound something or someone. It made him crazy with longing for her.

But he didn't push.

He was afraid to push. Because he was afraid, if he did, she would walk out for good.

He told himself that didn't matter either. And he believed it for about twenty-four hours. But that night when he'd come home and she wasn't there, he'd felt as if all the air had been sucked right out of him.

He'd stopped to pick up Chinese because he was early for a change. And he figured, since she'd gone back to work that day, that she wouldn't want to have to fix a meal. He'd expected to arrive home about the same time she did or maybe right after—soon enough that he could tell her not to bother cooking dinner.

But she hadn't been there.

An hour passed and she never came. He'd felt a niggling nervousness, a sort of free-floating worry. Had something happened to her? Had she been run over by a bus?

Had she left him?

It wasn't the first thought that occurred to him.

But it was the one that sent him bounding up the stairs to check the room she slept in. Memories of the abortive wedding with Carin played in his head. And he'd breathed a sigh of relief to see that everything was still there.

For now. Maybe she was just out arranging to have her things moved. He'd paced and puttered for another half an hour, wondering if he should go look, telling himself not to be stupid, before he heard the key turn in the lock.

At the sight of her, weary and exhausted and lugging that damned tackle box, he felt a whoosh of relief like nothing he'd ever felt before.

Later, though, he'd been annoyed with himself. It wasn't like he couldn't have survived without her, for goodness' sake.

Still, as the days wore on, he was glad she was there.

It surprised him, really, how now that he wasn't going to bed with her, he found other things about her to admire.

He knew from experience how devoted she was to her sister. But now he saw how devoted she was to her friends. There was, of course, the astonishing gift of his money she'd made to her friend, Pammie. That had been in a good cause, of course. But she was often busy doing something small but significant for someone else.

She took a psychedelic stuffed duck to work one day for Gib and Chloe Walker's little son, Brendan.

"Is it his birthday?" Dominic asked.

Sierra shook her head. "Brendan likes ducks. And I saw this one yesterday and I couldn't resist."

She brought home a sack of fresh fortune cookies one day and handed them to him.

"What are these for?" Dominic looked at them mystified.

"You like them," Sierra said. "You're always eating mine."

Which was true. He did like them. But he'd never had anyone notice before. "Well, er, thanks," he said. And because she was standing there expectantly watching him, he plucked one out, cracked it open and popped it into his mouth.

"And your fortune is?" she prompted.

"It isn't the fortunes I like," he said, his mouth full.

"Even so," she insisted.

He unfolded the tiny white paper. "'Don't look back.'"

Sierra laughed, delighted. "Sounds like my kind of fortune."

That was something else he liked about her. She didn't look back and brood. She looked forward and around her, and did what she could to enjoy life—and see that others did, too.

Later that week at breakfast—she was eating breakfast with him now, too—she told him she was going to be late that night, that she wouldn't be home for dinner.

"Got a hot date?" Dominic asked before he could stop himself.

She blinked, surprised, then shook her head. "I told Mariah I'd baby-sit so she and Rhys could go out to dinner. They really need a night out for themselves."

"Oh. Right." He felt foolish. He'd never thought about how demanding it must be to have twins.

He tried not to think about it—and while he was at work he did fairly well. There was always more than enough to keep him busy at work—as long it was interesting enough to keep Sierra off his brain.

It would be good for her to be gone tonight, he told himself when he came home. He'd done just fine without her for a lot of years. It wasn't as if he needed her there.

But he wondered if maybe she needed him.

So he called his brother's and asked Sierra if she'd like him to bring over dinner.

"You have time?" she sounded surprised.

"I have to eat," he said gruffly. "I might as well do it with you."

"Well, when you put it so nicely, I don't see how I can refuse," she said. But she wasn't really sarcastic. Her gently teasing tone just made him ashamed of his surliness.

He picked up some Burmese food from a place near Rhys's, and when he got there he found that she had set the picnic table in the back garden of Rhys and Mariah's brownstone.

"It's nice here," Sierra said. "Like being in the country."

After they'd eaten she stretched out in a chaise longue, balancing Lizzie on her thighs and letting the baby hold on to her hands as she bounced up and down, giggling and grinning. Sierra was grinning, too.

She looked young and happy and very maternal as she played with Lizzie. They rubbed noses and giggled some more. Then Sierra blew kisses against Lizzie's soft belly and got a full-blown gurgle out of her niece.

She was very good with children. It made Dominic wonder if she wanted some of her own.

They'd never talked about children. They'd never talked about much.

Experimentally he rolled a ball toward Stephen who was sitting on the patio banging a spoon. The little boy batted the spoon at it and the ball rolled partway back.

"Wow! Look at that. What a swing! He's going to be a ball player," Sierra said with a grin.

Dominic couldn't help grinning, too. "Of course he is. All Wolfe men play ball."

Sierra's brows lifted. "Even you?"

"Of course me," he said, affronted. "I pitched my team to the state semi-finals in high school. I won there, too. A three-hitter," he added, and was unaccountably pleased when she looked impressed.

"Did you play in college?"

He shook his head. "No. No time. I started working for the firm then, plus I was going to school full-time, double major in accounting and communications technology. Baseball was just a game. Dad figured it was time to grow up."

"Dad ought to mind his own business," Sierra muttered.

Sometimes, traitorously, Dominic had thought that, too. But he'd never ever articulated it. "The firm is important. It was Dad's sweat and blood. Long hours and a hell of a lot of determination. It's our livelihood. And I needed to learn it from the ground up."

"I didn't say it wasn't," Sierra said. "I just think it's too bad you didn't get to play ball if you wanted to."

"We don't always get what we want," Dominic said gruffly.

"Not always," Sierra agreed. She gave Lizzie one more bounce. "You have to decide if it's worth fighting for."

Her words stayed with him. They echoed in his head all that evening and for days afterward.

It would help, he thought, if he knew what the hell he wanted.

He'd thought he did—the business, freedom from parental harassment, and a wife who knew her place, which was in his bed.

But the longer he spent with Sierra, the less he was sure.

In spite of his resolve not to get involved, he spent time with her. The fact was, he liked spending time with her out of bed as well as in.

He liked coming home and eating with her, some nights even cooking with her.

He liked baby-sitting with her at Rhys's and Mariah's.

After they'd eaten, he could have gone back to their apartment. Instead he hung around.

Of course, there was a Yankee game on television and he had started watching it while she heated bottles and got the twins ready for bed.

Then she appeared next to the chair where he was sitting, handed him Stephen and a bottle and said, "Feed him."

"What? Me?" Dominic felt something vaguely akin to panic and tried to hand the baby back.

But Sierra shook her head. "He needs a little male bonding," she told him. "Besides, I've only got two arms, and I'm going to be feeding Lizzie. Relax. You're his uncle. He loves you."

Did he? Was being an uncle all it took? Dominic considered that as he considered the child in his arms.

He wasn't much of an expert on love. He wasn't really sure he believed in it.

Once upon a time he'd thought he did. Before Carin.

After Carin he'd given anything remotely resembling it a wide berth. As devastated as he'd been at Carin's defection, he couldn't imagine leaving himself open to caring again.

But it was hard not to care about a helpless child.

He rubbed a knuckle against Stephen's soft cheek, then

glanced up self-consciously, and felt even more so when he saw Sierra watching him.

She smiled at him. It was a warm smile. Gentle. Intimate. The same soft, satisfied look she had after he'd made love to her. As if they were sharing something special. Just the two of them.

Dominic tried to harden his heart against it. He didn't want this. He didn't!

So what the hell was he doing here?

He didn't have an answer to that.

She'd thought she was in love with Dominic before.

It was nothing compared to her love for him now. Every day that she spent with him—even when he was ostensibly trying to avoid her—she found more things about him to admire, to cherish, to love.

And, of course, she still wanted to go to bed with him.

She didn't dare.

Because the more she saw, the more she wanted. She wasn't settling for being a wife in bed only. She wanted the whole enchilada.

It was funny how things had changed.

Her first impression of him had been that he was rich, arrogant and, because he worked on the fifty-third floor, looked down on the rest of the world. She'd been determined to bring him down a peg. He'd been surprised, then intrigued, by her attitude toward him.

"Do most people bow and scrape?" she'd asked him once.

"The men touch their forelocks, the women curtsy," he'd replied, never cracking a smile.

She hadn't thought he was kidding at first. Then she'd realized he was playing to her prejudices, having her on.

The metaphorical gloves came off. They sparred with

each other first verbally, then, in Kansas after the wedding, sexually.

The battle lines were drawn.

Sierra had met her match.

She loved that. She loved his determination, his fierceness, his dedication to his work. She loved his dry sense of humor, his sharp wit. She loved his way with Stephen and Lizzie, tentative, gentle and unquestionably loving.

She loved him.

She hated that he didn't want to love her, that he thought her only value was in his bed.

She was determined he would learn otherwise. And she actually thought he might be.

He'd come with her to baby-sit, hadn't he?

And though he often came home late and disappeared to work in his study in the evening, some nights he brought home dinner so she wouldn't have to cook. And always he helped clean up after.

"My mother said boys should do their share," he told her.

"Three cheers for your mother," Sierra replied. "I wish I'd known her."

He told her about his mother and father, about what life had been like for the three Wolfe brothers growing up on Long Island as boys. As the oldest, Dominic had always been the leader, the responsible one, the one most like his father, and destined to follow in Douglas's footsteps from the moment he was born.

His mother had provided some necessary balance. But after her death, his father had held sway. And what was good for the business, had been good for Dominic.

But he never complained. He thrived on it just as his father had.

It made her try to explain her need to keep working to

him. He still didn't see the need for her to do it, but he actually seemed to listen when she tried to explain.

"I like making people look good. I like making them feel good about themselves. I like pleasing them. And I like working with hair. It's alive. Responsive."

He raised an eyebrow, but he didn't contradict her.

"I like the people I work with, too. Even the bitchy cranky ones like Ballou."

"Pardon my skepticism," he said dryly.

"Well, I like almost everyone," Sierra qualified with a grin.

And she saw Finn and Izzy, Gib and Chloe, and the others she worked with as often as she ever did.

But she didn't see Pam and Frankie much. She called and talked to them on the phone a couple of times a week, and Frankie always asked when she was coming down to watch *Star Trek* with them.

And finally, because she missed them, she said, "Tomorrow. I'll come tomorrow night."

She told Dominic the next morning that she was going to visit Pam and Frankie and watch *Star Trek*.

"Why don't you invite them to watch it here?"

She must have gaped, because he scowled and shrugged dismissively. "It won't bother me. I'll just be in my office working. Besides, I bet Frankie would rather watch on a big screen."

Frankie was thrilled. He was practically bouncing off the walls when they arrived. He looked brighter than he had in some time. He'd been through all the tests, Pam told her while Frankie, wide-eyed, looked around.

Everything was great, Pam said. Except she wasn't a good match to donate a kidney and neither was her sister. "So we just have to wait until the right match comes along."

"It will," Sierra said confidently.

"I hope so." Pam lifted her gaze to the heavens. "I'm counting on it."

"C'mere, Mom," Frankie urged. "Look out here. It's just like you're in my tree house. This is so cool," he said over and over till Pam shushed him.

"You'll bother Sierra's husband. He's working upstairs," she admonished.

He was. He'd disappeared straight after dinner. "I'll get out of your way," he'd said. She'd been going to invite him to stay, but given his eagerness to be gone, she didn't say a word.

She just wished. And then, sometime during the second episode, Sierra heard a noise in the doorway and turned around to find Dominic standing there.

"I thought I'd make some popcorn," he said. "Want some?" he asked Frankie.

The boy's eyes shone. "You bet."

Star Trek was put on hold while they made popcorn. Then the two of them sat side by side on the sofa, the popcorn bowl between them, engrossed in the video while Sierra and Pam looked at each other and shook their heads.

When the video ended, Frankie told Dominic how much his apartment looked like a tree house he'd drawn.

"You draw tree houses?" Dominic asked. And he opened a cabinet and took out a yellowed folder and showed Frankie drawings of house plans and tree house plans he'd drawn as a boy.

"Oh, cool. Way cool" Frankie exclaimed. "Lookit, Ma. Don'tcha like this one."

"I prefer this one," Dominic said, showing him an even more elaborate one.

"Oh, wow," Frankie breathed, looking at Dominic with hero worship in his eyes.

The bonding, needless to say, was mutual and intense.

"I thought he was supposed to be a stuck-up jerk," Pam

whispered to Sierra when they left "the boys" to their tree houses and went to the kitchen to make some cocoa.

Sierra smiled a little wistfully. "He tries to be. Sometimes. He keeps his assets well hidden."

"I like him," Pam said.

"I do, too."

Worse, every day, heaven help her, she fell more deeply in love.

She saw how hard he worked on the business. It demanded his attention most of the day and half of the night, but he didn't seem to mind. And while he expected a lot of his employees, he treated them like human beings, too.

He came home early one night after telling Sierra he'd be late because of a meeting.

"No meeting?" she'd said, surprised.

"Canceled it."

"Why?"

"Doakes's daughter had a dance recital," he mumbled.

Sierra's eyes widened. He'd canceled a business meeting so one of his managers could go to his daughter's dance recital?

"We can meet early tomorrow morning," he'd said gruffly. "The work will get done."

"Of course it will," Sierra said. She moved to kiss him, then stopped. She couldn't do that unless she was ready to resume intimacies with him. It would be teasing if she did, taunting, tempting. Even if she didn't mean it to be.

What she wanted it to mean was that she loved him.

But she still didn't think he was ready to hear it.

He made it difficult to stay aloof, though. Just yesterday he'd called from work right after she got home.

"I'm going to be late," he said, and she smiled because in the last few days he'd taken to calling and telling her if he wasn't going to be there for dinner. "I've got to stop by the hospital."

Sierra felt an immediate stab of panic. "Why? What happened?"

"Nothing major. My secretary, Shyla, had her baby this morning, that's all. But I said I'd stop in to see her. Admire the offspring. Do you think I ought to take it a Yankees' cap?"

Dominic and his Yankees. Sierra grinned. "By all means. Gotta start 'em young. Tell her and her husband congratulations. What did they name him?"

"Deirdre Eileen," he said. "They had a girl."

Probably the only girl to go home with her very own Yankees' cap, Sierra thought as she hung up the phone and stared out the window, smiling.

Oh, Dominic! Why are you making this so difficult?

She wanted a child with him. A child like Dierdre Eileen or Stephen or Lizzie. A child to wear the smallest size Yankees' cap. To cuddle, to hug and to love. A child with Dominic's dark hair and deep blue eyes.

So, go to bed with him, her mind argued.

There was no question that he wanted her to. He still looked at her with the same hunger. He didn't say a word. He didn't have to. She saw it in his gaze.

But later that evening when he came home, telling her it was as ugly a kid as he'd ever seen, and it was a good thing he'd given it the Yankees' cap to distract peoples' attention, she burst out laughing, and they smiled at each other, and the flames of desire rose between them hot and fierce.

But still she didn't go to him.

Because she wanted not just his child, but his love.

"Your father," Shyla's replacement said the next morning, "on line one."

Dominic didn't feel the usual instant clench in his stomach that he normally felt when he heard those words. Douglas had been lying low since the night he'd met his son's new wife. But Dominic knew better than to hope such reticence would last forever.

He punched in line one and said with all the good cheer he could muster, "Dad! What's up? Haven't heard from you in a while."

"I've been busy," Douglas said flatly. "Had a reception to arrange."

"Somebody getting married?"

"You did," Douglas replied. "So I thought it was only fitting that I give you a wedding bash."

A wedding reception for him and Sierra? "We don't need—"

"Of course you do." Douglas's voice was a smooth tempered steel. "We need to introduce your bride to our friends and colleagues. Don't we?"

Dominic felt ill. "It's not necessary," he began again.

But his father cut him off. "Of course it is. Unless you're ashamed of her?"

Dominic gritted his teeth. "I'm *not* ashamed of her!"

"But you are married to her?" There was a faint desperate note in Douglas's voice.

"Of course I'm married to her! What the hell did you think? That I brought her along just to make a point?"

"You married her to make a point, didn't you?" Douglas asked mildly.

Dominic shoved his fingers through his hair. "It's my business and hers why we got married." His response was weak, and he knew it. His father's snort of derision only underscored the fact.

"You damn fool," Douglas grated.

"I'd have been a bigger fool letting you tell me who to marry, how to run my life!"

"So you married someone entirely inappropriate instead!"

"Who says she's inappropriate?" Dominic couldn't believe how suddenly angry he was.

"You think she'll fit right in, do you? No one will even notice when she takes her place on the board of the charity foundation? No one will bat an eyelash at having a purple-haired woman on the hospital committee."

"Why should they care what color her hair is if our money is still green?"

"It's not them who will care," Douglas bit out. "It's the committee!"

"Too damn bad."

"Too damn bad," Douglas echoed mockingly. "For God's sake, Dominic!"

Dominic scowled, knowing exactly what his father meant, and resenting it furiously. Anyone who knew Sierra would know she was worth ten of those women. "They need to look beyond the surface," he growled. "They need to wake up and realize not everyone in the world dresses the way they do."

"And it was your mission in marrying Sierra to teach them that?"

"Of course not. But—"

"No, it wasn't. It was your mission in marrying Sierra to show me up. What I want to know is, did you stop and think how all this was going to affect Sierra?"

Oh, now he was going to make it seem like Sierra was a victim? Anyone less like a victim Dominic couldn't imagine. "She didn't have to say yes!"

"Why did she?"

It was like being socked in the gut. A simple mild question that cut straight to the bone. As if Sierra had had no more reason to marry him than Carin—who hadn't.

"Go to hell, "he said through his teeth.

"Sorry," his father said quickly. "I didn't mean—" He cleared his throat, but didn't speak.

What, after all, Dominic wondered, was there left to say?

But being Douglas, of course, he found something. ''I'm giving a reception for you, Dominic. For you and Sierra.''

''Why? So you can hurt her the way you think she shouldn't be hurt?'' Dominic said bitterly.

''If you believe that, you're no son of mine.''

''Then why?''

''To show a little family solidarity. She's your wife. She's my daughter-in-law. She's a part of Wolfe's now.''

''Lucky her,'' Dominic muttered. Then, ''Fine,'' he said recklessly, ''have a reception for us. Invite the whole damn city if you want.''

CHAPTER EIGHT

"A RECEPTION?" Sierra beamed at the news. They were walking through Central Park on Sunday afternoon. The sun was shining. People were playing Frisbee and walking dogs and tossing footballs and, according to Sierra, all was right with the world. "How nice of him."

Dominic didn't think it was nice at all.

For all that the old man had blathered on about family solidarity, Dominic knew the people who would be there—most of whom wouldn't be family, and a great many of whom would have an opinion about Sierra with her purple hair and her funky clothing—and the opinion wouldn't be good.

Personally he didn't give a rat's ass what they thought of his wife. But he knew they could freeze a polar bear's toenails in their dismissive, haughty, but very genteel way.

And he was damned if he was going to let them hurt Sierra.

The trouble was, he didn't know how to prevent it, short of telling her to dye her hair brown, paint her fingernails pink, and get a dress from some subdued, sophisticated designer. And if he did that, she'd think he was embarrassed to be seen with her.

He wasn't.

Admittedly, it made him a little self-conscious, knowing that peoples' heads turned at the sight of the two of them together. They were turning now at the sight of Sierra in her neon pink spandex top, black leather jeans and wide-brimmed floppy hat, walking alongside him in his Brooks Brothers' khakis and pale blue Oxford-cloth long-sleeved shirt.

"Mr. Buttondown and the free spirit," Rhys had called them this morning when they'd had brunch with him and Mariah.

"They're good for each other. A balance," Mariah had said approvingly.

A balance pretty much summed it up. He was still sleeping at one end of the hall and she was at the other. She talked with him, laughed with him, cooked with him, watched TV with him. But she hadn't touched him since the night they'd fought. It had been two weeks.

"When is the reception?" Sierra asked him now. "And where?"

Douglas had called right before they'd gone out, giving Dominic the final information. He told Sierra now, "This coming Friday. He's rented a yacht. A dinner cruise down around the tip of Manhattan Island and up the East River, then out by the Statue of Liberty."

Sierra looked delighted. "Fantastic. How romantic with the sunset and the city skyline as a backdrop!"

"And three hundred of the old man's nearest and dearest friends and associates."

Sierra blinked. "Whoa. That's a lot. But Rhys and Mariah will be there, won't they?"

Dominic nodded. "Nathan, too. Dad said he'd told Nath to turn up, and apparently he's going to."

Nathan, the middle brother, was a globe-trotting photographer, the one son who'd eschewed any interest in the family business—or the family, for the most part.

But apparently when Douglas meant family solidarity, he meant *all* the family, even if he had to haul them back from the ends of the earth.

"I'm looking forward to meeting him. Is he anything like you?"

"More like you. He doesn't own a suit."

"Heaven forbid." She laughed. "Still, it will be fun, don't you think?"

Dominic forced a smile. "Sure. It'll be great."

And if anyone gave her any grief, they'd better hope they could swim!

Friday evening. 6:00 p.m.

The moment of truth.

And as far as Sierra was concerned, definitely one of those *Anna and the King of Siam* moments. One of those mind-shattering, throat-grabbing, pure panic moments where she'd certainly have whistled a happy tune, if only she could have mustered enough spit.

They had boarded the yacht half an hour before.

"Yacht?" she'd said, gaping when she'd first seen it at the Hudson River pier. "It looks more like an ocean liner!"

Dominic had given her a grave smile. But his expression showed him to be almost as nervous as she felt, though exactly what Dominic had to be nervous about she was sure she didn't know!

They were, after all, *his* friends and *his* colleagues, *his* father's choices from *his* particular world. Oh, Finn and Izzy and the kids were coming. So were Chloe and Gib and Brendan, and two or three other couples whose names Dominic had got from her, including Sam and Josie Fletcher and their son, Jake. Not to mention, Rhys and Mariah, Dominic's brother Nathan and, to Sierra's surprise, her own parents.

"Of course I invited them," Douglas had said just minutes before. "It's only proper."

Proper.

That was what Sierra was worried about.

Ordinarily she didn't. Ordinarily she just went her merry way, did what she thought was right, and let the chips fall where they might.

But "right" wasn't necessarily the same in the world Dominic often inhabited. And she desperately didn't want to embarrass him.

She loved him, regardless of how he felt about her. And while she didn't think he had any great expectations of marriage—except of course the sex he wasn't getting at the moment—she didn't want him to regret marrying her.

So she was going to try to behave like some finishing school female for the next six hours, even though she thought she might croak.

She wondered again if she should have dyed her hair. She could have gone brown for the affair. It wouldn't have killed her. She'd been a blonde, after all, for Mariah's wedding so as not to shock a hundred impressionable Kansans.

But that had been for Mariah's wedding, because Sierra hadn't wanted to attract attention that should rightly have been her sister's. It had been right then to fade into the background.

Somehow, even though it might have made things easier, she couldn't bring herself to do it here. It would have felt like a copout. It would have seemed, even if only to her, that she wasn't being true to herself.

So her hair was still pretty purple—sort of more of a black cherry, actually—and she'd done it sleek and shining, then because they would be outdoors for a good part of it, she wore a broad-brimmed pink hat. Her dress was silk, purples and pinks, short and stunning, sleeveless with a high neckline. Very basic, yet very Sierra. Not as funky as some of her clothes, but not likely to turn up in the next issue of *Town and Country*, either.

It made her feel as if she could almost cope.

"They're boarding," Rhys came in to report. The guests, he meant. When they came on board, they would go through a sort of modified reception line, just Sierra and Dominic, her parents and Douglas.

"So everyone gets to meet the bride," Douglas said cheerfully. "Won't take long. Then you can move around and visit with people. Then dinner and dancing. You look wonderful, my dear.'' He gave Sierra an encouraging smile and looked as if he actually meant it.

She smiled back, then put her hand on Dominic's black tuxedo jacket sleeve and took a deep breath.

"You all right?" Dominic asked her. He sounded worried.

"Fine," Sierra said briskly. She gave him her best whistling-in-the-dark grin, and made up her mind that she was telling the truth.

No one was rude to her face.

Of course they were all too proper for that, too well brought up, too genteel. Dominic knew they wouldn't do anything so impolite as to say what they were thinking, nor would they be so obvious as to catch a glimpse of the bride, then turn and walk away.

But sometimes, out of the corner of his eye, he saw people looking askance. The women, of course, more than the men. He heard mutters. The occasional indrawn breath of astonishment followed, naturally, by disapproval.

He gritted his teeth, smiled politely, said all the appropriate things. And hoped Sierra didn't hear.

She gave no sign that she did. She was as warm and friendly and engaging as she always was. She sparkled in public, like a jewel.

Costume jewelry, Dominic imagined most people would think, looking at her.

But it wasn't true. Sierra was as deep and radiant as the finest diamond. Her beauty came from within, not from what she chose to wear.

"Whatever could he have been thinking?" he heard just then, the voice a carrying whisper almost right behind them. Dominic turned slightly to see one of his mother's old bridge club members, Sylvia Ponsonby-Merrill, using her driving glasses to take another look at his bride.

"I really can't imagine." This voice was even more familiar. Younger. Mellifluous and carefully cultured. "I'm sure he *wasn't* thinking," she said. It was Marjorie—she who'd demanded an engagement ring in return for her favors—disapproving now in honeyed tones. "Or," she added with a small laugh, "certainly not with his head!"

Sierra was speaking to Talitha Thomas, the widow of one of his father's oldest friends. Talitha was patting her hand and beaming up at her, and Sierra was smiling and clasping the old woman's hand. She didn't falter once, but all the same, Dominic was sure she heard the exchange between Sylvia and Marjorie.

He wondered if either of them could swim.

Then his father appeared and invited the two of them to admire the sunset from the top deck, and the conversation turned to other topics.

Sierra went right on talking to Talitha.

On her behalf, though, Dominic fumed.

At first it was awful.

Like the first day of school in kindergarten, when you knew hardly anybody, and no one wanted to know you.

But no one ever did, Sierra had discovered, if you didn't try to know them. So that's what she set out to do. Every person Dominic introduced her to was an interesting individual. And she made sure to show she understood that. Most of them responded politely and, if they were reserved at first, the majority, by the time she'd finished talking to them, responded with at least a little warmth.

A few, of course, did not.

She told herself she didn't care. For herself she did not. But she hated that they thought less of Dominic because of her.

Not all of them did.

Tally Thomas, for instance. What a delightful surprise to see Tally there. The sprightly octogenarian had been one of Sierra's first clients when she'd come to New York. Tally had been a regular at the little salon on Madison where Sierra had first found a job cutting hair, and one day when her regular stylist was ill, she'd made do with Sierra.

After that she'd insisted on Sierra always doing her hair. She'd followed Sierra through three more salons until Sierra had told her she was going to go to Paris. Then Tally had given her a series of French lessons. "So you don't let them get the best of you," she'd said, with a twinkle in her eye.

Sierra had loved the lessons and she hadn't forgotten Tally's kindness. Though she hadn't seen Tally much since she'd come back and was working on photo shoots now, she was delighted to see her first real client.

Tally was equally thrilled to see her. "Who'd have thought it!" she'd said, clasping Sierra's hands in her own. "Never would've dreamed one of Douglas's boys would have such good sense!"

"Dominic's brilliant," Sierra had assured her, watching her husband out of the corner of her eye. He had stiffened at the voices of two women behind them, and what they were saying made Sierra stiffen, too, though she did her best to pretend she hadn't heard.

They didn't matter, she assured herself.

Only people like Tally mattered. Kind people. Loving people.

And, of course, Dominic.

"My secretary, Shyla," Dominic was introducing her to now.

And Sierra put the other women out of her mind and took Shyla's hand. "I'm so glad to meet you. How does Deirdre like her Yankees' cap?"

Shyla laughed. They talked, compared notes on Dominic, and, Sierra was delighted to see, made him blush.

Then Mariah appeared and said, "It's time to go sit down and eat."

"You okay?" Dominic asked her.

And Sierra nodded. Yes, she was.

She'd said she was fine.

Then she disappeared.

They ate dinner, cut the cake, fed each other bites of it, and she was smiling and happy, then told him she needed to wash her hands, headed for the ladies' room—and disappeared.

"You're supposed to be dancing. The bride and groom lead out the dancing," Rhys said into his ear. Dominic was pacing the deck. He'd been over all of them looking for her when she hadn't reappeared. He'd seen everyone, smiled and shook hands and met some curious gazes, and he could hardly say he'd mislaid his bride, so he'd kept looking by himself.

But she didn't seem to be anywhere!

"You and Mariah dance," Dominic said now, brushing Rhys off.

"We're not the bride and groom."

"Well, pretend you are," Dominic said through his teeth. "Sierra's not here!"

"What the hell do you mean, not here? This is a boat, for God's sake! Where could she be?"

"How the hell should I know? She went to the head and she never came back."

"Maybe she's still there."

"It's been half an hour!"

"Did you look?"

"Of course not. I didn't go busting in. It's not a unisex bathroom."

"Did you ask?"

Dominic grunted. "You don't go around asking for your lost bride."

"Well, no, I never have," Rhys said cheerfully, "but I've never lost mine."

"Since you married her," Dominic said pointedly. He

wasn't going to allow Rhys very much smugness. His brother had screwed things up pretty badly with Mariah before he'd come to his senses and begun to live happily ever after.

"Since then," Rhys agreed. "Want me to ask?"

Dominic didn't want anything of the sort, but it was better to have Rhys ask than to do it himself. "If you want," he said offhandedly. "But don't tell them I sent you!"

Rhys crossed his heart. "And hope to die," he said piously.

"Just do it." Dominic gave him a push toward the stairs. He followed Rhys down at a discreet distance, ready to look the other way while Rhys knocked on the ladies' room door.

But before Rhys could do it, the door opened and three women came out, laughing and talking together like old friends.

Sylvia Ponsonby-Merrill, Marjorie, and Sierra.

Discreet distance and deliberate indifference forgotten, Dominic gaped at them while Rhys stepped back and let them pass.

"I don't know how to thank you," Marjorie, face flushed, was saying to Sierra.

"Not a problem." Sierra replied cheerfully. "The same thing happened to me at my friend Katie's wedding. Only worse. My switch fell in the soup!"

Both the other women's eyes bugged, then all three burst out laughing, and Sylvia patted her hand and said, "I'll give some thought to that rinse you recommended. I've never thought of myself as a blonde." She looked absolutely delighted. "It's intriguing." She gave Dominic a cheerful smile and, as she slipped past him, said, "Lovely girl, your Sierra, Dominic. Trust you to find her."

His eyes met Marjorie's for just a moment as she followed Sylvia. "I like her, Dominic," she said.

So did he.

But he was a little dazed and confused about how she had managed to convert the enemy.

"Marjorie's switch came loose in the breeze when she went up on deck with your father," Sierra told him simply. "She was in despair when I went to wash my hands. She couldn't get it up and fixed again. Neither could Sylvia." She shrugged. "So I did."

"You helped—but they were the ones who—" Dominic stopped as Sierra took his hand in hers.

She smiled at him, both her hands warm as they wrapped around his and she looked into his eyes. "They're guests. And it's true what I told Sylvia." Her eyes simply sparkled. "She would look good as a blonde."

It was a beautiful night.

Magical.

The skyline of Manhattan twinkled in the distance as the sun went down and the moon rose. People laughed and ate and drank and chatted. Children played and whooped and clapped. The band played lilting romantic melodies.

And for the first time in weeks Sierra was back in Dominic's arms.

It was required, of course. They had a duty dance down by the band, and he held her close and she could rub her cheek against the starched white of his shirt or the soft black of his tuxedo jacket. She did just that, couldn't help herself. But, all too quickly, the piece ended and her father was claiming her, and then Douglas and Rhys and Nathan and Finn and Gib and seemingly an endless stream of men.

Lovely men. Charming men. Dashing men.

She hugged her father, thanked Douglas profusely, assured Rhys that everything was fine, enjoyed a few moments with Nathan who, wearing a borrowed suit of Dominic's, looked remarkably like him.

But Nathan wasn't him.

And she wanted him. Desperately.

What Dominic wanted she had no idea. He was dancing with an equal number of women. She kept her eyes open, watching for him, aware every moment where he was—even when he was on the far side of the dance floor. She saw him with her mother, with Mariah and Izzy and Chloe and Pammie. She even saw him dance once with Sylvia Ponsonby-Merrill.

She wanted him to dance again with her.

It reminded her of Rhys's and Mariah's wedding when she'd danced all night determinedly with other men, but had only had eyes for him.

The difference was, she hadn't danced with him first—or at all—that night, until the very end.

Then somehow they just happened to be standing near each other at the beginning of the last dance of the evening. And their gazes, which had been connecting and avoiding all night, met once more.

And this time neither had looked away.

"Dare you," Dominic had said gruffly, a muscle jumping in his jaw. He held out a hand.

And Sierra took it and felt the electricity jolt through her.

"You're on," she'd replied and stepped recklessly into his arms.

From that moment she was lost. She'd probably been lost from the first time she saw him, but she hadn't realized it then.

She was still lost in love with Dominic and she didn't know how, after tonight, she would be able to resist.

She stood now beside the staircase leading to the upper decks and watched the other couples dancing. She tried to find Dominic, but for once her radar failed her.

And then, quite suddenly, he was there.

Right next to her, his shoulder brushing hers, his fingers sliding in to lace with hers.

"Dare you." The gruff whisper sent a shiver right to the center of her.

She whipped her head around to see him there, a wry grin on his face and a reckless look in his eyes.

She swallowed. "Dare me to what?"

"Dance with me." He took her hand, but he didn't lead her to the dance floor. Instead he drew her up the steps, not to the next deck or the next, but to the very top open air deck where there was no one else, just the music drifting up to them. And then he shut the door.

He held out his arms. "Dance?"

Sierra blinked. "Oh, yes. Yes, please." And she stepped into them again, felt one slide around her back and draw her close, felt the other close around her right hand, tucking it against his chest. Her hat bumped his nose.

He laughed. It was a strained laugh, rough with desire. And when she took the hat off and tossed it away, he wrapped his arms around her and they watched it float on the night sky into the water below.

Then he turned her in his arms and they danced. Alone. Together.

Then Dominic said, "I wonder if maybe we ought to go on a honeymoon after all."

Sierra's heart leapt. She stepped back and looked up at him, trying to see his heart in his eyes. But there were too many shadows. The night was too dark.

But not too dark to hope.

CHAPTER NINE

"A HONEYMOON?" Douglas looked surprised. He stopped fidgeting in Dominic's office and regarded his son with curiosity. "Where?"

"I don't know where," Dominic said irritably. He just knew it was a good idea. If he and Sierra were ever going to make anything out of this marriage, they needed some time alone together, to concentrate on each other.

He didn't stop to think when he'd decided that it was necessary that he and Sierra make something out of their marriage—something more than he'd originally thought, at least. He just knew it was. He knew she'd been right.

He only hoped he hadn't waited too long and blown it.

He didn't think he had. She had looked surprised but happy when he'd suggested it last night, which was why he was in the office on Saturday. He was trying to get things squared away, sorted out, finished up.

"You really want to put the past behind you and move on?" Nathan asked. He was lounging on the sofa, leafing through a magazine while he waited for their father. The two of them were going out to the old family home on Long Island to go fishing. They'd stopped by Dominic's place to see if he and Sierra wanted to go. Sierra had told them he was at the office.

"Idiot," Douglas had said when he'd first burst in. "What are you doing here, leaving your wife home on the Saturday after your wedding reception? You'll lose that girl, Dominic!"

"I'm trying *not* to lose her, damn it!" Dominic had retorted, jabbing a pencil in his father's direction. "I'm trying to get things sorted out so I can take her away from here."

"You should go to our place in the Bahamas," Nathan said.

Dominic snapped the pencil in half. He glared at his brother. "That's the stupidest damn suggestion I ever heard! Take her where I got *jilted* last time?"

"Have you ever been back?" Nathan asked him.

Dominic raked a hand through his hair. "Hell, no. And why should I have?"

Nathan shrugged. "To get over it?"

Dominic slammed his hand on the desk. "I am over it!"

"I can tell," Nathan murmured. He got up and paced the room, then tossed the magazine onto the coffee table, then glanced at his watch. "Come on, Dad. He's not going with us, and I want to get some fishing in. I'm only going to be here a week, then it's off to Antarctica."

"Right," Douglas said. He hoisted himself out of his chair, then regarded his son across Dominic's wide desk. "The honeymoon is a good idea." He turned and started for the door, then stopped and looked back. "The Bahamas is a good idea, too. For a marriage to work, it needs a clean slate."

She'd only been to the Bahamas twice.

In all the traveling she'd done on photo shoots all over the world, she'd only managed a week in Nassau.

"Nassau?" she'd said eagerly when he mentioned the Bahamas.

Dominic had shaken his head. "We have a place on one of the out islands. There's a small town, a fishing harbor, and a few houses scattered along the windward beach. Three miles of pink sand and usually deserted."

"Sounds heavenly," Sierra had said.

And now she knew it was.

They'd flown to the closest island airport, then had taken a water taxi to the island. It was called Pelican Cay, and it was picture-book beautiful, with rows of pastel-colored houses climbing higgledy-piggledy up the hill from the harbor, and narrow asphalt roads that wound through town and then in two or three directions out of town into what looked almost like jungle.

One of the islanders met their water taxi, an old man named Maurice, who drove a purple Jeep and gave her a deep courtly bow when he took her suitcase and helped her in.

"My car," he said, "she matches your hair." And he beamed broadly when Sierra grinned.

Dominic, for his part, was quiet. He seemed nervous, wary, a little gunshy, Sierra would have said. She watched him openly as he got into the front seat next to Maurice. When he turned his head, she noted a tight line at the corner of his mouth and the fact that he hadn't taken off his dark glasses since they'd set foot off the plane.

"It's lovely," she said, reaching up to put a hand on his shoulder and when he touched it automatically, she laced her fingers through his. "Thank you for bringing me."

"My pleasure," Dominic said. But he certainly didn't sound like it.

"It be our pleasure to have you back, Mr. Wolfe," Maurice said as they bounced through the narrow streets. "We miss you."

Dominic's mouth tightened even further. But at last he nodded at Maurice. "Thank you."

Maurice smiled again with great good cheer. "But now you here, it be like you never left. Only good things. And you enjoy it!" He slanted Dominic a sidelong look. "This be your honeymoon, yes?"

Dominic hesitated, then nodded. "Yes."

Maurice laughed, delighted. "You definitely enjoy then! My Estelle, she give you plenty of privacy. Estelle be the cook an' housekeeper," he told Sierra. "I tell everyone to give you plenty of privacy." He laughed again. And Sierra was enchanted to see Dominic blush.

"We've been married a while," he said stiffly. "We're hardly newlyweds."

"Hardly," Sierra agreed, but then the imp within her made her say, "But we'll enjoy all that privacy, you can be sure!"

She and Maurice laughed together. Dominic retreated behind his sunglasses, and Sierra wondered if she'd made a mistake by teasing him.

But she knew she had to treat him as she'd always treated him. They were having a honeymoon. They were getting to know each other. They needed to be who they really were for this to work. They couldn't try to pretend.

They had to be themselves.

Nathan, not for the first time, had been wrong.

Why the hell had he listened to his stupid younger brother? What the hell did Nathan know about being married or making things work with your wife?

Nathan wasn't married, never had been!

He was as footloose and free as a bird. He'd never even been engaged, never been in love, never even looked at the same woman twice as far as Dominic knew.

So where did he get off telling Dominic what to do?

And why the hell had he listened?

Because in New York City in a steel-and-glass building where he was strong and clever and in control, it had made a certain sort of cockeyed sense.

And so he'd finished up his work and gone home to tell Sierra he'd made arrangements for them to fly to the Bahamas. He'd made it sound enticing, charming, delightful—the perfect honeymoon paradise.

But the closer they'd got, the more he'd choked.

The sight of the town as they'd crossed the water had brought it all back. All the memories. All the hopes. All the disaster.

And then Maurice had been there to meet them, which

had been his father's doing, no doubt. Maurice, who had come to him with the news that Carin wasn't there. Maurice, who had patted his arm and said sadly, "I think maybe she panic, you know?" Maurice who had then gone and told his father who had begun to send people on their way.

Maurice knew.

Dominic didn't know if Sierra knew anything or not.

He didn't see how she couldn't. He hadn't said anything, but Mariah probably had. Mariah, married to Rhys, would know something. Rhys would have told his wife about the place in the Bahamas. He'd even brought her and the children down here a couple of months ago.

"It was therapeutic," he'd told Dominic after, because he'd had his own ghosts to lay to rest. "You ought to go back sometime."

But Dominic hadn't wanted any therapy like that.

Not then. He didn't now, either, suddenly. He only wanted to leave.

But it was too late.

Sierra loved it. He could see it on her face. She didn't wear sunglasses often, even when he thought she ought to. So her emotions were transparent. She was enthusiastic about everything. She looked around eagerly, pointing out this, asking about that.

And then, when Maurice turned down the long winding lane that led to the Wolfe house, she leaned forward eagerly, and exclaimed with delight when the cathedral of jungly trees opened onto an island garden and a low-slung peach-coloured house, with trailing dark burgundy bougainvillea all over one wall.

"This is it? It's beautiful. Gorgeous." And then she caught sight, beyond the house, of the beach and the turquoise water of the Caribbean. "Oh my! Oh, how wonderful!" And she leaned forward and threw her arms around Dominic's shoulders and drew him back into a hug.

It was oddly settling, the feel of her arms around him, the

whisper of her breath against his neck, the sound of her voice in his ear. She was Sierra, not Carin.

This was now. Not then.

They were married already.

They only had to make it work.

Maurice stopped the Jeep and got out. Dominic climbed out, then helped Sierra out, too. She stood, floppy hat clapped on her head with one hand, and turned in a circle admiring it all—the mangrove jungle, the shallow fishpond and stone patio of the garden, the white trellises with their bougainvilleas and the stands of multicolored oleander, the house, the hammock, the sand, the sea.

"I love it," she said, and she put her arms around him and hugged him again.

And one by one, as he stood holding Sierra in his arms, Dominic's fears, his memories, his humiliations seemed to recede.

It was hard to remember Carin in the presence of as vibrant a woman as his wife. It was hard to think of the wedding that hadn't happened, when Sierra still talked happily about the one that had—and the reception his father had given them.

It was hard to dwell on the past, when the present was so much more fun.

He hadn't considered that coming back to Pelican Cay would be fun. He'd thought about it seriously, determinedly, with earnestness and resolution. He was going to banish the past and make a concerted effort to get to know this amazing woman he'd wed.

But it hadn't really sounded like much fun.

But then, he'd forgotten what life with Sierra—when she wasn't trying to avoid him—could be like.

They barely got in the house and she said, "Why don't we go swimming?"

"Now?" He was surprised, then willing. He had no reason to want to remain in the house, after all. He just remembered standing here that morning, waiting for Carin—and Carin never coming.

"Swimming? Sure," he said. "Why not?"

She changed into a deep purple maillot, slathered her fair skin with sunblock, and rubbed something oily on her hair. "So I don't turn the ocean purple," she explained, then grinned. "I'm kidding. It's to protect my hair."

"Oh. Right." He grinned, too. But his mind was less on her hair than on her nearly bare body which he hadn't seen in far too long. Something he should probably not be thinking about right now. "Go ahead. I'll get my trunks on and join you."

She was waiting on the deck overlooking the beach when he came out a few minutes later. She was leaning forward, hands braced on the railing as she looked out down the beach which was empty as far as the eye could see.

"This is amazing," she said. "This is paradise and it's deserted. This has to be the world's best kept secret."

"We know it's here," Dominic said smiling at her, holding out his hand to her.

She put hers in his. "Then let's keep it just for us."

Once they were down on the beach she ran toward the water and he ran with her, remembering he'd probably been a teenager last time he had actually run into the surf.

It felt good. Liberating.

Then she let go of his hand and dove beneath a small wave, and he dove after her. They both came up sputtering and laughing.

"It's like a warm bath!" Sierra exclaimed. "It's heavenly." And she ducked again and came up, purple hair streaming as she smiled at him so eager and alive that his heart seemed to lodge in his throat.

They swam and played in the water. Then they came out and flopped, exhausted, on the pale pink coral sand beach. Lying side by side on their stomachs, breathing hard, they stared at each other. Then Sierra smiled. And he smiled back.

He didn't know how long they lay there. Sierra's eyes closed and he thought she had fallen asleep. So he got up and spread a light sheet over her to protect her from the sun, even though it was fairly late in the day. She smiled slightly, but she didn't open her eyes.

He just sat and watched. Traced the lines of her features, memorized them. Marveled at how young and innocent she looked. With the purple hair she reminded him of some sleek sea creature, a mermaid, perhaps. An enchantress.

From the very first she had enchanted him. Bewitched him. Got past his very well-developed guard. And now he couldn't imagine life without her.

He wished she would tell him again that she loved him. She hadn't said it since the night they'd fought.

Maybe he should tell her.

But he couldn't. He hadn't said the words in years. And every time he thought them, they stuck in his throat.

She was still sleeping by the time the sun went down behind the house, casting the beach in shadow. Darkness came early in the tropics. And as the sun fell a light breeze sprang up and blew in from the water.

Dominic touched her shoulder. "Sierra?"

Slowly her eyes opened and she smiled. "Hey." The way she looked at him made his toes curl with anticipation. He wanted her now with a depth he couldn't have guessed at when he married her. It was so much stronger than anything he'd ever felt before.

"Ready for some of that dinner Estelle left us?"

She hauled herself to a kneeling position. "Sure. I'm starved." She brushed off the sand from the front of her swimsuit. "I must have fallen asleep. Sorry. You must have been bored. You could have left me. Got some work done. Or—"

"No."

She looked surprised. "No?" She said the word almost hopefully.

Slowly Dominic shook his head. "No. This is our honeymoon, remember. It's just for the two of us."

The smile that lit her face then took his breath away. She stood up and drew a deep breath, then looked all around before her gaze came back to him. She held out her hands to him and went up on her toes to touch her lips to his.

"Thank you," she said softly.

"My pleasure," he replied.

And this time he meant it.

Late that night he realized as he was shutting out the light and preparing to go to bed with her, that he'd never once thought of Carin. He'd never remembered the last time he'd been here.

It was time.

All day she'd been waiting. No, actually longer. She'd been waiting since Dominic had suggested they have a honeymoon after all, since he'd decided to see her as more than a mere bed partner.

She didn't know if he loved her yet. But she thought there was a chance now that he might. They'd had a wonderful day on the beach, at dinner on the deck, then after, walking along the sand once more.

And now it was time.

Time to go to bed with Dominic again.

To make love with him for the first time.

There had been love in it before, subliminally, subconsciously—at least on her part. But it hadn't been like this. It hadn't happened with this need, with this depth, with this commitment.

She felt awkward as she prepared for bed now. There was none of the silly spontaneity of their earlier couplings. None of the frenzied need with which they'd wrestled each other down. He wasn't even in the room. He'd gone to shut out the light in the living room while she changed into the soft white gown that Mariah had given her yesterday afternoon.

"I know this isn't a traditional honeymoon," her sister had said. "But it means just as much—maybe more. You need to have a few trappings to make it special, besides Dominic."

The gown was special. Almost virginal in its simplicity.

Sierra felt oddly virginal. And she supposed emotionally she was. She'd never made love like this before.

She settled on the bed and lay waiting, hoping, praying that Dominic would feel as committed as she did, would want things to work as badly as she did.

And then he was standing in the doorway, looking at her, his eyes hooded, his expression unreadable. He wore only a pair of boxer shorts, and she could see that his chest and legs were slightly reddened from the sun. His normally neat hair was salt-stiffened and tousled. He looked gorgeous— strong and muscled and one-hundred percent virile male. All Sierra's hormones went on alert.

The need for him was as great as it had ever been, the depth of feeling, the seriousness of loving this man forever was still there. But as Sierra smiled, she suddenly didn't feel awkward at all.

"No tie?" she teased.

And Dominic's brooding expression faded. A smile touched the corners of his beautiful mouth. "I didn't even bring one," he said. "Damn it."

Sierra held out her arms to him. "Don't worry. I think we can improvise."

They improvised.

They kissed and stroked and touched and licked. Even though he'd showered earlier, she could still taste a slight saltiness on his skin as she nibbled his shoulder. And she gave a delicate shudder as he nibbled hers, then moved up her neck and along her jaw before covering her lips in a soul-searing kiss.

She drew him down over her and splayed her hands across the breadth of his back. His skin was warm to the touch and smooth. With her fingers she walked the ridge of his spine, then pressed her fists alongside it and felt his muscles bunch and flex.

Then he rose to kneel between her legs and part her soft flesh. His touch made her shiver with longing, and she reached for him. "Now, Dominic. Please."

There was no teasing tonight. No wrestling. Only hunger and passion and the need to become one as fully and quickly as possible.

He nodded and slid inside her, filling her, making her whole. It was as if some part of her that had been missing was suddenly there, found, home. The wonder of it made Sierra's breath catch in her throat.

She shifted to take him more deeply within and heard him draw a quick breath. "Dominic?" she whispered. "Are you all right?"

"Am I all right?" His tone was incredulous. "I've never been better in my life." And she heard a ragged little catch in his voice this time.

And then he began to move. Slowly, languorously, lazily almost. At first. But then there was a subtle change, an increase in tempo, a tension in his body. She could feel it just as she felt the change in her own. She locked her heels against the backs of his thighs as she rocked to meet him.

He drove down one last time, then stopped dead, quivering violently, shattering in her arms. Lost. Found. Shattered.

And, Sierra hoped desperately as her own body splintered, made whole.

Singing in the rain.

That's what they did the next morning. She actually got him down to the beach in the middle of a downpour—

"We're going swimming anyway! Who cares at what point we get wet?"—and danced along the sand.

He didn't dance. But he felt like it. His heart danced. And his soul. And every other part of him but his feet.

And even they did a couple of quick shuffles when he was sure no one—except maybe Sierra—was looking.

"You're a wonderful dancer," she protested when he wouldn't. "You danced on the *Sloop John B.*" That's what she was calling the yacht now.

"But there was music then," he argued.

"There's music now. In my heart." She grabbed him and pressed his head against her breasts. "Can't you hear it?"

He heard enough music of his own. He kissed the tip of her breast and then grabbed her up into his arms and ran with her into the ocean, then sank down, submerging them both.

They came up sputtering and laughing. And then they teased and tickled and wrestled and played. And when the rain stopped they came out and lay on the damp sand, breathless and hungry for each other.

"I could make love to you right here," he muttered.

"If we didn't have an audience." Sierra nodded her head in the direction of a couple of little girls down the beach perhaps quarter of a mile away.

"They'd never know."

"They won't know," Sierra said, hopping to her feet and pulling him up with her. "Because we're going back up to the house to do it. I'm not sharing you, even voyeuristically, with anyone."

That was fine with him. Dominic had no desire to be shared. They went back to the house and made love in the shower, then in the bed, and barely managed to be dressed and respectable when Estelle arrived to clean.

"You sleepyheads," she admonished gently.

"Oh," Sierra said brightly, "Dominic's been up for hours." And then she giggled, and he felt his face flush.

He pulled her into his arms and hugged her hard. "I'll take this hussy out of your way," he promised Estelle. "Come on. We'll go back down on the beach."

They didn't swim this time. They sat on the sand and dug tunnels and made sand castles because that was what he and his brothers had done here years ago and it seemed right that he do it with Sierra. She was family now.

"We can do this with our kids," he said.

She looked up from digging a tunnel and her eyes were wide. "Kids?" she said in barely more than a whisper.

"You want kids, don't you? I figured you did. You're good with kids. Frankie. Stephen and Lizzie."

"I'd love to have kids." She looked like he'd given her the moon. "I wasn't sure you…" Her voice died out and she shrugged a little awkwardly.

"I want kids," he said firmly. "I would always want them. No matter what. I couldn't believe Rhys turning his back on Mariah when she was carrying his child."

"I remember you didn't fight too hard to keep his whereabouts secret," she said with a mischievous grin.

Dominic remembered that day, too, remembered being astonished when this purple-haired virago had invaded his office and threatened his manhood unless he surrendered his brother's address.

"I wouldn't have given it to you," he said, "despite the turn-on, if I hadn't thought you were right. A man has a responsibility to his child. And to its mother."

Their gazes met across the castle. Then they were kneeling right in the middle of it, kissing with a desperation that might have led them to be a public spectacle if Sierra hadn't pulled back suddenly.

Dominic groaned, needing her now.

"I wonder if Estelle has finished in the house," Sierra said raggedly.

He hauled her to her feet. "She's done, whether she's finished or not."

*   *   *

They walked into the small harborside village that afternoon because Sierra insisted. "I know honeymooners are supposed to spend every minute in bed. But I do want to see where I've been."

"In bed," Dominic said, grinning. "Why does it matter where you've been?"

"It does," Sierra insisted. "We'll have a good time. We can pick up some groceries, and stop and tell Estelle we'll cook for ourselves tonight."

"And then she won't come back and…" Dominic could already see possibilities in that.

"And I'd like to find something to take home to remember this by. A souvenir."

"You might already have a souvenir," he said with a grin and a glance at her midriff.

The heat of his gaze made Sierra warm all over. And the thought that he, too, wanted a child thrilled her to bits.

If he would only say, "I love you."

She stopped herself even as she thought it. She knew of other men who couldn't say the words. Her own father, according to her mother, had barely managed to get them past his lips half a dozen times in his life.

Which was six more than Dominic had, she thought. But then she slipped her hand in his and leaned up to kiss him.

And he kissed her back with such fervor that she wondered how she could ever doubt.

He would never have told her it at all if she hadn't asked.

They'd gone out fishing that afternoon with Maurice's brother, Victor, and Victor had said, "Ain't seen you in years an' years. Not since your weddin' what wasn't." And then he'd clamped his mouth shut and seconds later when he opened it again, everything he'd said had to do with fishing.

But that night when they were in bed, lights out, hunger

sated, sleepy and warm in each other's arms, Sierra asked, "Will you tell me about it?"

He knew she wouldn't press. It wasn't so much of a question as an invitation, and though he would never have guessed he would take her up on it, now that she was asking, he did.

"It was the year after my mother died," he told her and felt the familiar lump lodge in his throat. "I was twenty-four. Finished with my M.B.A. I'd been working for Wolfe's since high school in one capacity or another, being groomed to take over, my dad directing every move. And that year I'd moved out of the subsidiary offices to New York. I was his right-hand man—and loving every minute of it. And he was missing my mother. We both were. Rhys had Sarah and Nathan had his photography and was gone a lot. But the two of us were sort of…lost, I guess. Him for sure, and I just wanted to be like him. And then he said, 'You ought to get married.'"

He rolled onto his back, folded his arms under his head and stared at the ceiling fan that moved lazily in the moonlit room. "Just like that. And I agreed."

He remembered it so well, how sure he'd been that his dad was right, that it was time to get married, even when he didn't even have a woman in mind.

"A few days later he told me that one of the men he did business with had this gorgeous daughter. 'You ought to see her,' he said. Then, 'You ought to marry her.' He was joking then, but I guess the seed was planted." He sighed, remembering how foolish he'd been, thinking it was going to be that easy.

"So I got introduced. And she was very pretty."

"How pretty?" Sierra asked in a small voice. She was lying against him, one leg over his, her head nestled in the curve of his shoulder. Her words stirred the hair on his chest. Her apprehensiveness stirred his heart.

"Pretty enough," he said because he had to be honest.

But she'd never made his heart kick over. She'd never made his pulse race. She'd been lovely in a grave, gentle way. Nowhere near as vibrant as Sierra. "Not like you," he said. "She was a student, a senior in college. An art major. At some Midwestern school. I can't even remember which. Doesn't matter. She was in New York for the summer, doing something at one of the museums, an internship or something. And we started dating."

It had been so pleasant. So simple to sweep her off her feet, to take her nice places, to invite her out to the family home on Long Island, to take her sailing. She'd been enchanted, had loved it all. And her fresh-faced innocence and enthusiasm had charmed him, too.

When his father had approved, had said the words that made Carin the perfect mate—"You know, she reminds me of your mother"—it had been the easiest thing in the world to propose.

He hadn't been surprised when she'd accepted. "And then we decided to get married."

Sierra raised her head briefly. "Just like that?"

"We had spent more time together than you and I did," Dominic reminded her.

She lay her head back down and he felt her nod. Her fingers played lightly across his chest. "Go on."

"She loved to go sailing, so I thought coming down here would be a great idea. We could get married here, I told her. And she thought that sounded wonderful. She didn't have a mother to plan a big wedding back in Wisconsin. Her mother and father had split years before and Carin had stayed with her father. So we just decided that Bahamas was it. I had work to do, so she came down early. One of us had to be in residence three weeks to qualify for the marriage license. So she came and stayed in the house. Then the week of the wedding everybody else came. Except me. I was putting together a deal and I didn't get here until the night before."

He stopped, swallowed, wondering again as he had so many times if that had been the problem. If he'd got here sooner would she have talked to him? Would she have told him what she couldn't tell anyone else?

"I didn't get here until the rehearsal was starting. And that was a crock anyway because her bridesmaid wasn't flying in until morning, and Nathan, who was supposed to be my best man, got a call from some magazine and took off, leaving Rhys in his place. I should have realized things weren't going to work."

But he hadn't. He'd gone through the rehearsal in a daze. He'd been exhausted, coming down with a cold, and short-tempered when anyone talked to him.

Including Carin.

Not that Carin ever said much. She'd asked him how he was, he remembered that. And he'd growled something about just being glad when the whole thing was over with.

He'd meant glad to be married.

He'd given her a chaste kiss on the forehead so he wouldn't give her his cold. "I barely spoke to her," he told Sierra now. "Except to tell her to get a good night's sleep." And he remembered mustering a grin that had promised she wouldn't be getting one on their wedding night.

"And then I said, 'See you in the morning.' But I didn't." He could still remember all the preparations, the last-minute things that needed to be done before he was left to stand by Rhys in the garden near the trellis of bougainvillea and wait for his bride. He'd stood still for the first time that morning, glad to have a chance to catch his breath.

And then he'd looked toward the house and waited for Carin.

He'd waited and waited.

The guests had waited, too. At first quietly, then with increasing murmurs and head turning.

Rhys had grinned and said, "Don't suppose she's ditched you, do you?"

Dominic had snorted then. But within moments it became increasingly clear that she had. Her father had appeared on the deck looking distraught. His own father had looked irritated, then furious. He'd glared at Dominic, then looked at Rhys and jerked his head for his youngest son to join him.

"Maybe she's sick," Rhys had suggested. "Nerves." And he'd hurried off to talk to their dad.

When he came back a few minutes later he didn't have to tell Dominic what had happened.

"She was gone," he told Sierra now, his voice flat. "Packed up in the middle of the night sometime and skipped out." His fingers curled into fists against the sheet.

"Oh, Dominic." Her voice comforted him. Her lips caressed him. "Oh, my dear." And then she moved right on top of him, as if she could shield him from the pain, from the memory, from the humiliation he felt at having to clear his throat and tell the assembled guests that there would be no wedding that morning.

And oddly, it helped.

The warmth of her body on his soothed ragged feelings. The gentleness of her touch healed a dozen years of pain.

It wasn't losing Carin that had mattered.

It was feeling unlovable.

Sierra took those feelings away. She loved him. She'd said so. And with her every act she reconfirmed those words. He rested his chin against the top of her head. His legs tangled with hers, and his arms came around her and held her fast.

"Oh, my love," she whispered.

And Dominic, throat tight and aching with love for her, could only manage two words, "Oh, yes."

CHAPTER TEN

THE phone woke them.

The morning sun spilled in the window and Sierra squinted at it as she untangled herself from Dominic who cursed and reached for the ringing cellular phone on the bedside table.

There was no phone line to the house. The only connection with the outside world was the cell phone Douglas had insisted Dominic take.

"You're head of the company now. You have responsibilities. But I won't call unless it's an emergency," he'd promised.

Now Dominic grabbed it and muttered sleepily into it, "This had better be good."

A minute later he was sitting up, raking his fingers through his spiky hair, saying, "You're sure? But that's impossible. No, you're right it's not impossible. Oh, hell. All right. Let me talk to Sierra and I'll get back to you."

He hung up and turned to face her, his expression rueful. "I thought I had it all taken care of, really I did. But Sorensen in Denmark is suddenly on the market and we've been trying to buy them for two years. Dad thinks they'd rather go to us than to anyone else, but they want to talk to the boss."

"You," Sierra filled in.

Dominic nodded reluctantly.

"So talk to them." She scrunched back up against the pillows. "You don't have to dance attendance on me every second."

"I want to dance attendance on you. I want to crawl back in bed and—"

166

"But you can't," Sierra said. "Not if you want Sorensen. Denmark is six hours ahead of us. The day is half over."

"You don't mind?"

"Go ahead," she told him. "It doesn't matter. I can go walk on the beach or go into town and find a souvenir…just in case I don't have another one already," she added with a grin. "I love you."

He flashed her a grin and gave her a quick kiss. Then he punched in a number on his cell phone.

Sierra took a leisurely shower, ate some yogurt and a banana, then drank a cup of tea. She could hear Dominic in the other room talking on the phone. She poured him a cup, took it in and set it beside him. She got a fleeting smile in return and an even more fleeting kiss on her fingers before he had to scrabble for a pen and jot down some figures.

"I'm going for a walk," she mouthed. "Back in a while."

He looked hassled and shrugged, then nodded. "Swim later?" he mouthed back. "Then bed?"

She grinned and nodded.

He said into the phone, "Run that past me again," and started writing furiously.

Sierra left him to it. She pulled on one of his T-shirts over her bathing suit, then stepped into a pair of shorts and slapped a broad-brimmed straw hat on her head to protect her hair and her face from the fierce tropical sun. Then she waggled her fingers at him and headed down the stairs to the beach.

Pelican Cay really was the closest thing to paradise she could imagine.

It was the perfect place to have come for a honeymoon. And the honeymoon was everything she'd hoped it would be.

They'd grown closer here. They'd shared stories of their childhoods. He'd told her about the adventures he'd had here and on Long Island with Rhys and Nathan and she'd told him about growing up in Kansas with Mariah. They'd laughed and played and held hands and kissed. They'd walked miles on the pink sand beach and they'd dug tunnels and built sand castles.

"We'll have to bring Pam and Frankie down here sometime," he'd said yesterday. "A budding architect should build a few sand castles in his youth."

And Sierra had smiled at the thought. "Yes, that would be wonderful." And she'd been pleased, not just because Frankie would love it, but because it meant that Dominic had accepted her friends as his.

Frankie would love it, she thought as she looked around at the nearly deserted beach, at the softly breaking waves, and the lumpy remains of yesterday's castles. She and Dominic hadn't brought a camera, but now she thought she would walk along the beach until she came to the road to town, then go to the little island drug store where yesterday she had seen a rack of disposable cameras.

She could send Frankie a postcard and take a few photos, and maybe she could find a souvenir for the apartment, something that would bring back this paradise every time they looked at it.

She could get there and back by lunchtime. If Dominic was done with his calls by then, they could spend the afternoon at the beach—or in bed. As long as they spent it together, it didn't matter to her.

She started out along the beach, but the weather was so warm and muggy that she decided a quick dip wouldn't be amiss. She stripped off Dominic's shirt and her shorts, set the floppy hat on top of them, then plunged into the surf. She didn't stay in long, just long enough to cool off, then came back out, hair dripping, plastered sleekly to the back of her head.

Three children stood watching her with wide eyes. They were about ten or so, a little older than Frankie, she thought. A girl and two boys. The boys stared at her in wide-eyed speechlessness.

The girl said what they were apparently all thinking. "Are you a mermaid?" she asked. She was staring at Sierra's purple hair.

"Only half," Sierra said with a grin. "Just the top. Look—" She did a little hop. "No fin."

They all laughed then and, realizing that she was as human as everyone else and just a visitor, they looked embarrassed.

"People have called me worse things," Sierra assured them. "Look, I'm just visiting. My husband—" she faltered a moment over the word, then said it again with pleasure and determination "—my husband and I are spending our honeymoon here. I want to take home a souvenir. Got any suggestions?"

"A T-shirt," one of the boys said promptly.

The girl and the other boy groaned.

"Everybody takes home T-shirts, Marcus," the other boy said.

"You got a better idea?" the boy called Marcus challenged.

"You could get a stuffed fish," the second boy said. "Go fishin' an' my grandpa will mount you a fish."

Sierra smiled. "Maybe another time. I think I want something besides a stuffed fish for this occasion."

"You could buy one of my mother's paintings," the girl suggested.

Now that sounded like a possibility. "Your mother paints scenes of the islands?" she asked the girl.

Long dark braids bobbed as the girl nodded. "Beautiful paintings. Want to see? She has a shop in the village."

"Why not?" Sierra said. She couldn't carry a painting back along the beach. But maybe she would find something perfect that they could pick up just before they left or could have mailed—if they were any good.

The girl, whose name was Lacey, was eleven. She had been born on the island. She painted, too, just like her mother. And someday she was going to be famous and go to New York and have a showing in a gallery there. She told Sierra this as they walked up the road toward the village. The boys had dropped out of the expedition, choosing to head for the fishing dock. Lacey talked nonstop. The boys weren't missed.

"Have you been to New York?" Sierra asked her.

Dark braids swung back and forth as she shook her head no. "But my mother has."

"Has your mother had shows there?" Sierra asked. She wondered if she might know the woman. She got invited to a lot of gallery openings by people whose hair she did. Sometimes they were multi-person shows. Wouldn't it be amazing to meet someone here whom she'd seen in New York? There had been a woman last winter...

What was her name?

Sierra tried to remember what she looked like. She'd been dark like Lacey. And Lacey did look oddly familiar.

"It's right here," Lacey said, leading Sierra up the steps to a small bright blue cottage with white shutters. It had a narrow front porch on which several island scenes were displayed on easels. They were primitives—bright bold colors and broad strokes—the sand a little pinker, the sky a little bluer, the houses a little brighter. But yes, it was Pelican Cay.

Lacey's mother had captured its heart.

And she captured Sierra's, too. She knew at once that one of those paintings would be the perfect souvenir.

"Come on in," Lacey said, pushing open the door. "Mommy! I brought you a customer!"

The inside of the small shop was as welcoming as the outside—natural wood walls held similar scenes from various points on Pelican Cay. Overhead a ceiling fan whirled around, making a shell wind chime by the door tinkle softly.

A woman pushed aside the bamboo curtain that separated the showroom from the back room and came out, smiling and shaking her head. "Lacey, when are you going to learn to be a little more tactful."

Lacey's mother was fairer than her daughter. She looked to be in her early thirties, with high cheekbones and a slender nose and long, loose honey-colored hair that Sierra would have loved to braid.

"Hi," she said, and offered Sierra a paint-spattered hand. "Paint's dry, I promise. It just doesn't come off. Nice to meet you. I'm Carin Campbell."

The thing about paradise was that it didn't last.

You couldn't expect it to. Seven days. That was pretty much it. If Adam and Eve had only got a week, what right did Sierra have to expect more?

She didn't.

And she didn't buy a painting, either, though they were lovely evocative pieces which captured the spirit and the beauty of Pelican Cay. Someday maybe she'd wish she had one—to remember.

Now all she wanted to do was forget.

She couldn't, of course. She had things to do.

Over the buzzing in her brain, she thought she'd managed to converse politely with the woman who had once left Dominic at the altar. She thought she'd said all the proper noncommittal things about not being able to quite make up her mind and wanting a while to think about it, and certainly being glad to have met her.

And Carin had said cheerfully, "Don't feel obliged. Just because Lacey is a hard sell, that doesn't mean you have to come back and buy one."

Sierra couldn't answer that. She managed a wan desperate smile, then let herself back out into the street.

The midday sun beat down on her, and she told herself it was the sun that was making her head buzz and her brain feel fried.

But it wasn't.

It was realizing why Lacey looked familiar.

It had nothing to do with the artist at the gallery opening she'd attended. It had everything to do with her having Dominic's dark hair and deep blue eyes.

Her features were her mother's. She had Carin's nose and Carin's generous mouth. But the hair color was exactly Dominic's. And thinking back, Sierra realized that when the little girl tipped her head a certain way, she had the Wolfe profile.

Dominic had a daughter.

And he didn't even know.

She leaned against the porch railing of the grocery store and the man at the counter inside looked out curiously. "You be all right, Miss?"

Sierra nodded. "Yes," she said faintly. "I'll be fine."

Someday. Years from now.

She remembered yesterday on the beach, when they'd talked about having children. She remembered Dominic saying, *"I want kids. I would always want them. No matter what. I couldn't believe Rhys turning his back on Mariah when she was carrying his child."*

And she knew he would want Lacey.

She knew he would want Carin.

She'd heard the pain in his voice last night when he'd told her about Carin running away, about losing her—his first love.

Maybe, she thought sadly, his only love.

Because as much as she'd wished he'd said those words to her, he never had. He'd given her his body. But she could only guess that he'd given her his heart.

There was always the chance she'd guessed wrong.

And even if she hadn't—even if he had come to feel something for her—it was nothing compared to what he would feel for Carin once he knew she was the mother of his child.

"He might hate her," she told herself. He might be so

angry that she kept Lacey from him for all these years that he'd want nothing to do with her. And for a split second she felt a stab of hope.

But then reality settled in—and reality told her that no matter how Dominic felt about Carin, they would have so many issues to settle that Sierra would only be in the way.

She drew a deep breath and started back toward the house. And on the way she tried to find the courage to do what she had to do.

He was still on the phone when she got there, but the minute he saw her coming up the steps he said something to whoever he was talking to and put the phone down, then got up and came to meet her, an eager smile—a lover's smile—on his face.

And Sierra took a deep breath and, eyes brimming, she said the words she'd rehearsed for the last mile.

"I think we should get a divorce."

He'd been dying for her to get back. He'd been sick to death of all this Sorensen stuff, he'd done his best to sort through it, all the while keeping an eye on the path from the beach where he'd catch his first glimpse of Sierra.

And the minute he saw her coming, he said, "I'll call you when I'm back in New York," and hung up on the head of Sorensen to go and take his wife in his arms, to kiss her and love her.

And she said she wanted a divorce.

Dominic stared at her, disbelieving, her words cutting like a knife in his heart. He, who had thought he was immune to such pain, who had taken care never to fall in love, knew he was wrong.

He loved Sierra more than he'd ever loved anyone. The pain he'd felt when Carin had jilted him was nothing compared to this. That had been embarrassment, injured pride, the humiliation of masculine ego.

This cut him clear to his soul.

"Why?" His voice was hoarse, desperate, frantic. He clutched her so hard that his fingers might be leaving bruises on her arms. He tried to loosen his grip, tried not to hurt her.

God knew she was hurting him!

"Because," Sierra said, her voice choked, as if she'd been crying. "Because there are things you don't know."

"What things?" He was baffled, shaking his head. "What are you talking about? Why are you crying?"

She wiped a hand across her eyes hastily. "I'm *not* crying! The sun was in my eyes!"

"What things?" he persisted.

"Things you haven't settled. Things that will make a difference." She struggled out of his grasp and moved quickly away, not looking at him.

He stared at her. "You always used to make sense."

She gave a quick desperate shake of her head. "Go into the village. There's a little house on Harbor Street. A shop where they sell paintings. It's blue with white shutters."

"Do you have sunstroke?" He tried to feel her forehead, but she pushed him away.

"Damn it, no! I don't have anything! Just go!" When he didn't move, she glared at him. "Do it, damn you! Go!"

Stubbornly he shook his head. "You come, too."

"No! I can't! I've got to—" She broke off and started into the house.

And he knew exactly what she was intending to do, and took three strides across the deck and grabbed her arm. "I'll go," he said fiercely. "But you'll stay. You have to promise me. You can't leave. Don't you dare leave until I get back!"

She glowered at him, but he wouldn't let her go until she promised.

"I'll be here," she said finally. "Just go." Her throat sounded tight, her tone agonized.

He went.

But not without a long and desperate look back.

* * *

She waited.

It was the hardest thing she'd ever done.

Harder than standing up to Terry Graff at the pool when she was seven. Harder than moving to New York when she was twenty. Harder than staying out of Dominic's arms when she'd so desperately wanted to be in them those weeks after she had learned he didn't want out of their marriage what she wanted.

She waited, and paced, and bit her nails and fretted. She didn't want to be there when he came back, didn't want to have to put on a brave face while he gravely agreed that she was right, they needed to get a divorce.

Even more she didn't want to be here if he came back and said they didn't. She didn't want to be the reason he was torn.

She prowled and fumed and agonized. And finally, because she could stand waiting alone no longer, she grabbed his cell phone and called Pammie. It would help to know what the outside world was doing. It would be good to know how Frankie was getting along.

So she rang Pammie on the cell phone she had now—the one she had to carry everywhere so that the transplant people could always get in touch with her.

Even so she was surprised when Pammie answered so quick and breathlessly.

"It's Sierra," she said.

And Pam said, "How did you know?"

"Know what?"

"They found Dan." Frankie's father, she meant. The man she hadn't seen in all those years. "He took the test. He's a match. He's here. We're at the hospital. They're doing the surgery within the hour!"

Abruptly Sierra sat down. And a good thing, too, or her legs would not have held her. "They found Dan?" she echoed. Were missing fathers turning up everywhere these days?

"Long story," Pammie said. "I can't believe it. But it's true. He came back the minute he heard. He's changed, Sierra. He's grown up." She sounded as wobbly as Sierra felt. "I'm not hoping for fairy-tale endings, you know—Dan, me and Frankie together forever—but at least Frankie knows his dad cares. And that's something, isn't it?"

"Of course it is," Sierra said. She felt faint and just a little bit hollow. "That's...wonderful." Her throat was tight. She thought she might start to cry.

"How did you know?" Pam asked again. "Did Dominic find out? He would. He's so good at everything."

"He didn't find out," Sierra said. "He's had...other things on his mind."

"Is everything okay?" Pammie demanded. "Are you having a good time? A good honeymoon?"

"Yes," Sierra said. "Oh, yes."

She was sure, under the circumstances, God would forgive her the lie.

"Give Frankie my love," she said a little desperately. "Tell him...tell him I'll see him soon."

"I'll tell him," Pammie promised. Then, "Love you, Sierra. And thank you. Without you this couldn't have happened. You and Dominic."

So something good had come out of it.

Frankie was getting a transplant. He was getting a father, maybe. At least that's what it sounded like. And Lacey was getting a father, too. And Dominic would, perhaps, get Carin back.

All because of Sierra.

It was just dandy being so useful.

But if it was, why did she feel lower than dirt?

She stood on the deck, clutching the railing and tried to swallow her misery, tried to be happy for everyone else—and then she heard the sound of footsteps, Dominic's footsteps coming up the path.

He was grinning. Laughing. Actually *laughing* when he spotted her!

Sierra shut her eyes. Damn him! *Lucky* him! she thought miserably. And as much as she knew she should feel glad for him, she couldn't show it.

Personal magnanimity had its limits. Sierra had met hers.

He came up the steps two at a time. "Sierra!" His tone was urgent. "Sierra?" Now it was questioning because she wouldn't turn around.

She felt his hand on her arm and had to force herself not to pull away. She held still, didn't move.

"Thank you," he said, his voice soft and serious and just a little choked up.

"You're welcome," she muttered, still looking away.

Silence descended. He still held her and she cried inside, *Let me go! Please just let me go!*

Then he said, his tone a little strained, "But I don't understand why you want the divorce?"

She whirled on him. "You don't understand? How could you *not* understand? That's Carin! *Your* Carin! The woman you loved—maybe still do! And there's Lacey! Lacey is... Lacey is..."

"My brother's child."

"What!"

He nodded and repeated what he'd just told her. "She's Nathan's child."

Once more Sierra sat down. Only this time it felt more like she fell. She stared up at him, shaking her head, disbelieving, astonished. "I don't understand."

"I do," Dominic said softly. "Now."

He sat down on the deck beside her, pulled her close, wrapped one arm around her and took one of her hands in his, as if he needed to hang on. Sierra thought she knew how he felt.

"Tell me," she urged.

"It finally makes sense. I don't know why I didn't see it

years ago. You know how I told you our fathers got us together? Well, mine proposed, but hers apparently did a bit more than that. He said he'd found her the man she was going to marry. And she, dutiful daughter that she was—besides being young and inexperienced—agreed.''

"She didn't…love you?" Sierra had to ask.

"She liked me. I liked her. I guess I thought I loved her. I didn't know what love was then." He gave her hand a squeeze. "And neither did she. Until she came down here to spend those three weeks. Nathan was already here. He'd been doing a shoot in Venezuela and he came up early to spend some time. He didn't know she was coming. Didn't know her! But what happened to them was, well—" he slanted her a glance "—a lot like what happened to you and me."

"Hormones?"

"Instant attraction. And instant resistance. She, after all, was supposed to be going to marry me. She said Nathan tried to stay away, but then the night before Dad and Rhys were going to arrive there was a storm and they ended up in very close confines and one thing led to another and it got…"

"Sort of like in Kansas," Sierra said softly.

"Sort of," Dominic agreed. "And as soon as the storm was over, Nathan left. He'd done the unthinkable—made love to my fiancée. And so he cut out, called Rhys, told him to take over. He had no idea what Carin was going to do. I don't think Carin even knew until after he was gone. She loved him. She liked me. There was never any contest." He sounded wondering and not at all hurt now. He actually seemed relieved.

Sierra touched his cheek. "Why didn't she just tell you? Why did she run?"

"Because there was no time. Because she was young and scared and her father was expecting her to marry me in the morning. Everyone was expecting her to marry me in the morning. And she knew if she said she wasn't going to, it wouldn't wash, Daddy would lean on her to do it.''

''She could have told you!''

Dominic shrugged. ''I didn't give her a chance. I brushed her off, told her to get some sleep because she couldn't expect any on our wedding night.'' He shook his head. ''God, I was an ass.''

''No!'' Sierra shook her head. He'd been hurt. But he didn't look hurt now. He looked almost happy. ''Where'd she go?''

Dominic's eyes narrowed just a little. ''To stay with Estelle and Maurice.''

Sierra's eyes bugged. ''Estelle hid her?''

''Just let her lie low. Dad and Mr. Campbell were checking ferries and seaplanes and boats and every damned thing you could think of, but no one remembered seeing her leave. No wonder. She never went. And—'' he grinned a little ''—she's been here ever since. Got herself a nice little shop and a decent career. And none of us ever knew—until now.''

They sat in silence then. The sunset sounds of the ocean and the jungle were the only things to be heard.

Sierra let it all settle in, reshuffled reality, put Nathan with Carin and Lacey and wondered what the future was for that. Then she redealt the hand that fate had played her—and wondered, too, if she dared hope.

''I thought Lacey was yours,'' she admitted. ''When I met Carin, I just thought…'' She couldn't say the words, because even though they were untrue, they still had the power to hurt.

''I never made love with Carin. I was never *in* love with Carin. I've only loved one woman in my life—besides my mother,'' Dominic said with a wry smile. He touched her chin with his finger and turned her face so that she had to look at him or shut her eyes. ''And that woman is you.''

He loved her.

He actually said he loved her. And she could see his heart

and his soul in his eyes, and she knew what he said was true.

It was scary being loved like that. It was scary mattering so much to another person. It was easier to love, she thought, than be loved.

"Have I waited too long?" he asked her. There was a hint of hesitation in his voice, a thread of nervousness.

"Too long?"

"Once you said—" he swallowed "—that you…loved me…" He stopped and looked away and she saw the fear in his eyes and understood.

"I do, Dominic," she swore. And it was a vow every bit as deep and passionate as the ones she'd made at their wedding. She put her arms around him and felt his wrap around her in an embrace that promised to last a lifetime. "I love you, Dominic. I do, I do."

She did.

When a man was lucky enough to be married to a woman like Sierra, he could have no doubts. Dominic's doubts were well and truly assuaged, that was certain.

He came down the sand of another beach—a Long Island beach—to find his wife was playing in the water with Frankie and his parents.

Three months after his surgery, Frankie's future looked bright. And not just because he had a new kidney. He had a father now as well.

"I don't believe in fairy tales," Pammie had insisted when she'd debated marrying Dan last month.

But Sierra had said, "You believe in love, don't you?" And she'd smiled over the top of Pam's head and her eyes had met Dominic's. "Then that's all you need."

That was what they had—the two of them. Love.

More love, Dominic thought, than any man had a right to. He basked in Sierra's love every day of his life, and he never stopped thinking how damned lucky he was.

He understood now how Rhys could have been terrified to love again after Sarah. It put that kind of fear into a man. It took a good woman to persevere, to remove one-by-one all the roadblocks men were so good at constructing. Mariah had done it for Rhys.

Sierra had done it for him.

The months he had been married to Sierra had been the best time of his life. He wouldn't trade Sierra for all the mergers and takeovers and positive balance sheets on earth. She brought joy to every day and pleasure to every night.

She had enriched his life in ways he never thought possible.

He hoped Carin someday might do the same for Nathan. If Nathan could ever get past the guilt.

"You did me a favor," Dominic had told his brother when he and Sierra got back from their honeymoon.

Nathan was just about to leave again and he'd stared, shocked, when Dominic had confronted him with the news that Carin was living on Pelican Cay—and that he now understood why all those years ago, she'd jilted him.

"It's all right," he'd told his brother. "We didn't love each other. We were friends, that's all."

But Nathan wasn't having any of it. "I betrayed you."

"Well, it didn't happen the best way it could have," Dominic conceded. "But that's past. It's over. That doesn't matter now."

Nathan had grunted, resisting just the way Dominic remembered resisting.

"I suppose you could just forget I told you," he'd said mildly. "Spend your life at the four corners of the earth and miss out on the best part of it."

Nathan had kept right on packing.

"Carin's made a good life for herself. She probably doesn't care if she ever sees you again," Dominic went on ruthlessly. "Can't say the same for Lacey."

Nathan stilled. He gave Dominic a narrow look. "Who's Lacey?"

Dominic smiled his best enigmatic smile. "That, ol' buddy, is something I think you might want to find out."

Nathan had left the next day. He was going to Tahiti, he'd said. After that he had an assignment in Lapland.

"Run as long as you need to," Dominic had told him when he drove him to the airport. "But don't run so long you miss the best part of your life."

Like he almost had.

He still couldn't be home as much as he wanted to be. He'd had to go to a meeting this morning. It had come up suddenly and it cut into plans he and Sierra had made for taking Frankie and his parents out to spend the weekend at the Long Island house.

"You go on," he'd told her this morning. "I'll finish as early as I can, and I'll come then."

"You're sure?" He knew she would happily have forgone the excursion, but he knew she wouldn't want to disappoint Frankie.

"I'm sure," he'd said. He'd done his job. Taken care of business. Then he'd headed for the house as quick as he could.

He knew she saw him coming because she waved in his direction just before Frankie soaked her with a huge splash of water. Of course, being Sierra, she gave as good as she got, drenching Frankie until he fell back laughing.

Then he dove under a wave and came up grinning. Then Dan let go of Pammie long enough to say he'd show his son how to body surf.

"Want to come?" Dominic heard Frankie ask Sierra eagerly.

And he was surprised to see his wife shake her head.

"I think I'll take a little nap," she said and came up the beach to stand over him and shake water all over his chest.

He squinted up at her. "Lookin' for trouble, lady?"

She giggled, shook just a bit more water his way, then said, "Move over," and settled on the beach towel beside him. He was still in his khakis and his shirt and tie.

She was cold and wet and it was like hugging a wet seal, but Dominic didn't hesitate to put his arms around her.

"Ahhh." Sierra burrowed against him, then she gave a little shudder. "Nice."

"Wet," Dominic said.

She smiled against his collarbone, then tipped her head to look up at him. "You know you don't mind."

He dropped a kiss on her nose. "You're right. I don't."

"How did the merger go?"

"We've merged."

"Fruitful, was it?" She was playing with his tie, loosening it, making him hot where he wasn't wet and cold.

He cleared his throat. "Very fruitful." He tried to sound calm and businesslike.

"That's the way with mergers," Sierra said. Her fingers had unknotted the tie now, and they were sliding it off his neck.

Dominic caught her hands. "Behave."

Sierra gave him an innocent smile. "Me?"

"We're on a public beach," he reminded her, though his body was more in need of the reminder than she was.

"Indeed we are," she agreed. "I have news about another fruitful merger." She was running the tie against the back of his neck.

He went suddenly still as the import of her words hit him. "Sierra?" He felt short of breath, punched in the gut. "Are you…?"

She gave him a heart-melting smile. "It appears that we are going to have a little dividend about six months from now."

He felt the color drain from his face and was glad they were sitting on the sand. He felt dizzy and delighted and scared to death.

"Try whistling," Sierra said, reading him perfectly. "It helps."

"Does it?" Dominic managed when he could form words.

"Oh, yes." She put her arms around him and nestled against him and he wrapped her in his arms and held her against his overflowing heart. "It will be fine. You and I together can handle anything, can't we?" She slanted a glance of pure love up at him.

And Dominic nodded, loving her with all his heart. "You bet."

MILLS & BOON® 0805/01b

Live the emotion

Modern
romance™

THE MILLIONAIRE'S PROSPECTIVE WIFE
by Helen Brooks

Nick Morgan was wealthy and handsome, but single
– and apparently not looking for a wife. And when
he did choose a bride she wouldn't be ordinary and
inexperienced, like Cory... Except Nick seemed to find
her innocence a real challenge...

A VENETIAN PASSION *by Catherine George*

A holiday in Venice was just what Laura Green needed.
But she hadn't expected a stunning Venetian, Domenico
Chiesa, to seduce her! It was a week of sizzling sexual
tension. But Domenico had kept a secret from Laura that
would have startling repercussions...

LESSONS FROM A LATIN LOVER *by Anne McAllister*

Visit the stunning tropical island of Pelican Cay – full of
sun-drenched beaches it's the perfect place for passion!
And Molly McGillivray is about to take some lessons from
her Spanish lover Joaquin Santiago!

THE CARLOTTA DIAMOND *by Lee Wilkinson*

Charlotte Christie had no idea how priceless the diamond
necklace she wore on her wedding day was. Simon
Farringdon didn't see her innocence until it was too late.
What would happen when Charlotte discovered that the
Carlotta Diamond was his only motive for marriage...?

Don't miss out!
On sale 2nd September 2005

*Available at most branches of WHSmith, Tesco, ASDA,
Borders, Eason, Sainsbury's and most bookshops*

Visit www.millsandboon.co.uk

MILLS & BOON®

Live the emotion

Tender
romance™

THEIR NEW-FOUND FAMILY *by Rebecca Winters*

As a single mum, Rachel Marsden has always tried to do her best by her daughter. So when Natalie's long-lost father, Tris Monbrisson, shows up, Rachel swallows her feelings and moves to Tris's beautiful home in Switzerland. But as she and Tris fall into the role of mother and father, the secrets of the past unravel…

THE BILLIONAIRE'S BRIDE *by Jackie Braun*

Marnie LaRue has come to Mexico for relaxation – but the man in the neighbouring hacienda makes her laugh, and *feel* more than she has in a long time. Mysterious JT doesn't know Marnie is a grieving widow – and she doesn't have any clue that he's a billionaire…

CONTRACTED: CORPORATE WIFE *by Jessica Hart*

Patrick Farr is happy with his bachelor life, dating beautiful women – but how can he make them understand that he'll never marry for love? A marriage of convenience! Lou Dennison is his cool and calm PA – she's also a single mum, so when Patrick proposes her answer's definitely no. Or is it?

IMPOSSIBLY PREGNANT *by Nicola Marsh* (Office Gossip)

Keely Rhodes has a new work project – to get up close and personal with the famous Lachlan Brant! He's invited her to spend a weekend away with him – but she's sure he has more than business on his mind… Keely's friends think Lachlan's her perfect man – and tell her to go for it. But after her trip, she discovers the impossible has happened…

On sale 2nd September 2005

Available at most branches of WHSmith, Tesco, ASDA, Borders, Eason, Sainsbury's and most bookshops

Visit www.millsandboon.co.uk

0805/055/SH112

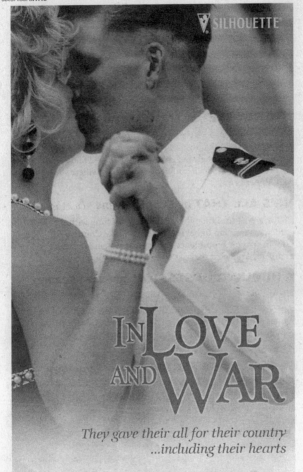

Desert
Heat

Susan Mallery
Alexandra Sellers

On sale 19th August 2005

Available at most branches of WHSmith, Tesco, ASDA, Martins,
Borders, Eason, Sainsbury's and all good paperback bookshops.

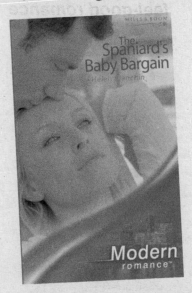